The Zarhunian Conflict

*Jedaf of Dolfi -
The 7ᵗʰ Lord of the Red Dragon*

David A. Stuhler

PublishAmerica
Baltimore

© 2011 by David A. Stuhler.
All rights reserved. No part of this book may be reproduced, stored in a retrieval system or transmitted in any form or by any means without the prior written permission of the publishers, except by a reviewer who may quote brief passages in a review to be printed in a newspaper, magazine or journal.

First printing

All characters in this book are fictitious, and any resemblance to real persons, living or dead, is coincidental.

PublishAmerica has allowed this work to remain exactly as the author intended, verbatim, without editorial input.

Hardcover 978-1-4560-9913-8
Softcover 978-1-4560-9914-5
PUBLISHED BY PUBLISHAMERICA, LLLP
www.publishamerica.com
Baltimore

Printed in the United States of America

The Zarhunian Conflict

Semedian Red Dragon — by Meghan Briggs

Recently after the death of our grandmother my sisters and I were given several manuscripts that were written a long time ago by our father. They were originally written for his and our amusement only but we thought that other fiction readers would enjoy reading them as much as we did.

**They are the adventures of Jedaf of Dolfi
The 7ᵗʰ Lord of the Semedian Red Dragon
Tears of Everro
The Culba's Soul Mates
The Zarhunian Conflict
Tabalis - The City of the Dead
The Histajonies Wars**

**Laura, Rebecca and Christine Stuhler
For
Emma Rukavena, Tate Wardman,
Abigail Wardman, and Leah Stuhler**

Table of Contents

Prologue 9
Chapter # 1: The Inn of the Athca 23
Chapter # 2: Valadis of Jeupa 41
Chapter # 3: Jeupan Spies 56
Chapter # 4: The Wasteland Road to Cathon 74
Chapter # 5: Motaluk — The Treskul of Pestilence 86
Chapter # 6: The Southeast Road to Tabalis 98
Chapter # 7: The Hand of King Dracar 111
Chapter # 8: The Village of Giehan 120
Chapter # 9: Princess Shayla's Bridal Caravan 131
Chapter # 10: Atus — The Royal Worezian Cook 144
Chapter # 11: The House of Traga 153
Chapter # 12: The Red Army of the Dragon Lord 165
Chapter # 13: Marshal Ebestar of Envar 176
Chapter # 14: South to the Kingdom of Jeupa 187
Chapter # 15: The Ancient Semedian City of Am Haas 203
Chapter # 16: Cystalen Queen of the Vourtre 216
Chapter # 17: Theisiah, Prince of Yoja 226
Chapter # 18: The Fleet of the Dragon Lord 236
Chapter # 19: The Vellastran Pass 248
Chapter # 20: King Eneas of Eastern Semedia 259
Chapter # 21: The Road to Envar 271
Chapter # 22: The Third Strata's Woman 282
Chapter # 23: The Green Envarian Army 290
Chapter # 24: The Ancient City State of Zarhun 307
Chapter # 25: Tenolfis North Point of Envar 315
Chapter # 26: The Red Dragon and Silver Sword 329
Chapter # 27: The Worezian Army Pincer 342
Chapter # 28: War Returns to a Devastated Land 359

Chapter # 29: Renvas The Capital City of Envar......... 370
Chapter # 30: Adathe the Capital City of Cathon 380
Chapter # 31: Worezian Insurrectionists 391
Chapter # 32: The Eye of the Storm 402
Glossary 416

Prologue

The first of three foretold ancient prophetic sagas had been fulfilled two thousand years ago. This predicted epoch led to the destruction of Lord Athumus's Trident and the old gods losing control over Palestus's inland seas and vast oceans. During the two thousand years that followed; the essential and most dangerous components of this trident were lost or disposed of where they would no longer bring harm to any kingdom.

Astroc, the King of Tark was a prime example. He was given one of the seven components taken from Athumus's Trident. During the five years the jagar ring was in his possession; his island kingdom experienced continual hot, dry, off shore winds and firestorms. His subjects were spending more labor hours fighting forest and grassland fires than planting crops. He ordered the ruby ring be dropped into an active volcano so this curse would be lifted from his lands. The other minor component parts of the trident's assembly were refashioned into ceremonial or decorative weapons.

The second prophecy foretold, of a frail, unwanted, malicious and sickly child. He would one day become a king through murder, guile and treachery. This dark lord would be the one responsible for spreading war and a dismal darkness over every continent. He along with a minion of underworld demons would wreak havoc upon the land, and generate an oppressive atmosphere that would last for generations.

The old gods had not envisioned how quickly man would spread throughout the world. The desecration of the old sacred forests had made them angry enough to want to start over. Most desired to reduce the population and return the survivors to a primitive hunter, gatherer of the dark ages. The proposed destruction to civilization would make the remaining humans once again more reverent toward them. The malevolent spirits that had been waiting beneath the Virkreb Mountains for eons had been biding their time as the dissatisfaction with the humans spread. They had been gaining strength and power as they waited for this expected malcontent to be born.

It was the tenth year of Gothorus and the sixth age of man was nearing its end. A failed revolt against King Kodus of Sylak in the year 2474 KC had been the cause of Prince Zaghar's banishment to the remote Kingdom of Eastern Wyloth. No member of the royal family had ever envisions his return from this harsh wasteland. It was the most desolate and last active volcanic region on the Planet of Palestus.

"The Northwestern Kelleskarian Wars" began once his cousin King Athar was killed in battle. Zaghar's hargot army swept over and defeated the decimated royal army of the Sylakian Kingdom, which made him heir to its throne. His first official act in the year 2477 KC was to enlarge his army and invade the neighboring pastoral western kingdoms. Nine years of bloody war followed before the remaining northern duchies and kingdoms of the Kelleskarian Continent signed a peace treaty.

Throughout the kingdoms and northland fiefdoms, a rumor had been spread that the mad King of Sylak had withdrawn his armies south toward more fertile lands. The cold mountainous regions and lowland valleys would now be spared the burning of their cities. The northern kings had no delusions of peace as long as Zaghar sat upon the Sylakian throne. An armistice was signed because it would give them at least a few years in which they could make preparations for the inevitable return of the Sylakian armies and the hordes of hargot flesh eaters.

In the year 2490 KC, the armies and auxiliary warriors of the Sylakian Empire invaded the west central kingdoms of Kelleskar. They sacked the monasteries of the peaceful Kingdom of Naros and had the entire contents of the ancient library brought back to Sylakia. Among the ancient tomes and prayer scrolls was a prediction relating to the third ancient prophecy. It was thought by one of the most influential monastic scholars, that this event would be fulfilled during the seventh recorded solar alignment in the Odea Galaxy. These ancient oral sagas told of a strange being with the unnatural ability to vanquishing evil and bring a lasting and tranquil peace to the land.

King Zaghar knew he must prevent this out-worlder from coming through the void of time during this event which occurred every five hundred years. Only a non Palestusian could prevent him from fulfilling his destiny, and this individual had to be killed quickly. The newest lord of the red Semedian dragon was the only being which could posses this power and meet the predicted expectations that would occur in the year 2,500 K.C.

The most important document confiscated from the library of Naros was the last known copy of the "Scrolls of Colinda." The Scrolls of Life, or better known as the "Scrolls of Colinda," were rumored to hold the secrets of life and immortality. Since ascending the throne, Zaghar had but two insatiable desires; to possess the "Scrolls of Life" and to reassemble Athumus's Trident. If he was able to translate Colinda's scrolls accurately, they could assist him in cheating death and give him the greatest power ever known to exist on Palestus.

In his first use of one scroll, Zaghar was able to evoke a mind bending incantation. This spell called forth and bound to him the souls and loyalty of the five evil treskuls of hate which had been created by Kebran the God of War. These demonic beings have been his constant companions since his cannibalization of King Nygouk. They feed off the energy of his life force for their strength, and inspire him to do perform more and more black magic. With the passing of each day the evil within Zaghar grows. This malignant wickedness is bringing him closer to his goal of becoming an equal with the immortal demigod treskuls.

Zaghar's second goal and desire of reassembling "Athumus's Trident" could take over a life time. To accomplish this task, he needed to find the "Scrolls of Colinda" which would give him immortality. The prince had found one of the most powerful parts of the trident inside the Virkreb Mountain Volcano. The jagar ruby ring gave him the power of fire, and an insatiable desire to posses all seven of the lost components. Sylakian agents have been scouring the planet looking for clues to the last known locations of the other six parts.

King Zaghar has made a treaty with King Magarus of Worez. He was to deliver two young virgin princesses of royal blood. They were to be used as an added enticement for the Worezian - Envarian wedding contract. Another part of their agreement related to parts of Athumus's Trident. Two of the relics that are in Magarus's possession will be given to Zaghar.

One of the outer tines of the trident was forged into a ceremonial short sword and given to Prince Ontiliac of the ancient Semedian Empire. The weapon had been lost in one of the last battlefield engagements of the second Zarhunian Revolt. This legendary black steel blade had recently been found in an excavation during the repair of the Zarhunian City State's barbican. King Magarus has already given this sacred sword to Zaghar. The blade was used as a downpayment for enough arms and war supplies to conquer the western kingdoms.

The other outer tine of the trident was forged into a long knife and given to King Sejand of ancient Envar. This sacred weapon is the sword of state for the Envarian Kingdom. It will soon be King Magarus's as part of a wedding contract he has signed with King Helidon. The heir of this royal union will one day rule over their united kingdoms.

A third part of the trident known to exist is the eston bone handle of Uthamus's pronged spear. This blessed staff now hangs over the royal throne of Bintar. It is the symbol of nobility for this centrally located kingdom on the Histajonies Archipelago. King Naphlus is the current ruler of this land, and the guardian of this ancient artifact.

If King Zaghar were to possess these components and reassemble Athumus's Trident, he would have control over all the oceans and it would aide him in his quest for world domination. The only known descriptions and picture of the infamous trident were also found in the library catacombs of Naros, along with the following three individual zeskarta, historical accounts.

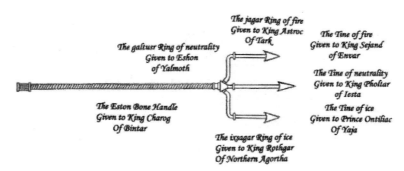

Athumus's Trident of Power

Uthamus Lord of the Sea

First born of the minor Gods Adarfus and Avello was given "The Trident of Athumus" at his birth. This trident made by his father, Lord Adarfus and his uncle Lord Megatharus controlled the tides and prevented man from sailing beyond the sight of land and kept intercontinental travel to a very few brave fisherman and naval captains. The staff was made of hand carved eston bone and blessed by prayers from his grandfather Athumus Lord of the Seas.

The three solid silver trident bars were forged by Megatharus, separating the rings of power below their point. The outer jagar or ruby ring was made by his uncle Lord Virros the God of Fire. It controlled the heat of undersea volcano lava and could bring frozen water to an instant boil. The other outer ixsagar or diamond ring was made by his aunt Worixsa the Goddess of Ice. It controlled the movement of icebergs and the frozen waters of Palesus's polar ice caps. It could bring boiling water to a hard cold frozen mass as soon as it was touched. The center galtus or blue steel ring was made by his great uncle Zestarius, the God of Time. The ring had minor effects on time and also insulated and neutralized the space between the tines of fire and ice.

Uthamus who was always intrigued by humans disobeyed his parents and became involved in man's second war on the Archipelago of the Histajonies. The southern continental Kingdoms of Gothor and Hampt swore to build temples to him and would make regular offerings of human blood in his honor. It was his task to sink any ship sailing to the continent with aide for the Kingdom of Bintar. For nine years he pulled ships to the bottom of the deep off of the west coast of the continent.

Eshon of Yalmoth was put in command of the armies of the Kingdom of Tark and its colony state of Bintar. The only way for cargo to reach Bintar was by sailing around the continent eastward and off loading in the ports of the far northlands. There it would be unloaded and packed on horses and wagons for the long journey south. Eshon knew that if Lord Uthamus's interference was not stopped the war would soon be lost. He also knew he could not kill him, but he might be able to trick the lord into stopping his aide for Bintar's enemies.

Eshon devised a plan to lure him into the shallow waters off the coasts of the southern Pharlon Isles. A large cargo vessel was disassembled and the upper half of the ship reconstructed on the reef. When Uthamus came to sink the ship he was entangled in cargo nets until he gave his oath not to sink any more ships and was made to surrender his trident. In his embarrassment and disgrace he swam to the underwater caves off the continental shelf and ate poison ogalto fish, turning him into a grey stone like coral. Never again would the gods have control of the tides.

ZK (zeskarta) Arestan — Circa 560 KC

The Second Histajonies War

Lord Uthamus become involved with man's war on the archipelago of the Histajonies in 542 KC. He had sunk all ships sailing with cargo to the Kingdom of Bintar for nine years before being captured off of the coasts of the southern Pharlon Isles. He made an oath not to sink any more ships and surrendered his trident of power. Eshon of Yalmoth, the commander of the armies of the Kingdoms of Tark and Bintar, was given the Trident of Athumus in the spring of 551 KC.

A great battle on the southern plains of Bintar was about to begin as soon as the spring ground hardened. The armies of the Kingdoms of Gother and Hampt outnumbered the army of Bintar four to one. They had almost two years in preparation for this battle because of the help from Lord Uthamus. They thought the outcome of the battle had already been determined. There was no way their armies could be defeated. They advanced into the center of the lowland plans from the southern heights confident in their victory.

Commander Eshon had positioned his flag ship off the southern Bintar coast, parallel to the plains. He had been waiting for this very moment. Using the Trident of Athumus he called upon the sea creating a huge tidal wave which crashed onto the coast flooding the center of the plain. Most of the enemy warriors were drowned and washed seawards devastating their armies.

To this day the once fertile southern plain is still nothing more than salt water marshes. Fighting continued in the mountains east of the swamp marshes for another nine years before a peace treaty could be signed. All kingdoms that had been drawn into this war attended "The Conference of Peace" which was held in the Yojan capital City of Joroca in 562 KC. It was decided at this conference that no one kingdom would have "The Trident of Athumus" and it was divided into seven individual parts and distributed to the rulers of various kingdoms.

ZK (zeskarta) Corvok — Circa 570 KC

Uthamus's Trident of Athumus

This trident was made by Lord Adarfus and Lord Megatharus to control the tides and prevent man from sailing beyond the sight of land and keeping intercontinental travel to a very few seamen. The staff made of hand carved eston bone was blessed by his grandfather the God Athumus. The three solid silver trident bars were forged separating the rings of power below their point. The outer jagar or ruby ring could bring frozen water to an instant boil. The other outer ixsagar or diamond ring could bring boiling water to a frozen block in the blink of an eye. The center galtus or blue steel ring effected time and neutralized the space between the tines of fire and ice.

Following the end of the second war of the Histajonies, all kingdoms that had been drawn into the war attended "The Conference of Peace" held in the Yojan capital City of Joroca in 562 KC. It was decided at this conference that no one kingdom would have "The Trident of Athumus" and it was divided into seven individual parts and distributed to the rulers of various kingdoms.

The blessed staff handle of eston bone was given to Charog the King of Bintar. One tine of the trident was forged into a knife and given to Sejand the King of Envar. Another tine of the trident was forged into a ceremonial short sword and given to Prince Ontiliac of the Kingdom of Yoja. The last tine of the trident was forged into a spear point and given to Pholtar the King of Iesta.

The jagar ruby ring of fire was given to Astroc the King of Tark. The ixsagar diamond ring of ice was given to Rothgar King of Northern Agortha. The galtus blue steel ring of time was kept by Eshon of the City State of Yalmoth.

ZK (zeskarta) Arestan — Circa 600 KC

A Ballad of Hope

*Civilization has crumbled once more
Death, destruction, and continuous war
Fate brings forth one of saga and lore
Through time space at callings room door*

*Half a life of war on the sea and land
Fingers of death from a mighty hand
Battles foe, old now new, of desert sand
About his neck forged, an iron band*

*Fields trampled, food rotten with mold
Charred lands, homes, cities, new now old
Men, women, and children chained and sold
Starvations door thrown open, by barons bold*

*Reborn of darkness from crypts old bed
Hates blackness has Yaldoc's marked head
White feather heart of the Dragon Red
Leads spirit army, lost once, thought dead*

*Man shall suffer many years to come
Natural disasters are expected by some
The war gods not finished, not yet done
Before peace returns the wars now won*

Unknown —Circa 1050 KC

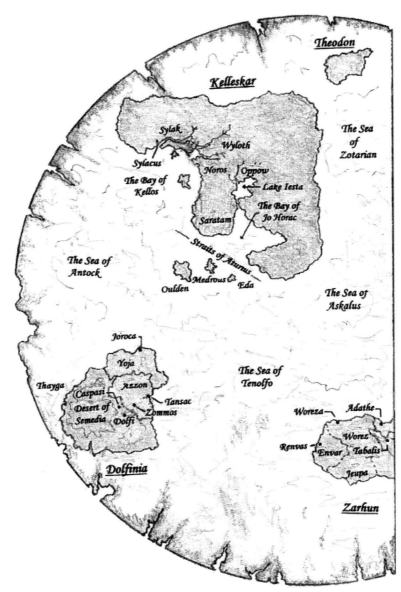

The Great Zarhunian Plain

Chapter # 1
The Inn of the Athca

Jeff had been quietly thinking about his companions and the past few days, as his horse trotted slowly along the dusty dirt road. It had been only a few months since he had been brought through the cold, dark void of time and space. Palestus was a small, strange planet that had evoled to a primitive, early feudal period in time. The voyage through the unnatural laws of this vast emptiness, physically transformed this twenty four year old student teacher. He was re-materialized into the body of a gangly, but muscular sixteen year old boy.

There was no literal translation to Jeff or his surname D'Afoe. Jedaf was the closest sounding to his own earth name. Unfortunately, this name had been used once before. Uttering this evil sorcerer's name, brought chills to most people. Jedaf was the name of one of the most hated men, born on the continent of ancient Semedia. His teachers in the Dolfi training compound fiercely disapproved of his choice. After several days of argueing their point of contention, they finally acquiesced and allowed him to keep parts of his first and last name forming this new identity.

Following several months of preparation and acclimatization on this world, he was ordained as the new Lord of the horned Semedian Red Dragon and Protector of the Dead. During his training and guidance at the calling center compound he had sworn a blood oath to the Council of Elders. As the 7th lord, he would fulfill his pledge to go on a religious pilgrimage. Above all else he was journey to the ancient City of Tabalis, located on the Continent of Zarhun. As the anointed one, he would pay tribute to the gods while respecting their deceased devotees.

Jedaf slipped from the back of his weary chestnut mare and began to walk alongside her. The salt streaked mount was glad for the rest. She gave the young rider a thankful look with her dark brown eyes, and whinnied softly. "Master your horse has only one rider and she's already sweating and breathing hard." Jedaf looked up at his two friends. They had been riding double at his side since leaving the Worezian city gates. Holding onto the bridle, he stroked her mane and gave his horse another gentile pat on the side of her neck as she restlessly stomped about.

Prince Kytos of Oppow carefully slipped off of the back of Ambassador Ajoris's mare. The grimy and smelly teenager was barefoot and dressed only in a mire rag of a stained and tattered, blue loincloth. His dignity, self esteem and possessions had been taken away from him. During his two month long captivity aboard the pirate ship Culba, he had been starved, kicked and beaten severely. This daily mental and brutal physical abuse left the royal teen, depressed and on the verge of suicide.

After a second merchant ship was seized by the privateers, Kytos had found another young man he could relate with and to share his concerns. Now his will to survive outweighed the ill treatment and manhandling by his captors. The squalid living conditions and rank smell below deck had almost become bearable. Being with someone his own age that had undergone similar harsh treatment made the last few weeks aboard this vessel more tolerable.

This all changed the day the Captain Tristos of the marine contingent on board the Culba punished the boy. Kytos's sister Princess Elona had refused to pose naked for a wedding portrait. In his retaliation, the marine officer used Kytos as an example to his sister and the other captive passengers aboard the ship. Ship Captain Sedran's orders were to be obeyed or severe consequences would follow.

THE ZARHUNIAN CONFLICT

For reasons unknown to him at the time; the young prince had been dragged from the ships galley. Two deckhands gave him a hard beating before taking him up on the main deck and pinning him down. As a crowd of marauding seamen and scruffy marines gathered about him, they severed his right hand with several chops of a cutlass. Luckily, Lord Jedaf had been standing nearby. Rushing to the boy's aide, he had managed to use his bandanna as a tourniquet.

Grabing the young prince around the waist, Jedaf tossed the limp body over his shoulder and rushed to the nearest hatchway. Most of the bleeding slowed by the time they reached the lower decks. In a panic, Jedaf could not think of anything else to do other than, cauterizing and stitching over the excess flesh and skin. It was the only way he was able to close the jagged wound.

The ships officers were pleased with the way this other slave had saved the younger boy's life. After that incident, it had been left up to Jedaf to care for the injured prince until the ship reached Woreza. This deep harbor and shallow anchorage was the ship's final destination. The port is the capital city for the Worezian Kingdom, and a safe haven for a majority of the privateer's.

The stitches were still oozing and his flesh was tender to the touch. The stump of Kytos's wounded wrist was beginning to throbbing below the leather strap to his wooden hand. Taking his arm from the frayed sling he loosened the ties a bit. Rubbing at the whitened skin, he tried to get some more circulation back into the limb. It was healing well but it had been less than a mursa or a Palestus month since his right hand had been hacked off.

The fifteen year old prince felt strange standing in the coarse gravel and silt. He was unaccustomed to being so scantily dressed and the hot suns were starting to redden his skin. Looking down at the road dirt on his bare feet and shins, he awkwardly brushed the pebbles and soil out from between his toes with his left hand. Bending down made the stump of his amputated hand throb all the more. He tucked his right arm back into the filthy white rag of a sling and he rushed forward catching up with Jedaf, his friend and new master.

"We've only ridden about three and a half thastas from the Woreza city gates and she doesn't look like she can go on much further. I think the livery that sold you these old horses must have over worked them. It's either that or they were wagon or coach mounts before being sold as riding horses?"

Ajoris the thin and dignified middle aged Yojan Ambassador nodded regretfully in agreement. "I was the one that picked these horses out at the corral," he said to Kytos. "At the time they looked perfectly sound to me. It makes me feel like a total fool being taken in that easily, and paying for these nags." The two year old mare turned her head toward the gaunt man and gave him a long blustery neigh. Jedaf chuckled at the sound. To him it almost sounded like she said, "You're the nag. Not me!"

The charge' d'affaires' met Jedaf on the cargo ship Tarpenya. They sailed together from the port City of Joroca in the Kingdom of Yoja, to the Continent of Zarhun. Jedaf saved the ambassador from drowning when their ship was attacked by the same pirates that had seized Kytos's and Elona's vessel. The two men were both been knocked into the sea during the collision of the two ships hulls. After having been hauled back aboard the vessel, they were held as hostages for ransom.

Since the pirates confiscated all of the ambassador's valuables, Jedaf paid King Magarus of Worez, the ransom for their release. The brigands did not bother searching through the boy's belongings, after hearing he was a commoner in servitude to the diplomat. For saving his life and paying for their release, the elderly man pledged his life and his allegiance to the sixteen year old Lord of the Dragon.

Disembarking from the pirate ship Culba, they decided to continue their journey to the City of Adathe by land instead of booking passage on another vessel. The Kingdom of Worez and the Kingdom of Cathon were not on friendly terms. Neither Jedaf nor Ajoris wanted to be caught up in another armed political dispute.

"I am sorry about that Master Jedaf; I guess I'm not such a good horse trader. Maybe I should have let you pick them out."

"No Ajor. It's me," the teenager replied half-heartedly. "The horses of your world just do not seem like me for some reason. As a matter of fact, this is the longest that I have ever ridden." Feeling kind of guilty, he stopped for a moment and looked back at her. "I think that she's a fine animal, and no one could have bought a better one." Jedaf gave his horse another gentle caressing pat and stroked her muzzle as he spoke.

"I am just sorry that she is this exhausted already. Maybe after she gets her wind back, we should change mounts until we get to the inn?" The older man dismounted and joined his two younger companions. They walked three abreast at a casual pace with their horses trailing behind.

Ajoris thought about the young lord's problem as they walked. It felt good to stretch their legs, and it was a warm, beautiful, late afternoon day. The birds were chirping and a cool, gentile breeze was felt as they made their way down the winding road beneath the sparse overhanging shade trees.

"Lord, how much do you weigh," inquired Ajoris? "You're a little taller than I am, and a little broader at the shoulders, but I've seen your boot impressions in the mud near the docks. At first, I thought that the ground must be totally saturated, and that's why you sank so deeply. I tried to be a little more careful where I walked, but no matter where I stepped, I hardly left a mark."

Jedaf hesitated a moment and turned toward them having a puzzled expression on his face. "You know mister ambassador; I think you might have something there! I had a good friend by the name of Gantilion back at the Dolfi calling compound center. He was much larger than I, but when we joked and wrestled around a bit, he had a lot of trouble lifting me off of the ground. How much do you weigh?"

Ajor adjusted his waist sash and patted the slight paunch protruding above his belt buckle. "About thirty two tarmets, in my stocking feet," he replied. "And how about you master?"

Jedaf pondered the question for a few zestas before answering. Then looking a little foolish and embarrassed, he replied sheepishly. "I really don't know how much I weigh. I know what they are, but

I've never physically seen or stood on one of your adufa tar scales. As a matter of fact, no one has ever asked me how much I weighed before this."

Prince Kytos looked at him skeptically. "Master, how could you not know your weight? The tallyman had to weigh you before you set sail from Joroca, otherwise how did you pay for your transportation tax?"

"Tax," Jedaf chuckled and commented cynically? "I don't know what you're talking about. I've never paid for any tax."

"But master, you had to. You could not have gotten aboard a ship without paying for it."

Jedaf sighed. "A friend purchased passage for me. He was the one that filled out all of the travel documents." His voice was subdued and having a forlorn tone. The young lord was thinking of Capitan Traga and his son Agar as he spoke. They were two Yojan friends, which he would never forget.

"You know Ky, maybe this friend of his just guessed at his weight," said Ajoris. "Not that many inspectors like to be up at the crack of dawn checking on the manifests or the passenger lists."

"You're probably right, mister ambassador. I guess they could have also just paid for the maximum. That way no questions would have to be answered."

At the crossroads over the next grassy rise were several buildings with thatched roofs. They were clustered closely together and having a split rail fenced paddock to one side. The assorted structures had been constructed in a shallow green valley near a wide brook. The small stream led to and fed a nearby, low, marshy, reed and cattail infested pond.

Swapping horses, they rode the rest of the way to the bottom of the hill and into the glade. A sun weathered marquee sign board swung over the main entrance door. On the blistered planking, the head of a large, dark brown and yellow turkey buzzard like carrion eater was painted. "That's it Jedaf, the Inn of the Athca!"

The stables were to the left side of the main building. A large exercise area for the horses was located on the opposite side. Ten to twelve saddle horses and a half dozen stockier draft horses ran about inside the enclosures. Most of them scattered into the higher grasses at the rear of the field when the travelers rode up.

The rusty wheels of the barn doors squeaked as they rolled open to the side. A skinny, eight to ten year old boy with his ribs showing through the open laces of his sleeveless vest, ran over to greet them. "Give them a rub down and some fresh water," Ajoris said to him. The boy smiled and held on tightly to the customer's reins while they dismounted.

"Yes sire. Is there anything else that I can help you with?" The older gentleman did not answer him; instead he tapped Jedaf on the arm and pointed inside the barn. "As long as were here, let's find out how much you weigh." Just inside the sliding double doors was a four foot square feed and grain scale. Ajoris led the way, and Jedaf stepped to the center of the wooden loading platform.

Kytos started to pile on the granite counter balance stones. Four, five, six, tarmet blocks weighing six tarmets each were added and the platform hadn't moved. Ajoris examined the chains and wooden scales cross beam leverage arm. "I think it must be broken? How much weight have we got on there?"

"Thirty six tarmets ambassador," answered Ky.

The stable boy scratched his unkempt hair and ran over, standing next to them. "No lord, the scales were balanced less than twenty days ago. You can see the date of the royal inspector's tax stamp seal on the weights."

Ajor placed one more six tarmet stone on the counter-balance platform. The scale dipped a couple of inches. The stable boy brought over two, one tarmet stones. The scales dipped the width of a hand. Two more stones were added by Ajor. It teetered a little low, but was almost balancing. The stable boy added two more, bringing Jedaf about eight inches above the ground. The arrow pointed almost straight upward. A half block balanced Jedaf as close as they could without going over.

The three of them stood back and looked at the stack of cut stone blocks in astonishment. "Forty six and a half tarmets, no wonder horses don't like you," said Ajoris. The Dragon Lord stepped off the scale and the platform jumped up with the balance stones making a loud bang. Then Ajoris stepped onto the platform along with the stable boy; their combined weight did not equal that of Jedaf.

"Master, the heaviest man that I have ever known was a strongman in a sideshow with a troupe of traveling entertainers. That muscleman weighted about forty five tarmets, and could bend a Theodian metal bar with his bare hands."

Jedaf didn't comment. His eyes rolled around as he made incredulous faces. Then he shook his head slowly from side to side indicating an Oh Well attitude. Pointing over at the tavern he asked, "Shall we get a late meal and a couple of ales?" There was no need for a reply. None of them had eaten since last evening, and they were all famished.

The "Inn of the Athca" was a large airy tavern with a high trussed ceiling of open, rough hewn rafters, collar ties and bottom chords. A dozen round wagon wheel chandeliers with five oil lamps to each were overhead. They were suspended from the beams with their lowering ropes tied off at the walls behind the tables. The conjoined boardinghouse and tavern had two separate fireplaces in the dining area. The second story over the kitchen was used as sleeping quarters. Large fieldstone hearths burned at each end of the great hall. Between the fireplaces were six rows of crowded long benches.

Along the rear wall of the gallery, was a row of individual round tables with chairs. There were also a few round tables scattered around in the front half of the dining area. In front of the fireplaces, and at the ends of the long benches, were three other individual round tables.

On the far walls, near the sides of the fireplaces were wall pegs for at least one hundred tankards, and mugs. None were the same size or shape, and the varieties were too many to count. Some were made of brass or tin, but the majorities were fire hardened, painted katmet ceramics. Jedaf looked them over. Most had scenes of hunting or pictures of wildlife on them. A few were made in the shape of an animal, or a human's head.

The front and back walls of the banquet room were covered with old, worn, dusty tapestries depicting famous warriors. Between each of the windows were an assortment of rusted weapons, leather skinned maps, charts, or animal hides.

To the right and left of the main entrance were four round tables. Half of them had been taken by the local clientele. Second lunch had ended zestars ago, and over half of the seats were still occupied. As they stood looking about the tavern, wood smoke and cooking fumes filled the air billowing up to the high ceiling.

Eight to ten serving women could be seen on each side of the building. The scullery maids were running around filling tankards, and mugs to the shouts of the patrons. Others were hurrying about with large trays trying to keep bread on the tables, or keeping the meat cauldrons covered and hot. Ajoris, Jedaf and Kytos seated themselves at one of the round tables in the corner. It had not been cleared yet, and one of the waitresses ran over immediately.

The woman's day was nearly half over. From her state of near exhaustion, Jedaf couldn't see how see was going to remain on her feet the rest of the day. "Will you gentlemen be staying at the inn tonight?"

"No," replied Jedaf. "We just stopped long enough for some hot food and to buy supplies, before heading east." She cleared the table, stacking the bowls, and wiping down the table with a damp rag which hung from her apron.

"The supply building is located directly behind the dining hall. We have all kinds of provisions, equipment, pack animals, and horses which can take you anywhere on Zarhun. Also, we can provide you with guides that could take you to almost anywhere in the remote regions. Because it is getting so late, you might want to reconsider staying and get a fresh start early in the morning."

"Thanks for the advice," said Jedaf. "We will think about it."

Jedaf, Ajoris, and Kytos had not eaten all day, and their stomachs growled at the mention of food. "We have roasting fowls, measan steaks, or fish today." All three of them made faces at the word fish. For two mursas the majority of the evening meals served aboard the

Culba where either calamari or bacalao stews with boiled oolets or some other rotting tuberous vegetable.

The other most common luncheon meal was a cold vichyssoise made with chunks of leftover salt preserved fish. Usually served along with the fish stew meals were stale, moldy rolls that had been suitably sized for dunking in the wooden bowls. A majority of the sailors used large gobs of spreadable lard or salted suet on them to hide the taste, or to cover the worm or weevil infestations. "Which would you prefer," she asked?

"The fowl," Ajor replied without thinking about it.

"I'll have one also," said Ky.

"Make it three," answered Jedaf. "We would also like a couple of fresh loafs, with sharp crock cheese, and three large tankards of ale." She smiled at the ambassador's servant and lifted her tray of dirty dishes. "Is there anything else that you need?"

"Yes, have your smith come in here and have these irons removed from my friend," said Jedaf. It was not long before the food was brought, and it only took the smith three heavy raps with his maul and chisel to sever the locking pin on Ky's slave collar. It had been put on him aboard the Culba just prior to being chained and taken to the slave market in Woreza.

Kytos was glad to be free of it and he kicked the iron band and ring chain under the table. Jedaf could see that chaffing marks were beginning to show. The smith assumed Ambassador Ajoris was the master, so the liveryman asked him, if he should also remove the collar from the other slave. Ajor was nervously embarrassed and momentarily at a loss for words. He looked down and around a little then quietly answered, "No," without looking at the smith or Jedaf.

The young Dragon Lord's one quarter inch diameter steel collar had been forged around his neck when he was in training at the Calling Room Compound. Suspended from the hardened metallic band were a short chain, a blackened swivel ring and a disk compass. This amulet attested to the fact, that Jedaf was the rightful heir to the throne of the Semedian Red Dragon. The smith nodded, gathered his tools, and left the building.

The meal was very tasty, and they ate hungrily. Their only distraction was the noise of the rowdy crowd, which made hearing any conversation difficult. It really did not matter much; all of them were too hungry to say more than a few words while eating. Not only did the food seem to vanish before them, the ales went like there was a hole in the bottom of each pint sized tankard. Jedaf was sipping his third ale, while looking about the great room at the patrons.

Most of those already seated were laborers, farm hands, or were from one of the local trade guilds. A group of twenty noisy customers seated at the far end of the hall appeared to be with some sort of traveling musical entertainment. Some of the tavern's clients were mercantile traders, or salesmen on some sort of business. Very few of them were wearing the apparel denoting traveling scholars, or men of the clergy.

None of the individuals looked particularly noteworthy except for one. A richly robed and refined looking woman was sitting by herself at one of the round tables in the opposite corner. Her slender back was to them, and the hood of her silver tread embroidered brown cloak was pulled up, partially shielding her face. She nibbled on a piece of broiled fish and occasionally took a sip from her wineglass. Leaning against her chair was a bleached white, walking staff with unique and distinctively ornate runic carvings.

Jedaf caught a glimpse of her aloof, dignified profile and recognized her instantly. The lady sat watching the main entrance while eating, and looked like she had been expecting someone to join her. Each time an individual came into the dining hall she would look up quickly in anticipation and then back down to her dinner. There was nothing left on her platter but a crust of bread, half a shallot and a few pieces of iretas fish skin with bones. Still no one came over to her table.

Jedaf watched as she buttered her last piece of bread in the wicker basket, and set it aside wiping her fingers on a cloth napkin. A feeling of anxiety suddenly came over him. Was she going to leave without saying a word to him? He had been waiting for her to make the first move. Then he thought the reason she hadn't was because she might not want to have any undo attention brought to her. A few zestas later she glanced in his direction, but she appeared to show no concern or further interest. He could not wait any longer; he had to at least say hello.

"Excuse me," said Jedaf to Ajoris. He had cut the diplomat off in mid sentence, then stood and left their table. Walking over to where the woman was seated, he tapped her lightly on the back of the shoulder and bent down low whispering in her ear. "I am glad to see you Mina. I have missed you and the others." He pulled out the chair across the table from her and sat down.

The lady was surprised by his touch and her hand instinctively reached for, and tightened on her stave which had been leaning near the side of her chair. She stared at him intently as she spoke. "Hydos rayos exparos eastra," she whispered softly then gave her walking stick a light rap against the side of the table. There was no apparent change in the behavior or mannerisms of the stranger that had invited himself to her table. He just went on speaking and disregarded her incantation.

"You've lost a little weight, haven't you? Has Dro stopped cooking?"

She raised her hand and waved it infront of his face, stopping him. "Sir, I do not know what you're talking about, and I do not know anyone by the name of Dro!" Jedaf stammered and was momentarily tongue tied for a zesta, as he looked at her a little more closely. The woman certainly had Minatis's nose and face, but her cheek bones were slightly higher. Her hair was a shade lighter, and her lips maybe a little fuller.

"I am sorry," he said when he heard her voice. It was also slightly lower but having a softer tone than that of his friend. She was at least five years younger than Minatis, and appeared to be in her mid to late twenties. "I did not mean to disturb your meal," he said nervously. "It is just that you look very much like a very dear friend of mine. In fact, you could pass for my friend Minatis's younger sister."

The secretive lady pulled the hood of her robe a little more forward hiding the majority of her face. "My name is Ciramtis. This Minatis you speak of, where is she from?"

Jedaf thought about it for another zesta, trying to recall the story Mina had told him about her childhood. "She was from one of the small northern kingdoms of Kelleskar; I think she said it was Naroe or something like that," he replied.

"You speak of her very fondly. Could it have been Naros?"

"Yes, that's it," said Jedaf.

Ciramtis relaxed a little. Her face muscles smoothed and she sat back in her chair slouching a bit. She dabbed the corners of her mouth with the hand towel. "Were you close?"

"Well we weren't lovers or anything like that, but I think we were as close to one another as you could get. I was fortunate enough to be able to spend some time with her. She taught me how to read, write, and to be thankful for some of the opportunities that I have been given. It was a pleasure consulting with her, and translating some of the ancient scrolls in her library. I also miss strolling in the conservatory and gardens with her."

"I still have some trouble with the Odea glyphs and the Kaybeckian runes, but they're coming with practice. I know if I had been able to stay with her longer, or had been able to spend more time with her, I'm sure that I would have been able to improve my reading and diction."

Ciramtis set her staff to the side while he rambled on. She folded her hands in the front and placed them in her lap as she listened patiently. "What really made you look so much like her, were the brown robe, the embroidered sash belt and the staff. Minatis's staff had carvings that looked much like yours, except her's was a little longer and had a polished metallic point covering one end."

A smile appeared at the corners of the woman's lips and her nose wrinkled slightly. "There, you see. You even smile like her. It's a kind of a half amused look. Mina used to have it on her face every morning. I would greet her, and say. Veajak, nosta ieja Esella, and she would use the same whimsical smile, as a reply."

Ciramtis staff glowed whitely for a tenth of a zesta giving off a burst of intense energy, as he spoke. Its brilliance was as if a photo flash had gone off. The sudden intensity startled both of them. "Please do not do that again. It is not proper using the name of the goddess in a tavern."

"Again I am sorry, you're absolutely right."

The smile appeared again, as Ciramtis took up her wineglass. "It's funny that you know this Minatis so well," she said nonchalantly. "The sorceress you speak of died well over two hundred years ago." She raised her goblet and sipped her wine, as she waited for a reaction from him.

Jedaf knew that he had let his guard down and spoken too freely. Taking a nervous sip from his own tankard, he paused trying to think of a way of changing the subject and recovering some of his self-respect and anonymity. It might be time to try one of Corella's white magic memory spells, but on the spur of the moment he was so apprehensive he could not think of one.

"Have no fear sir," Ciramtis said. "The Lady Minatis was a distant relative of mine. By what ever power you possess, I think that you really did know her, and I am happy to make your acquaintance. Good sir, may I know your name?"

"Oh, I'm sorry again, forgive me for not introducing myself," he said as he extended his hand in her direction. "It is Jedaf, Jedaf of Dolfi." There was an instant of concern on her face as she reached across the table in formal greeting. She recalled the fabled demonic treskuls and the evil sorcerer of ancient Semedia. The legendary story was a way to frighten ill mannered children and make them behave.

"I said, Jedaf of Dolfi, not Caspasi!" Her eyes sparkled with an inner knowing; she nodded and smiled politely at his unorthodox greeting. No one on the Planet of Palestus would have expected to shake the hand of a female, let alone speak to her without being introduced by a third party or a relative.

Over Ciramtis's shoulder, Jedaf could see one of the innkeeper's servants conversing with two Worezian border guards. They were looking in Jedaf's direction, and turned their heads away as soon as Jedaf noticed them. "Do you know that tavern worker or either of those warriors?"

Ciramtis casually looked to the side at them, shaking her head. "I think that they saw my staff glow, and went to get the royal guards. I'm wanted for questioning, and I have to get out of here as quickly as possible."

He touched the back of her hand compassionately with his fingertips. "I am sorry, for what I have done. Is there anything that I can do for you to make up for it?"

She looked around the banquet hall for an exit, and noted the narrow hallway near the back door to the kitchen delivery area. A soot and grease blackened, redwood plaque with two thin chains was hanging above the hallway ceiling. Painted on this sign board was a white upside down tankard, depicting the direction leading to the rear outhouses. Picking up her staff, she asked quickly, "Which way are you heading?"

"I am traveling to the high mountains toward the ancient City of Tabalis."

Ciramtis looked a little apprehensive and said in a hushed tone, "Then you'll be heading for the eastern roads. I don't have the time to explain further. Stay on the main road for a couple of days, and do not leave it. I will meet you along the way." She tied the front drawstrings of her hood, and tossed a garja copper coin on the table.

Giving him a quick wave goodbye she picked up her tartan, satchel style travel bag. Heading toward the opposite side of the inn, Ciramtis stepped around a waitress and walked by the kitchen food preparation sorting tables. She didn't look back and wasted no time in heading between the stacked crates of fresh vegetables.

Jedaf returned to his table and reluctantly watched the woman until she was through the crowd of customers. "Master, what ever you said to that wench sure put wings on her feet." Jedaf ignored Kytos's cynical comment. Leaning over the table closer toward Ajor, he whispered. "I think we should be going. The innkeeper's kitchen help has sent for the royal guards, and I don't want to get involved in anymore trouble."

The front door banged open, with six burley and rowdy sailors coming into the tavern. They were yelling for ales and muscled their way between the patrons to the service bar. Ajoris tapped Jedaf's arm, and pointed to the entryway with his thumb. At first glance Jedaf did not recognize them.

The seamen looked as if they had recently escaped from a prison or one of the pest houses. Their yellow and white tunics were in shreds, and they looked like they had not washed in weeks. Jedaf handed Ajoris a silver piece and said, "Get Captain Odelac and his crew a mug of ale. Send the captain over to our table."

The captain was a big robust, red headed, forty year old strongman. He stood approximately five foot ten, or fourteen hands, and weighing about two hundred and sixteen pounds, or about thirty six tarmets. His tunic, kilt, knee high stockings and boots were well made but they were of the simple working variety.

The dull yellow and white colored woolen cloths of the seaman's guild were filthy and ragged. The captain's hands were huge, rough, calloused and quite strong. The first time that they greeted aboard the merchant ship Tarpenya, Jedaf realized the man's fingers wrapped completely around his own wrist.

Ajoris walked over and spoke with the captain while he and a few of his shipmates stood drinking at the bar. After paying for the round of ales, the ambassador thanked the captain for saving their lives. The officer was led a few feet away from the service bar where the other sailors could not hear. While Ajoris's back was to the crew, Odelac was quietly told about Jedaf being the king and the rightful Lord of the Semedian Red Dragon Empire. For the sake of safety it was of the utmost importance that this information be kept confidential.

Captain Odelac had not known this before. Lord Jedaf had been traveling incognito, and had been introduced aboard ship, only as the son of a merchant from central Semedia. Once his vessel was seized, it was Odelac's idea of telling the pirates that Jedaf was the ambassador's servant. At the time it was the only thing the captain could think of that would save the young boy's life, and keep him from being thrown into the slave hold.

Ajoris paid for another round of ales and directed the remaining crew members to one of the long tables. The captain felt a bit foolish and ashamed of his past actions, but swallowed his pride and walked over to Jedaf's table.

From Odelac's appearance, he looked like he hadn't had a decent meal since sailing from Joroca, and he smelled even worst. Downing the ale that he had carried over with him, he pulled out a chair and sat down. Jedaf waved the waitress over ordering four more ale's for his table, and a fowl for the captain along with one of them for each of his men.

"Lord, I'm sorry for the trouble I've caused you in sailing here to Zarhun. The ambassador just told me who you are. Had I known earlier, I would have taken a lot more caution and not risked your life while trying to aide that other ship in distress. Thank you for the ales and the meal, Master Jedaf. It took almost every silver coin that I had in the merchant bank to buy my freedom and that of some of my crew members."

Jedaf looked in the direction of the captain's rag tag disheveled group, recognizing only two of them. "The rest of my crew went to the auction block first thing this afternoon. I only hope that some day I will be able to get my fingers around Mister Tristos's neck."

The waitress brought over a roasted fowl for the captain of the Tarpenya and brought the rest of the plicarens over to the long tables for the other seamen. Odelac twisted the broiled game bird in half, and took a huge bite of the breast. "Where are you bound for captain," asked Jedaf?

Odelac swallowed hard, wiping the hot grease from his mouth with the back of his hand. Then he took a sip of ale to wash it down, and clear his throat. "The men and I thought we might be able to work our way east and sign on board a ship out of Adathe. We would rather ship out of an honest port, even if the wages might be less." Jedaf pushed the bread and butter basket over closer to the starving officer. The captain nodded a thank you, and buttered two golden sections of salt crusted krastan.

Jedaf finished the last sip from his mug before setting it down and speaking. "As long as you're traveling east, how would you like to join up with the ambassador and myself?"

Odelac nodded his head affirmatively, his mouth full of food. Spraying some crumbs he replied, "Sire, you're the only one that's bought me a meal since I was a cabin boy. I owe you, and if I can repay you and the ambassador by providing you an escort to Adathe, it will be all the better. The only problem we have is we're short of funds. All the money I've got left will barely pay for a few ales and some journey breads."

Jedaf stood up saying, "You don't have to worry about the costs or provisions, but I have to warn you, we may be in for some trouble. It will be good being part of a larger party." Odelac's men came over to the table thanking the young lord after having eaten most of their pheasant. They appeared to be in as bad a physical shape as their captain. "Kytos get our bags," said Jedaf. The waitress came over to collect payment for the meals, and stood by quietly until Jedaf looked in her direction.

"That will be five coppers and three steels sire." Ajoris handed Jedaf the four bronzes change from the silver that he had given him earlier, and Jedaf dug into his purse for a few more coins.

"I will also be paying for the other fowls, bread and ales, which my men are eating." He handed her the additional two bronzes and three steels. "Captain, after your men finish eating have another round of ale on me. Then take a short rest. I'll be around the back of the inn at the supply buildings and dry goods store. You and your crew can meet up with us there later."

"Yes Lord." They raised their tankards in a quiet toast of thanks, as Jedaf, Ajoris and Kytos left by way of the kitchen exit.

Chapter # 2

Valadis of Jeupa

The supply building was almost as large as the inn itself, but the exterior had a more run down appearance. It was a dilapidated unpainted structure of rough sawn board plank siding without any advertising signs or indications that it was a mercantile warehouse. The building was a converted two full story barn with an additional rear half walkout story below grade. From the outside one would never expect it to contain anything other than farming equipment, horses, a few measa milking cows or some other domesticated animals.

Stacked to the ceiling beams of each floor, were palleted goods of all types. Many items were covered in cob webs, a thick layer of millet chaff, or wind blown fodder. The tax collectors of this district were obviously well paid for turning a blind eye toward this community. "May I help you gentlemen?" As they entered the door the head clerk and owner of the establishment called out and came running over quickly.

He stepped between Jedaf, Kytos and Ajoris, speaking directly to the ambassador. He was smiling and smelling the possibility of a large sale. "Yes," replied Jedaf. The balding man with bulging waist, turned away from the well dressed gentleman in the direction of the rather disheveled teenager, and the slave attendant standing at his side. "I will tell you what I want. You load it, and then we will negotiate the costs and the prices of the goods."

A gleam lit the corners of the older salesman's eyes as the youth spoke. A young inexperienced lord disguised as a peasant. With him in charge it would mean an even greater profit. "Yes sire, will you require supplies for a long journey?"

Ajoris stepped around the merchant and moved over closer to Jedaf. "Lord, we will need at least a weeks worth of provisions for us to travel to Tabalis, and an additional two to three days of supplies to get from there to the City of Adathe. With the eight of us you'll need supplies for half a month."

Kytos tugged lightly at his sleeve. "Lord, we're nine," he whispered. The clerk liked the sound of that; supplies, equipment and provisions to outfit an expedition of nine travelers for a half mursa. It would be his largest sale since the beginning of the Envarian War three years ago, and he did not have to bribe anyone.

"Gentlemen, if you plan on traveling the woodland and mountain roads to the east, I would suggest that you take along a couple of extra days rations. Many of the old roads have not seen a traveler in years and some have been entirely abandoned. The few roads that are passable are not as good as they use to be. Your journey will take longer than you think. The eastern woodlands are fraught with danger. You will have to be extra cautious with highwaymen and murderous vourtre still inhabiting the mountainous regions."

Jedaf gave his nod of approval. "Very well, we will make it food and supplies for twelve to fifteen days."

"Sire, do you have carts or wagons for your supplies," inquired the clerk?

"No," replied Jedaf making a cloud of dust as he tapped on a stack of folded tarps. "I would like to walk around and see what you have to offer, before making any decisions."

The owner led the way and showed them out of the side door. They walked down the grassy hillside around and behind the dry goods building. There were four smaller storage sheds, a large weather worn sun bleached lean-to, a half dozen coops, and a smaller fenced in livestock area. Between these out-buildings were a couple of older open sided wagons, three two wheeled carts, and two covered Conestoga style wagons.

One wagon seemed to be in fairly good condition. It had newly replaced support slats and tarpaulin covering. "How much do you want for the covered wagon?"

"Eighteen hundred coppers," said the owner with a straight face.

"With a price that high, I would expect the four horses, harnesses, the trace lines, and all the rest of the gear."

The clerk pretended to look a little shocked. "Why no, those are all extras. The horses are another one hundred and fifty a piece, and the gear is another two hundred."

Ajoris stepped between them, facing the clerk. "You want twenty-six hundred coppers for a broken down, rickety wagon and a few nags?" He turned back toward Jedaf. "This salesman is crazy," he said contemptuously. "Let's go down the road to the other supplier. The bartender in the Worezian market sector told me if we could not get what we needed at this supplier; there was another trade goods store off the path a little further to the south."

Jedaf laughed at seeing the disgusted look on Ajor's face. "Just a zesta, maybe the rest of his prices will even out the cost for the wagon and horses."

The clerk was a little worried and apprehensive. Taking a handkerchief from his belt he mopped the perspiration from his face, and tried not to look too concerned.

"How much do you want for a cart and team," Jedaf asked?

"Six hundred for the cart, three hundred for the team, and I will throw in all of the gear."

Jedaf walked around to the best of the three carts and shook it by the wheel. The cart rattled and bumped up and down in the dirt. "Are all of the carts and wagons made of softwood," he asked? Then, the teenager walked over to the larger and wider of the two wagons. Picking the rear wheel off of the ground he looked at the undercarriage and examined the vehicles rear axle and suspension system.

"The wagon's made of the same cheap inexpensive materials. Really shoddy workmanship, wouldn't you say Ajor?" The clerk had never seen anything like that in his life, and the thought of losing the largest sale of the year left a dumbfounded expression on his face.

"I must," he stammered, "have made a mistake. The really good wagons must have been sold already. This wagon with its team is only two thousand, four hundred coppers and the cart is only seven hundred."

Jedaf dropped the wagon. "I will tell you what I am going to do. I had planed on buying a lot of supplies and equipment here. So I should get a lot better price on the cart and wagon. Say twenty-five hundred for both, with the teams and all the gear."

The clerk tipped his head back and wiped the sweat from his flabby neck with his kerchief. "Are you going to fill the cart and wagon?"

Jedaf looked to Ajoris, for the answer. The ambassador grudgingly shrugged his shoulders. "With the amount of supplies we will need; we will probably fill them both, and we may need a few pack animals for the extras."

"You have your answer," replied Jedaf.

"Alright," the proprietor said reluctantly. "If you fill out the rest of your order here, and only buy supplies from my warehouse, I'll give you the price that you asked."

They walked around the lower foundation wall and re-entered the side door of the main building. "You there, bring the wide wagon with the yellow tarpaulin and the covered cart with the longer sided wheel base around to the front of the building." Two men sitting at the top rail of the paddock jumped to Jedaf's order.

"Ky, go over to the clothing shelves and pick out a few new outfits with boots to go with them; also get a good heavy travel cloak." Kytos did not have to be asked twice. The young prince disappeared behind a large stack of blankets and clothing racks, stripping as he ran.

While the wagons were being pulled around to the front of the building, Ajoris and one of the clerks went to pick out the teams. Jedaf walked up and down the aisles of the storeroom picking up, sorting and stacking miscellaneous supplies and an assortment of bottled herbs until they returned. The wagon was the first to be loaded, and it was good to have Ajoris take charge. It was quite evident that this was not the first time that he had outfitted an expeditionary party of this type.

Ajoris started yelling out orders, and clerks ran to fill the request as soon as Ajor called the item out. Four sacks of oolets, the potato like root with red skins, three sacks of krastant flour, three ceramic lined barrels of cooking oil, two kegs of ale, and two kegs of wine. The stabblehands loaded the provisions in the wagon as soon as the clerks carried them to the front of the barn.

Every one of the owner's warehouse clerks seemed to be busy at once, and the owner had to go over to the inn to get a few of the kitchen helpers for assistance. Cooking kettles with tripod stands, metal plates, utensils, and repair tools were fastened to the one side of the wagon. Then the ambassador gave orders for thirty tarmets of dried measan meat, a large bag of emen cooking salt, another two sacks of dried rena beans, two large burlap bags full of watull corn meal, and two more sacks of jes spli brown rice.

Nine extra heavy travel cloaks, two complete changes of clothes for Odelac's men, and twenty blankets were stowed in the front of the cart. A large water barrel was tied onto the side frame of the wagon and a smaller cask was lashed to the cart. Hand axes, saws, knives, swords, hammers, mauls, metal banding, and an assortment of miscellaneous hand tools were tied on the other side of the wagon for easy access. The owner stood to the side and kept tally scribbling down each item as they were loaded.

Slowly the covered wagon and cart were filling. Two large cheese wheels, sacks of dried fruit, two large oily tarps, several long coils of ropes having different thickness, pulleys, an assortment of oil lamps, lamp oils, and tallow fat candles; the list kept growing and growing, seeming to have no end.

Ajoris walked each aisle of the three floors examining the goods and making mental notes of material, equipment, or provisions he thought they might require. The clerks were quite satisfied, as well as the proprietor. It was the sale of a lifetime. Hynon, the owner, walked over to Jedaf and Ajoris as they checked off the items that had been loaded.

Jedaf was beginning to think he should have asked the owner to have both wagons brought around to the front of the barn. The vehicles were stacked nearly to the top of the canvas. If he had chosen the narrower wagon instead of the cart, they would not have been overloaded. But then again; if he had, he was sure they would have kept buying until it too was cramed full.

Jedaf and Ajoris wanted to make sure that they had not forgotten any of the basic necessities. They talked among themselves softly as the proprietor stood by quietly. Finally clearing his throat Hynon asked; "Will you need a couple of women, slave laborers or perhaps a guide? I have got two young females that would be good to have on a journey this long, and I also have a few strong backed slaves that I could let you have very cheap." Jedaf could imagine their health from what he had seen aboard the pirate ship Culba and at the slave market earlier in the day.

The economic conditions of this kingdom were now very poor. Manpower was in such short supply, the plantation owners and miners were buying slaves in any condition. They also did not ask any questions concerning their health, or where they came from. "No thanks! I do not need any more mouths to feed and I don't intend on filling another cart or wagon."

Looking over Ajoris's shoulder at the list, the portly owner noted the amount of items which had check marks next to them. It created a wide satisfying smile on the businessman's face. "Is there anything else that you will need, anything at all," Hynon asked?

Jedaf thought about it for a half zesta, scratching at the stubble of a beard that had grown on his face since sailing from Joroca. "Come to think of it, there is. Ajor, go back to the corral and pick out two more saddle horses and a few pack animals. One horse for Ky and one for Captain Odelac. Get blankets, saddles and everything else that they will need, and have one of the stable boys toss in a couple extra bags of feed grains into the wagon."

Kytos stepped out from behind one of the racks, with an arm load of clothing. Even though he still smelled like a sewer, he looked good in his new outfit and boots. "Master, is there anything else that I should get?"

"Yes, a large travel bag to keep your stuff together," Jedaf yelled back.

Ajor returned in a half zestar, with two dark brown riding horses trailing behind him. The stable boy followed behind with two stout, brown and white, wide backed pack horses on a leader. The mounts were a shorter and a slightly stockier breed than the two saddle horses that were purchased in Woreza.

These shaggy ridding horses had white stockings and lighter brown spots on their hindquarters. Their black manes and tails were also longer and coarser than the more domesticated variety. They had been bred for the rockier mountain passes and colder, rougher terrains of the interior.

"Ky take one of the horses from Ajor, it is yours." Running from the barn, the boy took the reins of the nearest horse held by the ambassador. It was a good gentile mount and Ky stroked its nose while the stable hands tossed blankets and saddles on them. The clerk added the additional costs to the lengthening list and tallied the bill of lading.

The young lord knew that Ajoris had picked out the best horses from the dozen or so running about inside the corrals. Jedaf could see the spiritual presence of Verolos, his old ridding teacher, walking at the animal's flank. A cloud of annoying, luminescent, firefly like insects buzzed about him, while the equestrian patted and stroked the mane to one of the mounts.

The old cavalryman didn't speak, but he gave Jedaf a wave of his arm and an approving nod of his head. Jedaf was glad to see the apparition of the old Oyaltan horseman again and yelled out to his spirit, "Jakib caska fa ata eiantan mu azzatus xin caskan gos." Hynon, the owner and his clerk, could not see anyone in the direction their customer was shouting.

The rest of liverymen standing around in the front of the barn looked nervously at each other after hearing the eccentric young aristocrat speak. A fearful expression crossed their faces. The possessed boy was suddenly speaking in the archaic language of the ancients. It was certainly strange for anyone to be thanking the thin air for picking out the best horses. The two sable hands leading the pack horses did not know why they should keep the east wind in their face.

The merchants also could not hide the greed on their own faces or the gleam in their eyes. Hynon had sold a majority of items that had been on shelves for more than five years, and disposed of others that had been in the barn since his father ran the business. It had been years since they had made a sale of this magnitude. The fact that this youth was more than a little crazy couldn't hurt business.

"That totals six thousand eight hundred and twenty one coppers exactly." Jedaf took the tally list from Hynon and began crossing out or altering the quantities that he had not seen loaded. Then he ran lines through some of the prices, and wrote in the costs that he thought were closer to the actual market value of the goods. "Three small gold, five large silvers, and six bronzes, would be nothing less than robbery." The teenager muttered as he readjusted the figures and struck out a few more items. Then he re-totaled the list of goods and materials.

"If I have to pay these prices for the few goods I have picked out, I might as well go all the way back to the city and buy them there." Handing the list back to Hynon, Jedaf said; "I figure that everything is worth about fifty five hundred coppers." It was the proprietor's turn to cross out prices adjusting the costs and re-tallying the bill.

A loud commotion started out of their sight during the negotiations. The noise and shouting was coming from the rear of the tavern. Ajor ran out of the barn and around the corner to find out what it was all about. Then he ran back to Jedaf and whispered in his ear. "I have to leave now, so you can stop your figuring. I will give you the three small golds and four small silvers, not a steel more."

Hynon gave his nodding approval. The owner knew it was a higher cost and profit for him than what he would have gotten had the bargaining continued. "Sold to the gentlemen with the large purse, and the generosity to match," said Hynon with a jovial smile on his face. Jedaf dropped the coins into Hynon's chubby hand and ran from the building.

Across the courtyard, three warriors were pulling and stretching a man of the clothier's guild over the hitching rail. A fourth warrior was holding the thin; five foot six man by his long brown hair, and a fifth was flaying at the man's back with a short riding crop.

"Where's the witch with the walking stick?" Another stinging lash fell across the man's back. The twenty five year old retailer jerked erect in pain as all his muscles tightened. Squirming sideways, the prisoner tried to pull lose of their grasp, but there were too many hands holding him.

The assistant cook and two of his kitchen helpers stood by on the kitchen back porch watching and commenting among themselves. They were quite pleased with how things had worked out, and had smug expressions on their faces.

Earlier in the morning the Worezian royal guards had stopped by at the inn. The border guardsmen had given descriptions of a woman they were looking for, and told of a high reward for her capture. The assistant cook greedily rubbed his hands together, and yelled out to the Worezian soldiers. "I have some boiling grease back in the kitchen, if you want to use it."

The whip cracked again as the detainee struggled, trying to twist free. "I don't know where she is! How many times do I have to give you the same answer," shouted the clothing vendor!

The second class warrior looped the braided leather whip about the prisoner's neck jerking his head backward. "You came here with her, where did she go?"

The man clenched his teeth, and yelled back at them after regaining some of his strength. "How stupid are you! I told you, I do not know!"

The senior warrior twisted the lash; cutting off the prisoner's airway until the man's face turned beet red. Then the guardsman gave him another hard backhand, cutting the captive's mouth. Pulling the loop tighter, the second class forced the retailer's face upward again, and then hit him with a full clenched fist. The blood flowed freely from the prisoner's nostrils. It ran down his chin onto his light colored orange tunic and the coarsely braided brown leather laces and trim.

"They must be asking about Ciramtis," Jedaf said as they ran across the courtyard. "If he is a friend of hers, we've got to help." The warriors let their prisoner drop to the ground and squared off for combat at seeing Jedaf and Ajoris approaching them. "Second class, what is the meaning of this?"

"Mind your own business you scrawny cur, or we will be whipping you next."

Jedaf took another step closer to the seasoned warrior. "This is my business. You're whipping one of my servants."

The hard scar faced, middle aged warrior straightened himself, coiled his black whip and fingered his sword hilt. "Then you know the witch wearing the brown hooded cloak?"

"Yes! Well sort of," Jedaf replied. "We just ate at the table next to hers in the tavern. I thought that I knew her, and sat at her table for a few zestas. Then the witch's magical staff glowed, and I realized that it was not the woman that I thought I knew. I got up and left her table as soon as she ran out the doorway. I have to tell you it scared the demons out of me. I thought that she was going to turn me to stone right then and there."

The warrior removed his hand from his hilt as he took a half step closer toward the bare faced youth. "How long have you known her," he asked in a boisterous tone?"

"Oh, we just met before sitting down to eat. If I had known she was a witch, I would never have spoken to her. All I wanted to know was how much she was charging for a night of pleasure." The explanation seemed to satisfy the non-commissioned officer, and his taxt of fellow border guardsmen.

"Now, if your men will release my servant, I will buy the ales." The two warriors that had pulled the prisoner to his feet let go of his arms again while Jedaf was speaking. The man fell to his face in the dirt after being let go. Blood seeped through the back of his tunic, as he lay there in a semi-conscious state.

"He is lying," shouted the short-order cook! "These travelers did not come here with that merchant. The man you're whipping was accompanying the witch when they rode up to the inn." As soon as the assistant cook opened his mouth, Jedaf pushed Ajoris backward out of harms way and had his sword in his hand.

The Worezian warriors were almost as quick, but slower to action. The man to Jedaf's immediate right never had a chance to pull his blade. Jedaf had cut his throat in one a long sweeping arc as his drew his sword. Three of the junior ranked swordsmen tried to position themselves around him quickly for best advantage. The fourth stood off to the side, with his boot on the back of the prisoner's neck.

A knife flashed for an instant in Jedaf's left hand then flew to the nearest royal guard that lunged at him. The young lord had aimed at his foe's upper chest but the warrior tried to duck. The short, double sided dirk found its mark in the jugular, and the guard was spitting blood before hitting the ground. Moving quickly through the opening in his opponent's defense, Jedaf parried one hard cut and spun between his attackers.

The men at his opposite sides now made their move. They were smart enough to stay out of thrusting range, but started to press their advantage and attack. A fast and furious clash of cold steel ensued until a heavy ceramic, katmet flower pot was thrown from the rear doorway of the kitchen porch.

The potted plant hit the second class warrior in the back of his head. Falling forward to his knees he dropped his weapon among the broken shards and loose soil. Jedaf attacked the other guard quickly and stuck him deeply under the left armpit. The warrior winced in pain for a zesta then fell to his knees in the dirt before slumping over.

The last warrior standing looked as if he was about to strike. Jedaf wield about to parry the blow but he did not have to defend himself. The stern Worezian warrior was standing and looking temporarily frozen, but was in reality dead on his feet. A large wooden handled bread knife was deeply imbedded in his chest. It had been thrown from the back steps by the youngest of Odelac's crew.

The sound of a horse and rider galloping off made everyone look up quickly. Through the trailing dust cloud, Jedaf could see that there was another member of the royal guards. He had been standing near the paddock tending to the patrol's horses, while the senior warriors questioned the prisoner. As soon as the last Worezian guard was killed, the survivor panicked and dropped the reins to his friend's horses. The other black war steeds scattered about the field as he quickly mounted and rode off to get reinforcements.

"I thought that you might need a little help," said the captain. The young Dragon Lord gave a quick nod of thanks to the wiry youth that had thrown the knife. From his vantage point it had not been an easy throw.

During the skirmish, the fearful assistant cook had slowly backed his way toward the rear entrance to the kitchen. He had not expected half a dozen royal guards would lose this fight, but he wasn't going to take any chances. Captain Odelac and his men had shoved him aside as they came out of the inn. Each of the sailors was armed with wine bottles and kitchen utensils.

The second class warrior groggily crawled up on his hands and knees and reached out for his sword. He had not been able to regain his stance since being hit by the flower pot. Vadeck took the last sip from his ale mug, before walking over and smashed his hefty ceramic tankard over the dazed warrior's head. The warrior collapsed again, as he was knocked out.

"Thanks men! We better get out of here, before that rider gets back with reinforcements. The cart and wagon are already loaded and hitched ready to go. A couple of you men gather those warrior's swords, cloaks, and horses. They won't need them anymore! The others get to the wagons."

"Aye, aye sire." A few of Odelac's crew trotted off after stripping the dead of any possessions that could be used. The others were able to round up three of the five, garrison's loose mounts.

The weak and battered prisoner on the ground slowly pulled himself into a sitting position. Leaning against one of the hitching rails uprights for support, he wiped the bloody mud from his face with his shaky hand. The merchant's right cheek bone and his eye socket were black and blue. Blood was still flowing from his swollen lips and nose.

Slowly the tradesman reached over and wrenched the second class's sword from the warrior's clenched fist. The merchant steadied himself momentarily while looking up the stairs toward the innkeeper's kitchen servants. The assistant cook nervously wiped his sweaty hands on his greasy apron as he edged toward the doorway. The prisoner swung the sword behind his head and let it fly. The long blade went clear through the cook's upper abdomen and sunk deeply into the planking of the building.

Looking down at the protruding hilt, the cook's wide eyes bulged with fright. He could not speak; he made a few gurgling sounds and started spitting up blood. He was about to die and he knew it. The pleading look on his face faded as his head drooped. The body slowly slumped forward but was unable to fall. The corpse hung on the sword until one of the cook's helpers pulled the blade loose from the planking. The rest of the kitchen helpers eased the cook's body down on the porch floor and covered his face with an apron.

The tradesman sitting in the loose dirt at the hitching rail yelled over at the cook and his helpers. "That is for sending the guards to beat me, and for offering the boiling grease." Jedaf reached down and helped the prisoner to his feet. "Thank you, Jedaf of Dolfi," he said in a shallow voice, before passing out once again and falling into the boy's outstretched arms.

The young lord looked at the retailer closely; he had never seen this man before. Two of Odelac's seamen ran over and helped carry the limp body of the injured man over to the covered wagon. Jedaf stooped down and pulled loose the Worezian guard's cape. Following the others to the wagon, he wiped his blade clean, sheathing his own sword. The swarm of little irritating insects that had encircled Verolos's sprit earlier, returned and landed all over him. It was as if he were covered in nectar. They had not lighted on anyone else as the men made room in the wagon for the traveling merchant.

The extra feed bags that Jedaf had bought and two, ten tarmet vegetable sacks had to be removed. They were tied over the back of one of the extra stockier pack horses along with some of the clothing he had bought for Odelac's crew. There was barely enough room at the tailgate, and the sailors had to bend the nearly unconscious man's legs for him to lie down.

The teenager swatted the cloud of pesky fireflies away. They seemed to disappear into the wooden cracks and crevasses of the wagon. He hopped they were not looking to make a nest in one of the burlap meal bags or wooden vegetable crates.

Jedaf reached over behind the merchant and tucked one of the folded blankets behind the stranger's shoulders and tried to make him as comfortable as possible. Opening his medical bag, he reached into the side pocket and withdrew a thin, four inch long, crooked and knobby purple carrot like vegetable. Breaking off about an inch, he put the rest of the thin root it in his waist pouch. Umaksepa was used as an anesthetic. The plants roots caused drowsiness while the boiled leaves created hallucinations.

The young lord wanted to do more, but he knew they needed to get underway pretty quickly. Another four to five zestars and the suns would be setting. The royal guards might wait until morning to pursue them, but they could not take that chance. Lifting his head a bit, the weary stranger spoke softly. "I'm Valadis of Jeupa. Ciramtis sent me to watch over you, I guess I did not do such a good job of it."

Jedaf climbed up on the rear bed of the wagon next to the injured man and put some folded towels under his head. "We do not have the time to talk now. Chew up and eat this piece of root. It will help ease the pain and help you to get some rest."

A crowd of spectators started forming outside of the tavern. Most of the staff and serving women had come out after hearing one of the cooks had been killed. Captain Odelac handed Jedaf the reins to his mare and mounted the broader backed mountain horse standing next to him. The two of them rode on the flanks of the wagon, while Ajoris and Kytos rode point. Odelac's crew rode up behind the wagon's forming the rear guard. They were finally on their way out of greater

Woreza and into the countryside. Jedaf was sure he was not going to miss this city.

Chapter # 3

Jeupan Spies

The injured merchant of the clothier's guild slipped in and out of consciousness as the wagon rattled down the dusty dirt road. A zestar from the inn, they stopped just long enough for Jedaf to dismount and climb into the back of the wagon. The young lord cleaned the stranger's wounds, and picked the larger pieces of dirt and stone from Valadis's back using a small penknife and a twig with cotton fibbers wrapped about it.

From the depth of the lacerations, it was quite evident that the riding crop's lash had been modified to deal with peasants and not horses. A rusted steel barb or a sharp stone had been embedded at the end of the second class's whip. Several of the cuts needed stitches to close, and one was deep enough that might have required a couple of additional sutures, but Jedaf was more afraid of the infection, than closing the wound.

One of the items that the "Inn of the Athca" and provisions supply depot lacked was a good medical supply. Jedaf had bought up what he could salvage, but most of the remedies, curative potions, and healing supplies were rancid, or had insect infestations. He bought a variety of herbs, tubers, purified oils, honey, and powdered minerals to make his own, but it would take time that he did not have.

It was a good thing that Jedaf and Ajoris had interceded when they had. Another few zestas and there would not have been enough skin on Valadis back to stitch together. While at the "Calling Center Compound," the young wizard had been taught the rudimentary arts of Palestus's medieval healing guild. Most of his medical knowledge actually came from his previous lives on Earth. Dealing with infections and dressing battlefield wounds on his planet, seemed to be as old as life itself.

Jedaf coated each of the gashes with bee honey and a sulphurous powder, healing ointment before bandaging the last of the lacerations. Then he left a clean yellow tunic out for the man to use once he woke. After covering the merchant with one of the blankets, Jedaf opened the rear canvas flap fully letting in some fresh air. The trade goods cart and rear guard were following the wagon. Dust clouds billow behind them, as he stood watching.

Holding onto the upper canvas supports he tried to think on happier times. It started out being a parched and hot morning, and had gotten warmer the further they rode from the coast. The road eastward was crusted with a hard packed, four-inch thick layer of finely compressed powdered silt covering the top surface. Not many merchants or travelers had been this way. It looked as if it had not rained in this area in ten days or more, and that it had been in a long dry spell before that.

Thick, black thorn brushes encroached on the edges of the road, and a tough fibrous knee high saw grass was growing in the ruts. Most of the vegetation had lost the new greenery of spring and was turning the greenish brown color which was typical for Palestus's first month of its two summers.

It had been over two zestars since they left the tavern, and it was good that Valadis had slept through most of it. Jedaf had enough of the stifling air beneath the canvas as he stood there. Waiving out of the back of the wagon, he tried to get Captain Odelac's attention. With the rattle of the wagon, the hoof beats and the dust cloud, the officer could not see or hear the young man.

Vadeck, the taskmaster of the Tarpenya caught sight of the teen and pulled up on his horse's reins moving nearer to the tailgate of the wagon. The boisterous marine was a short, crude, unintelligent looking fellow. He had a narrow forehead and his eyes were set to far apart. There were small hooped brass rings in his cauliflower ears. The straight, light brown hair on his bead had been bowl cut; giving him an almost Oyaltan look.

It appeared to Jedaf that the taskmaster had been in some sort of accident at one time. Part of his nasal cavity had been flattened, as was a section of his left cheek bone. Both areas were scarred and having a motley reddish purple discoloration to the skin. "Lord, would you like something," he asked in his heavy nasal voice.

"Yes. Have the captain and the ambassador pick a shady spot ahead. I think that we all could use a short rest and a stretch of our legs."

"Aye Lord," he said. Giving his mount a gentle nudge he rode to the front of the column. After the old seaman had spoken with them, Odel yelled back to Karadis. He was one of the deck cargo crewmen, and a part-time ship's carpenter. Kar, was a thirty year old muscular, seaman with a cracked weathered face and calloused hands. He stood about thirteen hands high or about five foot six and weighed about twenty-four tarmets, one hundred and forty-five pounds. The dark brown hair above his heavy brows hid his deep set eyes. They always seemed to have a serious look about them.

Jedaf had not spoken with this man since he had been assigned as the driver of the wagon. Looking up and over to Odel, the deckhand wiped the sweat from his face. "Pull your wagon under that large tree in the glade ahead," shouted the captain. Kar shaded his eyes, looking off to his right where Odel was pointing. Wild goats, boars, and werna red deer had cropped the tall grasses and had thinned the lower branches of the trees.

Valadis awoke from the bump of the first set of wheels leaving the road, and he sat up. At first he was a bit disoriented, but he accepted the water skin from Jedaf gratefully. The Conestoga made a turn to the left than a sharper one to the right before coming to a rest beneath the branches of a large and sparsely limbed, pin oak type of a tree.

Vadeck waived his arm at Baradic the driver of the cart, and the younger man seated next to him. He silently indicated they should follow after the wagon. Baradic was also a strong and wiry seasoned sailor. He was a little shorter than Karadis and a half a dozen years younger. His slicked back, greased hair was parted in the center and his thinly shaved; pencil thin, dark brown beard gave him a kind of a shady look. There was also his habit of questioning every order which didn't help give you a feeling of trust. Bara understood the taskmaster's meaning without speaking, and turned his team into the shade of the overhanging branches.

The twenty year old that rode on the brake side of the cart, jumped to the ground as soon as they stopped. He ran to the rear and held onto the pack animals until Baradic was able to climb down and steady the cart's horses.

Captain Odelac had been chained to this young slave as soon as they had been taken off of the Tarpenya. He was not a sailor, and no one really knew him or anything about him. Odelac's new companion had a soft voice. He spoke very seldom and kept mostly to himself. It was one of the things that Vadeck liked about him. Also, the old taskmaster liked the fact that this young man did what he was told and did not complain about it.

Near the port docking facility gangplank, a rope on one of the cargo pulley, boom crane's had broken loose. A large shipping crate swung over and almost landed on Odelac. If it wasn't for this grubby half starved stevedore, the captain would have been crushed.

The slave had seen what was happening. He ran over hitting and knocking the freight into the water while it was still in midair. The senior wharf taskmaster said that he had enough of the young troublemaker and had him chained to the old sailor that he had saved. Later in the afternoon, they would go to the slave market as a pair.

Myritt, the youngest members of the crew had been riding rear guard. He dismounted next to Trestan, and handed over the reins to his horse. "You can take care of mine along with the others," he said. Then he walked off into the shade. This sailor was twice as muscular as the young slave, but he did half the work. To call Myritt lazy would have been an understatement. He could not be found if something was needed to be done. The only time you knew he was sure to be around, was if a meal was about to be served.

Odelac only had enough funds in the merchant's bank to pay the ransom for the release of four crewmen. None other than Mister Vadeck, and seaman Karadis had been a prior crewman of the Tarpenya. Odelac had chosen to pay for Baradic, even though he argued a lot. He was a seasoned sailor, a hard worker, and knew what needed to be done without being asked.

Myritt on the other hand, was selected only because Mister Vadeck had vouched for him. The captain should have known better after seeing this young man standing by the prison door. After more than two weeks of captivity; Myritt's clothing was still fairly clean and the material had few stains and no rips or tears.

Jedaf and Odelac helped Valadis from the wagon. The two men allowed the merchant a few seconds to stretch and steady himself before they walked over to a secluded spot under the low boughs of a smooth barked burkat tree. Valadis sat, leaning his side against the tree trunk as he watched the other men tend to the horses.

It was a much-needed break for everyone. The young lord could see the others stretching their sore back and leg muscles as they swatted the dust and flies from themselves. The horses were unsaddled, and given a hasty rub down before they were staked out down wind, under the taller trees a little further ahead of their camp.

Val still carried the water skin with him and sipped at it slowly, trying to rinse the bitter taste of the anesthetic root from his mouth. All he could remember of the ride was the smell of the stagnant air beneath the oily canvas, and the sting of the alcohol on his wounds. "Feeling a little better," asked Jedaf?

"Yes. Thank you! Ciramtis told me that I could trust you. I thought Dastus had taken away the last of my luck, and that of my countrymen." Jedaf sat down cross legged next to him. A wide blade of grass was sticking out of the corner of his mouth.

Thinking momentarily about his vourtre friend Yanus and his people's patron god gave him a little chuckle. Dastus the Palestus

God of Fate certainly hadn't done him any favors. The grass shoot had a sweet minty smell as he twirled it around, between his lips. "And what country is that," asked Jedaf?

Valadis glanced quickly to the sides, than chuckled. "I guess I can tell you," he said softly. "Especially, since you've killed several royal Worezian guards." Shifting himself into a more comfortable position, he removed a large pebble from beneath his hip. Tossing it into the brush he replied, "I am from the southern Kingdom of Jeupa."

"I was sent north to spy on Worezian troop movements. We heard rumors that King Magarus is mobilizing his armies for war again. Why else would he need more fresh troops and supplies if he has made a treaty of marriage with the Envarian Kingdom?"

Jedaf thought of Kytos's sister Elona at the mention of the kingdom. He had fallen in love with the princess aboard the pirate ship Culba, and he was afraid that he would never see her again. His face flushed as his feeling started to get the better of him. Turning his head to the side he feigned a cough, shrugged his shoulders and tried to look emotionally detached and unconcerned.

Valadis sat up straighter pointing his finger at the young lord. "I will tell you why! First it is to help put down the rebellion in eastern Envar, and second it's to invade Jeupa." Jedaf was surprised to hear his conclusions. If Val's thoughts were true, it certainly would explain why King Magarus would be interested in receiving war supplies from the Sylakian Empire.

"Are you sure of that information," asked Jedaf?

"Yes, and so is Ciramtis. That is why the royal guards have been searching for us. We've learned much these three months of spring, and now I must get back to my people and warn them of the war. The Worezian Blue Army is already occupying the ancient Envarian City of Zarhun. We have also learned the Worezian Violet Army is moving down from the north coast through the Giehan Hills and into the Worezga Mountain foothills."

"Most of the rebel Envarian Army under the command of Prince Sesmak is still encamped on the western edge of the Great Zarhunian Divide. On the far western side of the Great Plain," he paused as he took a sip of water, "is the Envarian Royal Red Army. They are also moving into the Moland Forests. It is our understanding that when all these men get into position, the Worezian Tan Army will advance, invading from the northwest. The Worezian Blue Army will advance at the same time and take the northern lowlands of the plain."

"As soon as this happens, it will signal the advance of the Worezian Violet Army. They will start the first engagements with the rebels. With the help of the Royal Red Envarian Army, they will take the entire western plain. Ciramtis estimates Prince Sesmak to have between thirty five to forty thousand men with him."

"Worez has three invading armies totaling about three hundred thousand, and Envar has only one other standing army of about eighty thousand. The two kingdoms will have Sesmak trapped, and boxed in on three sides. The only escape route will be to the southeast. With such overwhelming odds, he won't have any choice but to retreat."

"That is exactly what King Magarus and King Helidon want. They plan on chasing Sesmak's Army over the border and into Jeupa. This will give them an excuse to declare war. They will invade our kingdom, claiming that Jeupa is giving aide to the rebel troops."

"Our kingdom is relatively small and has only four, half strength armies scattered over our entire countryside. By the time our good King Galthardon mobilizes the other warriors in the east, the Worezians will be over the border and half way to our capital City of Hyupeious."

Jedaf had been sitting quietly listening to the details and thinking to himself. How could Worez supply food for Sylak's war in the Histajonies, and fight a war of his own? "Are you sure that this information was not planted to throw a spy like you off the track? It seems to me that for such great powers, they broadcast their every movement. Something is starting to smell awfully bad to me!"

"No Lord Jedaf, you're wrong! Ciramtis does not make mistakes like that. Most of her information came directly from senior officers involved in the planning." Valadis took a few more sips of water before continuing.

"She opened up a gaming house for officers and gentlemen only, near the palace garrison. She let them think they were to have her or several other courtesans for a night of sexual pleasures. Instead they were drugged so all they could do was speak the truth and dream. They were beautiful and sexy hallucinations.

Soon word got around of this fabulous place. Money, wine and krasta en flowed freely. Even the commander of the Tan Army was on the list of preferred customers." Valadis tipped the water skin toward him again but it was empty. There was painful expression on his face, and he dabbed at the blood that was starting to flow from his nose again.

"Rest for a zesta, I will get a clean cloth." Jedaf got up and fetched a second water skin along with one of his travel bags, before returning from the wagon. "It sounds like she has you pretty well convinced. Have you any proof yourself, or is everything you know second hand knowledge?" Valadis snatched Jedaf's water skin and took a long pull before angrily tamping the stopper back in it. He was not sure if he had been insulted or whether this boy was just being overly cautious.

Valadis thought about it for a moment, and then gave a kind of half smile. "I know this all sounds suspiciously far fetched," he said as Jedaf handed him a clean cloth. "I can understand your apprehension hearing a fantastic story coming from someone that you do not even know. All the things that I have told you are the truth. The only reason I told you in the first place, was Ciramtis said I could trust you with everything that I know. I can also assure you that she was not the only one getting this information."

"I questioned one of the senior officers myself. It was late in the evening and Ciramtis had already drugged, and cast a spell over him by the time I had arrived. He was sprawled out in deep hallucinations and lying butt naked across the bed. This commander was so deep in his delusions that when I sat on the mattress next to him, he took my hand and started sucking on my fingers."

"He thought that I was Ciramtis or one of the other prostitutes. Kissing the palm of my hand he asked me to marry him. I told him that I was afraid to marry a warrior who was about to go off on a campaign, and that there were too many spies that already knew the invasion plans."

"That giddy buffoon laughed, and giggled while trying to lick my knee. I had to hold him off with both hands. He said; "What difference does it make? If Prince Sesmak's men flee to Jeupa before were ready to strike, the outcome will be the same. The southern kingdom's will assemble its first few armies and advance to the border. We will then claim that they are an invasion army coming out to rescue the rebels they have been supporting. Spies won't make any difference at all. In this war, we will out number them, ten to one."

"That was all I needed to convince me, and I hope it will be good enough to persuade you. I do not know who you are, or why Ciramtis wanted me to tell you everything that is going on. But, I do know her well enough to trust her with my life. I have done as she has asked, and if you don't believe what I have told you, so be it." Jedaf gave him quick thankful nod, and thought quietly about what he had been told before speaking.

"Your story sounds all too common and logical not to believe. Do you know when the Worezian's are planning to begin this campaign?" The doubts on Valadis's face faded. His smile widened and his eyes shined with anticipation. He poured some cold water on the cloth and held it over his sore nose and cut lip.

"We have just learned that today," he said excitedly! "That is why the Worezian guard is hot on our heels. In ten to twelve days a wagon train is expected to leave Woreza. This armed caravan will be escorting Princess Shayla and the royal wedding entourage. They will be heading for Renvas, the capital city of the Envarian Kingdom."

"The royal escort guards will be carrying the finalized peace treaty with them, and the last zesta changes for the invasion plans. At the same time, King Helidon will be sending almost half his kingdoms grain supplies to Woreza by ship. This boon is to be a partial downpayment to King Magarus for putting down the rebellion. Four moons after the royal caravan arrives in Renvas, the Envarian Red Army will sound their war trumpets and advance onto the Zarhunian Plain."

The young Semedian lord was once again silent for awhile as he thought and muttered under his breath, while counting his fingertips. "That is sixteen to twenty days after Sylak's fleet invades the Histajonies. The six cargo ships that Worez is sending to Maltarus will have plenty of time to unload their cargo, load up with the needed war supplies and return."

"I am sorry Master Jedaf; I did not quite hear what you said."

"It doesn't matter Val. How many days were you in Woreza?"

Valadis closed his eyes and thought for a zesta, "In the city itself a mursa; a full month, all sixteen days."

"Did you see any large shipments of food goods or other provisions, while you were there?"

The merchant toyed with the small mole on his chin while he thought. "No sire. I can't say as I had. As a matter of fact, now that you mention it, there were less baked goods and vegetable carts than usual. Even the taverns and hostels were having a shortage of meats and bread rolls."

Jedaf thought of Princess Elona and Diara, as Valadis spoke. "Have you heard any other details concerning the wedding contract or of the ceremonies?"

"No. Not really. I don't know anything about Woreza's Princess Shayla, but I do know a little about Prince Quayot of Envar. Word is he's a half-wit," Val said sarcastically. "Quayot is about thirty-two years old and is the only son of King Helidon. None of the commoners in the kingdom likes or respects him." As he listened, Jedaf took his shoulder bag, from the lower limb that he had hung it on. Then he and took out a short stack of papyrus, a stiff black quill, and an ink bottle. He wrote for several zestas while Valadis returned to sipping at the water skin.

The Jeupan spy had talked himself dry, and was starting to tire. "I would like you to tell me everything that you know about the treaty, or of the officers that you came in contact with," said Jedaf. "I am not familiar with the Continent of Zarhun, and I know even less of the countries or their kings. I would like to write it down, and than try to sort it out later for myself." Valadis slumped down a little against the tree trunk, making a noticeable sigh.

Jedaf took this as a sign that it was going to be a long story. "Where shall I start," Valadis asked?"

"How about the treaty itself; have you heard anything about that?"

Valadis crossed his feet at the ankles, closed his eyes and relaxed. "Yes," he said in a matter of fact tone, "But it's just what everyone else knows. The king sent out proclamations to all the towns and villages over four mursas ago. When the war began three years ago, it drained the treasuries of both kingdoms quite heavily. Worez conquered the six northern provinces of Envar, and the regional capital City of Zarhun. It's one of the oldest cities on the continent and was one of the most prosperous."

"Most of Worez's war supplies were used up during the siege, and with the loss of Zarhun City, Envar's economy went from bad to worse. This last engagement was the cause of the stalemate between their two kingdoms, and the reason it has lasted to this day. Envar could not afford a campaign to recover Zarhun City or the surrounding towns, and the Worezians could not leave a large rebellious provincial city behind their front lines and still expand their frontiers."

"After about a year of occupation, an armistice and treaty of marriage was announced. On the eve of the wedding the war will be officially over, and neither side will declare victory. The Worezian Kingdom will still keep all the territory that it has conquered, but only keep them in trust until a male heir is born to the royal union."

"The child's regent will rule all the territories conquered by the two nations until he reaches the age of twelve. The prince will also be the heir to both thrones, and will eventually assimilate both Envar and Worez into one kingdom."

"It's the part about the conquered territories, which worries us in Jeupa and the other nations of western Zarhun. That is why I was sent on this mission." Valadis slumped a bit and once again tried to lean against the tree trunk for support. He needed the rest and closed his eyes momentarily giving Jedaf some time to catch up with his hastily scribbled notes.

Jedaf set his quill aside for a short time as he looked patiently back at Valadis. He could see the lines of strain starting to show on the man's face and how tightly he held his eyelids closed. It made the teenaged lord feel slightly self-conscious. He was not sure whether or not to continue asking any further questions. The man looked played out. Then Valadis suddenly opened his eyes and said, "Where was I?"

"If your feeling up to it you can tell me what do you know about this rebel army of Envar, and how does this Prince Sesmak figures into this conflict?"

Valadis took another deep cleansing breath. "It's another long tale lord." Wincing, he made a grimacing face and tried to find a comfortable position, but could not find one. Slumping back where he was originally leaning, he inhaled deeply, than held his breath for a zesta. The blood had dried and stuck to the inside of his new tunic. He arched his back slightly and gently pulled the stiff fabric loose of the wet bandages.

"I know that you're not really up to another long story Val, but I have just arrived in this land and everything you know will be of help to me, and could save many lives. I have seen a pretty vague map of this continent, but it was hundreds of years old and did not have many of the current kingdoms or the cities on it."

"I don't mind sticking my neck out to help someone, but I would not want my head cut off for sticking it into a trivial matter that was really none of my business. If you could keep it short, and answer a few more questions, I would appreciate it very much."

"All right lord, if it will help." Jedaf flashed him a smile of gratitude. Picking up his eco quill again he dipped it into the ink bottle. "Why not start with this Prince Sesmak," said Jedaf?

The merchant nodded and waited for the young lord to look up at him before beginning. "The prince is the younger brother of King Helidon of Envar. Before the war, he was the governor and military protector of the northlands. Upon hearing that the Worezians had crossed the border and invaded the northern province of Tespaden, he sent out a call to arms."

"Nine tantaxes were hastily formed and marched north to meet the threat of these raiding parties. With Prince Sesmak at their command, the military won all of the minor skirmishes and most of the engagements involving a few thousand warriors. They had almost driven the invaders from their soil when the prince was wounded."

"This was when a change in the command took place. King Helidon decided that his son should be in command of the armies. Crown Prince Quayot arrived at the front, replacing all the senior officers. Most were personal friends or cronies of the diplomatic corps that could pay a high price for a leadership position. Prince Sesmak objected, refusing to relinquish his army to officers that had never been on a battlefield or that had no military experience."

"King Helidon sent the royal guard to arrest and to escort him back to the City of Renas. Sesmak was summoned to appear before a tribunal of the royal families on charges of traitorous insubordination. He was publicly reprimanded and assigned duty in the City of Yoathon. It's an obscure southern outpost in the murderous vourtre lands. This was where he remained serving until receiving word of the devastating defeat and slaughter of the northern Green Army."

"The first order that Prince Quayot gave, was to pursue the Worezian renegades at all cost. After three weeks most of the tadletas in his army were spread thinly throughout the north provinces and the men were exhausted. Every time the prince received word of an incursion, Quayot would order another one thousand horsemen in hot pursuit. His warriors chased the raiders about the grasslands of the Great Zarhun Plain at a break neck pace. They quickly used up most of their supplies, and the local inhabitants could no longer spare any feed grains."

"Two mursas after taking command, Prince Quayot's scattered units followed these retreating bands of Worezian's to North Point. The commander of the host had been led into a trap. With his army's back to the Sea of Tenolto, there was no escape. The three Worezian tadetas that they had been pursuing were smaller parts of eight other enemy tantaxes which now closed in behind them."

"The few veteran officers still in command of the Envarian Army ordered fainting counter attacks at the flanks, giving them enough time to withdraw. Quayot countermanded these orders and told them to hold their ground. Every day they lost more and more warriors as they were pushed back to the coastal waters. The Worezians were better equipped and out numbered the Envarian warriors' two to one. All hope seemed to be lost, and surrender looked inevitable."

"Prince Quayot told his men that he had been given a divine inspiration after sacrificing two senior officers that were personal friends of Prince Sesmak. Kebran, the God of War; had spoken to him personally and had promised victory. At first light his army would charge the center and heart of the Worezian forces, shouting "For Kebran" as they advanced."

"The orders were given, and at sunrise the Envarian Green Army marched forward with the sun in their eyes. They abandoned their fortified positions and made a mad dash for the southern plains attacking their enemy. They sacrificed themselves and died by the thousands."

"Only a handful of privileged officers knew the real plan. It was to get Prince Quayot safely back to the City of Renvas. The night before the battle, the prince and his close friends commandeered a clipper ship from the small fishing village. At the height of the battle, they slipped aboard and sailed it south around the combat zone."

"Of the original sixty thousand warriors, twenty to twenty-five thousand had been killed during engagements in the north woodlands, or on the battleground. Another fifteen to twenty thousand had been cut off from the main body and were either wounded or captured."

"Marshal Ebestar, who had been reduced in rank to a tadleta commander regrouped the remaining stragglers and retreated to the coastal fishing village. While the majority of his warriors held the grounds outside the Village of Tenolfis, Ebestar was able to evacuate almost five thousand men to the Continent of Dolfinia by boat."

"The rest were slaughtered on the shore or were taken as slaves. They were sentenced to a lifetime of work in the mines or the fields of the Worezian royal estates. Less than fifteen thousand of the hardest fighting men escaped south, making their way through to the plain."

"Sesmak ordered the southern Blue Army under his command to abandon their fortifications and to assemble all the auxiliary troops in the area. A third of them formed under his banner marching north in a hurried rescue attempt. His army was halfway across the great plain when news reached him that he had been accused of being a disloyal renegade and a traitor."

"Prince Quayot blamed Sesmak for training the men poorly, and for abandoning the southern borders. King Helidon ordered Sesmak's wife and all her immediate family members executed. A price of a thousand large silver pieces was placed on his younger brother's head. Sesmak was blamed for the defeat at north point on the grounds that his officers would not obey orders."

"King Helidon awarded his son the acotaxarus; the Gold Seal of Valor, and promoted him to Lord Commander of the Host and Protector of the Northlands. This was for his brilliant tactics in preventing the Worezians from marching south against the capital City of Renvas."

"The new Lord Commander was also given the ancient ceremonial long knife of King Sejand. This knife was re-forged from one of Uthamus's trident prongs, and is the symbol of his authority and ancestral right to the kingship of Envar."

"The revered and blessed knife is to be turned over to King Magarus after Sesmak's Army is defeated. The black blade will then be presented to the heir of Prince Quayot and Princess Shayla. It shall be returned to the peoples of Envar once their two nations become one."

"Sesmak's warriors continued marching north until they joined forces with the last survivors of the Envarian Green Army. They formed a rear guard between the Worezian Army and the Capital of Renvas. For two years now, he has held the great plain and kept the Worezian Army from overrunning the countryside. During this time King Helidon has left him alone, because if it weren't for Sesmak, Helidon would not have a throne or kingdom. The proposed marriage will change all of that."

"Thank you Val, I will let you rest the rest of the day." Jedaf removed the remaining piece of umaksepa root from his belt waist pouch, and handed it over to Valadis. "Break it in thirds and chew a piece while were riding, it will help with the pain."

"Captain Odelac," Jedaf called out for the burly seaman! The captain had been resting under the low boughs of a tall green pine tree at the edge of the clearing. He was speaking with the young slave that had been riding with Baradic. When they were dragged off to the auction blocks in the City of Woreza, Odel bought the boys' freedom as thanks and repayment for saving his life.

The captain jumped up and waived, until Jedaf located him. Odelac had taken the young man under his wing and was one of the few in the group that actually spoke with him. The rest of the seamen were all crew members of the Tarpenya and usually left him out of any conversation. They also took advantage of him, by giving this quiet slave most of the dirtier jobs or the ones that would take the longest to accomplish.

Jedaf walked over to the grassy spot where the two men were sitting. He wanted to discuss some of the problems he was having understanding the Zarhunian war preparations and the information that Valadis had just told him about. Jedaf knew that he could talk these matters over with the ambassador later, but Captain Odelac had been sailing the seas between the Continents of Dolfinia and Zarhun all his life. Odel had been in most of the ports on both continents. His perspective might add some understanding before these future events unfolded.

The twenty year old slave stopped speaking as soon as Jedaf ducked under the largest bough. "Lord Jedaf, I don't think you have met Trestan," said Odelac as he introduced them with a wave of his hand. Jedaf got down on his hands and knees and crawled below the lower branches. As the teen neared the tree trunk, he extended his arm in greeting.

The young slave was a little surprised by the lord's behavior. Who would ever greet a lowly serf in such a manner? "I'm Jedaf of Dolfi," the young lord said as he smoothed out some of the pine needles and cones. Trestan took on a more surprised look as the young lord spoke. A far off kind of blank expression crossed his face.

"Are there people living there now," he asked timidly? This question was even more of a surprise for the Dragon Lord.

"Have you ever been to Dolfi," asked Jedaf? The twenty two year old squirmed and closed his eyes for a zesta, trying to shut out some bad memories. Then he answered softly, "I was once there with my father before he was killed. It was a very long time ago."

"Trestan? Trestan," said Jedaf over and over? I know that name from somewhere, he thought. "Are you from one of the Dolfinian Kingdoms?"

The bony slave wearing grimy, threadbare rags, nodded. "I was born in the City of Joroca, in the Kingdom of Yoja. I was captured and sold into bondage by the Azzonian Army. Since then, they shipped me here to Zarhun, where I have lived and worked in the Worezian shipyards and docking facilities."

Jedaf looked at him a little more closely, and saw a slight resemblance to one of his friends. "Trestan, your father is not dead," he exclaimed! "Recently your mother Myra and your father Traga gave me lodgings until just before sailing here to Zarhun."

The man's face suddenly whitened loosing expression. Then his eyes widened with tears running down his cheeks. "They're not dead," he stammered between sobs? "I was told by the Azzonians that all of the warriors of Yojan Army of the Green had been slaughtered." Jedaf crawled over closer to him, placing a strong gripping hand on the young man's bony shoulder. Neither he nor Captain Odelac could say anything to Trestan. They let him sob quietly while his hands covered his eyes.

"Captain I came over here to speak to you about some other matter, but it is not that important now. Trestan, I'm going to be sending my friend back to Joroca today with letters for your father. I have written out instructions for Kytos on how to get there and how to find your families residence. It would be a lot easier now that I know who you are, and if you were to accompany him on this journey."

"Now I know you have a thousand questions, but I need to speak with the captain. He has a lot to do for me today and he can fill you in on what I need done later. Please forgive me for being in such a hurry, but I need Kytos to get back to Joroca as quickly as possible. I am also sure that you would like to get back to your family just as fast. Now give me a few zestas with Odel. Tell the men to load up and get ready to ride."

Karadis and Vadeck helped Valadis walk back to the wagon. He was too exhausted and sore to stand for himself. The ride was peaceful and quiet, for the next zestar and a half. The Jeupan merchant slept through most of it. Jedaf wrote several letters, reorganized and encoded his notes in English. After reading everything over once more, he folded, sealed, and wrote protective spells over each before tucking them away in his rucksack.

The teenager was satisfied; that he had covered all of the possibilities and scenarios for the situations as he saw them. He was suddenly very depressed and feeling alone. Jedaf could not get his mind off Princess Elona and Diara. How he wished he could do something for them. He sat for the longest time not moving. It was as though a paralysis was creeping through him.

"I'll bet Myra has a hug put away in the pantry for you."

The sound of Drocilus's motherly voice started a warm glow in his chest and a smile appeared on his face. He missed the shining eyes and warm smile of his teacher and mentor of herbs and medicine. He looked around quickly, but was disappointed at not seeing even a wispy spiritual presence. "I hope your right Dro," he said out loud. "At least she will have her youngest son back home."

Chapter # 4

The Wasteland Road to Cathon

Jedaf climbed into the front of the wagon and waived at Odelac. The captain slackened his reins and allowed the wagons team to pull up even with his horse. The spotted stallion walked at an easy gait while the two men spoke quietly. After a few zestas of whispered conversation Jedaf asked Karadis to pull up. Odelac dismounted and changed places with Jedaf.

Jedaf fetched two bags from the rear of the wagon, took Odel's horse and rode up to the front of the column where Kytos had been riding. The prince clearly liked riding point. When he was at the front of the column he seemed to ride taller in the saddle and it gave him a look of confidence and authority. It made him feel like it was he that was leading the wagon train.

"Ky, I would like a word with you." Jedaf reined up and turned his horse into the trees along a narrow game trail. The young Oppowian followed until the branches became too low to ride beneath. They both dismounted and tied off their reins on the limb of a fallen tree. Jedaf straddled its moss covered trunk and sat down. "Ky, I need a favor." He motioned the younger boy to the space next to him, by patting the trunk.

"Anything lord, just name it." He sat down and watched as Jedaf searched through his backpack. "It will be very dangerous, but I trust no man better for this task." Taking out a bound leather folder, Jedaf untied its laces. "Lord Jedaf, I owe you my life, and everything that I have is yours. I will gladly do anything that you ask of me, no matter what the danger."

Jedaf removed several folded letter envelopes from the folder and fanned them out before him. Ky could see the embossed red wax seals on each of them, before Jedaf tucked them back into the leather folder. "I want you to deliver these letters, and I can only spare one of the men to go along with you. The only ones I know and trust are Captain Odelac and Trestan his younger, skinny slave."

"The both of you will have to ride north to the nearest fishing village and purchase passage on a ship bound for the City of Joroca, in the Yojan Kingdom. Once you reach the city, I want you to deliver these letters to the House of Traga. He is a friend and the Commander of my Red Dragon Army. He also happens to be Trestan's father."

"I don't think that you will find him at his home, but his wife Myra can direct you to his bivouac area. Give the folder to Commander Traga or his son Agar, but no one else. Traga's instructions are in one of the envelopes and he will take care of all of the details. You are to remain there with him and his family, and may answer any question he asks." Kytos started to protest, but Jedaf shook his head. "I know you want to stay with Ambassador Ajoris and I, but this is more important, and I need you to do this for me!"

"There is also a letter in the pouch that is addressed to King Jeston of Saratam outlining your brother Pinthos's treachery and the threats to your father's kingdom. Once you get to the safety of Joroca, I want you to write a couple of letters. One of your letters should go to your Uncle Rastos and the other one to King Jeston. These can be included with the dispatches that I have asked Traga's son Agar to deliver. I'm hoping that with the addition of your letters and the support from your uncle, that King Jeston will believe what is written."

Jedaf tied the laces of the folder in a bow, and then slipped the loop end over Kytos's head. Ky tucked the dangling pouch in under his tunic through the neck hole and patted it flat. Taking a twice folded sheet of loose parchment from his bag, Jedaf handed it to Ky. I don't think you need this with Trestan along, but I want you to have it just in case you're separated. "It's is a rough map of the City of Joroca, with directions to Traga's house. Memorize it, and than destroy it." Ky quietly folded the map back up and tucked it into his waist belt pouch.

Jedaf removed the pinkie ring from his right hand, and handed it to his friend along with three large gold coins, and three large silver coins. By using his mouth, Kytos placed the ring on his bony index finger and dropped the coins into his purse. "Get these dispatches to Joroca as quickly as possible." Jedaf placed his hand on Ky's shoulder and looked deeply into the other boys saddened brown eyes. "Every day, every zesta counts."

Kytos gave him a slight smile and a worried but apprehensive nod of his head. "You can count on me lord," he said somberly.

"I know I can Ky." They stood and walked over to the horses, untying them. "The road forks just ahead about a quarter of a thasta from here. Captain Odelac has scouted it out for a short distance and says it leads northeast towards the smaller Worezian coastal fishing villages. Trestan will be waiting for you on the road ahead."

Jedaf gave him a parting bear hug and helped him back into the saddle. "My friend, I don't know if we will ever see each other again, but I want you to know that I will never forget you or your sister. I wish I could have done more for her. I don't know if it will do any good, but I have said several prayers. I hope your gods look kindly and take care of the both of you."

Jedaf draped Ky's travel bag over the saddle horn, along with a meal sack and gave his mount a pat on the side of its neck. He stood to the side stroking its coarse mane, as he spoke. "There is a water skin, dried meat, cheese, and some journey bread in there for you and Trestan." Ky extended his left arm and Jedaf clasped his wrist. "Remember, keep that arm in the sling, and have Trestan change the bandages every other day until it is completely healed."

As they parted, Jedaf could see tears welling up in the corners of the Oppowian prince's eyes. He swallowed hard and replied. "Thanks again lord! Goodbye! You can count on us." Grasping the reins tightly, he nudged his mount forward into a trot. Shouting back, "We will get there as fast as we can," he rode back to where Jedaf and he had left the road.

The Dragon Lord stayed for a few emotional moments standing quietly at the side of Odelac's horse. His arms were draped over the saddle and his forehead was resting at the seat. Doubt's and fears flooded his mind. He wished he knew if he was doing the right thing in sending Ky off on this mission, and whether he should be asking Traga and his family to be risking so much for strangers that they have never met.

Finally, he gathered enough courage for him to grab a hold of his saddle horn and mount. The skittish stallion turned his head and whinnied in long, drawn out, anxious tone. "There's a wolf about!" The young wizard wasn't quiet sure he had heard or interpreted these sounds correctly, but he was not going to take any chances. Riding slowly back through the thicket, he looked about warily from side to side, and kept a sharp eye on the denser brush.

Making his way eastward Jedaf followed the wheel ruts. At the main bend in the trail a flock of frightened picrican took flight in front of his horse, startling him and his mount. Their vivid feather colors and wing flapping seemed to bring him back to reality.

There was no sense in rehashing his decisions. Whatever the outcome he could not change them now. His heels nudged Odelac's horse forward until he caught up with the cart and wagon. They had slowed their pace since Jedaf and Kytos had broken away from them. The wagon train had only advanced at the most, two thastas beyond the fork.

The wagon's dust cloud was not that far ahead of him, but his horse was already exhausted by the time he sighted them. Captain Odelac stopped the wagons at the sound of the hoof beats. Standing to the side of the road he waited for Jedaf to ride up to him.

Neither spoke, while Jedaf dismounted and climbed back onto the wagon. Odelac removed the saddle and tied off the reins at the rear warkmeg cleat near the back flap. There was no way that this horse would carry anyone the rest of the day.

Ajoris and the rest of the men had also dismounted or had climbed down from the cart stretching their legs and backs while they waited for Jedaf to climb back into his wagon. They hadn't known why Jedaf and Kytos had ridden off alone, or why Captain Odelac had left their new companion Trestan at the fork in the road by himself. They kept turning their heads to the rear of the column to see if Ky and Tres were going to catch up with them. Ajoris told the grumbling men that if the young lord had wanted them to know what was going on he would have told them.

The ambassador now rode point at the front of the column; he was followed by the cart, than the wagon. It was his duty to see that they took the right roads and did not stray too far from their intended destination. He was not about to question any of Jedaf's decisions. Picking a route at each fork was enough of a problem for Ajor. It was hard keeping the wagon and cart from going into the ditches and they didn't need a broken axle. Several times it was easier for Vadeck to remove the limbs or larger rocks, than trying to get around them.

The further southeast they traveled the denser the forest became and the narrower the road. Ajoris halted the wagon and cart after another zestar of riding. It felt good to relieve their bladders and stretch their legs once again. They had ridden through most of the afternoon with few respites and having eaten only at the "Inn of the Athca."

It was now nearing the twenty first zestar. Another zestar and the suns would be down. There didn't seem to be any reason to be pressing on any further. Finding another camp site at dusk was risky, and would leave them vulnerable and unprepared for an attack, if one came.

At first glance they could not have found a better campsite. The clearing was a bit small but there was a thin stream, and a large patch of wild tu tia, blue berries nearby. The horses were unhitched and led to a natural watering hole, widened by wallowing animals. The water was clear and undisturbed. From the split hoofed tracks in the mud, these animals must have been as large as water buffalos, probably a small herd of long horned wild measan.

This was not their main concern. Where there are game herds there are carnivores. A watch would have to be posted all night. Just down stream and over a flat rocky area the men re-filled the water barrels. After washing the travel dust and the stench of captivity from themselves, they changed into some of the new clothing that had been purchased at the supply depot.

Jedaf decided to take first watch. He knew he could not sleep with all the thoughts racing through his mind. From his vantage point on the top a large boulder he could tell there was an argument going on in the camp. He could not hear the words clearly, but he knew there was some sort of a heated dispute. Odelac and Ajoris were standing face to face, poking at each other with their fingers. He jogged in their direction and yelled over to them, "Hold on there!"

"Lord, we have a slight misunderstanding or problem here," said Odelac. "I thought that we were going to camp here for the rest of the night. Now, the ambassador tells me to get the men mounted up again." Jedaf looked questioningly at Ajor, but didn't ask. He was just as surprised as Odel.

"Captain, I know you're not going to like this," said Jedaf, "but if the ambassador says we move on, we do. I have put him in charge, and I expect you and your men to follow his directions as if they were my own. That is, unless the men are too tired to carry out the orders."

From the tightness of the captain's face, he was clearly not happy with the answer but didn't say anything. Being a man use to giving orders, he knew there could only be one person in charge. Jedaf was bone tired himself and his muscles were stiff and aching. The cold stream refreshed him but also drew a lot of energy from him. "How are they holding up," asked Jedaf?

"They will make it sire. I'll have them hitch up the teams again. I hope the horses have not bloated themselves." He turned to walk away, but Ajor reached out and stopped him.

"I am sorry for the confusion captain, but before you give the orders I want you to know the reason." Odelac paused and waited for the explanation, but his facial expressions hadn't change. "I think that we are being watched and followed closely," said the ambassador.

"I've had this sensation for half of the day now, and it has gotten worse and more intense in the last half zestar. At first I thought that it might be a Worezian patrol, but we're now too far from the city. There is something eerie about this particular stretch of woods and watering hole that just does not feel right."

Ajor rubbed at the back of his neck as if he were trying to smooth the hair back down. "Have you noticed how shriveled, knotted and stunted the trees are? There is also a sick moldy smell to the dust clouds that the horses have been kicking up. I just don't like the feeling of the atmosphere, and I think the faster that we get through this patch of woods, the better off we'll all be."

Odelac looked about the clearing noting the changes in the shrubs, bushes and trees. The leaves were small and withered; the boughs were twisted and intertwined with a pale yellow colored tendril like thorny vine. Then he noticed and pointed out some faded wind abraded and rain eroded ancient writings beneath the weeds on the face of the hillside. The symbols had been etched into an outcropping of shale and were barely discernable beneath the thick overhanging vegetation.

Jedaf walked over to the rock shelf and gave a swipe of his sword to the hanging and creeping vines. A cloud of insects burst forth into the sunlight. The fireflies surrounded and landed all over Odelac and Ajoris while he swatted at the biting horse flies. The other insects did not seem to bother either of the other two men and they just ignored them. Below the chiseled characters were two vine covered skeletons sitting in an upright manor and embracing one another.

The young lord had seen a form of this ancient Odea glyph writing but even his teachers and the council of elder could not translate it fully. This form of pictogram script was only known to be written by direct descendants of the old gods. The pre-Kaybeckian language had not been spoken in several thousand years, and it was considered a sacrilege to deface the text.

The Dragon Lord timidly reached out his hand running his fingertips lightly over three of the glyphs. He tried to sense their meaning or the author's motive. He knew it was not wise to try to verbalize the characters, because he could release their power from the rock minerals and bring their meaning to life.

"From what little I know about these characters, I think these symbols imply that the longer anyone rests at this location, the less one will ever want to leave it." Odel could feel the need and impulse to lie down and rest as Jedaf spoke. As soon as his lord cut away the vines and exposed the font to sunlight, the feelings had intensified. Fighting off the urge to do nothing, he nodded to Ajoris. The fireflies took flight again and the captain reluctantly went to give the orders.

The rest of the men were as disgruntled as the captain, but they did as they were told and broke camp. Karadis stacked the deadwood branches and logs that he had scrounged, and loaded them into the back of the wagon. He had the feeling that they would be riding until the suns set and he did not want to be wandering around in the dark looking for fuel for the campfires.

The rocking of the wagon caused Jedaf to fall into a restless agitated sleep. He did not open his eyes again until a few zestas before the two suns merged and dipped over the horizon. Ajoris had found another fairly large clearing, but it was fifty odd paces from the roadside. They had to clear a path for the cart, and had to cut down two small trees for the wheelbase of the wagon to fit through.

Setting up camp was a rushed but orderly affair. Odelac first put his men to clearing the brush, and gathering as much firewood as they could. While they could still see, the men unloaded the tripod spit, kettles, blankets, oats and drinking water for the horses. Vadeck started the cook fire, and started preparing the meal with some help from Valadis.

Baradic ran a rope from the rear of the cart to the tree line for tying up the horses. Unhitching them, he gave each a good rub down. Karadis cut up and carried over several armloads of the tall cut grasses for the teams, and brought the feedbags over to them.

Myritt, the clumsy twenty two year old deckhand, with big feet, was standing around as was his usual. He was not a self starter, and if no one gave him directions, he would never do any work. Vadeck yelled at him to go help Baradic. He at least un-saddled the horses, held onto their reins or walked them about, while Baradic did most of the work. The older seaman seemed to have a way of knowing what the animals needed. Even though he was not very sociable around most people, he took good care of the horses. It was as if he could sense their needs or read each of their minds.

Odelac and Ajoris scouted the edges of the clearings and set up a picket detail, while Jedaf chopped wood, stacked it, or stood guard between breaks. It looked like total confusion for awhile, but each kept to the tasks assigned, and soon they were all sitting or lying down warming themselves near the main campfire. Captain Odelac now stood the watch and paced about in the deepening shadows at the camp perimeter. The young Dragon Lord was now too preoccupied with his own thoughts and was mentally overwhelmed.

Vadeck's thick vegetable stew was boiling by the time the bedrolls and blankets were pulled from the cart. Each sat quietly eating, too done in and fatigued to speak. Jedaf sat with Ajor, filling him in on what Valadis had related to him. They both agreed that they could trust this Jeupan, even though they had just met him.

Jedaf's head was throbbing and pounding at his temples while he and Ajoris spoke. At first he thought that it was because he was so hungry, but the headache still lingered after his second bowl. The more he thought about their situation the worse and more agonizing the migraine became.

"That is all this land needs now is another prolonged war," said Ajoris. Jedaf stood and folded up his notes. Then took out a clean sheet of parchment, and started scribbling on it at a frantic pace. The young lord seemed to have a kind of tired half dazed and confused look about him. Standing stiffly he sauntered off toward the wagon without another word.

Vadeck called out to him; "Lord, will you eat anything else tonight?"

Jedaf stopped a moment, clearing his thoughts before replying. "No. I think I will write for awhile, and then get some rest. Do me a favor and ask the men to keep the noise down, my head feels like its splitting."

The old taskmaster looked at the ambassador and raised an eyebrow. The wily marine knew there was something decidedly wrong. The men were half asleep, and none had spoken a word in at least the last ten zestas. Jedaf's exhaustion was not just physical, it was mental as well. In this deep and overwhelming morass the boy could not seem to make a decision. Nor did he know what to do, or what steps he should have taken.

Reaching the wagon he sat near it on a large boulder in the semi-darkness. Then he finished writing down his thoughts and the comments that the ambassador had made when they discussed the impending wars. The council had warned him, that he would be responsible for and would be the cause of great strife or war. Were these monumental conflicts, contentious bickering discords, and future wars entirely his fault?

Two new large wars were developing and he could do nothing to stop or prevent them from spreading. He had no more control over them than a cancerous growth. Most of all, he couldn't even save Princess Elona from bondage. The thought of his loved one in the hands of the Envarian royalty turned his stomach.

If he stayed to fight against the Armies of Worez, the seafaring Kingdoms of Bintar and Lyda would fall. That would mean; the greater portion of the Histajonies Archipelago would be under the direct control of the Sylakian Empire and King Zaghar his sworn enemy. Thousands were going to die needlessly or be enslaved for life. Many more would be made starving refugees that had been driven from their destroyed homes.

If he sailed to the Kingdom of Bintar, the Worezian Army would massacre the freedom fighting Envarians and invade the peaceful lands of Jeupa and the southern nations. Half of the Continent of Zarhun would then be under the thumb of King Magarus, and Jedaf was sure this rotund mad man would not stop there.

On the other hand he was under an obligation and sacred blood oath to go on a religious pilgrimage to the City of Tabalis. The Council of Elders had told him that above all else, this was his priority. Perhaps it was all for nothing, maybe he should just die there and stop the suffering and misery that his existence had caused.

Jedaf thought of all that had happened to him since he had arrived on this world, and of the people he had grown to love. How he wished he could have just stayed in Joroca with Traga's family. Then he thought of Elona, Diara, Kytos and Ajoris. He would have never met her or any of them if he hadn't sailed for Cathon. "I wonder; if I have written a death sentence for Kytos, and Traga's family."

Crawling over the rough planks on his hands and knees, Jedaf pulled the back of the canvas flap drawstrings tight. It would at least cut down on the wind. It had been good of Vadeck to unload some of the crated supplies for the night giving Jedaf and Jeupan spy-merchant a little more elbowroom.

Propping himself up on a sack of krastant flour, Jedaf took a last look at Valadis. The injured man seemed to be sleeping comfortably. Laying back down and pulling one of his blankets over his own head, the boy thought about his first long day on the Zarhunian Continent. "By all the gods, it's getting cold," he said softly and closed his eyes.

Repositioning himself he thought he could see the mist of his breath coming out from under the blanket. The light of the cook and sentry fires could barely be seen through the side openings in the canvas. The flames were low, flickering and hugging the ground. It looked almost as if they were not getting enough oxygen or the wood was too green or wet.

The cold seemed to penetrate right down to the bone leaving nothing but a throbbing numbness. Jedaf pulled his blanket tighter about him. A large black nimbus cloud rolled across the sky shading the moons, and hiding the stars. Every living creature seemed to know it was going to be an unseasonably cold, damp and dismal evening.

Jedaf's last conscious thoughts were of Ajoris and Odelac. They had set up some sort of shelters in case it rained later in the evening. The land and countryside needed the water badly, but a cold downpour before dawn and three inch deep mud on the road were certainly not going to raise the morale of the men or lift his spirits.

Jedaf could not think anymore; pulling the blanket tightly about him, made him shudder. A fleeting memory of coming to this world through the numbing cold of the black void crossed his mind and he finally drifted off to a restless sleep.

Chapter # 5

Motaluk — The Treskul of Pestilence

All of the men had covered the ground below their bedrolls with the softer ends of fresh cut pine branches before braking out the extra blankets. They huddled as near to the three fires as they could without fear of being burned in the night. More wood had been gathered, cut and stacked before they turned in.

Karadis stood up shivering and flapping his arms across his chest. He had been assigned the first guard watch for the inner campground and was to tend all the fires. Captain Odelac circled the outer clearing at the perimeter. Occasionally he walked amongst the picketed horses keeping them calm, and making enough noise to ensure the woodland predators knew that he was nearby.

The two, four inch diameter, four foot long logs Karadis had just leaned into the flames had not made him feel any warmer. Finally he fetched the largest branch he could pull from the wood pile, and tossed into the blaze. The red hot embers burst high into the air but only lasted for a moment before dying. The additional fuel seemed to have no effect; neither the air temperature nor the height of the flames increased.

Karadis sat back down on the half rotten stump in a hunched over position and pulled his blanket about his shoulders. Then he leaned closer toward the dull yellow flames and extended his hands. His calloused fingers were stiff and numb as he clapped his hands together rubbing some warmth back into them. In the center of the campfire, the snapping and popping sounds of the fiery brands seemed to have been muffled.

The smaller tinder in the central campfire was quickly consumed leaving mostly light grey ashes but almost no hot coals. Slumping silently, the burning logs fell inward upon themselves and the flames stopped radiating heat.

Jedaf was sleeping in a restless agitated state, dreaming of ice fields and frozen wastelands in thin crisp mountain air. He could feel his whole body trembling and shaking beneath his blanket. The freezing cold and hypothermia reminded him of the void of time, and the endless darkness that he had traveled through while being transported to this planet. It appeared that this miserable weather was going to last all night.

It was in the middle of the evening at about the twenty-eighth zestar; that a bone deep numbness and feeling of dread crept over his entire body. All at once his dismal and somber dreams turned more terrifyingly gruesome, and distinctly morbid. Half frozen decaying corpses were sitting by the roadside calling his name. The putrefying odor of incense mixed with the smell of vomit and gangrene churned his stomach.

Rolling over on his back, Jedaf tried clearing this icy battlefield carnage from his mind. The young lord's heart stopped racing and he settled into a deeper REM sleep. He heard the soft sounds of thrumming stringed instruments and the rhythmic beats of a soft skinned bongo drum. Jedaf was now dreaming that he was standing amongst friends attending a funeral service. It appeared to be one of the more traditional ceremonies, for the rights of the dead. Burials or cremations were usually held at night because this was the time that Kebolus the Palestus God of Death ruled.

The air was cold, crisp, black, and silent. He stood close to the body of the deceased, as the mourners and loved ones filed by. Each one in turn, tossed a hand full of flower seeds and whispered a private tearful goodbye as they passed the raised platform. The corpse had been anointed with scented oils and had been tightly wrapped in layers of thin white cotton; one layer dedicated for each of the four winds.

This was one of the nine requirements for the bolusa or soul to reach Odea, the home of the gods. From head to foot the alia stambur embalmers cloth was tightly spun about the organless body, giving it the look that it had been prepared by an enormous spider. The corpse rested on a wooden delclot platform decorated with runic prayers which had been carved into the side rails. Each one of the four support posts were carved in the perceived likenesses of the wind gods and dedicated to them. Surrounding the deceased were cama offering baskets, crocks of cooked foods, fruit, clothing, wine, and spiced meats.

At the foot of the funeral platform were the painted katmet ceramic lined rectangular coffers containing most of the internal organs. The xinu stramus was always the first to be removed. This body organ was believed to be the cause of all illness and death because of its snakelike appearance. The intestines along with the wooden blood collection bucket were burned the day before in a separate ceremony in preparation of the burial site.

Below the platform, a great quantity of seasoned and blessed clotis hardwood was stacked. It had been cleaned of its bark, scented and properly tied with arisdi flowers and vines for the ritual krem rocala pyre.

Dark shaped spirits that should have been the claura or priests, worked diligently around the body directing the funeral party and stacking the fuel. Jedaf knew these paranormal beings were not human, but was not sure in his mind, if this was not a normal occurrence. Most people did not see these supernatural entities, let alone conversed with them.

The creatures wide, slanted, red eyes were clearly glowing and radiating. They drew in absorbing the flames energy, while increasing the sorrow of the mourners at the same time. The beings walked in a single file, slowly circling the fire pit. The firelight reflected off their peened silver, gold armor, highly polished chains, merimec pendants and ornamental religious amulets.

Jedaf was compelled to watch; he was transfixed and unable to divert his eyes. This was his first experience with the sacrificial rites of death and the ritual practices of cremation. Becoming very emotionally depressed, and saddened he regretted his past behaviors and actions. Wanting to weep and rub his dry, burning eyes, he found he couldn't. Even with the dense smoky air, and sorrow bottled up inside him there were no tears.

Knowing in his heart that the death of this loved one was probably caused by him, he recalled what the Council of Elders had predicted would happen because of his non-beliefs. Only the flapping sounds of the creatures thin skinned, translucent bat wings and an occasional scraping of their nails could be heard.

At the outer perimeter of the ritual circle sat other dark grey shapes that appeared to have more mass than the funerary spirits. They were also more humanoid looking than the grey wispy skeletal creatures nearer to the corpse. One large blacker and more solidified, ominous individual presided over the ceremonies.

This being remained silent as he directed the other entities. The creature did not speak, but gave non-verbal hand signals. He casually leaned on his trident while the others worked. The gruesome looking forked weapon was constructed of human bones. The illium, femurs and tibias had been fused together with silver inlays. The glazed, brittle bones were then banded together with wire and wide riveted stripes of blackened iron.

The demonic master of ceremonies looked away from the ritual momentarily, turning back and looking in Jedaf's direction. The hellish creature smiled at him displaying his sharp, yellow, fanged incisors. Raising the butt plate of his trident above of the ground, he tapped a nearby rock with three quick downward thrusts.

The metallic report echoed and reverberated loudly, breaking the silence. All the mourners now looked to him and knelt quietly in reverence. The tridents barbed silver forks began to glow, radiating heat. The pitch blackened tines smoked, changing orange, then to red, then to an intense white hot color.

Stepping forward the creature touched the crumbled tinder below the woodpile with the glowing weapon. The dry twigs and smaller kindling branches smoldered than ignited. The burning embers in front quickly spread to the sides, and soon the whole outer edge of the crematory woodpile was ablaze.

The master now walked around the outer ring of the pyre circling the body counter clockwise. At each of the four sides he stopped, intoned an ocrotiej prayer, and tossed a small papyrus scroll of scripture into the pyre.

Jedaf's eyes burned and his throat tightened from the smell of the acrid smoke and the rut ana incense oils. Attempting to raise his hand and rub his dry eyes, he found he could not move. Looking down, he found himself wrapped in the white muslin embalmers cloth and he panicked. Now the full realization came to him that this was his funeral.

Fumbling at his side for his knife, Jedaf was able to touch the end of the pommel but he could not unsheathe the blade. The cloth was woven so tightly about him; he could not bend his wrists. The heat intensified, bringing the aroma of the singed cloth and hair to his nostrils. "I am being burned alive!" No one looked in his direction, as he screamed.

It was as if Jedaf was not there physically. All his muscles tightened, straining and trying to stretch the scorched muslin cloth. It was no good, it had become like another layer of hard calloused skin. "The only way I will ever get out of this would be with some sort of a spell or an incantation." He hurriedly mumbled this out loud, while trying to calm his heart and gather his thoughts.

Cold perspiration beads formed on the teenager's anxious brow. Wetting his lips, Jedaf could taste the salt and potassium dripping down his sweaty cheeks. He would have to direct his meager efforts toward the lesser black shapes. Even though Jedaf had been anointed as the Protector of the Dead, he knew that he did not have the ability or strength to influence the minds of these other creatures.

The more Jedaf stared at these lesser figures, the more familiar they became. The master closely resembled the malicious black apparition he had encountered in the City of Caspasi, and the humanoids represented the darker sides of his companion's souls.

The cruel specter shrugged as he felt Jedaf's eyes on him. Turning about, the creature sauntered over in the direction of the wagon. The evil demigod wanted to gloat, while getting a better look at the young Dragon Lord and new Protector of the Dead.

"King Zaghar told me recently that somehow you have managed to send my younger brother Lufarus beyond, to the other side. My master has searched the land, sea and air. So far he has been unable to locate any of the remains for resurrection.

My lord also warned me that even though you are but a mere boy, I should not underestimate your abilities or power. It was very thoughtless of you forgetting to weave a spell of protection over your men, or yourself. But I do appreciate all the help you have given me. It has made my job a lot easier, and has made my revenge all the sweeter."

Jedaf's whole body tightened becoming more rigid in the sizzling, perspiration soaked embalmers cloth. Once again he tried freeing his hands as he strained at the constricting fibers. The malicious treskul just laughed at his efforts.

Patting the boy's chest with his long, gaunt bony fingers, he hissed. "Your men sit there freezing. The more wood and fuel they stack on the pyre the faster and hotter you will burn."

Jedaf looked again toward the smaller shadowy, figures. They were shivering and huddled beneath their cloaks and blankets. The larger winged creatures which had been created by the treskul were standing between the men and the fire. These invisible, lesser demonic beings stretched out their wings, blocking the heat and absorbing all of the radiated energy. Of the lesser humanoid figures, one stood out among the others. This man was further away from the central fire, but had the same blank and dull emotionless expression on his face.

Jedaf's skin was beginning to sear and scorch. He could feel the perspiration soaked shroud smoldering and could hear it sizzling as it started to blister his skin. The specter continued to chuckle at his efforts. "Go ahead Master Jedaf," he said in an amused sarcastic tone of voice. "Show me some of your magic!"

The creatures head tipped back as he laughed hysterically at the empty blackness above. Slimy, drooling saliva oozed from its two inch long canine teeth and its eyes glowed with intensity. Raising his taloned hands skyward, the treskul thanked his father Kebran, the Lord of War for allowing him the honor of claiming this tantalizing soul.

Jedaf concentrated and focused all his efforts at the lone figure; he knew to be Captain Odelac. "Burn out-worlder! Burn! I am already savoring the taste of your scorched delicate flesh, and I promise to give you a prolonged, agonizing death. I am going to especially enjoy devouring your sweet compassionate soul."

The malevolent being moved closer bending down slowly over Jedaf. Their faces were now only inches apart, almost eye to eye. The foul odor of its strong smelling putrefied breath was almost enough to break the young wizard's concentration. The drooling beast panted deeply as its eyes roved over the surface of the skin at the youth's neck. Its own large veined throat throbbed ever so quickly as it located the beating pulse of Jedaf's jugular.

"The time has come, and at last you're mine." The specter slowly opened his mouth wide, tipping his head slightly sideways. Jedaf could feel the heat of the beast's exhaled breath. Saliva started to run down the teenager's throat as the fangs began to close. Suddenly a deeply pained expression crossed the demons face, and the radiance in his eyes diminished.

A loud splashing and sizzling sound made him turn his head suddenly. The treskul screamed out loudly, dropped his trident. Then he stood erect with a pained expression on his face. At the same instant, Jedaf pushed himself backwards and avoided the gnashing sharp teeth. The horrid and vile humanoid wield about yelling at the figure standing by the pyre. Captain Odelac stood next to the central campfire with the smaller water cask in his arms. He was slowly tipping and pouring out the contents, dousing the hot embers and flames.

The facsimile of the funeral immolation vanished, and the specter ran screaming for Odel to stop. The creature grabbed hold of the strong human sinking its strong sharp talons deeply into the officer's shoulders. Its fangs sought for a hold at the nape of Odelac's neck.

The captain fought back at the invisible assailant. Rolling on the ground through the hot wet firebrands and coals made the rest of the stupefied men jump out of the way. They thought that their captain had gone stark raving mad. Throwing water on the fire was bad enough. Now he was rolling about in the ashes and kicking smoldering logs at them. It certainly was not the act of a sane man at any rate.

That is when his crewmen noticed the injuries. Blood was starting to appear and flowed freely from wounds on the captain's arms and back. Karadis and Vadeck ran to the captain's aide trying to help him. They were both knocked over backwards by a hard unseen blow to their chests. Baradic stepped away from the mayhem and drew his sword, but there were no adversaries to see or fight. Myritt grabbed his blankets and ran for the safety of the woods.

At the start of the commotion, Ajoris rushed off to the wagon to wake Jedaf. Pulling back the canvas flap, the ambassador found the young master wrapped up tightly in his blanket. The teen called for Ajor's help with all the strength he could muster. He could not move a muscle and was barely able to inhale or speak in his constricted position.

Ajoris drew his long knife and quickly sliced through the blanket material. The young lord burst from the cloth like a butterfly from a cocoon. Jumping to his feet Jedaf grabbed his medical bag and ran toward Odelac. While running he took a sparkling blue glass vial of liquid from it. Then he tossed his bag to the side and pulled out the stopper. Spraying about a third of the fluid on Odel and the specter made the vile creature loosen its grip.

A shrill piercing scream louder than a thunder clap knocked Jedaf backward to the ground. The terrifying high pitched shrieks were followed by another and yet another. The reverberations were so intense and sharp; everyone had to cover their ears.

The horses whinnied out a loud terrified "Demon" like sound and bolted in every direction! They pulled loose the picket tethers and scattered in every direction. The mounts were running off in the darkness as the camp became nothing less than total bedlam.

Odelac lay on his abdomen, face down, bloody, and exhausted, but still alive. Jedaf rolled the large man over gently and wiped the blood, soot and wet ashes from his face. Odel looked up. His eyes rolling about and moved but, he could not see. "Take him to the wagon, and get some fresh water," yelled Ajoris.

The ambassador helped Jedaf to his feet, while the others carried the captain. In the mean time, Myritt came slinking out of the shadows with his sword drawn. As he looked about the camp he tried to hide the nervous expression on his face. "I don't think that creature will be coming back now that I have driven it into the woods." Vadeck gave him a stern, disgusted looking glare but did not say anything.

The massive black cloud over their head, started to dissipate. In the streaks of moonlight Jedaf could just makes out the rise and fall of Odelac's chest. "Baradic, Karadis, get a new fire going. Myritt get the oil lamps. Ajoris, find my medical bag. I tossed it over there somewhere. Vadeck see to the horses." Everyone moved quickly, to his orders, and in no time the area looked like a campsite again. The one exception was the fact that there were no horses.

The captain's physical condition appeared worse than it really was. He was covered from head to foot in blood, wet ashes and mud mixed with bits of charcoal. Most of his injuries were superficial shallow slashing wounds which had bled a lot.

His heavy weather cloak and leather tunic had protected him from the claws, but two of the talons had raked the right side of his face clear down to the check bone. There were also several deep lacerations on his upper arms, and a long slashing bite mark at the side his neck.

This jagged wound was where the young lord started working. A steady stream of blood was spitting upward. Jedaf applied and held a compress tightly over the area. The skin had been ripped back exposing some of the flesh and muscle.

The wound was shallow but the sharp fangs had nicked a vein or artery just above Odelac's right clavicle. It had been a grazing blow from the creature's upper fangs. It was fortunate that the beast's bite had been deflected by the captain's collarbone. There were no actual puncture marks, but Jedaf did not know if trekuls were venomous.

"Master, shall we hold him down while you sew him?" Jedaf looked to the side at the concerned face of Odelac's oldest and closest friend.

"No Vadeck. I don't think that will be necessary." Jedaf poured some of his sparkling fluid on the compress and held it firmly. A short time later, the bleeding slowed and Jedaf timidly uncovered it. The wound was still raw and jagged but was already starting to show signs of healing.

Odelac mumbled and started thrashing about, as one possessed. "Hold this Vadeck," said Jedaf. The taskmaster moved to his friend's side applying pressure to the bandage. The young lord lifted the captain's head, and poured a small amount of the luminous liquid between the old sailor's lips.

Odelac's eyes widened with fright and Jedaf forced him to swallow. It was no more than a sip, but it made the captain cough and gag. For a short moment, the muscular seaman stopped thrashing and seemed to be at ease. Then a tremendous shudder started to go through his whole body.

The captain's torso convulsed from the antidote while his body began to harden, like the beginning of rigormortis. His skin color changed to a light grey matching the ashes near the fire pit, and his eyes clouded over. Jedaf ripped open the captain's tunic and placed his ear to Odel's petrifying chest. The skin was cold and clammy, but there was a weak noticeable heartbeat.

Lord Jedaf closed his eyes and bent his head low letting Odelac's aura appear. There were no internal injuries and most of the captain's life sign colors were slowly becoming normal. The worried young man was very thankful for that. Jedaf dressed the arm and facial wounds and wrote some healing symbols on the bandages.

While dressing the wounds, some of the old seaman's golden skin color returned, and twice he opened his eyes while trying to speak. Vadeck washed his friend's face and asked him not to talk. If there was anything needed his life long friend was there at his side.

Ajoris and Karadis helped remove the captain's muddy clothing and they washed him as best they could before covering the captain with the warmest blankets. Vadeck and Karadis stayed quietly at Odel's side until he appeared to be resting comfortably. The others members of the crew went about tending the fires and walking guard posts.

It was many zestars before the camp fully settled down again. The men slept restlessly or not at all while Jedaf walked the camp reciting scripture and casting spells over the trees and rocks. Ajoris stood guard at the opposite end of camp. Vadeck sat tending soup or tea kettles between trips from Odel's bedside to the new main fire.

The Dragon Lord would not be caught again without any warning or protection. After cutting a branch from a burkat tree, Jedaf stripped it of its bark and fire hardened its point. It took a zestar to scribe one complicated symbol at each of the four points of the compass around the camp's perimeter.

Another tense and uneasy zestar followed. The men were wary and unsure of the teenaged wizard's abilities. Convincing them the unseen evil demon would not come back to take their souls, was made more difficult because of Myritt's comments and constant grousing.

Once Jedaf started reciting verses of ancient script from one of Corella's books of white witchcraft, luminescent insects of all varieties started gathering and flying about the clearing. They lighted the entire campsite throughout the night and continued assembling in the darker recesses until all the shadows had vanished.

At sunrise Jedaf stopped back at the wagon and checked in on Valadis and Odelac. The injured men were both sleeping comfortably. In the twilight, he decided it would not be wise to break camp this morning. After what the crew had gone through, it would be best to stay bivouacked here for at least one full day if not two.

Vadeck still tended the fire, as he had all night long. His facial muscles and heart were hard with hate. The guilt of not being able to stop this evil spirit from hurting his friend made it all the harder for him to let go of his anger.

This scarred and hardened ship's taskmaster was not a religious man. Yet, he solemnly thanked the gods for his friend's life, and promised to do penance at the nearest temple. Sitting on a tree stump near the cook fire the old marine eased his frustrations by throwing knives into the ground at his feet while trying to remember how to pray.

"Are you all right, Vadeck?" The harried taskmaster jerked and looked up suddenly. It was as if had been caught drowsing off while on guard duty. His thoughts cleared and the marine reached over for the dried jerky strip that was resting on the stump next to him. "I am all right, master. A bit tired maybe, but still ready and able if you need something."

Wiping the dirt from his knife on his kilt, he cut a slice from the jerky and handed the piece of hardened measan to Jedaf. Then he cut another strip from the thick, preserved meat off for himself, and pointed at the other stump with his dagger.

Jedaf accepted the silent offer without speaking and sat down heavily. They were both haggard and bone tired. The weary teenager watched the old seaman's eyes as he stared blankly into the red hot embers. It looked like the old warrior was asking himself the same questions and wondering what more could he have done.

Vadeck put away his sharp curved bladed rigging knife, and was now twirling around the blade to his short sword. The point tossed up a small dirt mound as it spun about. The firelight reflected hypnotically off the blades sides, as it rotated. Streaks of yellow, white and orange light danced around the camp, giving off a kaleidoscopic effect.

It was the last thing Jedaf could remember about that evening and early morning. Slumping forward he had fallen asleep sitting up. A short time later Vadeck noticed the young lord's eyes were closed. He carefully lowered the teenager to the ground near the fire circle and fetched a blanket to cover him.

Chapter # 6

The Southeast Road to Tabalis

The ambassador touched Jedaf on the shoulder causing him to jump in his sleep. The young man immediately swung out a blocking arm as he reached for his weapon. His friend was lucky the youth was not armed. Jedaf had been sleeping on the ground near the fire, and could not seem to awaken. Ajoris was not surprised at seeing the boy's bloodshot eyes, the dark circles below his master's lids, or the fatigued expression on his face.

"Sire, by the suns dial, it's about the eleventh zestar. That woman Ciramtis is here in the camp, seeing to Captain Odelac and mister Valadis."

Jedaf stood slowly, rubbed his eyes and handed his blanket to Ajoris. The drinking water keg was near the stump where he had slept. Taking a few sips from the ladle he rinsed his mouth before bending down and dumping one scoop over his head. The water ran through his hair and down his face. Even though it burned his eyes, the cold water made him feel a little better and more awake. Ajoris handed him a hand towel while the boy stood and arched his aching back.

Over at the wagon, he could see the side canvas flaps were fully open and a stepping crate had been placed at the tailgate. Everyone in the camp was up and going about their assigned tasks, except for him. His whole body seemed to be one mass of hard, knotted, bruised mussles. Brushing off the loose dirt and dry pine needles from his kilt and socks was a painfull ordeal.

Walking over toward the wagon, Jedaf stopped half way in mid stride. Cramping up, he suddenly felt nauseous and feverish. There was a fluidic pressure in his lungs and the skin between his breasts was stinging. Stooping and holding onto his knee, he opened the lasses of his tunic with his other shaking hand. Over his sternum was a red to purple three fingered hand print with round black bruises where the demon's palm and talons had touched. The sensation reminded him of the dry ice burns he had received while unloading refrigerator trucks when he was in college.

Inhaling deeply he wheezed and coughed several times as his vision blurred and white dots darted about. His stomach cramped up and Jedaf doubled over in pain while holding his abdomen. Thinking he was going to be sick, the teen staggered to the nearest tree. Vomiting up a pint of foul smelling sour liquid, he held onto the tree trunk for support as the world spun. Then the boy started coughing again and spiting up mouthfuls of thick pasty yellow phlegm.

Ajoris ran over and held him tightly while the youth retched and his body trembled. "Lord should I get your medical bag?" Jedaf didn't answer right away. He just stood there and shook his head no, while waiting for the delirium tremors to stop.

"I'm alright. Just give me a zesta to rest and another ladle or two of water." Ajor hurried over to the water cask. He filled two metal cups and wrung out a wash rag before running back. Jedaf rinsed his mouth with one cup and drank the second one as the spasms returned. Ajor lowered him gently to the ground, and knelt quietly at his side. The ambassador wiped the perspiration from the boy's pasty white face. Then he held the cold wet cloth over Jedaf's feverish forhead. After fifteen to twenty zestas, he stood and took a second apprehensive look at the boy.

Jedaf could see the worried look on the older man's face. "Thanks Ajor! I think I will be fine shortly." The ambassador nodded but made no comments as he turned and walked over to the cart. He spoke quietly with Vadeck for a few moments before returning to the fire circle. Jedaf knew that they were talking about him but, he did not want them to be unduly worried.

The crew had emptied the wagon of most of its contents the night before. This created sheltered sleeping conditions for the two injured men and would keep them high and dry if heavy rains came. Last night's dark cloud cover turned out being an atmospheric anomaly created by the evil treskul. They were not nimbuses, and the black masses had created nothing more than cold, heavy dew this morning.

Near the Conestoga a makeshift lean-to had been hastily constructed in a small clearing. At a height of twelve feet, a thick adubur rope had been stretched taut and tied off, between two tall clotis trees. Over the thick hemp cable the extra tarpaulins had been pulled and branch poles had been cut to support the sides. The canvas covered the supplies and provided a warmer and dryer area where Vadeck could prepare the meals.

Jedaf stood a little uneasy at first. Then he straightened his tunic and composed himself before walking toward the wagon. His legs were still a bit wobbly, but by the time he reached the rear wheel he was steadier on his feet and thinking more clearly.

Climbing onto the back gate of the wagon Jedaf found Ciramtis in the act of re-bandaging Valadis's back. The captain was sleeping quietly at the opposite side of the wagon. She had administered a pain medication and muscle relaxer to each of them. They appeared to be comfortable, warm and well rested.

"The morning light pales in your presence and the kindness of your heart warm more than brandy wine." Ciramtis's eyes shined as she smiled at the age-old compliment.

"You have tended their wounds well, but they are still not fit for travel," she said. Placing the last bandage on Valadis's back, she gently pulled his tunic down and covered him with a blanket. "Val and Ajor have told me what happened last night. You have very powerful enemies Jedaf of Dolfi. They are so powerful," she said just above a whisper, "That they can send their servants or their spirits over great distances. Neither mountains nor oceans deter them."

"I was within a quarter days ride from here when the shock wave of the power force could be felt. It took all of my will and concentration to keep my mount from running off in the opposite direction. Still, I was only able to advance for another half thasta or so before a searing wave of pain shot forth. It was so intense that it took my breath away and dropped my horse as if his legs had been knocked out from beneath him."

"I hit the ground hard and it loosened my grip on the reins. By the time I regained my stance, he had managed to get to his feet and gallop off. I'm just glad I wasn't nearer to your wagons when it hit. Walking to the camp, I saw a lot of weaker animals that died at the roadsides."

"What did you do to that fiend to cause him such great pain?" Her joints were becoming stiff from kneeling on the rough planking. Sitting down next to him she rubbed the redness from them, as she spoke.

"I splashed some water of Hespa on him," the teen replied in a matter of fact tone.

A puzzled and almost startled expression crossed her thin face. "Hespa, where did you get that?"

Jedaf reached over next to her and fumbled through his blue leather, medical bag of the healing guild. Retrieving the light blue ixluk glass bottle, he handed it to her. "It was given to me by an old friend just before leaving Dolfi. Her name is Corella of Bintar."

The shimmering iridescent liquid glowed brightly as she held the half empty bottle aloft looking through the rippled glass. "Cora said that I did not deserve to have it, but she gave it to me anyway." The tone of his voice tightened and crackled as if he were speaking as an old woman would. "Use it sparingly, because Hespa's spring only gives water once a year."

Ciramtis clutched the container close to her breast saying a silent prayer. "Do you know where the spring is, and the time of year?" She was so excited and full of anticipation that when she leaned forward quickly it caused the hood of her cloak to fall back. A large raw abrasion and bruise was revealed on the side of her face.

Jedaf reopened his nedika medical bag and took out a jar of ointment. "Yes, the spring is in the coastal mountains just north of Eshon's landing in the Bintarian Kingdom. Every third day of Asursa, the geyser erupts. Cora told me that the priestesses of the Daughter's of Divine Justice had built a small stone chapel at the side of the spring. I have never been there myself, but from Cora's directions I'm sure I could find it."

Rubbing the salve gently on her face as he spoke, she sat watching his eyes. "Thank you Jedaf. You don't seem to know the significance of this knowledge. The location and the day the geyser erupts have been forgotten for at lease three generations. I have been searching here on Zarhun for the last two years, just for some small clue. Ostical of Cathon was said to be the last priestess to hold the secret. No one knows if she ever passed the knowledge on, or to whom."

Jedaf placed the lid back on the ointment jar. "Did you get that bruise when your horse threw you?"

She touched it lightly with the tips of her fingers, and winced. "Yes, does it look as bad as it feels?"

Jedaf held her by the chin and examined the scuff a little more closely. "I did not think so at first but, you might have some fine grains of sand imbedded in the skin. Why don't you wash your face again and reapply another layer of salve."

Jedaf handed her a clean cloth and Ciramtis washed the abrasion as she spoke. "You placed yourself in great danger, by using Hespa on him. The creature was of great power and could have gone mad, sending out his evil in all directions, and contaminating half of the countryside. Why did you choose that weapon to fight him?"

Jedaf leaned back watching her. It was nice to just relax and chat for a change, she reminded him so much of Minatis, that she totally disarmed him. It was just like talking with a dear old friend again. "First of all, I did not know or think of it as a weapon, and second, I didn't expect that kind of a reaction.

Corella only told me the blessed water would keep most demons away, and heal any wound caused by their fangs or talons. I don't even know who Hespa was or why this holy hot spring geyser is so important."

"I was just as surprised as Motaluk to see what it was doing to him. The creature was attempting to bite Odelac when I doused him with it. Some of the water hit the back of his head and ran down the side of his face. The rest splattered and splashed down his back. It was as if I had dumped acid on him."

"His left eye, cheek, part of his jaw and neck fell away along with the top of his left shoulder, and parts of his wing and trapezium muscles. I also saw some holes open up in his back when he retrieved his trident. While limping away, his hip and thigh were dissolving before he reached the edge of the woods. That is when he began screaming the loudest. I don't know if there is enough left of him to bury."

Ciramtis applied a new coat of tessa ointment on her cheek as she spoke. "Jedaf, Corella meant for you to rub the water on yourself or the person you meant to protect. You say this demon's name was Motaluk? How did you know his name?"

Jedaf paused thinking for a second before answering. "I really don't know, he said that I had killed his brother Lufarus, and as soon as he spoke, the runic letter M came to me. The only treskul I knew whose name started with an M is Motaluk, the evil of pestilence."

Ciramtis's eyes widened, "You mean that creature was one of the five evil treskuls of hell?" She took on a more frightened but concerned look. "Again you may have caused this land greater pain than you realize. If he no longer can leave the vicinity, the land will be contaminated because of his malevolent presence. All creatures might die of his diseases, and no one may be able to dwell in this land ever again."

She bowed her head and said several silent prayers under her breath, before looking at him once more. "I do not think that you will see that enemy for a long time. Motaluk knew if he did not get to a poison waterhole or some filthy swamp, Hespa's waters would continue to eat at him until a foul or a noxious liquid could dilute it.

At best, he will be crippled for eternity and unable to ever fly or move about on his own."

"You see, Hespa is the place where Athamus the God of Water, married Iesta the Goddess of life. Once a year on the anniversary of their union, the geyser gushes forth the gift of life into the rivers, lakes and seas. What you did by sprinkling Hespa's water on him, was to try to bring something to life that had been long dead and turned to dust. There were no cells for the water to rejuvenate, so they just washed away the fabric of his being and left nothing in its place."

She finished applying the second coat of the tessa honey bee salve. Ajoris lifted a portion of the canvas back flap interrupting them and flooding the wagon in sunlight and fresh air. "Master, would you and Ciramtis like to have something to eat? Vadeck still has a pot of tea, some biscuit bread and some hot food in the skillet by the fire."

Jedaf nodded, and thanked him. "Sounds like a good idea, Ajor." The Ambassador helped Ciramtis down and out of the wagon. Then he tied up the canvas flap up on top before following them over to the cooking area.

The sun's light was bright enough for both of them to shade their eyes as they walked over to the cook fire. "Lord, first lunch has been prepared. Will you eat now?"

"Yes. Thank you Vadeck, and fix a plate for Ciramtis."

Vadeck gave a nod to her acknowledging the young woman's presence. "That's already been taken care of sire." Ajoris caught up with them and draped a cloak over one of the stumps for Ciramtis to sit on.

Vadeck was handing out sour dough biscuits to the rest of the men, and stopped long enough to fill plates for Jedaf, Ciramtis, and Ajor. A thick and pasty rena bean and wild measan meat, chunk, stock stew had been prepared. The men sat eating silently, and after Jedaf tasted the meal, he knew why. The flavor was terrible. It had too much blyga black pepper and had a burnt taste. No one complained knowing Vadeck had done the cooking and they knew they could not have done better themselves.

Ajoris returned to the wagon and fetched one of the wineskins. He poured everyone a large cup of deep purple lusumak, which helped clear their palate. The remainder he poured into the iron stew pot making the rest of the portions more digestible.

Karadis and Myritt had found six of the horses earlier in the day and two more just before sitting down to eat. After tasting lunch, they decided it was the right time to see if they could not find at least one or two more of the missing mounts. Otherwise one of the saddle horses would have to be hitched to the cart.

Jedaf leaned over nearer to Ciramtis as they ate, and whispered to her softly. "Yesterday I sent a dispatch pouch with several letters to friends in Joroca. If it reaches them, they may be able to help you, Prince Sesmak of Envar, the people of this land and the Kingdom of Jeupa."

"I am afraid that I may have chosen a bad time for their arrival, and they must be warned. Will you be willing to ride to Envar's North Point for me and carry another message to my friends? You may have to stay there and hide out for a few days to a week."

Ciramtis stood and warmed her hands at the fire pit. "Why not send Vadeck or one of the others?"

Jedaf stood and moved closer to her, and once more lowered his tone. "Frankly I don't know any of these men very well. I completely trust Captain Odelac, and his friend Vadeck, but I don't know the rest of them. They have pretty much stayed to themselves, and I guess that has been beneficial to everyone."

Jedaf scraped the remains of lunch from his dish into the fire. "I was pondering sending one of them before you showed up, but now I think it would be better to have the men take Odelac and Valadis south to Jeupa. They will be able to get medical attention and warn the people of the impending war. They can also help them make some fortifications at the border lands, or warn the people further to the southwest."

Ciramtis handed her plate and cup to him. She had not eaten much of Vadeck's cooking either, but had managed to eat a few mouthfuls and the biscuit. Jedaf scraped her plate and dropped it and her wooden spoon into the wash bucket near the fire. "I have to continue my pilgrimage to Tabalis, and nothing is supposed to deter me from it. I ask again. Will you take Odelac's mount and deliver the letter for me?"

Ciramtis turned to him looking deeply into his bloodshot eyes. "You have a strange power about you young master," she said quietly. "It is hard to resist your green vourtre eyes. Prior to the rumors of this new Worezian War, I had planned on traveling northeast to Cathon's, City of Adathe."

"I have been seeking the last known whereabouts of Ostical, and any clue to the location of the legendary spring of Hespa. Everyone that I know thought that the spring was here on the Continent of Zarhun. If we could have found it, we might have been able to help cure or heal many wounded and might have been able to ease the pain and suffering of their dying."

"Now you come along and give me the answer without asking any questions, as if I had been a long and trusted friend. Now, there is no longer a reason for me to take a month long journey to Adathe and back. I can stay here and continue working with the Jeupans. How could I refuse your request, you're the one that is doing most of the helping?"

Jedaf placed a light hand on her shoulder, and looked back into her shining eyes. "Thank you. I hope when this is over we can meet in Bintar next Asursa and search for the ruins of the temple." She smiled back, then lowered her head and gave a quick nod of acceptance.

"Ajor," Jedaf called out. "Have the men pack some supplies on the saddle horses for you and me, and have them pack Odelac's horse with some supplies for Ciramtis. You and I will be going on alone from here. The rest of the men will be taking the cart and wagon, and heading south to Jeupa."

Ajoris stood brushing off the loose bark from the back of his kilt. The tree log that he had been sitting on was partially infested with large ants and there were georgs clawing out from under it. These foul smelling, legless slugs seemed to crawl into everyone's pockets or purses while you were sleeping on the ground.

As the ambassador looked down at the slime on his boots he hoped they had not gotten into any of the uncrated goods or meal bags. The thought of these long legged insects and the nauseating gastropods had been giving him the creeps throughout lunch. Setting his plate aside he said, "I will have them take care of it right away."

Jedaf waived an acknowledgement and walked off behind the wagon to be alone for awhile. Ciramtis sauntered off with Ajor to pick out a mount for herself and to get a few supplies. Jedaf sat on a stump, writing a letter to Traga. He had to inform him what was about to happen. It was a lengthy letter explaining everything that he knew of both impending wars.

In the letter he had written and given to Kytos, he had given Traga orders to assemble his army and have them embark for Envar's North Point as quickly as possible. It was his intention for them to help Prince Sesmak in any way they could. Now Jedaf knew these efforts would be in vain. They would still be far outnumbered and might be massacred before they could to do any good.

It would be best for all, if he were to just worn Sesmak, and have him move his army to the south as expeditiously as possible. The meager force that Traga would be mustering could only provide a holding action at best. Jedaf wanted them to avoid doing battle with the Worezian or Envarian Armies that were gathering on the Zarhun Plain. They were to take up defensive positions and help the Jeupans in any way that Traga thought best.

Standing he folded the letter inward and melted a small amount of red wax on the seam. To it he pressed his signet ring deeply, and waived his hand over it in a clockwise circular motion. The Kaybeck runic symbols fell softly from his lips, formed in mid air, then fell to the envelop staining it a rusty brown. To the last five lines of the protective spell he added, treskuls curti yie enom fasic. He was not going to let this letter fall into the hands of the enemy kingdoms, or any of their demonic helpers.

"Such a powerful protective spell on a letter addressed to a friend?" Ciramtis had come up on him from behind, and he had not known of her presence until she spoke. Jedaf jumped to the rear, sword flashing clear of its scabbard. He was totally surprised, she moved as quietly as a breeze.

"Are you in the habit of sneaking around scaring people out of their wits?"

Ciramtis did not speak at first, but cleared her throat. "My Lord Jedaf, are you in the habit of wearing silks and silver to slay one unarmed woman?"

Jedaf looked down at himself, tightly gripping his hilt. Closing his eyes momentarily, he relaxed and let his mind clear. His enchanted traveling clothes returned as if they were a blurry vision. "My Lord, I knew who you were when we first met at the inn," she said. "No one but the Lord of the Red Dragon could have stayed at my table without receiving pain once I touched it with my staff."

She extended her hand and took the letter before kneeling. "I Ciramtis of Iblac, swear allegiance to the Lord of the Dragon. May my eyes shrivel and my fleshes rot with disease, if I ever fail to serve him. I swear this in the name of Iesta Goddess of life."

Jedaf reached down and pressed her clasped hands between his. "Arise Ciramtis trusted friend and ally." She smiled broadly as he helped her stand.

"Lord." It was Ajor's voice coming from the other side of the wagon. "Our horses are ready." Jedaf took a hold of Ciramtis's arm and they returned to the cook fire area. Karadis and Myritt had returned to the camp and had found one more of the pack horses, and one of the wagon horses.

"You will be able to recognize my men by our standards. Give the letter to Commander Traga." Ciramtis went to fetch her travel cloak, which she had hung at the back of the wagon. She said her goodbye's to Valadis, and told him she would meet up with him in about a mursa, a sixteen day Palestus month. Then she mounted, waived to the men and rode off making her own trail through the trees heading to the west.

Jedaf walked over to the old taskmaster while Ciramtis was saying her goodbye's to Valadis. "Vadeck, we have not really had a chance to speak very much to one another, but I know that I can trust you. I'm expecting you to take care of Captain Odelac and Valadis. Get them and the men to the Kingdom of Jeupa for me. Valadis will give you the directions." He extended his arm, and Vadeck took and held his wrist firmly.

"Don't worry Master Jedaf, we have more than enough supplies, and I won't let anything happen to the captain. We will stay here the rest of the day, and then break camp first thing tomorrow morning. Goodbye, and may the gods protect you when you reach Tabalis." He clasped Jedaf arm again a little tighter, then he gave him a sharp salute, more out of respect than military protocol.

Ajor stood at the horse's side holding both reins, while Jedaf spoke with Odel and telling the men farewell. It was going to be a long lonely ride. Jedaf wove a protective and strengthening spell and sent it forward into the horse's ears. They tried not to listen, but Ajor held them firmly. Mounting, Jedaf took a last look at the sundial that was set up near the fire pit. It was the fourteenth zestar and the suns were almost directly overhead. They both knew that it was going to be a hot, hard day. "Let's go Ajor; I would to like to be over the Worezian border before the suns set."

The road that they followed to the southeast continued to deteriorate. Hynon, the proprietor of the "Inn of the Athca" was right. There seemed to have been some travel eastward to Cathon, but not much. King Magarus of Worez did not like King Samalis of Cathon. He had cut off relations with him after a dispute over the fishing villages that had been built on the coasts between their two capitals. Naturally King Magarus claimed most of these small communities were in his empire but did not have enough warriors to station beyond the Lestran Mountains to enforce those claims.

There were only two major easterly passes through these mountains. The northern pass which had the main east-west road connecting the Loceran Plain of Worez and Vellastran Plain of Cathon. The other was the southern pass which also connected the two plains. But it swung far south into the ancient lands of the Eastern Semedian and the vourtre kingdoms, before heading back north through the mountains to Cathon.

This second pass was the one that Jedaf and Ajoris intended on taking to Tabalis. If Ajoris's information was correct this second pass and road would branch off of the main road about five thastas, or just over four miles ahead of them. They would locate the fork in a rocky area of the foot hills to the higher still snow capped Tabal Mountains.

The endurance spell that Jedaf had woven over the horses worked better than either of them had imagined. Instead of having to stop and walk them every two thastas they were able to ride a half a day without them tiring. After eating the meal that Vadeck had given them, neither wanted to stop to fix anything to eat, so they rode through second lunch and into the late afternoon.

They had been riding more than three zestars, climbing the foothills steadily upward before stopping for their first real rest. The trees had thinned to a shorter variety of scruffy ponderosa style pine tree and the ground was noticeably harder, with broken bits of rock mingled with a crusty reddish-brown potter's clay.

Chapter # 7

The Hand of King Dracar

From one of the higher ridgeline overlooks, Ajoris could see what he had been searching for. "There it is!" Jedaf looked far off in the distance where the ambassador was pointing. It was an enormous stone hand extending out of a rocky shelf face of bare grey speckled adarf mountain. Another two zestars ride from their location, a flat palm with the fingers extending to the west had been carved by the ancient vourtres as a gesture of peace before man inhabited these lands.

Three of the fingers were now broken at the knuckle joints from weathering and rock slides. This was the landmark that the ambassador had been seeking. At the Worezian border, the hand divided the two mountain passes. The pass to the north headed to the Vellastran Plains of Cathon, and the pass heading southeast was toward the City of Tabalis.

Arching his soar back, Jedaf decided the mountain divide was as far as they would be going today. They had ridden in silence most of the way, stopping only twice to walk the horses. This was the location that travelers had used for hundreds of years and they knew they would not find a better campsite within riding distance. It soon would be too dark and dangerous to follow the mountain trail.

The ambassador knew that something was decidedly wrong. He did not think or feel this thick apprehensive atmosphere was caused by the presents of evil, bad weather, or any sickness. The young master had ridden most of the way in deep thought, and sometimes he would just let Ajoris take the lead while riding single file on the narrower tails.

It was disheartening and disappointing to see that nature was slowly reclaiming this resting place. Now after only a decade of infrequent use it was starting to be over run with thorn bush and dry scraggily weeds.

Since King Magarus of Worez had been crowned, minor conflicts with each or the neighboring kingdoms had occurred. He especially did not like King Samalis, the ruler of the eastern Kingdom of Cathon. This was partially due to the fact that since the Worezian — Envarian War, Cathon had become one of the most powerful kingdoms on the Continent of Zarhun. The other being their sovereign would not be bullied by demands from King Magarus.

Reaching the rocky shelf beneath the stone hand, Jedaf dismounted walking his horse about fifty paces down the southern fork. He removed the saddle, blanket, packs and bridle from his tired mount. It was not the distance they had traveled that had worn them out. The horses were still skittish from the previous evenings encounter with the demon. They had not settled down or really rested until just before dawn. They had walked about in the darkness fearing the carnivores that had been aroused by the treskul's evil.

Jedaf was equally tired from this encounter and the apprehensive emotion of leaving their friends and companions behind. Sitting on a large rock near the old fire pit he watched the ambassador go about setting up camp. Ajoris tended to his horse then started gathering wood, and clearing some of the brush. No matter how bad he felt, Jedaf could not let the older man finish doing all the work.

There was a lot to be done if they were to have a comfortable and safe rest. The most important of these tasks being the weaving of a spell of protection over the camp. He would never again be left vulnerable to an attack while they slept. The enchantments alone would take over a zestar to complete. Each went about their tasks without speaking.

Finally Ambassador Ajoris could not contain his questions any longer and turned around to speak to the young Dragon Lord. The teenager was nowhere to be seen. He was no longer in the camp and he hadn't finished clearing the fire pit. Ajoris suddenly became very worried, and started shouting for him. There were no answers to his calls.

The ambassador started searching frantically for him. He knew that Jedaf could not have gone down the road that they had come from, he would have seen him. Heading to the south between the trees that grew along the cliff, the weary diplomat climbed up the next several layers of sharp, jagged rock shelf. Above him were the overgrown remains to the ancient stone cutters path. It was littered with broken sections of petrified scaffolding and stone fragments.

Ajor hoped this was the trail that Jedaf had taken. He followed it upward for another half thasta, where it ended at a large pile of broken shards and loose rubble. Ajor ducked under the twisted boughs of a dwarfed tree that was leaning against cliff face. Then he climbed up the two more sedimentary layers of the rock bluff that ran upward along what was left of the stone cutters path. Rounding a large chipped and fragmented boulder he could see the young lord's back, which gave him quite a relief.

Bending down and holding his knees, Ajoris caught his breath. His master was on the craggy shelf above of him. Jedaf was sitting in the palm of the large ancient stone hand with his legs dangling over the edge of its broken fingers. His head was bent low, as he looked into the ravine and down the deep chasm to the widening valleys. The youth was sobbing softly and wiping his tears on his sleeve.

Ajoris stood quietly off to the side behind him. It was not what the ambassador had expected, and he did not wish to disturb him. This man was the Lord of the horned Red Dragon, the Protector of the Dead, the leader of warriors and armies, and the destroyer of evil. Ajoris was about to storm right up to him and ask him what was wrong, but decided to just sit down and keep silent. He thought; if the great lord needed something all he had to do was to command me. Jedaf did not move other than rising his head a few times looking out over the mountains or down one of the two passes.

The gentile middle aged man remained sitting behind Jedaf for what seemed the longest time, watching and waiting patiently. It then dawned on Ajoris, that this Lord of the Dragon was not really a man. Sitting there at the precipice of the cliff was the back of a lonely sixteen to seventeen year old boy that had never been born to this world. He had no parents or any relative that he could turn too, or speak to from the heart. Ajor walked over to him from behind and put his companionate hands on Jedaf's shoulders holding onto him tightly.

"Don't turn around master Jedaf," he said with a calming and sympathetic tone to his voice. "Just look out over the mountains toward the horizon and listen. When I was a little younger than you, my father was killed during a raid by Azzonian warriors near the eastern border. My mother had died of fever when I was too young to remember her. I did not have any brothers and my much other sister had been sent away to live with my uncle."

"All I had was my grandfather on my mother's side of the family. He was very old, and in poor health, but he was my best friend. He said jokingly that I should not be afraid of death or the unknown. The only thing to fear was having no one to remember you, or no one to leave offering cakes at the tomb."

"On his death bed he said to me that one day we would all be together again in Odea, and there would be no more suffering, just tessom honey cakes and beer. They were his favorite snacks." Ajoris smiled at the fond memory of him. "His last words to me were, just because you can't see me anymore, doesn't mean that I am not around. Look to the wind and you'll find me."

"I know you don't really believe in the old gods, and I guess you really don't have to. When I need an ear, I speak to my grandfather and Atrusa, Goddess of the Wind. Tell her what is bothering you." Ajoris kept his hands on Jedaf shoulders, and remained silent. Jedaf sat for awhile, the tears still flowed and ran down his cheeks, but he made no sound.

Finally he yelled out at the top of his lungs, "What do you want of me? You drag me to this world and everything I touch is either killed, or destroyed. You killed Sarasa's father and brothers, you tried to kill Agar. You ruined Odelac's ship the Tarpenya and the ship that Elona and Kytos were sailing on, just to make slaves of us all. Now you you're going to start wars on two more continents, kill thousands of people, and for what? So I can be blamed for that too." The echo's continued while he shamefully lowered his voice.

"I have no way of helping or stopping these events! You made me fall in love with Elona, then you take her away and I will never see her again. Why not just take my life now? You want it, take it!" He tried to fall forward off of the great stone hand and into the ravine below. Ajoris held on to him firmly.

"I know that you are in pain, but think what you're doing," said his friend. "If you die now, the evil that is upon the land will have won, and Elona will die for sure. All you can do is the same that we all try to do. That is doing the best we can and help when we are asked. Yes, we lose sometimes, but think of the good that you have done in the short time you have been with us on Palestus."

"You told me how you saved Axeth from the slavers. You spared Sarasa and her mother from a fate worse than death. You saved Commander Traga's son Agar from being tortured to death. You rescued me from drowning. You prevented Prince Kytos from bleeding to death. You cured Princess Diara of dying from blood poisoning and fever. You can not protect and save everyone. Princess Elona is not dead yet! If you really love her, don't give up on her. She has more gumption and fight in her than you give her credit."

Jedaf reached up and gently took Ajoris hands away from his shoulders. "Thank you Ajor," he said without looking at him. "I will be alright. I guess I was just feeling sorry for myself and just don't understand your world. I did not intend this being a pity party. If you don't mind, I think I will stay up here for awhile in the vourtre's hand and wait for the suns to set."

"Then again, I might take your advice and talk to the Goddess Atrusa. I think I will end the evening by yelling at Lord Krebolus for awhile. I guess the only thing left for me to do is to go to Tabalis and tell death, King Zaghar and his friends where they can go. Thanks again and good night mister ambassador."

It was a cold and almost sleepless night for Jedaf of Dolfi. After the smaller sun Myastus caught up with and merged with the larger sun Horastus there was an immediate ten degree drop in the temperature. The twin suns were in alignment at the horizon for less than another ten Palestus zestas, or twenty earth minuets before going over the horizon.

There was almost immediate darkness. A heavy black cloud bank had rolled in obscuring, the stars and the smaller slate grey moon of Palea which was in half crescent. The larger moon Mursas was on the other side of the planet.

Killing King Zaghar with his bare hands was his last conscious thought. Every time his eyes closed it was as if he were reliving each moment of his short past. He had been on this planet now for less than four of their months, or mursas and he didn't think he was going to get used to their way of life. All there seemed to be was misery and death.

In his dream he looked behind the horse he was riding and saw Ciramitis. He had just met her at the "Inn of the Athca's Head." Ciramtis was the great grand daughter of Minatis, a member of the council of eleven and one of his teachers. In his dream, she was dying; lying on her back. She was in the center of the road waving something at him.

The teen could see his crest of the horned red dragon on the outside of the dispatch, but it looked strange. It really wasn't a correspondence envelope. It was an intravenous blood bag that had been punctured and was spraying the contents on her. He yelled "No" out loud and awoke sitting up quickly. It was almost dawn but still very dark; the stratus clouds still covered the stars.

"I wonder if I have now written a death sentence for her also. I should have sent one of the men to deliver that letter to Commander

Traga." Rubbing the sleep from his eyes and the stiffness from his muscles he looked about him. Sleeping on the rocks all night was not one of his smartest ideas. He did manage to notice that he had a thick brown blanket over his legs. Ajoris must have come back here late last night. Jedaf took it and wrapped it about him, waiting for the sunrise. He didn't think he could find his way back in the dark.

It was worth the wait. It was a beautiful sunrise, with bright red and orange streaks coming over the horizon driving out the shadows behind him. Then from far back in his memory he had second thoughts about the morning light. Red sky at night, sailors delight, and red sky in morning sailors take warning. I wonder if it is going to rain today. He smoothed his blanket out on the flat stone and folded it.

Beneath his blanket were six large lines of runic characters, caved deeply into the stone. Leaning over them he blew the dirt away, reading the lines of text out loud. "The great hand of King Dracar bids you welcome. Come in peace. Take only the wisdom of age when you leave." It was then that Jedaf remembered that he had been sleeping in the palm of a giant stone hand all night.

What was that old epic Thargos use to speak of? Oh yes, the vourtre king of ancient Umzath Ra. He had his people carve it around six hundred twenty after the second western Zarhunian revolt on Megath. The open left hand was supposed to be a sign of peace to the humans of the west during their civil war. The gesture was meant as a sign that these people did not have to fear any interference by the vourtre.

He thought that it was a shame that the monument was now half broken. What would his old vourtre friend Yanus say? Probably something to rile Gantilion like; "No good humans probably broke it trying to steal the rings, only to find out they were made of painted stone." The thought of both his teachers giving each other good natured jibes, brought a smile to his face as he walked back down the trail to the campsite.

Ajoris was awake and he had a hot tea kettle on the fire grating. He was sitting on a log and toasting sliced bread on a stick. Jedaf's bags were still off to the side of the fire pit where he left them. The ambassador had most of his possessions in his bag, and it looked like he had been waiting for hours. Jedaf suspected that his friend hadn't slept at all last night, but he was too ashamed of himself for the way he had acted, to ask any questions.

The weary diplomat did not say anything about it; he just held the hot toasted bread out in front of the boy to take. "Lord there is honeyed lusarus raisin spread near the bags and some salted redolga jerky that I boiled earlier. I have eaten already. You should sit, for a few zestas while I saddle the horses. We should get going, a storm is coming and I don't want to be caught in a flash flood down in this arroyo."

The tea, bread, and boiled bacon strips tasted better than he thought they would. It might have had something to do with how hungry he was. Thinking about the long lonely ride that they had getting to this site, he decided to once again weave an endurance spell over the horses. They did not like it any better than the first time, but were getting used to having Ajoris hold their heads making them look at Jedaf. The last spell lasted more than half a day allowing them to cover over eight thastas, a little over seven miles.

They rode down the southern pass for less than half a thasta only to find that it had been blocked. From the looks of the way the rock face had been scared, the western humans had created an avalanche to prevent the vourtres from coming down out of the mountains and onto the plains. This way man would have total control of the hunting and fishing grounds. There were tons of gigantic stones in the debris field. Some boulders were as large as wagons.

The avalanche was over sixty feet high and it would be very hard to get over them without climbing ropes, and impossible to get a horse over. They had to back-track the entire length of the pass. Half of the morning had been wasted, and they were right back where they started. Jedaf looked up at Dracar's hand with the missing three fingers and said, "It looks like the humans bit the hand that fed them for a thousand years." The ambassador gave no reply; he just nodded in agreement as they rode beneath it.

Since they had lost the morning, it was decided they would ride down the north pass for only another two zestars before taking another break. Now that there was no way they could get to Tabalis from here. They would have to travel all the way north to the City of Adathe. After buying addional provisions, they would have to go back up the pass from the other direction if they were to reach the city of the dead.

Ajoris laughed, "You see Dastus, the God of Fate, knew what he was doing when he had you originally purchase passage on a ship for Adathe." Jedaf pictured Odelac's ship the Tarpenya, his crew and the pirate Sedran that had captured them on the voyage from the City of Joroca.

Suddenly the image of Elona and the Goddess Everro came into focus from out of nowhere. Placing a hand over his breast pocket, he closed his eyes tightly for a moment. Inside his tunic was her painted likeness. The small scrap of canvas was all that remained of the wedding portrait. The remorse he felt, tightened his stomach as thick blanket of tearful emotions covered him. He was deeply pained. Knowing there was nothing he could do for her, and leaving her aboard the pirate ship was the hardest thing he had ever done in his life.

Jedaf knew he would love her all his life, and probably would never see her again. Then he thought of Elona's brother Kytos. He had sent him back to Joroca carrying letters for Commander Traga. Was the boy another friend that had been sent off to his death? The dour possibility brought on the deep depression again, causing him to ride in silence until the next rest stop.

Chapter # 8
The Village of Giehan

The narrow path that Kytos and Trestan followed was more of a wandering game trail than a road. It branched off the main highway and meandered almost due north. Kytos knew this because for most of the afternoon ride the suns were to his left moving and setting in the western skies. Riding until it was nearing dusk took the two of them most of the way back to the coast. Trestan the twenty two year old young Yojan slave that had saved Captain Odelac's life was not much of a talker. He had ridden most of the way in silence, following behind the fifteen year old Oppowian prince's horse.

They discussed lighting a fire, but they both feared highwaymen would see it or smell its smoke. Once they rode from the thicker woodlands the path they followed had more frequent east-west tee intersections. At two of these locations they could tell that other travelers were in the vicinity. The first encounter they could smell campfire smoke, and the second they could hear loud voices and music coming from down the eastern path. It was better to continue riding away from everyone else, until they reached a more remote clearing.

The young men tied off their mounts under a large shady burkat tree and hoisted their travel bags up into the higher branches for the night. This is where the two of them made a small platform ten feet off of the ground. Trestan cut some thicker support branches from a nearby clotis tree. Then he lashed them to the upper forked limbs in their make-shift hideout. They lined the tree stand sides of the tree blind; padding the smooth trunk and heavier limbs with softer cut pine branches. It was a bit uncomfortable but would have to do for the night.

The tree stand was away from where the horses were staked out, but still within their eyesight. They were close enough to protect the mounts from predators, but far enough away from the animals for them to slip into the woods if found by a group of marauding thieves. Being hidden from sight, and resting in the seclusion of the thicker foliage, made them both feel a lot safer.

They knew it would be colder and windier in the tree tops, but still better than sleeping unprotected on the ground. The horse blankets helped, but both of them were stiff and soar when they woke up. They stayed in the upper limbs munching on journey cakes until later in the morning, and did not climb down until Horastus had fully risen.

Breaking camp and saddling the horses helped them get over their anxieties. The early morning physical activities seemed to get their blood pumping and made them feel even better. Kytos had been able to sleep for at least half of the night, but Trestan barely slept at all.

Traga's son had been a slave for more than five years and had become accustomed to sleeping chained, body to body in a stinking and crowded confined space. The openness of the treetops, the fresh air, and not feeling constrained and cramped, brought out hidden fears that Trestan could not cope with.

Kytos wondered how long it was going to take for Trestan to just speak openly. Being a bond slave had taught him to be quiet and at times almost invisible. If Kytos did not turn around once in awhile he would never know there was another horse and rider behind him. After a zestar of riding north they came upon a watering hole, and a large berry patch beneath an old rotting butkat tree.

They both wadded into the cold water and washed thoroughly. While their clothing dried and aired out, they picked and ate several handfuls of berries. It was to be the longest respite of the day, and they did not know how much further it would be before reaching a coastal village.

Another six zestars of ridding with only a few walking breaks had made them both saddle sore. They were lucky to have arrived at the outskirts of the small fishing Village of Giehan without an incident. The area surrounding this hamlet had been the target of numerous raids by local bandits. The brigand's had become bolder recently due to the fact that King Magarus had ordered the Worezian Army of the Tan re-deployed to the south western borders. This left the eastern provinces at the mercy of local thugs, looting bands of homeless displaced tenement farmers and seasonal pickers.

Among the three small fishing trawlers, the half dozen barges and ten to fifteen rowboats, was a sleek looking and fast passenger schooner. It stood swaying at the small dock as they entered the village. Its crew was preparing to make sail and had already cast off the stern lines. Its hull had been painted two shades of dull grey and the narrow white trim made it blend into the backdrop of the sea.

Dismounting and stretching they rubbed at their aching backsides as they viewed its tall masts, sails, and rigging. All were painted in the same dull grey, but they had dark blue wavy bands painted horizontally every two feet right up to the banner. A sailor standing at the port side bow above a fish shaped beakhead pulled loose the mooring line at the front cleat, and tossed it to the dock.

"Wait there," yelled Kytos! "Can you tell me if there is a ship bound for Joroca?" A bare face young man in his mid twenties stuck his head out of the small passenger quarters hatch at hearing Ky's voice.

"Yes, there is," replied the curly haired seaman. "This is the Sydolla. She's the fastest ship in the east mercantile fleet. We're sailing for the Cities of Tansac and Joroca. We've just started setting the sails. No pirate has ever been able to match her speed or agility."

Kytos looked around quickly. There were no stables nearby, only a combination dry goods—trading post, and several small warehouses. "Can you wait for us for a few zestas? We want passage, but have to sell ours mounts." The captain, standing at the wheel called out to the other seaman at the stern. "Hold on there Timis, we have a few more paying customers."

Ky ran over to the retail shop, pulling his horse along with him. Tying the reins off on the front corner post cleat, he darted inside. The trader and owner of the establishment bought their horses for two thirds of their value, saying it was all he could afford. Ky did not have the time and knew it wasn't worth bargaining over. They just could not leave them at the dock.

They did get full price for the saddles, but practically gave away the saddle blankets, and reins. Trestan wanted to call the salesman a thief, but the young Oppowian prince reminded him that one of the horses actually belonged to the Worezian garrison. There really wasn't a loss, there was a profit.

Running as fast as they could, they headed back to the Sydolla with their travel bags and cloaks. The crewmen of this sloop tossed the last coiled line to the dock upon seeing them approach. Kytos and Trestan jumped over the ship's rail. They steadied themselves on the main deck, with their backs against the cabin wall as eddies pitched and swayed the sailboat.

The small vessel seemed to come alive all at once as the mooring anchor was pulled aboard and they got underway. Rocking with the swells of the tide, the wind started filling and flapping the fore-and-aft sails. The thought that he would never again set foot on another ship, crossed Ky's mind. He closed his eyes tightly and pressed his throbbing stump and wooden hand across his chest. Swallowing hard, he tried to keep down his undigested biscuit breakfast.

Timis finished coiling the mooring anchor rope as he watched Kytos's face whiten. Then the middle aged sailor standing at the stern grabbed a hold of the rail and gave a final push to the dock with his foot. The ship settled into a gentle rocking motion as the sails billowed. They smoothed and stretching wide as the ship surged while moving out into the deeper waters.

The Sydolla moved slowly at first, but as the tall sails caught more and more wind, it cut threw the waves easily. The captain had not given any orders. It was a small ship, with a crew of only five. They all knew the ships routine, and went about their tasks. The captain turned the wheel over to Timis before walking over to where Kytos was pressed against the cabin wall.

Ky stood for a moment rigid in fear and frozen against the planking of the wheelhouse. His eyes were open but he was unable to loosen his grip on his travel bag and couldn't seem to set it down. Trestan stood nearby him not saying anything and waiting for Kytos to do all the talking. The captain stretched out his hand. "Fare's four rebest small silvers each." Ky swallowed hard and let the bag slip slowly from his hand while reaching for his purse.

"How many days to Joroca," he managed to ask as he counted out his coins?

"I can have you there in nine or ten days if the winds right."

Ky dropped the coins into the captain's leathery hand. Pulling the draw strings with his teeth, he shook his purse jingling the coins. "Everyday you arrive in Joroca ahead of the nine days; I will give you another small silver."

The chinking coins made the captain smile even wider. He tapped the bottom of the bag making the metallic clinking sound once more while feeling its weight. "Lad if your willing to pay that much to get there, I'll stretch every inch of canvas I have got." He escorted Ky and Trestan to the wheelhouse, and held out the kartbaco logbook for them to sign. The young prince held up his wooden hand. He didn't have to say any more. The captain turned it toward himself and looked over to them.

"Kytos of Oppow, twenty three and one half tarmets," he said. "This is my friend Trestan of Yoja. Just write down the same weight."

The captain scribbled as Ky spoke, then blotted the wet ink, with an eca and ran his finger down the chart at the right side of the logbook. "That will be two coppers each for travel taxes."

Ky took another small silver from his purse and flipped it over to the captain with his thumbnail. "Keep the change." It was a sizable tip, and Kytos knew the captain would do what he could to earn more. He also did not want the captain to think he needed the money.

"Erret!" The captain shouted. "Take these gentlemen to the best cabin." Captain Zabus Tay was good to his word. The trip was mostly uneventful, and full sail was maintained in spite of the weather. He was not only the captain; he was also the owner of the Sydolla.

The captain and his father had built her, fifteen years earlier, but from her looks, it could have been built yesterday. Zabus Tay also changed the destination in the ship's log. It now read Joroca and Tansac, instead of the other way around. Ky knew that by doing this, he would owe the captain at least two more silvers.

The third day out, they caught the tail of a south-westerly gale. The sea roughened a bit, and the rain stung everyone's cheeks, but the captain kept full sail. Ky thought that the masts would break under the strain.

The canvas was so tight on the spars it had lost all its wrinkles and folds. They looked like one molded part of the ship. The two of them stayed up on deck most of the time. Not only didn't they like the other passengers, being below deck gave Kytos a claustrophobic and a tight chested feeling of apprehension.

There were three other Azzonian passengers from Tansac, aboard. They were merchants returning home after selling a sizeable amount of leather hides to the tannery on the outskirts of Giehan. Fearing robbery, they kept to themselves for the most part. Ky had seen them up on deck once getting fresh air, and once to complain about having to sail to Joroca first. Captain Zabus had to promise them that they would not be staying over night, and he would not bring any other passenger aboard while they were in the harbor.

The Azzonian skinners had not spoken to Kytos or Trestan at all during the voyage and they both thought it best to leave the other passengers alone. Timis, the first mate had been instructed to leave their food on the tray outside of their cabin door. They allowed no one inside.

Kytos was glad for the rain; it kept the Azzonian's in their cabin, and gave him more room to walk the decks. The rain felt good and had a good clean smell to it. It had been raining since they caught the tail wind of the storm.

"Nothing like a good wind to take your mind off your troubles," It was the captain's voice; Ky turned away from the rail as he heard him speak. Prince Kytos had been thinking about Captain Wova and the Sulaga that he and his sister had sailed on from their home port in the City of Jesilla. Wova was a good man, and he was sorry that Captain Sedran's pirate crew had killed him when they took his ship. Ky swore he would never forget him or his good natured laugh.

"No. I guess your right captain, but it also brings to mind some painful memories." Zabus noticed the boy rubbing at his stump and wooden hand. A strong gust came up and he turned his face into the wind allowing his long brown hair to blow over the rail toward the open sea.

Zabus took a leather strip from his belt tying his hair back as he spoke. "If this wind keeps up we may make it in six days. I can almost taste that cask of wine your extra silvers are going to buy me." He licked his lips and laughed loudly. It was good to hear and Ky laughed awhile with him, chatting until near dusk.

Trestan was a bit seasick and he could not fight off his anxiety and agoraphobic attacks. Earlier in the afternoon he had stopped at the galley and fetched a cheese crock and some biscuits before going to their cabin for the rest of the day. Munching on the hard dry breads helped keep his paranoia and nausea in check. After vomiting on and off for the past two days, he decided to stay in their cabin for the rest of the voyage.

Trestan also did not like the Azzon merchants and their presence kept reminding him how he had been taken as a young boy to be sold into slavery by one of their kingdoms raiding parties. Erret, the wiry sailor-handyman yelled over to them that kreb had been prepared, and they headed for the lower deck.

The last meal of the day seemed to be aptly named, especially at sea. Being named after Krebolus, the Lord of Darkness, it quickly became pitch black with the setting of the suns. Everything turned dark as far as they could see and if it weren't for the one oil lamp they would not have been able to find the hatch.

Below deck in the common space, a portable table had been set up with six folding chairs. The captain's son was the only one seated but four bowls had been set out. Erret lifted the lid from the cook pot, serving out large ladles into the bowls as they gathered around the table.

The meal was a thick bouillabaisse fish stew with spiced and diced oolet potatoes, femelis onions, ja sebus red cabbage plus a couple of hard cracker style rye breads with veavara efbur fennel seeds. They were too crisp and crumbly for dunking, but smelled delicious.

Ky stared into the tureen, not speaking. The last time he had eaten this type of dinner was with his sister Elona. He stomach turned over suddenly and he set his spoon down, unable to eat. "I am sorry Zabus. Suddenly I feel a little sick like Trestan. I don't think I will eat tonight either. Too much sea air today I guess." Picking up a stack of the crackers to keep the butterflies in his stomach under control, he retired to his cabin.

Trestan had the wick of the oil lamp turned down low and it was very dark inside their room. Kytos could barely make out his companion's silhouette in the shadows. Trestan had finally found a place that was confined and comfortable enough for him to sleep. He was curdled up on the deck in a corner, wedged between a highboy chest of drawers and their stacked baggage. Lying on the bunk Ky closed his eyes hoping to fall a sleep quickly. It took awhile to clear his mind of the past few days activities and thoughts of his friends. Finally a restless sleep came over him but it was filled with too many dreams.

On the evening of the fifth day they could see the lights of the City of Joroca on the horizon. Kytos and Trestan lingered along the rail looking at the cubic shaped buildings as the ship drew nearer. Most of them looked like plain white rectangular boxes stacked up on the shoreline. Zabus ordered sails trimmed, as they headed over the reef into the large bay.

There were at least fifteen other large mercantile ships at anchorage in the harbor, and more than two dozen barks and sloops. The Sydolla being one of the smallest; tacked in and out between them and chose an anchorage just leeward of a very large and agedly Tarkan or Zureathian merchantman.

The sight of the shoreline at night was the most fantastic thing that Kytos had ever seen. The polished mica imbedded in the zarmet marble of the building stones reflected the suns reddish light far out to sea. The scenery had a twinkling effect that was almost indescribable. It was as if the entire coast was ablaze. No wonder the ancients called Joroca the city of lights or the city of fire.

This was to be their last day aboard ship. Captain Zabus had originally promised his crew a day's leave in the city before sailing on to the City of Tansac, but now he had to take back that promise. The Azzonian's would not wait and were fearful that the only reason they had been brought to Joroca was murder and robbery. They had decided not leave their cabin again until sails had been set. Also, they would not eat anything brought to their cabin unless they saw Zabus Tay tasting it first.

Kytos and Trestan stayed at the bulwark rail watching the magnificent city in awe. There were no cities as large, or as beautiful in his Kingdom of Oppow and Trestan had never seen his homeland from the sea. The setting suns darkened the city almost at once. Ky thought it was though a candle had been snuffed out. Reluctantly returning to their cabin, Ky flopped down on his bunk and quickly fell into a deep sleep, while Trestan curled up next to the dresser.

The prince dreamed of his family and of being home in his Kingdom of Oppow among his family and friends. A load had been taken off his mind, at seeing the shoreline. The last two evenings all he could dream about was pirates, and he would waken to a cold sweat and shaking in fear. Tomorrow he and Trestan would be safely ashore.

The creaking of the gaff woke him. It was already daylight and they both had slept contently. Ky was so relaxed; he expected to wake up in bed at home. Jumping from his bunk, he woke Trestan and they washed and dressed quickly. Zabus had raised the mooring anchors and had hoisted only one sail. It was all he needed for the wind to carry the Sydolla to the docks.

The morning wind swept the coast of the bay in a circular pattern. It gave the harbor a good clean scent from the flowering jorocana shrubs that the city was famous for. The air currents blew out to sea following the eastern cliffs, swirled around and headed back to the mainland and into the center of the city.

Ahead of them a small merchant ship, hoisted anchors and made ready its sails to catch the eastern winds. A ragged edged two tone blue flag with a sharp toothed, white avaka in flight was flapping at the masthead. The ship was from one of the Jolacian fishing ports. Most likely she was taking on a load of emen cooking and preservative salt.

They hailed Zabus in passing, and he in turn yelled back the latest weather that they had sailed through. There was no news regarding the northern continental wars, but the other captain did have one interesting tale of resent events. It had to do with a large party of Azzonian's that had just crossed the southern border of Yoja.

There was nothing unusual about an incursion like this. Raiding parties had been sacking and looting the region for generations. The Yojan King would protest to the Azzonian Ambassador and he would always deny it. His answer was always the same. If you can prove it was a mistaken crossing by one of our officers; Akeska the King of Azzon, would be all too happy to make restitutions and pay for any of the damages.

The Azzonian's never left any survivors, and the Kingdom of Yoja no longer had the wealth or power to declare war. This time was different. The raiders ran into a newly formed Yojan border patrol. Seventy five to one hundred Azzon warriors had lost their lives. Close to another one hundred had been captured.

The prisoners were being sold on the slave blocks and the whole city was celebrating. Kytos had been wondering why he had heard music so early in the morning. It was not too early to start; it just hadn't stopped from last nights festivities. Zabus tacked one last time, before Timis, and Erret dropped sail. The dock master pointed out a berth next to a small grain barge and they headed directly for it.

With swift hands at the wheel, Zabus swung the bow in sharply. Dropping anchor, the Sydolla gently bumped the pier as stevedores caught and quickly tied fast the lines. Kytos was anxious to be on his way. He had already given Zabus the small silvers that he had promised, and had said his goodbyes. Both he and Trestan jumped the rail to the dock and gave a last wave to the crew before heading into the crowd of merrymakers.

Lord Jedaf had given Ky a map and description of the docks before they parted. On the right side of the drawing were directions from the docks to the main avenues and streets leading to Traga's home. With Trestan along Ky no longer needed the map, so he tossed it into one of the hand warming burn barrels at the end of the pier.

There was twice the normal number of people in the main square, with most of them still drunk, languishing at the roadside curbs with empty beer crocks. It looked like the celebration of the Azzon defeat was going to continue throughout the day and into the night.

At one point it looked like they would not be able to push their way through the tightly packed slobbering throng of revelers, but a santax of warriors from the First Army of the Yojan Red cleared a path for a royal coach. They were able to run between the crowds and follow the vehicle before the avenue was blocked again.

It only took Trestan a short time for him to reconnoiter and get his barring. After reaching the main thoroughfare near the palace fortifications, he remembered which streets and lanes led to his home. They did not have to follow Lord Jedaf's directions; Trestan knew a few short cuts through the city to the western suburban districts.

Chapter # 9

Princess Shayla's Bridal Caravan

    The banging on the solid wooden panelled door came earlier than it should have. It was still dark inside their dismal sleeping quarters. Diara; the fifteen year old petite princess from Eurkus, rubbed her sleepy eyes and turned up the wick of the oil lamp. The security guard unlocked the door to their room and entered. He was followed closely at his heels, by two female scullery slaves.

    The overweight kitchen attendants set the heavy meal trays down at the foot of the sleeping mats. Then they stood up breathing hard from the exertion and gathered the waste buckets, dirty towels and linen that were stacked and folded by the doorway.

    "You two it is ies. Time to get up and eat breakfast," shouted the young prison cell attendant.

    Diara looked over at her friend Elona. The seventeen year old Oppowian Princess was still asleep, or just did not want to open her eyes. "It can't be time to eat," said Diara? "What time is it?" The guard walked over to where they were laying.

    The junior officer had intensions of throwing her off of her sleeping matt. Diara read his mind; rolled to the side, and she was on her feet before he was able to take two strides. Kytos's sister was not as fortunate. The guard pivoted slightly and kicked Elona instead.

Elona woke up holding her ribs to see Diara adjusting her waist sash and their jailer about to kick her again. She jumped to her feet, standing eye to eye with five foot six sentry. She was tall for a cartolean woman and more muscular than most. Sweeping her long light brown hair behind her shoulders she stood arrogantly before him.

The jailer sneered at the Oppowian princess and was about to hit her with the back of his hand. Elona defied him and didn't back down. After being denigrated and treated as a captive prisoner aboard the pirate ship Culba for more than two mursas, she had become a lot more self sufficient and feisty.

"If you ever lay a hand or foot on me again, I will tell Princess Shayla that you called her a swollen and sweaty smelling redolga."

The guard's cheek twitched on one side of his face. It tensed than whitened a bit. Being skinned alive was not the way for an honor guardsman of the royal family to die. He cleared his throat nervously and tried to look unconcerned. "I am sorry for being over zealous and exceeding my authority, but Princess Shayla has decided that today is the day we are to leave for Renvas, Envar."

The centurion backed away from Elona and stood off to the side of the doorway. The scullery slaves carried in and set down a clean bucket of wash water and a stack of towels before leaving the room. "This is to be your last meal in Woreza. The wagons are already loaded." The captive princesses knew that the guard would not be leaving until everything had been eaten. This young officer was a lot more attentive and wasn't going to be as fooled as easily as the other older jailers had been. Elona sat cross-legged on her matt, and placed a folded towel over her lap.

Pulling the breakfast tray closer Elona began eating in earnest. Diara did everything in a likewise fashion and the guard was satisfied that this was going to be easier than he had been told. The warden had given him strict orders. The young officer was to see everything that was served was eaten. He had also been told that these two sorceresses were not to be provoked into making any more trouble than they had already. The women started asking all kinds of questions about the

City of Renvas, and the guard relaxed answering them as best he could.

What he did not know was, by alternating their questions, the ladies were not eating. He would look from one to the next answering their questions, giving each woman time to hide a small portion of their food. Half a zestar later they had given the appearance of having eaten the large meal and were complaining that they couldn't finish another bite.

"You will soon get used to that bloated feeling," he said. "You know that Worezian's eat six meals per day, unlike the backwards kingdoms that you come from. Gathering their bowls and trays, he stacked them and left the room. No sooner had the door closed behind him and the bolt was thrown, when they were on their feet. They raced to the window with their towels and emptied out the scraps of food into the moat below.

"I thought we were going to be here in Woreza six to eight more days?"

"I thought the same thing," said Diara. Picking up her hairbrush, she started removing the snarls from her light brown hair. "It sounds like Princess Shayla is starting to get anxious. She might also be afraid that her prince has change his mind and decided to break the wedding contract."

Elona laughed at that, but then became a little more serious. "I wonder if she will order us to go to back to her royal suite before we leave."

Diara finished parting her wavy hair in the center and set the brush down. Then she turned confidently back to Elona. Her delicate face had a smirking expression and she answered in a cocky sounding voice. "I doubt it, witch! After all, look what you did to her in her own bedchamber. Once that streak of blinding light froze the branding irons, I thought she was going to have a heart attack and die right on the spot. Then after her fat rolls stopped shaking, she wet herself. I don't think the Worezian princess will ever want to see us again and I am happy with that."

"But, that was not my fault," said Elona! "It was Jedaf's enchanted ring." Diara finished tying the laces to her bodice and put her hands up in the air, as if she could stop her girlfriend from talking. "I don't care how or why it happened; all I know is that they have not tried to brand us since that first day at the palace."

Elona's lower lip protruded slightly as she thought about Jedaf and Kytos. She knew that she had fallen in love with him aboard the privateer ship Culba. It no longer mattered that he was only a slave and personal attendant of the Yojan ambassador. The princess thoughts turned to her brother and how he had been punished because she had refused to pose for the wedding portraits. Her eyes were welling up and Diara knew Elona was about to start crying.

"Come on El you should be, just as thankful. Let's finish getting washed and get dressed before the security guard comes back. I have a feeling that we will be leaving shortly." She flipped open the lid to one of Elona's trunks, removing a brown, skirt and pair of long stockings. Then she placed them on Elona's matt and fetched a clean hand towel for her.

Elona dipped her hands into the washbasin and splashed some cold water on her face. "I guess you're right. Being locked up in this stagnant room for the past few days has turned me into an ungrateful wretch. It will be good to get out into the fresh air and sunshine again." Within a zestar four sweaty, strong backed eunuchs returned to carry the trunks from their quarters. Two Worezian royal guardsmen and a junior officer accompanied the slave bearers. These warriors provided the escort for the two captive princesses and made sure of their safety.

The pageantry and courtyard departure ceremonies were very brief. The wagons had been painted, decorated with fresh flowers, silken ribbons and bows, and had been preloaded the previous night. The royal army escorts were dressed in their finest uniforms, and their horses were saddled and waiting. Walking out of the palace servant's entrance at the east gate, the women were surprised to find out that the official ceremony had ended zestars ago.

Elona and Diara were led to the last wagon in the bridle train, and helped through the rear canvas flap. Inside there was just enough room for them to sit facing each other. Both sides of the wagon were lined with trunks, and the front was stacked within eighteen inches of the top canvas braces. The sides of the tarpaulin were tightly lashed from grommet rings to side cleats, and the guards had tied the rear flap to the point where little light was able to penetrate the thick canvas.

Elona climbed up over the trunks and looked out over the drivers' head. Princess Shayla was hugging and saying goodbye to an old woman and some other family members. All the gentry were dressed in their finest, trying to impress one another. The standards for each of the regal household coat of arms had been unfurled, while the royal musicians played and celebratory ballads were sung.

King Magarus stood by on a decorative raised platform overseeing everything. He was looking quiet pleased, and giving last zesta instructions to a young captain of the guard. Elona saw the rather short and corpulent king hand the officer a bright mint green leather dispatch pouch. The captain tucked the correspondence into the inner breast pocket of his leather tunic and gave the king a short bow. Mounting his horse, the officer saluted smartly and rode to the head of the column.

Princess Shayla was escorted to the first wagon amongst cheers and the waiving of silken handkerchiefs. A stepladder was provided for her with two strongmen holding the sides. She barely had the strength to ascend the steps, but managed and stepped below the lavishly decorated canvas of a custom built royal coach style wagon.

The princess's wagon was wider and longer than most vehicles of this type. The majority of it was richly painted in a high gloss dark green with mint green and gold piping trim work. The canvas was a golden yellow with a coat of arms on both sides. The Worezian, silver crossed battle axes with leather bound handles were embroidered in high relief.

Along side of the family's crests were the Envarian royal emblems of a silver sword over a six pointed silver crown on a mint green field.

The coach was pulled by six stout, shinning black horses dressed in green silks with, gold skirting and bright yellow leather harnesses.

Two of Shayla's personal attendants removed the steps and hung them across the back bracket, lashing them securely. The captain waived his arm in a circular manner and then pointed south. Each of the drivers gave their whip a crack, and the wagons lurched forward in unison. A loud cheer started and continued until they had exited the main city gate. Elona tried to climb back down from the stack of clothing trunks a little too quickly. She lost her grip and footing. Falling down almost head over heals, she partially landed on Diara.

"Owe," she groaned as she rubbed her banged arm and elbow.

"You're lucky you did not break your fool neck." Elona was flat on her back with her right foot caught up in one of the rear canvas ties. She tried to sit up and kick herself free, but her foot was tangled to high above the wagon bed.

"Did you see anything?" Diara helped lift her enough for her friend to get her ankle free, but they almost lost her shoe. She sat back down, pushed her heel in and retied the laces.

"Not much, the princess is in the lead wagon, and we have an armed santax escort. There are five other wagons between hers and ours. What have you been able to see out of the back?"

Diara shrugged. "Nothing, the flap is tied to tight." The two of them stood and with each of them pulling with all their strength and weight, they managed to stretch the fabric enough to have a three inch wide air gap that was two foot long. Taking turns in front of the opening they described to the other what was going on outside.

Woreza was like most of the mid-sized cities of Zarhun. Its narrow streets and lanes were crowded with the every day merchants, peddlers and people arguing prices. It smelled of outdoor cook fires, damp cobblestones and drainage sewers. Most of the buildings were less than three stories in height, and in need of a coat of paint. The escort had cleared the way and the bridal train only had to make one stop because of an overturned vegetable cart.

Through the rear flap they could see the void cleared by the wagons fill quickly with buyers and sellers. Everything returned to normal.

The only thing that Diara thought was strange about Woreza, was the fact that all the inhabitants were under the impression that the whole world envied them for having built the most beautiful and magnificent city on the planet.

Their wagon passed through the southern gate and they both stood peaking out of the crack together. The surrounding countryside looked as modest as the kingdoms capital. The dirt road was narrow, the tilled fields were small, and the farmhouses and barns needed repairs. Elona returned to her seat and two remained quiet for some time. Each of them, were lost in their own thoughts and memories.

With the noise and the hustle and bustle of the street gone, there was little to distract them. The only sound they could hear was the knocking of the trunks against the sides of the wagon and an occasional shout from their driver. "How long have we been riding Di?"

"I guess about two zestars," she answered back in a kind of a forlorn monotone voice. Diara stood arching her stiff spine and backside.

"What did that guardsman say when I asked how far it is to Renvas?" She turned around to see that Elona had fallen asleep from the stuffy atmosphere. "That is terrific. Now I am talking to myself." She sat back down, curled up and put her head on the end of a rolled up carpet.

The sunlight streaking in the back of the wagon woke the two of them. They shaded their eyes until they could see a little more clearly, and watched a young warrior untying the rear canvas flap. "Hora, first lunch, get out and stretch your legs," said their guard. A large fully bearded soldier, with his belly overhanging his weapons belt was watching the youngster handle and interact with the two female slave attendants.

When they did not jump out immediately, he ran right over. In his left hand he held a greasy leg to a pheasant, which he used as a pointer while he yelled at them. "Didn't you hear Nemak, get out of the wagon its lunch." Elona climbed down first. Her legs were stiff, and her back and arm hurt where she had fallen on them. She helped

Diara to the ground and they both stood for a moment looking around at the camp.

Most of the drivers and escorts were clustered around the cook fires, but they could not see the princess. The guards led them over toward the spits where they could see at least ten more birds roasting. They both could feel the ogling eyes and hear the heckling from the troop as they walked by. It made them both feel like they were to be the dessert.

The young warrior led them between two other wagons, to a shaded area where the princess's table had been set up beneath a colorfully stripped pastel awning. Shayla was already seated and the food had been set out in trays ready to begin serving the meal. They walked over to the table and bowed their heads to the princess. Elona took the right seat and Diara reached for the other, but she did not have a chance to sit. She didn't have the time to.

Shayla instantly swung out her heavy forearm quickly knocking Elona and the folding chair over backwards. Diara took her hand off the back of the other chair and stepped backward away from the table. The princess glared at her for a moment then turned her attention back toward Elona. The Oppowian princess lay flat on her back momentarily stunned.

Shayla started laughing along with her eunuchs and specially selected bodyguards. Craning her neck, Elona looked up at the Worezian princess. Her plump face was smeared with poultry grease and her cheeks were crammed so full of meat she could barely breathe let a lone laugh.

Shayla suddenly returned to glaring, and everyone stopped laughing as if on cue. The princess was trying to finish chewing so that she could speak. It seemed to take forever, but finally she swallowed hard with half the food chewed. She was furious; breathing heavily threw her nostrils and making a wheezing sound.

Elona thought that she sounded like a bellows with a hole in it. Rolling over she crawled up on her hands and knees. Princess Shayla looked over to her confidant, body servant and nodded. He stepped forward quickly and kicked Elona in the belly knocking the wind out of her. The young woman slumped to the ground and curled into a fetal position holding her abdomen.

Shayla took another bite, and chewed as she watched Elona gasp for air. "Slave if you ever sit at my table again, I'll have you whipped until your skin is raw to the bone." Elona crawled over on her hands and knees to where Diara was sitting. The ground was dry and hard without any moisture. The parched yellowed grass was coarse and fibrous. Shayla took two of the chicken like legs with thighs from her platter and tossed them over to the women.

Diara caught hers but Elona's landed full in the dirt. "That is your lunch, start eating!" Shayla watched them both for a zesta, and then returned to filling her face. One of the other servants handed Elona and Diara a four inch diameter baked oolet potato and a thick slice of bread that was saturated in butter. They both ate in silence watching the princess finish her second foul, four smaller baked potatoes and three glasses of deep red lusverus wine.

Something nudged Elona's leg and she looked over to see a thin legged and scruffy young slave boy with two wine cups in his dirty hands. She took them and said softly, "Thank you!" He smiled showing a chipped front tooth, and ran quickly back to the other wagon.

"I said eat that picrican," yelled Shayla! Elona looked over to where it lay in the dirt and reached over picking it up. The skin had reddish brown road dirt all over one side. Carefully Elona pealed the skin from it and tossed it on the grass. Then she half heatedly ate while keeping her head bowed and occasionally looking in Diara's direction.

Shayla took a sharp knife and cut a large fruit filled pastry into quarters. She kept two for herself, and then tossed the other two into Diara's lap. "Excuse me your majesty for interrupting the meal." A scrawny male servant dressed in a floral patterned tunic and dark brown kilt stepped forward. His arms were behind his back as he bowed his head and spoke. Elona looked at his gaunt face, high cheek bones and thin nose. If it was not for the sparse red moustache, she thought he would make a good characterization of a gass rodent.

"Mistress this slave can not have dessert; she has not finished her foul yet." Shayla looked up at her body servant. From behind his back, he produced a penknife with a dirty piece of the birds' skin on it.

"Thank you Hyeasan, for having an attentive eye!" She mumbled spraying cake crumbs as she spoke. Hyeasan walked over and dropped the greasy skin in Elona's lap.

Elona and Diara changed sides of the wagon before it got underway. Elona was not feeling very well and she wanted to sit closer to the opening in the canvas. The air felt good but within five zestas of the wagon swaying, she was vomiting out of the back flap. She couldn't seem to get the taste of the dirt and animal fat out of her mouth. The more she thought about it the more she gagged. The more she gagged the more she thought of ways to kill Hyeasan.

She would never forget his laughter while she chewed on that filthy skin. She was still having trouble closing her mouth fully. Something had become lodged in one of her molars, and she picked at it with her fingernail until it came free. It was a small reddish brown piece of a sandstone pebble. Upon seeing what it was, she vomited once more.

After lunch when they crawled into the wagon, Diara noticed that someone had hidden a small wineskin behind one of the trunks. She thought the driver had put it there in the hope, that no one would find it. Diara pulled it up and over the trunks and handed it to her. "Here rinse out your mouth before you make me sick too."

Elona uncorked it taking a small sip. It was warm but tasted good. As good as any that she had ever had. It probably came from Shayla's personal wine barrel. She swished another mouth full around and spat it out the rear flap. "Where did you get this?" Diara raised an eyebrow and took the leather bag taking a small sip herself.

"While everyone was watching you eat, I noticed that someone had taken one of Shayla's wineskins and hidden it in our wagon. Taste rather good doesn't it?" Elona took another small sip. It was not only good; it helped soothe her throat which was starting to burn and become sore from all the vomit.

"Don't drink too much of that, it might make you sicker or give you cramps. We should save it for a better time." Elona tapped home the stopper and tucked it between the trunks again. She knew that Diara was right, and she certainly did not want to throw up again.

Pulling back the flap once more, she began watching the road. It all looked the same, never changing. Closing her eyes, and trying to find a comfortable spot was impossible. There was nothing to cushion the bone jarring bumps of the wooden bottom or the sides of the wagon. She slouched to the side and started getting used to the cramped quarters and long boring quiet spells with nothing to do but sleep.

The wagon finally jostled to a halt. It was another time to use the bushes. It was their only break in the monotony. About every two zestars they would halt for a quick respite. "Are we going to ride all day or what," yelled out Elona. No one responded to her question. Diara looked over at her. Elona was a nervous as a caged cat. "Not that I am complaining" she said, "but aren't we going to stop for second lunch?"

Diara smiled at the way Elona pinched off one side of her nasal passage and mimicked Princess Shayla's voice. "That is just what you need. Get caught making fun of her, and she will make you eat dirt without the bird."

Elona grabbed her stomach and leaned forward with her mouth open and her tongue sticking out. "Ahhhh," she said in a long drawn out tone, and they both laughed.

"The cook slave said that we would be riding for at least six zestars before resting the horses. That is fine for horses Di, but how about us?" She just shrugged, and peaked out of the canvas. Nothing had changed behind them and there was nothing to see but dusty swirls on the road.

They had changed places once again at the last stop, so Diara could get some air for a change. "Do you want some more of that wine?"

"No." answered Elona. "I think that I will wait awhile. I do not want a full bladder either." She stood up and leaned over Diara's head, peaking through the crack along with her. There were no riders or rear guards near their wagon.

Kneeling down next to Diara, Elona whispered. "I saw you standing near the chuck wagon before we were loaded back into this wagon. Do you think that you could get as close to the dowry wagon as you did to the cook's wagon?"

"I don't know," Diara replied. "The only reason I made it that far was they were all watching you. Why?"

Elona's face tightened. "I want to get even with Shayla, and I think the best way of doing that is through her wealth."

Diara took a hold of Elona's shoulders and looked sternly into her eyes. "Don't be such a fool! If you're caught, you will die a horrible death." Elona stood up without saying another word and held onto the overhead canvas supports, before returning to her seat. She leaned back and folded her arms in a disgusted fashion. Then she tipped her head back, took a deep breath and let it out quickly threw her nose as if she were blowing off steam.

Something moved, just over her head at the top of wagon. Elona watched a little more closely. A large brown spider darted out from above the wooden canvas supports. It paused a moment then ducked under one of the braces. As she watched it, it reminded her of the sneaky Hyeasan. "I have got it," she said jumping to her feet.

"Give me the wine skin, hurry!" Diara didn't know what was going on, but quickly reached behind the trunk and tossed her the bag. Elona pulled the cork and took about three sips then handed it back to Diara. "Here take a few sips, hurry."

Diara did as she was asked and gave it back to Elona. "You are not thinking of poisoning her?"

Elona gave her back a smirking grin. "Of coarse not. Where would I get any poison?" Pulling the stopper, Elona positioned the spout straight up, and lifted the sack to the ceiling.

"What are you doing?"

Elona moved over a few more inches, still looking upward. "Just a zesta, I've almost got him." Diara tried to see what Elona was talking about, and stood up next to her. She was just in time to see the dark brown furry arachnid crawl into the spout.

Elona reached up slowly, and pushed the cork stopper in place. "There we are," she said softly. Then she carefully wedged the neck of the wineskin in an upright position between the trunks. "We wouldn't want the poor little spider to drown, would we?"

They both had a good laugh. "I would bet that she is not going to like your friend."

Elona stopped laughing and winked at Diara. "That is not all. Wait until she gets my real surprise."

Diara became suddenly serious, "What are you going to do?"

Elona leaned back and refolded her arms. "I am not going to tell you. If I get caught, I don't want you getting any of the punishment." The wagon slowed ending their discussion.

"It must be time to empty our bladders again," Diara said. Elona did not comment, she was contriving and planning but not talking.

Chapter # 10

Atus — The Royal Worezian Cook

The same young guard that had been on duty earlier in the day came over and untied the back canvas. He didn't have to say anything, Diara was up and out before he could open his mouth. Elona followed, noticing the tingling in her legs. The vibration and the cramped space had slightly cut off the circulation. They stretched, and moved away from the wagon, walking slowly. They both had guessed wrong. It was second lunch, not just another rest break.

The princess had decided that it was to hot for her to eat outside, so she stayed lounging in her wagon. The eating tables were not going to be set up. The cook slaves handed out dried meat and fruit, along with buttered bread, and large mugs of ale. Both women were allowed to roam freely, as long as they didn't leave the proximity of the camp.

When no one was paying any attention to her, Elona returned to their wagon. She carefully lifted the wineskin and returned it to the cook wagon. No sooner had she finished propping it up, when someone came up on her from behind. "I hope you do not make the princess any angrier. She takes it out on all of us." Elona jumped, startled white with fright. It was the ten year old slave boy that had given her the wine cups at the last meal.

"No I won't cause any more trouble, er a."

"Caysa; mistress." Elona wiped her clammy, nervous hands on the sides of her skirt. "Is there something that you were looking for?"

"Yes Caysa. I was looking for a water skin. Do you think we could have one put in our wagon? It gets awfully dusty in there."

"I will see to it myself mistress." He turned quickly and ran off.

"Phew," she said softly and hurried off to her own wagon. Caysa came over to the women's wagon a half zestar later. He had the water skin that he had promised and also a sack full of dried avna. The light orange colored, apricot like fruit was delicious, and they both thanked him for the added kindness. Most of the camp had remained packed. All they had to do was stand around and wait for the guards to tie up the back flaps for them to begin the next leg of their journey.

The zestars past agonizingly slow once they were back on the road again. There was little to see that they had not seen before. The farms became less frequent the further west they rode, and it was quite evident these houses needed more repairs. Occasionally one of the escort riders would ride up from behind and ride rear guard, but he wouldn't last there too long. The dry dust cloud was just too much for them.

"The cook fire attendant told me that sometime tomorrow night we will be reaching the old Worezian, and Envarian border. I wonder if we will have a reception party waiting for us. You know, with a changing of the guard and everything."

"You have to be joking Di, these two backward kingdoms have been warring for years, and Envar's Army is in revolt. If it was not for this marriage, the war would continue for god knows how long."

The wagon slowed down to a crawl again, and they both instinctually held on tight. The wagon jarred bouncing from side to side as it hit a furrow. Diara looked back out of the crack. The countryside had changed slowly to more rolling hills and trees, with an occasional wooded area. It was one of these glades that they were just starting to ride through. Trenches had been dug across the highway to slow down the army supply wagons.

As the wagons approached each of these trenches, the escorts would fan out searching the area thoroughly before allowing the wagons to cross. The captain could not afford an ambush on a member of the royal family. Most of these trenches had been filled and repaired by previous military convoys, but the rains had washed away a lot of the loose topsoil, leaving ruts six inches to a foot deep and three foot wide.

The women stood and looked out the rear canvas. The wagon turned slightly paralleling the road, avoiding several felled trees. It was the site of an old battlefield. The barn in the distance was nothing but a pile of charred timbers, and not much remained of the house. Two stone walls still stood, but the rest had collapsed along with the blackened roofing timbers. "You know Di. The more I look out, the more depressed I become."

Diara took her seat as they changed sides again. "I am beginning to think you're right. This is certainly going to be a long trip." The wagon hit another rut knocking Elona off her feet. "Damn, it is bad enough being cooped up in here, why can't they at least tie the back flap open?"

She got up on her knees and looked out again. "Is the rear guard still back there?"

Elona shook her head, no. "He has moved off out of sight again. All that is back there now is the road and the weeds." She sat back down and crossed her legs. She looked bored and disgusted as she rubbed her kneecaps.

"If you're looking for something to do, why not climb back up in front and see what is ahead?" Elona shrugged her shoulders and slowly stood. Placing her foot on the lower trunk handles, she carefully pulled herself over the top of the luggage. It was twice as hot up there, and the air was stifling.

"Be a little more careful this time." Elona waived her hand, and signalled Diara to be quiet. She crawled along on her hands and knees, until the wagon hit another large bump. Landing full on her face, she almost tumbled out through the front flap. It was lucky for her that the wagon driver and brakeman had jumped down right away.

They would have seen her hanging over the top trunks. Up ahead of them, Elona could see a group of several sentries talking amongst themselves but they were too far away for her to make out their words. There was no one standing within the immediate vicinity their wagon.

Elona called back to Diara. "I can't see anything from up here, anything out of the back?"

"No," responded Diara! "You better climb back here before someone sees you."

Elona inched her way backward until she felt her feet clear the last trunk. "Give me a hand will you?" Diara caught her friend's foot and guided her downward. The corner on the top trunk snagged Elona's long sleeve blouse under the arm, and as she slid down it ripped open making an eight inch long hole.

"Now look what you made me do!"

Diara looked at the tear. "Its not ripped that bad, just the seam. When we get started again, you could take it off and we will try to sew it with one of the wagon splinters."

Elona looked out the back canvas again, still nothing. "Maybe there is trouble up ahead? Do you think that the guards went to fight?"

Diara put her hand over Elona's mouth. "Quiet. Maybe with the guards gone we could untie some of the canvas straps and escape into the woods?"

Each went to opposite sides of the rear flap, and stuck their arms out. There were five knotted ties on each side, and after tugging and straining at the tight straps for half a zestar, they were only able to undo two of them. "It is too bad we couldn't get out. I do not like the idea of being, a slave very much."

"Neither do I El. How about over the top?"

Elona shook her head. "Na, the trunks are stacked almost clear to the top, and the opening in the front is only large enough to get your head and maybe one arm threw." They both sat down feeling dejected and waited, quietly.

Another half zestar went by without them hearing anything. The temperature had risen, from the lack of air movement and perspiration dripped from their faces. They took turns breathing out of the back, but it did little to cool them. Large circles of sweat started to show under their armpits. Elona felt like fainting. Standing at the flap she started yelling for help. The wagon jumped foreword and turned sharply to the left. It knocked Elona off of her feet again and she bumped her head. The wagon hit another clump of hard sod then came to a halt.

A round, rather beefy looking guard undid the ties this time. They jumped out quickly, to see the sentry Nemak sheepishly standing to one side. He was the young warrior that had been the occasional rear guard. "I told you that they would learn a little manner's if we left them in there for awhile!" The younger guard did not say anything, he just held the reins of both mounts, and kept his chin lowered. Elona looked at Diara, then about the rest of the camp.

Just about everything had been set up. The escort riders sat in the shade of the trees and a tent with scalloped canopy had been set up for the princess. "You mean that we are camping for the night and you left us in that sweltering heat?"

Diara put her arm around Elona and turned her away from the guard. "Be quiet for a change will you. We are out and can breathe some clean air."

The wagons were arranged in a semi-circle and the teams of horses were staked out in a wooded area on the other side of the circle. The warrior escort was camped on the other side of the horses, completing the circle. At least eight cook fires were going and the sentries had already been posted around the camp, and behind some of the wagons. The guard that had been walking with them, called out for Atus. A short pot bellied, balding man in his early forties, jumped down from the cook wagon next to them.

Turning his head slightly he spat between his missing front teeth, and looked them over. "So you're the skinny twigs that are going to fill the water barrels for me." He walked around the back of the supply wagon and climbed into it. Four black iron pots came flying out, landing in the dirt. Each container was capable of holding about a gallon of liquid.

"The stream is over there, about fifty paces from the tree line." They looked up to see him pointing at the hedgerow behind them. Then they looked at the row of eight wagons. There were two barrels on each, but luckily they were of the smaller twenty-gallon variety.

"You want us to fill all of those barrels?"

Atus looked over at Diara. "No. The barrels on the royal wagon are for wine, and the two on the cook wagon are for vegetable oil. Just fill the rest, and get started. This is the last good drinking water, for the next three days. It will be getting dark soon and you do not want to be out there." They both picked up their pails and headed for the hedgerow. Looking at each other, they read the other's mind and smiled.

"Do you think that we should go right on walking?"

"I was thinking the same thing myself." Elona parted the bush and started to step threw the dense foliage.

"You two!" It was Atus that was yelling over to them. They stopped and looked back. "Don't dawdle around the stream too long, there are banta in the area, and they like to rip men up just for spite." A loud deep throated growl filled the glade causing them to look around quickly.

"I think we should fill the barrels as fast as we can," said Diara. "I don't want to be something's dinner." They ran off in the direction of the stream and found it shortly. It was clear, cold, had a good swift current and low banks. They filled their pots and hurried back to the safety of the camp. The barrels had been filled in Woreza, and it was fortunate most still had over half of their water.

Two zestars later, they had made over twenty trips, both were exhausted and having blistered hands. They were covered in mud to their knees, and their sandals were soaked and caked with river silt. "You two, that will be enough water." It was Atus's voice. They stood panting a moment, listening to him as he dumped a kettle of boiling water into a wash bucket. "You can go over to where the royal table has been set up. Rest and get yourself something to eat."

Instead they walked over and seated themselves next to the cook wagon. Both were too tired to eat. They just wanted to sit on the ground and lean against the wheel. "I don't think I could have made another trip." Elona did not answer her. She picked the dead skin from her broken blisters, and nodded in agreement.

"You two had better start eating!" They looked up to see it was Shayla's man servant yelling at them. Helping each other up, they walked over next to the princess's personal attendant. He was standing there with two wooden bowls of stew in his hands. "Shall I sprinkle a little bit of dirt on yours?" Hyeasan smiled broadly and handed each of them a bowl.

"No, that will not be necessary," she replied. Elona took the bowl and walked over, and sat in the dirt next to Diara.

Hyeasan walked off toward the other wagons and they began to eat. They ate half-heartedly, until Diara looked up to see Hyeasan standing at Shayla's side with a wine sack in his hands. She gave Elona a nudge with her elbow as he pulled the stopper out. At first Elona did not know what was happening. She had completely forgotten about the spider.

The large furry creature jumped out onto the rim of the drinking glass and onto Shayla's forearm. Screaming she jumped from her chair knocking over the table. Servant and soldiers came running from all over as she screamed. The campsite was total pandemonium and panic.

Elona suddenly set her bowl down and crawled under the wagon, coming out on the other side. The time had come, for her to get even. She ran over to the cook fire, selecting a two inch diameter firebrand that was glowing brightly. Grabbing the end, she pulled it from the blaze and wrapped the glowing end in a hand towel.

It was still hot and smoldering as she walked slowly toward the dowry wagon. The security guard was preoccupied trying to keep everyone from getting too close to the wagon, and he didn't see Elona slip up from behind on the woodland side.

She untied the strap at the corner of the rear canvas flap, leaned inside quickly, and tucked the firebrand between a stack of embroidered carpets. Then she quickly retied the knot and ran back where Diara was still sitting.

"Where have you been? I thought that you might have got trampled in the crowd."

Elona wiped the charcoal from her hands on the grass. "I had to run a little errand." The servants were cleaning up the area, but Elona could not see Shayla. "Where's the princess?"

"She fainted and had to be carried to her wagon," replied Diara.

Caysa ran over to them. In his hands were a piece of roasted measan on a stick and a half loaf of bread. "Ladies this is all that I could save of the meal. If you have not eaten, you could take it back to the wagon with you."

Elona gave him a pat on the back. "Thank you, but we really don't feel like eating right now. We will eat it a little later." She took the meat and bread, rolled them in a towel and set it next to her. "I can not see Hyeasan. Where did he go?"

The slave boy looked around to see if anyone was watching. "I do not know where he is now, but I saw a guard drag him off awhile ago. I heard that he tried to kill the princess."

Diara looked at Elona. "Is that so," she said in a sarcastic voice.

Elona smiled. "I guess you can't trust anyone these days." Diara turned her face away to keep from laughing. "Come on Di. Let's go back to our wagon." The three turned and strolled off at a leisurely pace, until they heard someone shout at them.

"Where are you two going?" It was Atus. Caysa ducked under the nearest wagon slipping out of his sight. The cook stepped in front of them blocking the way. "We were told to go to our wagon, and finish eating"

The cook grabbed the women's arms and led them off. "You're not getting out of work that easy. Who do you think is going to clean up all this mess?" They scoured all the cook pots, carried firewood to each of the campfires, and returned all the utensils to the cook wagon. They were about to slip into the darkness with their wrapped dinner, but Atus caught sight of them again. Wiping the sweat from his neck he said, "Before you leave, I have only one more thing for you to do."

Before the cook could say another word someone yelled, "Fire!" Three warriors ran by them with drawn swords. Diara and Elona looked in the direction the perimeter guards were running. She could see a reddish glow with hot fly ash coming from over the top of one of the other wagons. Everyone ran over to see what was happening.

Six guards were pulling on the wagon tongue, and several were pushing at the rear wheels. Slowly the wagon turned and started to roll. It gained momentum, and was soon clear of the semi-circle.

Bucket after bucket of water was tossed at the fire, but there was no controlling it. It was only a matter of a few zestas, and it was totally engulfed in flame. "My dowry," shouted Princess Shayla! She came up from behind, and the crowd parted. "Save my dowry!" A muscular first officer, in a hand embroidered silken shirt and embossed leather tunic, walked over and saluted.

"Princess, I am afraid there is nothing that I can do to save it."

She glared at him. "This is your fault. I hold you personally responsible!"

The officer knew his life would be forfeited for this accident, but he showed no fear. "There has been a guard on this wagon since we left Woreza. The only way it could have caught fire was by flying embers. Some must have landed on the canvas top. It was an act of fate destined by the gods."

She waived for the guards to take him. "Is that what you call it? Tomorrow when your head falls from the chopping block, I will send word to your family notifying them, how the gods, had your head removed. Take him and the security guard for the dowry wagon. Chain them with that other traitor, Hyeasan. Tomorrow morning at sunrise, see to it that their heads are removed and posted on pikes"

"Have the pikes driven into the roadside ahead of us. Let it stand as a warning, that I will not tolerate any more accidents." Looking at the burning wagon one more time, she stamped her heel deeply into the dust. Then she turned and stormed off toward her wagon. The entire group was watching the princess's tantrum, giving Elona and Diara time to slip off into the darkness.

They decided not to go back to their wagon. Atus was sure to go there first, and the women had no intention of letting the cook find them for the rest of the night. Instead they would sleep hidden in the tall weeds, under one of the supply wagons with the urchin slave boy.

Chapter # 11

The House of Traga

    A zestar after disembarking from the Sydolla in Joroca's harbor, Kytos and Trestan were opening the rear garden gate to the house of Traga, the commander of Lord Jedaf's Army. Rapping on the door several times with his wooden hand sent strange tingling sensations down Kytos's arm. He rubbed at it while they waited.

    Trestan had decided that it would be best, not to just walk into his family's house. He stood behind Kytos with his head lowered and the hood of his travel cloak pulled up. After being gone for more than five years, he thought that if his mother was the first one to see him, she would think he was a spirit and faint.

    A plump, dark haired woman of middle age opened the door. "What do you want," she asked in a peevish tone of voice? "I am not feeding anymore strangers today! Just because you buy my husband a few ales, you think I'm supposed to fill your belly when you are sober."

    Kytos blurted out, "I am looking for Commander Traga, or Captain Agar. Can you tell me they're whereabouts?" She wiped the soapy dishwater from her hands on a small hand towel and looked them over rather skeptically.

    "One moment sir," she said in an indignant tone. Then she lingered for zesta, while giving them a second look before shutting the door and walking off in a huff. Ky could hear the bolt being thrown, as she called out to husband Traga. Myra walked into the living area. "There are two young men out there looking for you or Agar." The old commander kicked the stool away from his feet climbing from his over stuffed chair.

"Well woman, what do they want?" Dropping the last bite of his hot buttered cake into his mouth he mumbled, "Do they want to join the army?" He brushed the crumbs from his lips and straightened his uniform.

"I don't think so," said his wife. "Neither of them looks like they can wield a sword."

Traga went to the fire mantle, picked up his weapon and strapped it on. "Show him in, I will see them anyway." Myra returned to the living area with Kytos and Trestan to find her husband standing to the side of the doorway with his blade drawn. She moved to the opposite side, two steps at a time until she reached the kitchen door, then went quickly through it. "State you name and your business," said Traga.

Ky was a little surprised at the greeting, but did not object. Extending his clenched left fist toward the commander he said, "I am Prince Kytos of Oppow, friend of Jedaf of Dolfi, Lord of the Dragon Host."

Traga was completely taken aback. He stood eyeing the steel dragon head ring on the boys' index finger. It was a smaller duplicate to one that was on his ring finger. Not knowing what to say, he stood momentarily frozen. Ky turned to the side a little letting the man behind him step forward. "And this gentleman, I think you know already."

Trestan pulled his hood back and stepped in front of his father. He had tears in his eyes and could not speak. Reaching out he put his arms around the older man and placed his head on Traga's shoulder. The old warrior could not speak either. He held his son tightly, and closed his own eyes and swallowed hard. Ky could see him mouthing a few silent prayers, but he could not contain the tears any more.

"Would you both like an ale?" Traga turned about to see his wife with a mug in each hand. She dropped them both at seeing her son. Her eyes widened and her trembling hands covered her mouth. Trestan walked over to her quickly and put his arms around her. She looked like she was about to swoon. Traga walked over and put his arms around both of them and they all cried. Kytos stood by watching and wishing he too would some day be welcomed the same way back in his own home.

After a few quiet zestas they let each other go and Traga and Myra stood to the side looking at their son. They had no idea what had happen him since he had been captured by the Azzonian raiders. Trestan was now taller and thinner, but more muscular having lost his boyish face. Other than having a scar on his cheek he appeared to be in good heath and was dressed in well made clothing and boots.

The commander knew in his heart that Lord Jedaf had something to do it, but did not ask. They had their son back and that is all that mattered. Trestan said to his mother, "Can we sit down now?" He pointed to the table then to Kytos. Traga walked over to the other young man and extended his right arm in formal greeting. Kytos grasped it with his left hand and held it tightly. That is when Traga noticed the boy's wooden right hand.

Myra, leave the mugs on the floor and fetch a couple of pitchers. It is a bit early, but I think, we all can use a few drinks about now. Traga pulled a chair out away from the table, motioning Ky to take a seat. Then he took the one next to it. Trestan took one on the opposite side of the table.

"I take it from the description my Lord Jedaf gave me, that you must be Traga."

The Commander rubbed a hand over his leathery face. "Yes, I'm sorry for the greeting, I can't trust to many people these days. You see things have been pretty hectic around here lately. I am Commander Traga, and this is my wife Myra." She nodded and brought over a tray with two large pitchers and four pewter mugs. "Best woman the gods have breathed life into." He put his arm around her waist as she set the tray down in front of them. Then she stood at Traga's side.

"How is our Lord Jedaf, Master Kytos?"

Ky took a sip, licking the foam from his upper lip, and looking up at her. "He has had some difficulties since he left you, but it's nothing to worry about. He is in good health and is continuing his journey eastward. He gave me a letter pouch to deliver to you, and said it was to go into your hands or the hands of Agar only." Reaching into his tunic, he pulled the pouch out through the neck hole. It hung from around his neck by a thin leather thong.

Bracing it against his chest with his wooden hand, he untied it, and pulled the letters out. Traga took them, examining the outsides of each, opening only the envelope with his name printed on the outside. It was a long letter and Traga was a slow, farsighted reader.

It gave Ky and Tres time to finish their ale and to look around a bit. The home was clean and spacious, with simple furnishings. To Trestan nothing had changed. More than half of the furniture had been handed down for at least two generations. This was exactly the way he remembered it in his dreams.

The Commander mumbled and cursed under his breath as he squinted and read the letter at arms length. Ky knew the warrior, wanted to strike something. His hand kept flexing into a fist. Then he pursed and bit at his lower lip, while he read.

"Sarasa," Myra called out. "Will you fetch a tray of cheese, fruit and biscuits?" Five or six zestas later a slim young woman with long, soft, curly brown hair came into the room. She was very pretty. Her pleated bright yellow and green floral dress with scalloped white lace collar and braided sash moved as if she were being carried by a breeze. Setting the tray down, she timidly stepped to Kytos's side.

Neither spoke, they just watched each other's eyes. She did not even look at her cousin more than a fleeting glance. It had been a long time since they had seen each other and she did not recognize him. "Thank you," said Myra as Sarasa broke eye contact. Blushing she backed away toward the kitchen, attempting to leave the room.

"Master Kytos. I would like you to meet my niece Sarasa. Sarasa, this is Prince Kytos of Oppow. He is a friend of our Lord Jedaf."

She returned to the table quickly, having a thousand questions. "You know my Lord? How is he? Will he be returning here soon? Does he need anything?" Her eyes sparkled, and widened while she spoke. It made her all the prettier. She leaned on the table moving closer to Ky. "Do I have time to put on my new dress, before he arrives?"

Myra reached over and patted the back of her niece's hand. "Is this how you welcome a guest? You interrogate and treat him like a criminal! You should be ashamed of yourself. You also have not given your cousin a hug after not seeing him in years."

Sarasa looked at the young man seated opposite Kytos. He was a total stranger to her. Trestan stood and walked over to her, took her hand and kissed her on the cheek. She did likewise, but felt totally embarrassed and uncomfortable.

Sarasa's face had a deep blushing glow. Lowering her chin she said, "I am sorry" in a soft muted voice. "It's just that we have been so worried about him. It made me lose all my manors." Kytos stood up and walked over to them. "It's all right Sarasa; I can understand your feelings. Lord Jedaf is fine and in good spirits, but I'm afraid he won't be returning here for quite some time." She gave him a little pouted smile, and he took her hand giving it a comforting squeeze.

"Myra," said Traga; "Master Kytos will be spending the next few nights with us. Put him up in the quest room. Tres your old room is as you left it." His son smiled, with an inner knowing that his mother would never have cleared the room of his belonging. "I have to ride to the camp this morning. Start packing my campaign gear. I will be returning late tonight." Carefully folding the other letters, he tucked them into his belt, and strapped his sword back on.

The woman of the house looked concerned but did not say anything at the moment. "Fetch me a travel cloak." Myra ran to the pegboard near the fireplace and selected the warmest, and ran back to him. He could see the wrinkled brows and worried look on her face.

"My husband, is it war again?"

Traga handed the letter he had been reading to Kytos, along with one with his name on it. "Burn it when you are through." Traga pulled Myra to him, holding her tightly in his arms for a moment. "I can't say. Lord Jedaf has asked us to get the men ready to sail for North Point Envar. How can I know what it will lead to?"

She kissed him quickly and stepped back. "Don't worry, I'll be back soon," he whispered. Tying the cloak about himself he reached into his belt pouch taking out a coin. It was an arus ixsagar, a gold and diamond coin of the highest valve. He placed it on the table in front of Ky, and hurried for the door.

The young prince looked up from the letter only long enough to see the coin, before he continued reading. Tears formed at the corners of his eyes as he read but he didn't make a sound. Myra, Sarasa, and Trestan sat down at the table across from him. They remained quiet while waiting for him to finish reading.

"My lord writes that soon my sister will be taken from the City of Woreza as a concubine slave. The wedding caravan will be heading south for Renvas, Envar. He has ordered your husband to use all the men and resources available to intercept them before they reach the safety of Envar's capital.

He has instructed me to procure a couple of large fast ships capable of carrying at least two thousand men each. We have approximately ten days in which we must reach the coast or it will be too late." Kytos let the letter slip from his hand, as he finished the last sip of his ale. He felt suddenly very drained and tired.

Myra stooped down, picked up the letter and tossed it into the fire as her husband had asked. Then she left them sitting quietly at the table returning to the room with another pitcher of ale. It was an awkward and uncomfortable moment for everyone. Bending low near Trestan she whispered in her sons' ear. He nodded then followed her back to the kitchen leaving Sarasa and Kytos alone.

"Ky?" Hearing her faint timid voice, he looked up to see Sarasa pouring him another ale. "Does Lord Jedaf love your sister so much that he is willing to start a war over her?"

"I don't know," he replied. We rarely speak of Elona. She thinks he is a slave and she doesn't speak to slaves." Kytos picked up the other letter that Traga had place on the table in front of him. It was sealed like all the others, and having no writing on it except for his name.

Breaking the wax hallmark stamp he opened the thrice folded paper. It was a bill of sale for a damaged young male slave having one hand. Total cost one bronze, plus a two steels tax, and an official inked logo of the Worezian crossed battle axe flag at the bottom. He folded it back up not saying anything about in and tucked it into his belt.

They sat for a long time talking about some of their resent experiences. Kytos told his tale of how he had met Lord Jedaf, aboard the pirate ship Culba, and how they had become friends. Some of the words were hard to find and the memories were painful. He had been unconsciously tapping his wooden hand on the table as he spoke. Sarasa could see he was not holding his ale very well.

His words now slurring, she moved on the other side of the table closer to him. Placing her arm around him she put her head on his shoulder. She held him tightly and let him pour out his soul. It was not yet first lunch; but he was totally drained of emotion and mentally exhausted. The ale made his head swim and he closed his eyes. Placing his head against Sarasa's he fell asleep in her arms at the table.

Commander Traga's sister and her daughter had been living at his home since the resent death of her husband. She returned from the market with her basket heavily laden with fresh vegetables. Setting it to the side of the door, she untied her cloak, and hung it on the wall hook. The living room was partially visible from the front entrance. From it she could see Sarasa sitting at the table, her arm around a young man with his head resting on her shoulder.

Erthea stepped out into the open doorway, giving her daughter an angry stare. She was very upset and about to tell Sarasa, just what she thought. A frightened look came over the young girl's face. The dreadful sight was enough for the older woman to change her mind. Instead of complaining, she returned to the entryway and fetched her basket.

"I thought that it was you coming in!" Myra stepped out of the kitchen. "That basket looks awfully heavy!" Running over, she grabbed a hold of the side handle and let her sister-in-law shift the weight getting the other handle. Together they carried it to the pantry.

"I suppose you saw Sarasa," said Myra. "I can tell by the flushed look on your cheeks." They set the basket down on the counter in the storeroom.

"How could you leave my daughter alone in the dining room with a man?" She started to sort the vegetables, brushing the soil from them and stacking the tubers on the shelves. "I could hardly believe my eyes, under your own roof? What kind of a mother would do such a thing?"

Myra reached into the basket taking out a head of sebus. "Sh, you'll wake him, and embarrass her all the more." She picked a bug from the dark green leafy vegetable, dropped it on the floor and stepped on it. Then she turned it upside down shook it and quickly looked to see it there were any other insects hiding in the leaves before handing it to Erthea.

"I left her alone with him, because he seems like a nice boy, and he is a friend of Lord Jedaf's. He's a prince from one of the northern kingdoms, and he is about the right age for her." Erthea didn't comment. She tipped the grocery basket over tapping the loose dirt from it into a pan that had been laid out on the counter for the vegetable peals and garden mulch.

"It will do her good to have a young man to talk to for a change. She never leaves the house or yard. You should have seen the way he watched her. I thought he was going to ask for her hand, right then and there." Erthea took up a corn broom, sweeping in a frustrated fashion as she listened. "His name is Kytos. He brought Traga a letter. In it, the letter mentioned the boy's sister being abducted and sent off as part of a marriage agreement."

"After reading it, he needed a soft shoulder. It was a good thing Sarasa was around. She has been holding him for over a zestar now. He has not moved. You should be happy she is with the kind of a man that will treat her well." The dust from Erthea's sweeping was starting to settle, as was her anger.

"But Myra she is too young!"

Myra reached over taking the broom away from her hands. "Too young, she's seen her fifteenth summer! How old were you when you married Hagnar?"

Erthea selected an arm full of assorted vegetables for the evening meal while listening to her. "That was different," said Myra with a quivering tone to her voice. "My mother and father were killed in the border war, and my younger brother, Traga was off fighting somewhere else." Tears formed in her eyes, as she thought of Hagnar, and their two dead sons.

"I'm sorry Erthea, but it's not much different today." She put her arms around her sister in law, and led her back to the kitchen. "I think he likes Sarasa, and I am sure she likes him."

Erthea wiped the tears away. Setting the vegetables in a wash basin she turned back to her sister in law and composed herself before speaking again. Myra stirred a flat pan on the hearth grate, and then released some of the steam from the kettle of vegetable chunks she was preparing. "He is awful young himself." Myra could see that her sister-in-law was weakening and becoming more tranquil as they spoke.

"Not so young. He's already been to war and has been injured during a battle! I could tell that after seeing he has a wooden right hand."

The sound of voices in the other room, made them lower their own. "He is awake now," Myra whispered. "Go in there and introduce yourself." Erthea straightened her dress and wiped the vegetable dirt from her hands. She knew that Myra was right. Opening the door to the dining room, she could see a timid and yet nervous look on her daughter's face. They both were a bit startled at first and stood as she entered the room.

Dropping their arms to their sides they both looked uncomfortable at being found in the compromising situation that she had seen. Smiling at them, Erthea nonchalantly walked over and gave Sarasa a hug. "You must be Prince Kytos," she said turning toward the young man. "I am Erthea, Sarasa's mother and Commander Traga's sister. I understand that you are a friend of our good Lord Jedaf." Pulling out the chair next to her daughter she motioned for them to sit back down.

Sarasa could not speak; her mother had totally surprised her. "I'm sorry I did not have the opportunity of greeting you earlier; I've been out to the public market." Kytos gave her a short bow then re-seated himself.

"I'm also glad to meet you; your daughter has been a perfect hostess during your absence." Myra was right again. After a long relaxing chat she knew that Kytos was a very special person. He was well spoken, and had a sincere light hearted laugh. Erthea also noticed the way he looked most of the time at Sarasa, even when speaking to her.

Kytos talked of Lord Jedaf, his own family, and everything that had happened to him since sailing from his Kingdom of Oppow. Erthea started to recount how Sarasa and she had met Lord Jedaf, but her daughter started biting at her finger nails. "Mother," she said softly. "Master Kytos doesn't really want to hear all that."

The young woman stood and pushed her chair back into place. "It's almost first lunch. May I fix something?" Ky patted his stomach with his wooden hand, "Not only beautiful, but a mind reader." Erthea laughed, but Sarasa did not think it was all that funny and blushed at being called beautiful.

The kitchen door banged open and out stepped Myra. Her sixth sense was also in top form. She juggled two trays and a slender pitcher of ale. Sarasa ran to her taking the meat, vegetable and biscuit tray. Then she went back to the kitchen fetching the glass steins. The four sat and ate a light lunch together.

It was the best food that Kytos had eaten since leaving Oppow. The venison was sliced as thin as butterfly wings, and had been sautéed in lusarus, a sweet bright yellow wine. The fresh steamed vegetables seem to melt in his mouth. He had two helpings before realizing it.

"Master Kytos, would you like some more?" He leaned back taking a deep breath.

"Myra if I take another bite, I'll split open." Her laughter reminded him of his own mother's. "I hate to leave such lovely company, but I have got some business down at the harbor. Do you think that Trestan would like to accompany me, and show me the most direct way?"

Erthea immediately looked to her sister-in law. A surprised but questioning look crossed her face. "Yes he's safe and at home. I will tell you about him later," Myra said. "I will get him up. He is lying down in his room upstairs but said that he did not feel like eating anything this afternoon."

"Your not leaving so soon, are you?" Sarasa's voice wavered a little. Erthea reached over taking her daughters hand, giving it a gentle squeeze.

"What my daughter means is your not leaving before we can show you some of the hospitalities of Joroca. You should see the ancient castle and some of the city statues, and the markets. Also you could not leave before seeing the garden of the Goddess Locises. It is the most beautiful sight in the city."

Traga's wife stood up, stacking the dishes. "Being a stranger though, you will never be able to find your way around. Myra let Trestan sleep. Sarasa, go upstairs and fetch your cloak. It will be chilly by the harbor."

"Mother," she said tugging the side of Erthea's dress. "I have the dishes to wash and the."

"Forget it daughter." She held up her hand, interrupting. "We can not let a guest and friend of our lord getting lost in our city. Now get your cloak."

Myra picked up the trays. "You heard your mother, now hurry. Master Kytos does not have all day to wait for you." She didn't have to be told again. She took the steps two at a time up to her room, and ran all the way back. Kytos took the cloak from her arm and held it out for her.

Sarasa looked for her mother and aunt, but they had returned to the kitchen. Kytos swung it around her shoulders and she tied the drawstrings in a bow below her chin. "There. I always did like orange." She looked down, straightening the sides, not knowing what to say. "Shall we go?" He held out his arm, and she took it. They walked off at a leisurely pace, being watched from the window by her mother and aunt.

Chapter # 12

The Red Army of the Dragon Lord

Traga rode into the encampment about the fourteenth zestar. It had been a long hard ride. His mount was covered with sweat and breathing heavily. An aide ran over grabbing the reins and holding the horse steady as he dismounted. "Have him rubbed down and cleaned up, he deserves it." The third class saluted, and led away Bastec, the commander's high spirited fast black stallion which he named Lightening.

Traga hurried toward the central dispatch command post. The officer's tent and adjoining lean-to structure was a patchwork of differing shades of yellow, green, brown and tan ragged canvases that gave it a kind of camouflaged look. The ten by twelve foot rectangular tents were hardly noticeable in the foliage of the shrubs and trees. It took an even keener eye to pick out the smaller irregularly shaped supply and cook tents.

His oldest son Captain Agar had instructed his men well in covert operations. Looking around the main compound, Traga could only make out thirty five to forty men as they went about their duties. He was sure that if an alert were to be called, hardly any of his men would be seen amongst the foliage. Satisfied with its appearance, he pulled back the tent flap and entered. Everyone inside immediately stood to attention saluting him. "Captain Drayus. Give orders to assemble the men. We're breaking camp. Have all officers' report here immediately."

Drayus set the morning log aside, capping the inkwell. "Yes sir." He along with two other junior officers and four senior enlisted men darted from the tent to give the orders. Traga pulled out the folding chair from beneath the portable campaign desk and sat down heavily. Pouring himself a goblet of deep bluish lusemtus wine, he read the reports stacked at the corner, and the half-finished morning's log.

The officers started to file in. They stood to the side of the command tent remaining quiet, until all in the immediate vicinity arrived. Traga folded the reports and tucked them into the companies travel valise. "Drayus, are all of the officers present?"

Captain Drayus looked about counting faces. "No sir. Captain Agar and his subordinate, First Officer Bygin are not in the camp. They've taken fifty warriors with them to Joroca. They escorted the Azzon prisoners to the slave market this morning and were to purchase some supplies before returning. All the others are present."

Traga set his goblet down and waited for the officer to finish speaking. "Good. Have Agar's, and Bygin's aides pack their belongings, and load them on the carts." Standing, Traga folded his arms behind his back, and looked at the men in front of him as he chose his words.

"I know some of the men are wounded and still healing from our engagement with the Azzonian Army, but we have been given our marching orders. Get back to your units and have them pack up. We will be breaking camp as soon as possible, and marching to a staging area on the parade ground at the outskirts of Joroca."

The officers saluted in unison and started to file out of the command tent. All accept for one junior officer. "Wait a zesta," he said while muscling his way to the front of the senior officers. It was Second officer Theisiah, the prince and youngest son of their Yojan King.

Having been notified of the defeat of the resent Azzonian Kingdoms raiding party; King Vestrak had sent instructions to Commander Traga. The king's son was to be allowed to enroll at a senior officers' rank and that his enlistment would be back dated to a time before the battle engagement.

King Vestrak had already awarded his son an acotaxarus gold metal for valiant actions during the battle against the Azzonian's, and a purple ribbon for meritorious service in defense of the Yojan Kingdom. It would be his son's duty to keep King Vestrak informed concerning all orders, decisions and troop deployments. As long as the Dragon Army of Semedia remained on Yojan territory and were loyal to King Vestrak, they could remain posted at the frontier.

Another obligation of the Dragon Army was to fly the King of Yoja's royal banner along side that of Lord Jedaf's. Commander Traga enlisted Theisiah as a second officer, the lowest rank in the officer's core. He knew this would cause problems, but he told Theisiah that he would not be given a higher rank until he earned it no matter what requests his father made.

"Where are we going after reaching Joroca?"

The other officers stopped to listen after hearing the question. "I can't tell you that, as of yet. But I will let you all know soon." Traga ignored Theisiah. Instead he addressed the question to the group as a whole. "There will also be no leave once we reach the city. We will be departing as soon as we are re-supplied. That will be all."

Prince Theisiah stepped in front of the group. "I said wait a zesta, you still haven't answered my question. I have to inform the king, commander. It is my duty to let him know where we're going." Traga turned his back and returned to the campaign desk. He sat back down, picking up his pen, ignoring the young officer.

"Have it your way commander. If you won't tell me, I will have to ride to the palace. Maybe by the time the army reaches the city there will be another in command that will answer my questions." The crusty, hardened officer turned his head toward him, standing with his facial muscles tight and waves of anger crossing over it.

"Captain Drayus." The captain stepped forward snapping to attention. "Yes sir!

Recite the oath of loyalty," said Traga, through his clenched teeth. "I think Second Officer Theisiah has forgotten it."

The captain stood taller and straighter. "I Drayus son of Sebo, son of Athenax, dwellers in the land of Yoja, Village of Duera, do here pledge my sword, my life, my family, and the fortunes of my family to Jedaf of Dolfi, Lord of the Red Dragon Host of the Semedian Kingdom. I will serve no other master during the five years of my enlistment in the Red Army of the Dragon. I will obey every order, of my superiors without question. I will come to the aide of, and will fight to the death, any or all that scorn or shame any of my fellow warriors."

Traga smiled cynically, walking out from behind the desk. "Now tell Second Officer Theisiah, what will happen to him if he disobeys my orders and rides away from this camp."

Captain Drayus looked over at the arrogant overly well dressed junior officer. "Sir, the punishment for desertion at the time, a battle ready, march order has been given, is forfeiture of all pay and booty accrued during the time of enlistment, and trial by Yara Zo!"

Traga stepped closer to the king's youngest son, and stood eye to eye with him. The prince had been standing at ease with a grinning childish smirk on his face and giving Captain Drayus a sneering and disgusted look, while he recited the oath. "Second Officer, do you know what trail by Yara Zo is?"

Prince Theisiah tipped his head cockily from one side to the other. "No commander. Why don't you have this illustrious peasant officer inform me?" At the snide comment, Drayus's hand immediately went to his weapons belt. Traga gave him a sharp glare. The captain fingers loosened on the knife's grip. It slid silently back into its scabbard, as he resumed his stance at attention. Traga nodded for him to answer the question.

"Sir, Yara Zo is the tribal rite of the ancients. When a warrior disgraces the tribe, every member is obligated to draw blood from him. The oldest account is a tale about a warrior named Derocan of Cathon. He was banished from the tribe after receiving over one hundred knife cuts." Traga could see Theisiah's face out of the corner of his eye. The young man at his side, swallowed hard and he shut his mouth.

"Thank you captain, hence forth Second Officer Theisiah will report directly to you and only to you. The rest of you, you have your orders. We march in a zestar."

The officers filed out of the tent quickly as Traga re-seated himself behind the desk. Picking up the quill again he dipped it in the ink and wrote an order for Captain Agar and First Officer Bygin. Bygin was to stay in Joroca with the men, and Agar was to take the money from the sale of the Azzonian warrior slaves and buy supplies for the army that would last for a month's duration. Bygin would march his warriors to the eastern outskirts of the city and set up a camp in the royal parade and fairgrounds. It was to be large enough for Jedaf's entire army.

Folding the written order and applying hot wax, Traga yelled out to the guard as he pressed in his signet ring sealing the envelope. "Fetch the company courier, and be quick about it." The soldier saluted and ran off. It was then that the commander noticed the small stand near the corner of the tent. It still had a tray of half eaten food and fruit on it. Pouring another goblet of wine, and fetching the tray, he settled far back in his chair and put his feet up on the desk. He had not eaten since first light.

The cheese was hard, and discolored. It had been sitting for a long time. Pulling off a couple of hunks, he folded them between two stale pieces of bread, and took a big bit. Most of the bread crumbled and he had to use both hands to keep it from falling apart. It tasted terrible and was dryer than expected. Taking a sip of wine softened it enough for him to swallow. It brought back a few unpleasant memories and the knowledge that it tasted better then what he had eaten on other campaigns.

A thin spindly-legged man having short, dark curly brown hair ran into the tent. "Sir, I'm Ledric, the tantax courier."

Traga swallowed and took a sip of wine to wash it down. "Do you know where to find Captain Agar?"

"Yes sir, he is probably still in the Jorocan slave and mercantile quarter." Traga handed him the sealed envelope. "Take this to him immediately." Ledric tucked it into his belt and ran to the horse waiting outside.

Two warriors entered the tent as he left. The elder was scared and had a noticeable limp. "Sir, have we permission to pack the command post?"

Traga grabbed a couple more pieces of bread, the cheese wedge, and the wine bottle. Tucking them under his arm, he said, "Yes, go ahead. I'll just take this outside."

The suns were still shinning brightly. There was not a cloud in the sky. An old uberan tree grew next to where the tent had been pitched. Its three foot girth and low wide branches offered the only patch of shade. It felt good to just sit for a change. The commander stretched out his legs, sitting with his back to the truck. At least the wine was good, and helped get the taste of the cheese out of his throat. He watched as his men broke camp, packing the supplies.

Most of them he knew by name, others he could recognize even at a distance. Suddenly he felt very old. Most of the men he watched had fought at his side during one battle or another. The others were sons of dead friends, wearing their father's faces. Some where young men that he had helped carry out of taverns or had loaned money to, keeping them out of debtor's prison. He didn't have to know their names. All he needed to see was the red dragon head on their leather forearm guards.

As armies go, this one had a lot of older warriors. The average age being thirty-five, compared to the youthful twenty of most units. More than half of the men had fought in at least two other conflicts. They knew from experience, their first duty was obedience. Punishment for rebels, and rabble-rousers, could at times be worse than death.

The two that packed the command tent were good examples. He did not know either of them personally, only by reputation. The elder limped from a pike wound in the hip. Narmetay was his name. It was rumored that, in the last Azzonian war, he had killed eight, Kubika lancers before dropping from a lack of blood. The other younger warrior was named Vytom; he was the son of an old friend that had given his life on the outskirts of Doretta. Traga owed him employment.

Over twenty percent of his army had been captured and sold into slavery at one time or another, and at least another ten percent, had been convicts. They did not walk in straight lines, nor did they walk with spring in their steps. Most did not laugh and joke on the march. These battle hardened warriors just shuffled along keeping silent.

The men also did not carry their own armor or any personal supplies. This was one of Traga's innovations. The commander used extra carts for the equipment. It was a little more costly paying for the extra horses and feed, but his men were more battle ready after a long march. Tired men with heavy backpacks don't fight well. It was the prime reason why they had won the battle against the Azzonians.

Traga had marched his men for three straight zestars, just to get into the right battle position. The renegade invaders, turned out to be warrior's of the Forth Army of Azzon. They were caught in an ambush at the old east road gorge. After hearing reports of the raiding parties' direction, the commander knew they would return by way of the eastern road, instead of the more mountainous western route.

The Red Dragon Army marched to the gorge and waited. They used their carts, wagons, and thorn brush to form a blockade at the southern exit. Then pike men where stationed in the woods at the northern entrance. The rest of the warriors were stationed behind boulders at the sides of the gorge, with an archer every thirty paces.

The Azzonians marched into the gorge's clearing, with their packs full of loot, and slaves in every pair of shackles that they had brought with them. Their six wagons were loaded to the bursting. It had been a good and lucrative raid. Their king would have been proud of them had they returned.

Instead, when the last wagon rolled into the gap the pike men attacked closing off the northern entrance to the pass. The bowmen let loose their arrows, turning the raiding party into a total wrought. Azzonians were falling at all points along the road. Each archer killed or wounded five to six of the enemy before Traga ordered the swordsmen to attack.

The battle engagement lasted two and a half zestars. Traga set free all the prisoners that the Azzonians had captured, and gave them a portion of the treasure wagons, along with anything that had actually belonged to them. It would be a long time before another surreptitious raiding party would be formed. Runners were sent to King Akeska of Azzon, to see if he would pay ransom for his soldiers, but he would not admit they were part of his army.

This being the case, all officers and members of royal Azzonian households that were captured were allowed to buy their own freedom. Those that refused this disgrace were allowed to take their own life or were beheaded. The other surviving warriors went to the slave blocks.

The wagons were nearly packed, and the men were beginning to mill about. With a forced march, they would make it back to Joroca, just before the suns set. The last patrols were starting to come in. It was what Captain Drayus had been waiting for. He waived his arm, giving the signal to begin the march. Axeth came running over when he caught sight of Commander Traga. "I have heard were moving out against another enemy!"

Traga placed an arm on the young boy's shoulder as they walked. "Yes. Our Lord Jedaf has sent word that he needs us."

Axeth bounced ahead of him, turned and walked backwards as they talked. "Is the master back in Joroca?"

"No," said the commander. He's still somewhere on Zarhun, but he has sent us a messenger." Traga noticed the way Axeth fidgeted with his shoulder harness, as he jumped about. "What is the matter with you boy? Have you got lice?"

Axeth stood still a moment, a bit embarrassed. "No sir," he said sheepishly. "I just wanted you to see my new harness and scabbard. I've joined the Army of the Dragon."

A wide smile appeared on Traga's face. "Boy you've been a dragon warrior longer than I have. I was wondering how long it was going to take you to realize it."

The twelve year olds smile returned. Axeth jumped about, circling Traga as he spoke. "Then it is all right for me to wear the uniform? Captain Agar said that I was too young."

Traga gave him a pat on the back of the head as he ran by him. "Well you are, for swinging a sword, but we always need fast runners."

Axeth jogged on ahead calling back, "Thanks commander!" Then he jumped into the back of the moving supply cart. Traga's aide ran forward leading two mounts, and waited for commander to climb into the saddle. They would ride straight through second lunch.

Commander Traga met up with his son Captain Agar at the parade grounds. He was glade to see that the cook fires were going and a hot meal had been prepared for his men. After a long march, most did not feel like setting up their tents immediately. The cooks and serving attendants dished out measan stew, with buttered dakalug bread wheels, and tall tankards of ale. They sat on the ground eating hungrily while Traga walked around and inspected the camp.

The one thing that was missing was a good supply of drinking water, but First Officer Bygin had already made arrangements with the family living nearby. A dozen men that were on the prison detail remained at the family's well bucketing out and filling barrels. As soon as the wagons were loaded they were driven to the camp, where they distributed the water to the tired warriors.

The army had arrived at the site near sundown. While the warriors were eating, the rest of the men that had escorted the Azzonian prisoners were tasked to set up the tents for their comrades. Traga expected that they would remain here for two to three days at most. If they tarried any longer, they would not be able to intercept the Worezian bridal caravan and rescue Kytos's sister, Princess Elona. Everything depended on how fast they could purchase enough supplies and find a means of transporting them across the sea.

Luckily a good supply of food and quite a bit of war equipment had been seized from the Azzonian Forth Army. Procuring the rest of the perishables would not be an insurmountable problem, but finding cargo vessels on such short notice were going to be hard to come by. This dilemma was wearing on Traga's mind as he paced through the camp.

Within three zestars the warriors had settled in and most of the campfires were banked. The sentries that had been posted about the perimeters had little to fear, but were having problems trying to keep sightseers and local women from roaming the camp. Traga and Agar met with the Captain Drayus who was the officer of the day, before having two fresh horses saddled for the short ride home.

They briefly discussed the situation and the urgency of keeping the men occupied and busy until sailing. There were to be no general overnight leaves, except for a few of the warriors that had family in Joroca. Traga didn't need to have hundreds of men with hangovers trying to load horses and equipment aboard a ship.

They rode into the city and were surprised to see hundreds of Jorocans still celebrating the defeat and capture of the Azzonians. It had been more than ten years since the citizens of this city had shown any pride in their army. The Yojan Royal Red Army had been reduced by half, and the Blue Army was a mire skeleton force stationed in the western provinces.

The Yojan Green Army that Traga and Agar had been part of were reduced to half a tantax totaling less than four thousand warriors. This minute armed force was now stationed on the southern border but had been given orders by King Vestrak not to engage or infuriate the Azzonians, because he did not want a war on his hands.

Now the people were taking credit for this victory even though the Yojan Army had not been engaged in the battle. Riding down the main avenue, many men and women ran over to them offering mugs of ale at seeing Traga's and Agar's uniforms. They waved off the cheering crowds of drunken revelers.

Both of them had a very long day and they wanted to get home and kick their boots off. Agar's back still hurt from being pulled from his saddle during the fight, and Commander Traga was thinking about the worried look on his wife's face when he asked her to have his campaign gear packed.

Neither of them had eaten the meal that had been served. Each was handed a few segment of buttered bread as they walked about, but they were more interested in seeing to the comfort of the men. Traga knew if he stopped long enough to eat and have a few ales, he wouldn't be home before ies, and he did not want to worry Myra more by staying out all night.

They finally reached the alley behind their home, and led the horses over to the vacant lot across the road. It didn't take long to unsaddle them, and fasten a tether to the fence post. Traga's aide had been accustomed to having a groom sent to the commander's home and one was scheduled to be there at first light.

Chapter # 13

Marshal Ebestar of Envar

It was late in the evening when Traga and Agar returned to their home. They quietly entered the darkened residence to find Axeth was already there. The boy had eaten quickly and had run back to the house before the suns had set. He was sleeping in Traga's favorite overstuffed chair in the parlor and immediately jumped to his feet when they came into the house.

The commander gave him a knowingly raised eyebrow, but did not complain. Walking into the living room, the men startled Kytos. He had been so deep in thought; he had not heard Axeth or the men enter the house.

The commander was covered in dust and smelled like his horse. They hung up their cloaks and looked around. The women had gone to bed zestars ago. The table had been cleared and the leftovers put away. Kytos remained awake by the fire. He sat sipping hot ale with his eyes closed. He had memorized Jedaf's letter before Myra destroyed it.

Now in the quiet solitude of the firelight, he recalled it, mulling each word over in his mind while he waited for them to return. Pulling out the chair at the side of the table, Traga sat down heavily. His lower back was aching, and he flexed his shoulders stretching the muscles. Agar sat down next to him. Axeth helped pull off both of their boots. Traga's were full of silt. The boy had ridden in the back of the supply wagon the whole way to Joroca. He was the only one of them that had any energy left.

Fetching a wash basin from the dry sink in the corner, he set it in front of Traga, and ran to the kitchen for the water pitcher and some hand towels. While Traga and Agar washed the boy ran off to the pantry returning with a pitcher of ale and four brass tankards.

Kytos watched him scurry about. He was half in a dream world when they had come in, but after seeing Axeth he could not help sitting straighter, and taking more notice of the goings on. The ales sizzled from the fire pokers Agar had fetched. They each took one while Traga stood and moved over to the hearth. He turned his backside to it, rubbing his behind.

"Prince Kytos. This is my son Captain Agar, and this is Master Jedaf's servant, Axeth. They both gave a nod as their name was spoken.

"It's good to meet you," said Kytos as he extended his arm and clasped the captain's wrist. I feel that I already know you from all that our lord has told me."

Traga sat back down sipping his ale. "Axeth would you fetch another pitcher for us? I feel like the walking dead." The boy jumped to his feet and disappeared into the kitchen. "Agar has set up camp for our men on the outskirts," said Traga. "He has also purchased some feed goods and some supplies. Have you found us a few ships, or do we swim to Zarhun?" Belching, he rubbed his soar feet looking to Kytos for the answers.

Axeth burst threw the door running over with the pitcher. "So we are off for Zarhun," he yelled, butting into the conversation. "I hope it will be a short fight. We have only nine hundred men, and that includes fifty to sixty that have been wounded""

The commander glared at him. It was enough; Axeth shut his mouth, and went about refilling everyone's tankard. "Father," asked Agar. "What exactly are our orders?"

Traga drained half his ale. "I will tell you after I have Ky's answer."

"I have picked out several vessels commander, but every time I ask about a crew, they refuse to supply one. Lately there have been too many pirates raiding the shipping lanes off the west coast of Envar. What makes it worse is that they haven't been taking any prisoners. No one ever comes back, not even in slave chains. I have offered as much as one small silver to each sailor that would sign on, and a bonus upon returning. As of this afternoon, I think I have a total of only eighteen willing to go."

The Commander thought a zesta while still rubbing his feet. "How many do we need to fill out a crew?" Kytos pulled his chair up closer to the end of the table, taking the ale pitcher. "Two of the captains that I spoke with said, they could get by with about twenty five seasoned sailors. They would need about another ten in training." He reached over taking the ale pitcher pouring as he spoke. "The third captain, the one with the largest ship said, he needed a minimum of forty, plus officers."

Agar had been listening quietly. "You don't have to worry about finding a crew," he said. I know that at least one out of ten of our men have had sea duty, which means that we have over ninety to choose from.

Traga slapped the table edge. "Good, see to it that they are singled out first thing tomorrow morning. When will you need the men Ky?"

The prince took a sip and set down his mug. "I put down a large deposit on the two smaller ships. The third, I have to meet with the captain again tomorrow." Kytos walked over to the hearth, picking up his dispatch pouch. Reaching into it, he pulled out several sheet of folded parchment.

"Here are the names of the two ships, and the sales contracts. The owner's were not willing to lease them knowing the destination. I think I paid too much for them, but I didn't have much of a choice. You can have your men report to the ships as soon as you round them up and pay off the remaining balance of the sales agreements." He handed the papers over to Agar.

"Everyone that I have spoken to said it will take a minimum of three days for the stevedores to load the cargo. That is what worries me the most." Kytos took the last sip of his ale. Lord Jedaf told me that his ship was attacked on the first morning out. It took us twelve days to reach Woreza. If the Culba's captain hadn't zigzagged around looking for another ship to prey on, we could have made it in less than ten days."

He banged his wooden hand on the table, loosening the wrist strap. "The ships that we will be sailing are old cargo vessels. Their big square rigged sails will be fighting the wind all the way. I wonder if we will have time to intercept the bridal caravan."

"Luckily we only have to sail to North Point," replied Traga. "That is three days less. If we use our men load the ships, and if we work day and night we may be able to save another day."

Agar stood and tossed another log into the fireplace. "Seven to eight days sailing," he said. "A half month, and were traveling light. It will take one whole deck for food and another for the horses and wagons. We will loose another couple of days unpacking, at that small seaport. How large are these ships?"

"There first rate," said Kytos. "There will be plenty of room for the men, as a matter of fact; one was originally a Yojan war freighter. It hit a sand bar coming into the harbor, and had some damage from shifting freight. After some caulking and painting it will be sea worthy again the day after tomorrow. The deck cargo broke up some of the bulwark rails and hatches, plus crushed two of the dinghies. There is no structural damage to the hull."

Ky pulled the draw stings to the leather wrist strap of his wooden hand with his teeth, and tied them a little tighter before standing. "Now I've got one more question. I have been wondering about, since Axeth came through the kitchen door. Why am I leasing or purchasing shipping to hold four thousand men when you only have nine hundred?"

Traga looked to Agar then back to Kytos. "I really don't know. In the mail pouch there were two other letters, one for a man by the name of Ebestar, to be delivered at the "Inn of the Ceratus," and one for Agar. I dropped off Ebestar's letter before ridding to the camp." He reached into his belt and pulled out Agar's letter, "I almost forgot it. Open it up it may have Ky's answer."

Agar took the half inch thick packet and looked at the seal, it was still unbroken. Unfolding the parchment, he read it quickly. "No it does not say anything about the ships, but it does say that I won't be going with you. Lord Jedaf has appointed me his ambassador. It says here that I am to purchase clothing befitting the guild position and that I am to have the seal of ancient Semedia embroidered on them."

"I'm than ordered to sail by the first available ship for the Kingdom of Saratam. There is a letter enclosed for King Jeston, and it says that Kytos is to write a letter that is to accompany it. After meeting with the king, I am to take the next available ship for the Kingdom of Agortha. Once there I'm to seek audience with the king, and deliver this other letter."

He held up the two small sealed envelopes, covered in runic symbols that were enclosed with his letter. "It goes on to say that I am to give them only to the kings and that if I am captured or run into trouble that I am to destroy them." Three rebarus large gold coins were enclosed. He jingled them in his hand, turning to Axeth. "It also says in the letter that you are to go with me, as my aide."

The boy looked a little disappointed at the news. He wanted to go with Commander Traga and the rest of the Dragon Army. Agar took another look at the smaller envelopes. There were no names on them just several rows of strange characters on each side below the name of the kingdoms. They were also sealed with red wax, having an impression of the horned dragon. Placing the coins and letters into his purse, he handed his father the letter that he had opened.

"I am going to miss you son. You're the most capable and trusted officer that I've got." He finished reading it himself than tossed it into the hearth's flames. "I'll be expecting you to be naming and recommending your replacement."

Axeth had gone back into the kitchen on a scrounging raid. He found more than expected. Myra had prepared two large trays for them. She had covered them with a towel and had left them on the pantry food preparation table. Traga's wife knew that with Axeth's nose for vitals, the trays would be empty by morning. He carried them back to the table, along with two loaves of bread and a cutting board.

They all re-seated themselves and ate quietly until a light knock was heard at the rear door to the kitchen.

"Who could that be at this zestar," asked the boy?

Traga gave Axeth a push from his chair, then stood by the fireplace mantle. "If you go to the door Axeth, we will all know." The youth picked up one of the two oil lamps from the dining room table and headed for the kitchen. Lifting the wooden cross bar from the door he opened it a crack and stood to one side. There were three hooded gentlemen standing outside with their heavy green woolen travel cloaks pulled tightly about them.

"Is this the house of Commander Traga," inquired the man in the center?"

"Yes it is sir. May I ask who's calling at this zestar?"

"Marshall Ebestar," he answered keeping his face partially covered as he spoke.

"One zesta," said Axeth closing the door. He ran back to the dining room to inform Traga, and quickly returned asking them to come in. Each pulled their hoods back, as they entered the house. They followed Axeth back to the dining room and living parlor area. Traga, Agar and Kytos were standing waiting for them.

The tall, slender and dignified man in the center was in his early seventies. He had silver grey hair and bushy eyebrows. His face was weathered and wrinkled. The other two men were forty-five to fifty years old and had equally stern faces but they had more muscular builds. They kept one hand in the folds of their clothing while they stood waiting to be introduced. Traga knew that they didn't have gifts beneath their cloaks. The three looked about the room a zesta then dropped their hands to their sides.

"I am Marshall Ebestar," said the eldest stepping forward. "This is Captain Azt on my right, and this is Captain Psydek on my left." Both men remained silent while they were introduced and they did not extend their hands in formal greeting. Neither did the senior officer after the official introductions had been made.

Traga waved his hand in the direction of the dining table. They accepted the invitation of his gesture and all walked toward the seating area as he spoke. "I am Commander Traga, this is Captain Agar, Second Officer Kytos, and my Lord Jedaf's servant Axeth." Kytos was a bit surprised being introduced as an officer, but he did not question it. "Will you and your men have an ale marshal?" Traga pointed at the pitcher in the center of the table.

"Yes Commander. I will have a small one." The other two captains nodded in agreement. Axeth fetched three more mugs from the kitchen along with a fresh pitcher. The three guests sat down on the side of the table with their backs to the fireplace. Captain Azt and Captain Psydek removed the single chairs from the ends of the table, placing them against the walls. This left only the chairs on the other side for Traga, Agar and Kytos.

Axeth sat on one of the chairs away from the table feeling left out, but he knew this meeting and discussion was for officers only and it would not bode well on Commander Traga for him to speak.

"I suppose this visit has something to do with the letter that I dropped off earlier," said Traga.

"Do you know what was written in the letter," asked the Marshal?

"No, I don't. I was instructed by my Lord Jedaf of Dolfi to deliver it to the inn. I did what I was ordered." Ebestar leaned nearer toward his aides, speaking and conferring quietly amongst them for a few minutes.

Captain Azt intentionally spoke louder than a whisper keeping the same expressionless face. "I'm not sure they're telling the truth. It could be a trap."

Agar placed his hand on the hilt of his knife. An insult like that needed to be challenged. Traga swept his son's hand away; leaning over and speaking softly in Agar's ear while his guests conversed. "I have never heard of a Marshal Ebestar, and I have served in two out of the three Yojan Armies. He could not have been much of an officer. Someone must have bought his rank for him."

Captain Azt and Captain Psydek reached for their knives. Ebestar latched onto their elbows and held them to their chair. "There will be no blood letting here," said the marshal.

"One does not draw steel in the home, unless it's to the death." Captain Azt gently pulled his arm free, as the older gentleman spoke. "I would not expect Commander Traga to know the name of any Envarian officer." Traga looked at the scowling expression on Captain Psydek's face, and could see that further insults were not necessary.

"Than you're Envarian," asked Agar?

"Yes," replied Ebestar. "We are the last remaining survivors of the Envarian Third Army of the Green. We have been on the Dolfinian Continent now for close to three years, waiting for an opportunity to return to our homes and to regain our dignity and pride. It was our army that was trapped and massacred at North Point. Now we vow vengeance on Prince Quayot, and his loyal following. After three days of hard fighting we found out he had abandoned us, and fled for the safety of Renvas."

"If it wasn't for a twist of fate we would all have died in that last battle. We were out numbered three to one, when the order came for all tantaxes to attack at once. The messenger that was supposed to deliver our orders had been killed. We marched forward one half zestar later than everyone else."

"When we crested the hill, we saw the Worezian Army swallow the last of our units in the valley below and close in behind them from all sides. There was nothing we could do. We retreated to the fishing village, and with their help we were able to escape here to Yoja."

"Your King Vestrak has allowed us to remain here as long as we protect his southern border near the city of Doretta, and make no trouble. It took two crossings to bring my men here, and many died in that little village so that others could escape. Their sacrifice will be paid for in full."

"It is time to avenge their deaths. The letter your Lord Jedaf sent me told us of events now happening in Envar. King Magarus of Worez and our King Helidon of Envar have made a treaty. They plan on surrounding our Lord, Prince Sesmak and slaughtering the rest of our warriors on the Zarhunian Plain."

Captain Psydek refilled his and the other two officers mugs while his senior officer continued speaking. "Prince Quayot will lead the

Red Army of Envar against our commander and the remainder of the warriors that are loyal to him. Your lord has asked me if I would like to fight under two banners, that of the Third Envarian Army and that of the horned Red Dragon of Semedia. I have come here to accept those terms."

Traga refilled his mug, Agar's and Kytos's. Axeth left the room to see it he could scrounge up some more cheese, fruit or biscuits. Ebestar paused for a zesta sipping his ale, and letting Traga digest the information he had just been given. "My informants have told me that you have one tantax stationed outside of the city, and you're preparing to sail."

"That is right," said Traga. "We plan on loading supplies tomorrow and hopefully boarding the day after. If you decide to sail with us, we will have to buy more food and supplies."

Ebestar stood and his officers followed his lead. "We will sail with you; I relinquish my command to your leadership." Captain Azt and Psydek looked incredulously at their Marshal. They could not believe what he had said.

Traga stood, and extended his hand in friendship. "Marshall Ebestar I think, what my lord meant, was that you are to remain in command of your own warriors. You have far more knowledge of the countryside, and therefore are better to command. If you agree, I think we should share this burden of responsibility equally. How many men can you muster under this short notice?"

The marshal took Traga's wrist, and clasped it tightly. Then he looked to his captains to do like wise, and each extended their own hands in a more formal and friendlier greeting.

Captain Azt turned to Ebestar. "Sir, since receiving the letter riders have been sent all down the coast, with a call to arms. So far we have been able to account for thirteen hundred of the original four thousand. We've left word at every tavern, and meeting hall. By tomorrow we should have about thirty four to thirty five hundred."

Kytos lifted his mug. "That is terrific," he said. "It quadruples our forces."

Ebestar looked surprisingly at the young second lieutenant's face than to Traga and Agar. "You don't know how many men were going to be fighting against?" Ky shook his head shamefaced, and a little embarrassed that he had spoken before considering the consequences.

"Your master estimates the enemy forces at about four hundred thousand."

Traga picked up the pitcher topping off everyone's mug. "It looks like it is going to be a short battle," he said. "Don't tell the women!" Commander Ebestar and his officers left to make some notifications and last zestar plans for their departure. It was almost dawn before Axeth and Kytos went to their room.

Traga and Agar remained at the dining table for the next two zestars. They discussed provisioning their warriors and added another thirty-five hundred men to the enlistment rolls. Counting and stacking the coins from the slave sale, and the money left in the war chest brought them to the same conclusion. They needed to find wild game and harvested goods on the Zarhun Plain to help supplement their diet; there were not enough funds to sustain them for very long.

The slave sale netted them, twenty rebarus large golds, and two leather bags containing an assortment of silver and bronze pieces. Another eighteen small golds were added to their coffers from royal officers that had bought their freedom. From the sale of the booty and trade goods, another one hundred and thirty four rebest large silvers had been added to the fund.

The Azzonian wagons had four small chests of coins, along with silver candelabras, platters, flatware, utensils and ewers that had been pillaged from one of the wealthiest estates. These chests contained a handful of small gold pieces, thirty to forty silver pieces and several hundred bronzes and coppers.

There were two hundred rebarus large golds, and about sixty rearus small golds still in the strongbox below the floorboards. In the false wall compartment behind the fireplace wood box were four bags of silver coins and two large metal boxes containing coppers and bronzes. In the corner base cabinet of the pantry was a large wooden chest filled with steels for daily purchases and two boxes of bronzes for specialty needs. The household funds were not counted or added to the general accounting. Something had to be left for an emergency.

Agar had spent sixty-five rearus small golds on supplies already. They tabulated a list of supplies, the men's wages, and miscellaneous expenses until Horastus rose. There was not going to be much left, after purchasing supplies for Ebestar's men. "It is a good thing it's going to be a short war for us," said Traga. "We can't afford enough supplies to keep us going for more than a few more mursas."

"It looks like you right father. I had better get the change from Kytos's diamond and gold, we're going to need every copper." I will keep and spend two of the three golds Lord Jedaf enclosed in my appointment letter. I believe that will be more than enough money for Axeth and I to sail Saratam and Agortha, plus it will keep us clothed and fed for several mursas. The other gold coin, I will save for the expenses of our return voyage.

Chapter # 14
South to the Kingdom of Jeupa

Ciramtis had ridden to the west in hope of getting around the enemy army's advanced guard. Only then could she change directions, and ride far enough into the Envarian north country to deliver Jedaf's letter, with the new orders for his warriors. What she had not counted on was the Royal Worezian Guard. The one warrior that had ridden away from the confrontation at the "Inn of the Athca" was able to rouse the southern gate outpost and return with a strata of Worezians.

The thirty five guardsmen were now riding hard after Lord Jedaf's wagon train. She crested one of the higher wooded glades, and could see the dust cloud of the troops far to her south circling the woods and following the south eastern road. She knew Odelac's men would not have a chance against so many.

The letter and orders could be delivered later; she would have at least eight days before they would arrive by ship. With some hard riding back the way she had come from, she could have the dragon lord's men moving out within another zestar, and still have time to send forth a spell to distort the enemy's vision and judgments.

Back in the east woods Odelac's crew had been breaking camp and re-packing the cart and wagon. All of the horses had run off during Jedaf's encounter with the evil treskul, and scouting parties had been formed to find them. The majority of the draft animals had been retrieved and one saddle horse that was not theirs. Karadis thought that it might have been Ciramtis's mount because it had a perfumed smell about it. Everyone except Captain Odelac and the merchant Valadis had been up and working since dawn.

The aroma of vegetable soup on the cook fire awoke Valadis. The Jeupan was hungry and it smelled good. Tossing the canvas flap back, he jumped from the back of the wagon. A few stitches pulled, and he reached over his shoulder gently pealing his tunic loose of the dried blood. Then very carefully, he arched and flexed the muscles of his aching wounds. "Still sore aren't you?" Valadis nodded as he walked stiffly over toward the campfire.

Vadeck was fixing him a bowl of soup to eat. Blowing away some of the hot wisps of smoke he said, "I'm glad to see you up and about." Valadis took the wooden bowl, sipping and looking over the rim. It did not taste as good as it smelled or looked but at least it was hot. "I did not want to wake you," said the old taskmaster. Valadis downed his thick, onion, pinto bean and potato vegetable stock. His eyes were tearing from the heated broth.

"Did Lord Jedaf have time to speak to you, Val?" The merchant took the ladle from the kettle and refilled his bowl. "Yes. He told me my first duty was to my king, and to get back to Jeupa as fast as I can. The border outposts must be warned, and the eastern armies mobilized. If I can get there fast enough, we might be able to have them on the western border in time to have King Magarus rethink his invasion plans."

Taking a small sip he continued. "He also asked me to take Captain Odelac and you men south with me. I still don't agree with him about that, but if those are his wishes I will do as he has asked. I think you and your men should have gone with Ciramtis. She's the one that has to ride through Worezian territory to get back to Envar, and she will need your protection more than I do."

Odelac had crawled through the front opening in the canvas and had been sitting at the bench seat of the wagon. One foot rested on the dash and his other leg was draped over the side of the bench seat.

He had been listening to them, since he heard Valadis jump from the wagon. "I agree with you Val, but for different reasons." Dropping to the ground, he winced and painfully walked stiffly over to them. Pouring himself a mug of the soup, he motioned for them to sit down as he spoke with them.

"While we were sailing here, Lord Jedaf became friends with that young man Kytos. I do not know if he told you or not, but Ky's a prince of the royal house of Oppow. The same pirates that captured us also captured him and his sister in addition to another princess.

Lord Jedaf has vowed to help free Ky's sister, Elona and her friend Princess Diara. But, he said to me that he may not be able to leave Tabalis, or ever be able to do anything to help them." Leaning over the iron kettle he gave it a stir and added another ladle to his bowl.

"The two princesses are to be delivered to Renvas as part of this marriage contract treaty. Now I know that Lord Jedaf had my health in mind when he asked to have me taken to Jeupa, but he is wrong. Ambassador Ajoris told me that the caravan would be leaving for Renvas within six days. If we break camp now, it would take a day and a half to return to the outskirts of Woreza.

Instead I propose we return by the south western roads. They may not be as good as the more traveled northern and western routes, but we will not meet as many soldiers. It will take us a day longer, but we should be able to intercept the bridal caravan north of the old Zarhun City and free the two princesses. Then we can head northwest to join up with Jedaf's friends. They will have sufficient strength to protect the women until Jedaf returns."

Valadis tossed his empty bowl into the wooden wash bucket. "Sounds like a good plan to me captain, but you forget one thing. You have only four men. The bridal troop will have at least two stratas of warriors. You will be out numbered fifteen to one."

Odel rubbed the stiff bandage and wound on his neck. "I thought that witch friend of yours might be able to help us with that minor problem. Perhaps she can create an elusion that we're five hundred instead of five."

Ciramtis laughed at Odel while, riding up on them from between the dense trees. "That would be a good trick and some powerful magic, but it's beyond my abilities." Standing in her saddle stirrups, she waived to Vadeck.

They were a bit surprised at her appearance coming through the thicket, and stood to greet her. "Don't ask, just divide up the supplies like you have suggested and make ready the cart. Be quick about it, the Woreza suburban guards are not too far behind. They will be here in a few zestars. Valadis, you will be taking the cart south to Jeupa. We will take the wagon and the rest of the supplies, and head to the southwest."

Vadeck grumbled under his breath, "Now we've got a woman in charge and giving orders." Looking to Odel, the captain gave a nodding assent. Myritt and Baradic found it easier to finish emptying the cart and wagon. After organizing the supplies, they divided them up. Odelac did not object. It gave his men something to do other than complain.

They were repacked within half a zestar. A few last adjustments to the trace lines, harnesses and belly straps and they were ready to depart. It would take Valadis four to five long, hard days to reach the southern border, if he did not run into any trouble.

Vadeck used a bottle of dark blue horse liniment to stain a picture of a loom on the side of the canvas cover, and to everyone's amazement the drawing looked rather good. Val changed his clothing and tied a colorful kerchief about his head making him look like more like a peddler of used equipment and rags than a trade good's merchant.

The cart was almost empty but the wagon and pack horses now carried one and a quarter times their original load. The supplies in the wagon were stacked as far forward as possible, and some of the grain sacks had to be packed on the extra two horses. This gave just enough room at the tail gate for Odelac to lie down in a kind of scrunched up fashion.

Vadeck rode the captain's horse, and Ciramtis rode at his side after thanking them for finding hers. Karadis drove the wagon with Myritt sitting next to him. Baradic tied the trailing pack horses behind the wagon and rode a few hundred yards beyond the trailing dust cloud. He provided the rear guard and would give them advanced warning of an attack.

Before leaving the area Ciramtis wove a spell. She whispered several lines of ancient Kaybeckian verse which formed into a large, misty, grey-green cloud. The fog swirled around the fire pit, several times growing in strength until it engulfed the entire campsite. Then the hazy particles merged with the trees and bushes billowing down the road to the west. It obscured the charred remains inside the rock fire circle, the wagon wheel ruts and made the bent grass stand tall and straight again.

No visible signs were left. It looked like it had been many years since anyone had visited this area. Following the mist, thickened wild grape vines quickly sprouted and grew spanning the road from tree to tree. They said their goodbyes under a clear sky with each of the drivers giving a quick flick to the reins. Valadis took the cart down the first forked road due south. Karadis veered off the main thoroughfare, and took the lesser traveled road to the southwest.

Odelac was still weak from his and Jedaf's encounter with the specter. Laying down to the swaying and rocking motion of the wagon he kept his eyes closed. He was right about one thing. The southern roads were not used much these days and the further southwest they rode the worst the condition.

The ruts deepened as well as the holes and fallen timber. There were also washed out gullies and areas that were so overgrown the direction southwest could not be easily identified. They had to scout ahead and make their own way between long stretches before they could call it a road.

Myritt and Baradic had to walk most of the way, removing rocks and fallen limbs. The jarring and pounding of the rough road made Odel wonder if the glue joints were going to hold and he feared that they would break an axle. Half a day out and they were already having trouble with one of the wheel's slip ring, roller bearings. The wagon had to be jacked up, the wheel pulled, pact and the axle re-greased.

It gave him second thoughts about whether he had picked the right road. The bridal party would be taking the only good road from the south western gate of Woreza. It had been primarily maintained for the military. If they were to intercept the caravan, it would have to be before they reached the old capital of Zarhun, and he was beginning to have his doubts.

"By all the Gods," he said. "I hope we can make a little more speed."

"What's that Captain," asked Karadis? He could not quite make out what Odel had mumbled.

"I said, can't we make any more speed! At this rate the bridal party will beat us to the border outposts and double their escort."

"Sorry Captain. This mountain road has not been used for long time. The weeds have grown across it, and in some places they are over two feet high. I can't see the rocks or holes anymore."

Odelac swore, and propped himself up looking around. "Where is Ciramtis?"

Karadis flicked the reins seeing a clear stretch of road ahead. "She rode up ahead trying to make sure there are no surprises." They had decided earlier that they would ride right through dinner and not stop until dusk. The two suns were starting to merge in the western sky. Hanging just above the treetops, the blazing orbs gave the dry grass an orange cast.

"Campfire smoke ahead," yelled Vadeck. Odelac could see the windswept black wisp over the treetops near the next bend.

It was Ciramtis's fire. Her unsaddled mount stood nearby in the lengthening shadows of the trees. Its reins were tied off at the lower branches. Karadis stood up as he drove. "I can not see her captain, but this is her camp." Turning his team, he directed them to the small clearing and tied off the reins on the break handle.

Looking near the fire the men could tell that she had been here for quite some time. A large stack of dried kindling and fallen branch wood had been gathered. Some of the brush and undergrowth had been cleared away from a hastily constructed fire pit area. Walking out from the wood line, Ciramtis had another armload of broken boughs. They were too heavy for her and the captain could see the strain on her face. "Myritt let Baradic take care of the horses, go and help Ciramtis with that wood."

Myr pulled the wagon tongue, lynch pin and pointed it at Odel as he spoke. "Wood gathering is for women. Let her finish it."

Odel swung out the back of his large beefy fist, hitting the young man on the side of the face. It landed hard, knocking him down and making him roll under the team of horses. "When I give an order, I expect you to jump, not mouth off."

Crawling out from under the horse's legs, Myritt wiped the blood from the corner of his mouth. Then he toyed with the hilt of his knife in a foolish burst of anger as he brushed away the dirt with his other hand. "Go ahead," said Vadeck to his younger friend. "If you think you'll live to talk about it." Myritt looked to his right. Vadeck stood there, his blade already drawn ready to protect the captain. Myr loosened his hand on the grip, as the sorceress approached.

"If you two are through arguing, I would like some help. There is a large dead tree over behind that hedgerow. See if you can't break loose some of the bigger limbs or get the axe and go cut them up." Myritt kicked the dirt in a huff and walked off in the direction she had indicated. "Captain you look better in spite of the ride."

Odel curled his arm, showing his bicep muscles in a comical troupadore strongman stance. "I feel a lot better too. I'm even getting some of my strength back." Baradic ran over taking the armload of wood from her, as the three walked over to the campfire.

"I am glad; you're going to need all the strength you've got. I have got some bad news." She knelt down and started stacking the wood, with Bara's help.

"What has happened," he asked?

"The road forks ahead around the bend. The way to the far southwest is clear, but will take us three to four days out of our way. The other branch, which follows the edge of the mountains, to the west has had a rockslide. The way it is now, the wagon could never get through. The whole face of the cliff has given way, closing the old road at the narrowest point."

"It had to be a tremendous avalanche, because some of the boulders were large enough to knock the trees over." She sat cross legged on the ground next to him. "I think all is lost. You might as well turn around and head for Jeupa. We probably could still catch up with Valadis before he reaches the frontier."

The captain thought in silence listening to her then paused for a few moments before speaking and asking her a question. "How long do you think it would take to clear enough to get the wagon over?"

Ciramtis lowered her head brushing the dirt and bark from her clothing. She avoided his eyes not wanting to answer or see his face. "I'm not sure," she replied. "My best guess," she said in a sullen tone, "Probably a whole day, maybe ten to fourteen zestars if we all worked on it."

Odel rubbed his chin, scratching the stubble of a beard that was starting to grow. "Vadeck," Odel called out. The taskmaster tossed the stack of blankets he had in his arms near the rear wagon wheel.

"Aye captain," he gave a quick salute and ran over.

"Ciramtis tells me there's been a rockslide around the bend in the road. Take a walk and see if you think we might be able to clear enough of it by torchlight tonight to get the wagon over. We would have to have it cleared by mid morning if we are still able to catch up with the wedding party."

"Right away captain," he answered. "Karadis," he yelled! "Follow me." The two trotted off down the road and turned at the bend.

"If we can clear the road, we may still have a chance. Have you been thinking about that spell for us?"

The young white witch laughed in good humor, shaking her head negatively. "No, I have not. But I think the best way to free the prisoners would be, to drug the bridal train's water supply. Perhaps we could sneak in during the night and pour sleeping powder into their barrels."

Odel listened, interjecting some suggestions and a few ideas of his own. The two discussed it for almost a zestar before seeing the men coming back up the road. "I think we have the start of a good plan" she said. "Here comes Vad."

She was surprised to see how fast the old bowlegged seaman could run. "Captain, it will be hard work," he panted, "but I think we can do it. Karadis can start cutting rollers and Myritt can start making the torches. We may be able to rig a boom crane. With the use of some good leverage poles, we will be able to move some of the larger boulders." Holding on to his knees Vadeck tried to catch his breath before going on.

His old broken nose was whistling as he panted. "Should we go ahead?"

The captain looked to Ciramtis for support. "What do you think? Should we give it a try?"

The sorceress shrugged her shoulders, and then nodded. "Might as well give it a try," she answered.

The captain agreed. "Yes, have all the men get to it. Ciramtis will put some food and tea on the fire and I will be up to help as soon as I can. Is there anything else that we should know?"

Vadeck straightened himself arching his back; he was still trying to catch his breath. "Yes captain, there is. With the men working all night, they're going to be dead tired tomorrow, and no one will be walking. I hope we don't run into a fight."

Odel stood by watching his men laboring at the rock pile. He guessed that about thirty-foot of overhanging cliff shelf had tumbled down closing off the road. Whether it was an act of nature or by a tactical design of the regional warring factions, he could only guess. At this point he really didn't care how it fell, all he knew was they had to clear enough by morning or they would not be able to intercept the caravan.

With five zestars of hard backbreaking work they were able to use the wagon to haul away eight loads of smaller rock. The larger ones they had pried up and rolled to the side until the smaller rocks could be carried away. No rock larger then what two men could lift was moved, before then.

Ciramtis drove the wagon and fetched water while they worked away at the pile. The captain had become tired very early on.

Unloading the wagon supplies all by himself, had taken away what little strength he had recovered. About all he could do to make himself useful was to make replacement torches, keep the cook fire going, and the teapot hot.

Occasionally one of the men would carry a piece of grey polished stone to the wagon. There must have been some sort of a building against the cliff at this spot, but it was now totally crushed and unrecognizable. They worked on into the night until Karadis yelled out. His shout made everyone jump; they thought he had been seriously injured.

"Look what I found!" Everyone dropped the stones in their hands going over to Karadis. There up against the cliff face, was the top keystone and the side of a small stone arch.

Most of the top and right side of the doorway had fallen inward. Squatting down low, Odelac stuck the torch into the black hole. The yellow light revealing a small anti chamber with a large hardwood door in the center of the opposite wall.

"Ciramtis; come over here, part of this building is still intact."

"Don't touch anything. The interior could be bewitched," she yelled! Hurrying over the rocks and loose rubble she took the torch and looked inside for herself.

"What's it look like to you Cira," asked Karadis?

She waived the torch to the sides trying to get a better look. "I am not sure. The front of the room contains mostly debris and broken furniture. The rear is too dark to make out much.

Myritt muscled his way between Karadis and Baradic. "I'll bet it's the treasure room of the tollhouse." He leaned on Ciramtis, and tried to peak over her shoulder.

Baradic grabbed him and pulled him backwards. "You're always thinking of treasure, you beggar."

Myritt swept his hand away; "That is better than dreaming about food and women all day. You wouldn't know what to do with one anyway. It has been too long since one has let that ugly mug of yours come within slapping distance."

Baradic pushed Myritt hard enough to cause him to fall backwards against the rocks. "That's enough," said Odelac stepping between them. "Before any of you thinks about doing anything to that chamber door, we have to clear enough of this slide to get the wagon over."

"Vadeck, how about that block and tackle, are you ready to start lifting some of the larger stones?" Vadeck helped Myritt up from the broken rocks, and made sure the young sailor was not injured before answering.

"Just about to captain, but before we start rolling and dragging those larger boulders, I would like to fill in some of the holes and pockets with loose dirt. While we do that, you and Ciramtis could cut up the blankets into strips to help protect the horses' legs from the sharp stones."

Odel gave him a pat on the back. "Good idea Vad. We will get right to it."

Myritt tossed his shovel down in disgust, "How come we have to do all this work tonight? We still have about four days before the caravan reaches the border! I've already got cuts and blisters on both hands, and my back is killing me."

Odelac picked up the shovel and was about to hand it back to him, but thought the better of it. It seemed for once the lazy young man was right. They had been working hard, and they've only taken two other rest breaks.

"We have to finish tonight, because the road continues south for another half day before it curves to the west. I would like to be there at least a day early, for us to rest and make our plans." With the sole of his boot, he pushed the spade of the shovel into the loose gravel, and let it stand.

"You men have done a lot of work, but there is still a lot to be done. You can all have another half zestar rest, but after you get something to drink, I will be expecting you to finish it without stopping again." Grumbling beneath their breath, they walked off to the campsite leaving Odelac and Ciramtis standing at the top of the slide.

It was the morning of the eleventh day of Kebran. Ciramtis noted it in her logbook, while she watched the last of the torches burn out. For the first month of summer it was still unseasonably cold. Aligning her small sundial to the east, she watched as Horastus, the larger of the two suns rose.

Sixth zestar, in another fifteen or so zestas and it will be light enough to start moving the wagon. Odelac had let the men sleep for the last two zestars of the night. They had reached the end of their endurance and had done all that they could. The center mound of the slide was still six feet higher than where the old road surface had been.

Odel had kept the cook fire going throughout the night while the men worked. Early this morning, he made a salty measan broth with Vadeck's assistance, and they baked some whole oolets at the edge of the fire pit. Most of the men were too tired to eat anything last night.

It was time to begin another day and it looked like it was going to be a hard one. At dawn Vadeck woke the men. Each of them half-heartedly managed to peal and eat one of the salted and baked thick skinned red potatoes, along with a buttered hard roll. They made faces at the unappetizing breakfast, as they silently washed it down with a small cup of the broth. Ciramtis made a pot of strong, black herbal tea that was high in caffeine.

The captain poured half a crock of krasta en into it, and the men thanked him for the added hot alcohol. The bitter elixir helped numb their aches and pains and kept them from arguing with each other for most of the morning. They had slept very little, and although they were irritable and moved slowly at first, they managed to walk up the hill.

While the men ate, Ciramtis and Odel led the horses' single file down a steep and shear drop off. The path wound its way south through a few stunted trees and smaller rocks around the base of the avalanche. This was all that was left of the of the cliff shelf, which had not dropped to the valley gorge thirty feet below.

Before turning in for the night, they had filled in each side of the mound, and Odel hoped the wagon would take the pounding of being hauled over it. Vadeck rigged a fifteen foot tall tripod stand with a block and tackle near the top of the hill. Then he had them stand at the ready near the back of the wagon.

The lines of the block and tackle were fastened to the front axle. The other ends were tied to the horse harnesses. When everything was ready, the old marine yelled out to Odel. The captain steadied the horses and walked them slowly taking up the slackened lines. The wagon rolled slowly forward and started to ascend the mound.

The men at the rear helped guide and push the wagon with leaver poles and muscles. Ciramtis ran from wheel to wheel blocking them with stones, and preventing them from rolling backward. It took three and a half, long zestars for them to get the wagon to the top of the rubble pile.

It was nearing mid morning and everyone was exhausted, and ready to drop. As soon as Vadeck locked the wagon break, all of them sat down where they had been standing. The men were unable to move. Odelac could see they could do no more; they didn't have much stamina left.

The captain ordered the tired men back to the campsite. He decided to let them rest for next two zestars before asking them to lower the wagon to the other side. It would be about time for first lunch when they finish, and maybe they would be able to eat something.

Standing guard had been left to him. Captain Odelac was the only one that could stay awake and still move around. The weary old seaman sauntered between the scattered crewmen and walked over to the cook fire. The tea kettle was still hot and half full. Pouring out a large tin mug he looked about.

The men tossed and turned on the cold hard ground. Blankets were pulled over their heads shielding the sunlight from their eyes. Ciramtis rested up against the supplies that had been unloaded from the wagon. She had amazed him from the time of their first meeting. The white witch had done more for the captain and his crew than anyone had ever done. She had put in longer hours than most of the men, and had not made one complaint.

Even Vadeck had mentioned the fact that she had done more work than Myritt and he wished she was a member of the crew instead of the lazy misfit. It was than that Odelac noticed the form beneath Myritt's blankets wasn't moving at all.

Odel walked over and kicked the covers from a pile of dried brush. The young sailor was missing. Vadeck was not sleeping, but he was resting nearby and having one eye open. He tossed his blanket off, stepped over the still sleeping form of Baradic and walked over next to his friend. The taskmaster had not slept either. He looked as if he were about to drop from exhaustion.

"Vad, where is Myritt," whispered Odel?"

"I saw him get up awhile ago. He said he could not sleep either. He wanted to get a better look at the roadhouse. Do you want me to get him?"

"No Vad, try to get some rest yourself. I will go myself." The captain could feel the calf muscles and tendons on the backs of his legs tighten as he walked. The road had only a slight incline leading to the slide. Reaching it, he wondered if he had the strength to keep his footing and climb in the loose soil.

As each foot went forward he cursed Myritt. He almost wished he had purchased the freedom of one of the other crewmen at the slave blocks. Vadeck had vouched for him, saying that even though he argued a lot, he was a good seaman. The shiftless sailor could not be seen anywhere. From the sounds of pounding and the echo's, Odel could tell he was most likely in the anti-room.

"I thought that I told you to get some rest!"

Myritt turned around to see Odelac sitting on a large rock near the entrance. He laughed at seeing how out of breath his captain was.

"I am resting Captain." Myritt sat cross-legged at the inner chamber door. He was gouging out pieces of wood around the locking mechanism. "As soon as I get to the other side I can stop thinking about this and get some sleep." Odel looked at the piles of splinters next to the torch. The young sailor must have been working at it more than one time. He probably spent all his rest breaks right here.

"How is it going?"

Myritt removed the sweaty kerchief that he had tied around his forehead and wiped his face. "Woods pretty hard and dry," he replied. "I have broken the point off one knife and my short sword is already dull. I had to borrow Baradic's knife this morning." He ran his thumb over the new blade as he spoke. Its rounded point didn't look like it was going to last too long.

"Captain!" Odel and Myritt turned around to see Vadeck running up the hill toward them. "Captain," he shouted again. "I think you should know that were being watched. I've seen several things moving along the top of the cliff and the birds and animals are moving away to the east of us.

If we don't get this wagon moving soon; we will be trapped here against the cliff with nowhere to escape. Better arm yourselves, if we don't finish in time." Odel stood looking about him. He couldn't detect anything unusual or out of the ordinary.

"But what are we going to do about the treasure," asked Myritt in an excited voice? "We are almost inside! I'm not going to give it to the first highwaymen with a blade."

Vadeck grabbed Myritt by the scruff of his neck and pulled him up and over the rocks, and out of the room. "You fool! If we get caught in this gorge, I wouldn't give you one in ten odds of ever seeing another sunrise. Now get over to the wagon."

Myritt sheathed the knife and ran over where the other men were standing. They were already on the alert, carrying the supplies over the mound. If there was going to be a fight, they wanted all the provisions on their side of the avalanche where they could protect them. It was the first time in weeks that Odel had seen his men hustling without complaint. There was no talking, and no slowing down.

The block and tackle was hastily moved to the rear axle, and breaking poles slid under the front wheels. The weight of the wagon kept the momentum going, rolling the heavy weight quickly down the other side. It was going too fast and the men were having trouble with their footing, but Odel knew they had to take the chance. They should have taken more time and care but he could not afford any. Luckily no one was injured, other than a few scraped knuckles and shinbones.

The loose supplies were hastily tossed inside as soon as the wagon hit the flat road surface again. Ciramtis had the horses in harness, and Odel hitched them while the others did the loading. Baradic jumped to the drives seat, grabbed the reins and released the break.

It was too late, they were trapped. A party of hate filled vourtre archers turned the bend. Their laminated rams horn re-curve bows at the ready and fitted with grey and yellow, feathered shafts. They were now bent to their fullest extent as the bowmen awaited the order to kill the humans.

Chapter # 15

The Ancient Semedian City of Am Haas

Baradic pulled up on the reins, calming the horses. One vourtre archer stepped forward of the battleline, directing the aim of his shaft at Bara's heart. There was nothing they could do but surrender. He tied off the reins on the break handle and raised his arms. Since the war party had not killed them at first sight, there was still a chance of getting out of this alive.

Ciramtis dismounted, walking over where Odelac stood. "What do you think they want?"

The captain slowly removed his hand from his hilt. "I don't know, maybe the supplies? One thing for sure, if they wanted us dead, we would not be talking now."

Vadeck was in the back of the Conestoga restacking vegetable crates. He crawled out threw the front canvas flap onto the bench seat next to Baradic. "Don't do anything hasty, he whispered. There are another twenty warriors behind us."

Vadeck raised his hands and sat very still. "What do you want us to do," asked Odelac? He raised his hands turning slowly about to his men. "I said, don't do anything, and do not move until you're told to do so." Karadis stood at the back tailgate of the wagon, with his arms raised over his head. "Where is Myritt," he asked in a quiet level tone? Odel looked questioningly from Ciramtis up to where Vadeck and Baradic sat on the wagon.

Bara answered softly with out moving his lips, "He went back to treasure room. He said he would catch up with us later."

"That damn fool! Don't say anything. They may not have seen him." Odel's tense and worried thoughts were answered by the sound of a man's scream. At first there was a sort of a groan, than one long agonizing and blood curdling horrific scream, after another.

"What do you think they're doing to him," asked Bara nervously? His hands were shaking almost uncontrollably while his eyes were looking about for a place for him to run. He drew his knife slowly and laid it across the folds of his tunic in his lap. Vadeck watched him and the bowmen, out of the corner of his eye.

No one seemed to have noticed, except Ciramtis. Bara wiped the sweat from his palms on his kilt. He didn't want the woman to notice his lack of courage. It would not have helped. She could see the fear written all over his pasty white face. If it came to a fight, she had no doubt; he would jump from their wagon and flee for the trees.

Vad cautiously swung his legs over the side of the wagons' bench seat and dropped slowly to the ground. Bara followed his lead, while palming the knife. They moved over toward Odelac and Ciramtis, standing closely behind them. "If we give them the wagon, do you think they will let us live?"

Ciramtis sneered at Baradic, hearing the cowering waiver in his voice. Brushing him back she took a step away from him, while whispering to Vadeck. "I have heard vourtre skin their captives alive, and then crush the life out of them in wine presses." She got the reaction that she expected. Out of the corner of her eye, she could see Bara's face whiten and his skin start to crawl, as he cringed in fear. She had not liked him from their first meeting.

Vadeck turned his head aside, and fained a cough. He didn't want Bara to see his smile. If they hadn't been in such a dire situation he would not have been able to contain his laughter. She turned back toward the captain, taking a step closer to him, and clutching her staff tightly. If she were about to die she was happy and proud to be at his side.

A short, burly, broad chested, officer stepped out from behind the wagon, and walked over to them. His pleated two tone woodland brown kilt and tunic had fresh blood on them. He was not wounded. They knew whose blood it was without asking. Standing to a height of about five feet six inches, he looked at them with a sneering disdain. He may have been a bit tall for a vourtre, but what he lacked in height, was made up for, in meanness and strength. He looked like he could have lifted the wagon from the ground all by himself.

The left side of his stern face and neck were deeply blotched and scarred by fire, his left eye dead white, with no hair growing on the scar tissue. Where his pointed ear should have been, a dark motley lump of grayish-green flesh grew. Clenching his teeth, he pointed his razor sharp dagger at them. "You are all going to die for desecrating the tomb of King Dracar."

Waving his arm, four men crawled quickly from underneath the wagon grabbing the sailor's ankles, and knocking them down to the ground. The rest of the perimeter guards ran forward pinning them in the dirt. After binding their arms behind them, a braided leather noose was slipped about each of their necks. They were kicked, disarmed and dragged to the rear of the wagon where they were tied alongside Karadis, to a lead line at the rear warkmeg cleat.

Odel's party marched for the next zestar and a half eating the dust cloud kicked up by the wagon and horses. At the next major fork in the road they were cut free of the wagon and marched off in a more westerly direction. The wagon and horses continued following the southern route, leaving them in a more distressed and depressed state. If they were ever able to escape, it would have to be on foot, and without their supplies.

The western route that the officer had chosen was little more than a narrow winding footpath with a steep downward grade. It led to a lower valley that was entirely overgrown with moss covered trees, having large white and orange fan shaped funguses. The wide, green leafy underbrush grew to a six foot height and tall ferns were thickening at each bend.

The war party turned off the path at a point where an old rotting burkat tree grew. Baradic tried to step around the captain in order to get closer to Ciramtis. He figured the closer he was to a woman the more likely he would be safe. Odel tripped over one of the exposed tree roots and bumped into one of the escorts. The guard pushed him back hard and the captain fell to the ground.

Odelac was kicked until he regained his stance and was able to stumble forward again. Vadeck had seen what Baradic had done. The old taskmaster took two quick strides forward and purposefully stomped on the back of Baradic's heel. It caused the sailor to fall on his face and having to limp until they stopped.

The forest undergrowth was so dense that nearing the eleventh zestar there was hardly enough light to see their footing. How long they continued to march Odel could not tell. There wasn't a true path anymore. They just plodded ahead keeping quiet. If anyone started to stray from the direction the guards intended, they would be poked with the point of a broadsword.

The Village of Am Haas was not too far ahead of them. They couldn't see it, but they could smell the campfire smoke and aroma of roasting vegetables. Women at the edge of the clearing started making shrill calls, sounding like the birds that these humanoids were named after. Word had been sent on ahead, and now the children joined in following the procession. They poked at the prisoners with the points of sharpened sticks, laughing all the while.

One short legged, ugly, and spiteful ten-year-old took particular delight in antagonizing Ciramtis. He would maliciously jab her in the kidney from the rear. As soon as she would turn about she would be shoved forward by the guard. The gangly boy would then run to her other side giving her another poke. She thought of casting a spell setting his clothes on fire, but they were in enough trouble.

The rustic village was constructed almost entirely of moss covered rough-hewn stone blocks. Each building was circular in shape, with a tree growing in its center, the trunk and main branches forming the roof. Other branches and thatch were woven into them filling in the bare spots. Gardens of wild flowers were at the sides and walks leading to the dome shaped structures.

Large old growth trees with thick trucks lined the main avenues leaving barely enough room between them for the width of two carts. Thick, wide leafed and twisted corkscrew shaped vines filled the treetops forming a canopy over the entire village.

The shade protected the delicate skin, and green eyes of the vourtre people, but the dim light made Odel feel uncomfortable and ill at ease. There was nothing he liked better than a clear warm sky. That is why he became a sailor, no trees overhead.

The side streets and lanes were very narrow, and darker than the main avenue. Not much sunlight reached between the dwellings. Most of the walls were covered with thick tapestries of green or a golden colored moss and having many varieties of thin variegated ivy vines growing in the mortar joints. Gardens of large tuberous vegetables, mushrooms, and gourds grew on trellises and in the moist black soil near each of the homes.

The prisoners were hauled over in front of an abandoned semi-dilapidated hovel which had a low roof. It did not have any windows, and had only one narrow slatted door with a very low lintel. Eneas, the blood spattered officer, dismounted from Odelac's horse, before pushing them inside and striding off.

It was a musty smelling, single roomed eight-foot diameter lodge with a damp dirt floor. The only furnishing being two oil lamps hanging from hooks mounted on the rear block wall, and two thatched oval shaped burkat fibber floor mats. A chipped unpainted pottery basin was resting on a crudely built small wooden tripod stand that had been placed between the mats and lanterns.

Two armed guards stood outside, leaving the door open. The seamen were all thankful for the fresh air; the atmosphere was rank inside and the stinking mats were mildewed. A large angry crowd was forming outside, and they were starting to surround the building. Some of the bystanders were praying aloud, while others were shouting, "Gelkula phicoparr, Kill the violators!"

A gaunt eighty year old woman with skeletal arms and a prune like wrinkled and weathered face led the chanting mob. She shook her walking stick at them, and then was the first to start throwing rocks. They came through the door opening with one of the sharper stones, nearly hitting Vadeck. Ciramtis drew a protective circle around the inside wall with the toe of her boot. Then she recited a few magical spells softly.

A few moments later, the anger and shouts of the crowd seemed to lessen. Most villagers went about their business until something up the road aroused them once again. They gathered around the building as before, but this time thicker than ever, as they shouted their rage with renewed vigor and determination. The situation was getting out of control and two additional warriors came over to help guard the door opening and to keep the near rioting throng back.

Ciramtis stood at the entrance watching the mob. Using her mystical and spiritual powers, she kept them from overpowering the guards and attacking Odelac's crew. A brass gong sounded three times, quieting the closely packed irate horde. They stopped shoving their way toward the cell and looked about for Prince Eneas's guidance. He wadded through the villagers dragging an almost unconscious Myritt.

The horribly beaten and bloodied taxzy sailor was almost unrecognizable. Two guards grabbed the near lifeless body by the arms and legs, tossing it into their cell. Myritt landed face down in the dirt without making a sound. Odel and Ciramtis immediately rushed to his side. They could not turn him; their hands were still tied behind them.

"Cira turn your hands to me," shouted Vadeck! She did as he asked, and in hardly any time at all he had bitten through the leather binding straps.

Ciramtis carefully rolled Myritt over. His face and hair were caked with mud and covered in blood. The crowd had stomped on and beaten him while he was dragged. He had no front teeth, his uppers and lowers had been knocked out. An ear and a piece of his nose were also missing. His arms, legs, and chest were covered with ever darkening purple bruises.

The sailor's right thigh and hip had been cut down to the bone. There was almost nothing left to his shredded kilt except blood soaked cloth. The young seaman's feet were bare; his tunic had been ripped open before a flaming torch had repeatedly been put to his chest.

Myritt's eyelids fluttered open for a few zestas as he groaned. Recognizing his friends, he managed a slight smile with his swollen lips. "I was right;" he said hoarsely. "The room was full of jewels and golden goblets. All I needed was ten more zestas and we would have been rich." His words trailed off, while his fists remained tightly clenched as if they still held the precious gemstones.

"Is there anything we can do for him?"

"I am sorry captain, I can stop the bleeding but it looks like he has a fatal head wound." Odel could see crushed and exposed bone splinters at the left temple near Myritt's hairline. He knew his young man would not suffer very much longer. Ciramtis walked around to the back of the captain and untied his hands before going over to Vadeck.

"Help me get him out of the doorway," she said. Odel untied Baradic and Karadis. The four men carried Myritt to one of the mats at the back wall and they gently laid him down. Odel covered him with his cloak, and Cira bound up his leg wound. Stroking his forehead, she kept the hair from the wounded man's eyes as he slipped in and out of consciousness.

There was nothing left for them to do but wait. All Ciramtis's medications and pain killers were in her bags at the back of the wagon. Odel sat at his crewman's side, holding onto his hand and talking about their ship and the next voyage they would be making out of a Jeupan harbor.

Myritt's breathing became a little easier for awhile knowing that he was with his friends. He died within the zestar. Cira covered his face, and said the prayers of the dead for him. The others sat sullenly with their backs to the masonry walls. Occasionally they got up to stretch or to look out of the doorway. "I told that fool to leave the door alone," said Karadis.

"Forget it Kar. He's dead now. No sense in telling him, I told you so."

Karadis could see the sorrow and angst on Vadeck's face. He knew that the tough talking taskmaster and younger sailor had argued a lot, but had been friends for the last ten years or more. Kar also knew that Myritt's father and Vadeck had been shipmates of many years.

The same accident that had killed the young man's father was the one that had nearly killed, and had severely maimed Vadeck. "Your right Vad, I'm sorry for your loss." Karadis sat back down with his elbows resting across his knees. He lowered his head placing his chin on his forearms and closing his eyes.

Baradic stood and paced about in a nervously agitated and frustrated manner. He wanted to talk and vent his fears, but no one wanted to listen to him. Finally he went to Vadeck's side, sat and whispered quietly. "We have to get out of here before they skin us. You heard what Ciramtis said. She knows everything about these green savages. Maybe we can get her to make a run for it tonight. She can draw the guards away, giving us a chance to escape into the darkness."

Vadeck grabbed a hold of Baradic's neck with both of his hands, dragging him to his feet. "You sea slug, if you weren't a good top man, Odel would not have paid for your ransom. I told him you were not worth two bronzes let alone twenty. You better stay away from me or I will skin you myself." Vad tightened his grip on the sailor's throat lifting Bara's feet off the ground.

Baradic gasped for air pushing himself free of Vadeck, and falling to the moist loose soil. Vadeck gave him a hard kick and spat on him. "If you bother me again, I'll finish the job." Bara crawled away on his hands and knees, to the opposite side of the cell away from the others. He sat by himself watching the door opening and trying to think up a plausible escape plan.

An elderly seasoned warrior entered the cell looking for Cira. He was dressed better than the average men at arms. His tunic was decorated with small glass and stone beads, and the head of a sharp toothed featga timber wolf was embossed in the leather over the area of his heart.

Cira sat near the young man's body praying quietly with Odel. Her eyes were closed and her face was streaked with tears. She had not known Myritt very well, but she knew he had a good heart even if he never seemed to do any work. She hated to see such a useless death.

"You there, woman," the guard shouted disdainfully! "Our queen demands your presence."

Cira slowly stood up to comply, but Odel was on his feet first. He stepped between them, baring her way. "Tell your queen, we have chosen to die together, here in this cell if need be. You're not dragging us off one by one to die alone."

The guard drew his blade taking a step forward. Vadeck, Karadis, and even Baradic stood surrounding him. The warrior could not take them all. He knew he could cut at least two of them down, but that was not what he came for. Sliding his sword back into its sheath, he withdrew and ducked threw the doorway. Within five zestas, he returned with a young, five foot tall woman. She was about twenty five years old, and was as thin as a willow wisp.

The guards remained outside, while she entered unarmed. Her long forest green robe hung a hands width above her slimly adorned sandaled feet. It gave the illusion that she floated as her garments billowed behind her. The hood of her cloak was pulled back, revealing her beauty. Her features were delicate for a vourtre. The lady's skin was smooth and having a slight olive-green sheen to it. Mint green Ivy had been woven into her dark black hair, highlighting her eye color. The soft greenness to them gave the impression of patients and intelligence.

"I am Lavea, daughter of Queen Cystalen. The leader of the vourtre peoples on Megath." These humanoid beings still did not recognize the change of the continents name to Zarhun. "I have come here to escort you to her. I swear on my ancestors, that no harm will befall you while you are away from your friends."

Ciramtis stepped forward and asked, "And after that?" Lavea extended her hands palm upward toward Cira. Crossing them she struck the back of one hand against the palm of the other, separating them once more in a matter of fact gesture. "When you return to your friends, all will be the same as before. I promise you nothing. Your fate will be decided by our queen."

Ciramtis waved her hand to the side in the direction of Myritt. "Alright, I will go with you, but first we would like to be allowed to bury our dead."

Lavea looked over at the covered body of the dead sailor and nodded. "Thay Taret," she called out!

One of the security guards entered. "Yes mistress?"

"See to it that these men are given shovels, and escort them into the woods where they may bury him. But you must come with me," she said to Cira. "The queen waits for no human."

Ciramtis followed the vourtre princess from the holding cell down a wandering flagstone path through the village. It led to an ornately carved grey stone building, with two honor guards standing sentry duty near the front entrance. The warriors both looked hard and stern, and were not pleased to see that a human was about to be escorted inside. Lavea whispered something softly to them, and ducked below the low archway. Ciramtis had to stoop even lower, but followed.

The ceiling was low and vine covered like all the other dwellings. Cira had to stay hunched over, while Lavea could stand tall with two hands of headroom to spare. The Interior was dark and sparsely furnished. An old woman sat on a plush brown cushion resting on a rectangular stone block near the rear wall.

In front of her lay a round cable braided rug, which was faded, thread bare, and loosing the orange fringe from its edges. An oil lamp hung from the branches overhead at each side of the room. The smoke had an herbal incense aroma to it. Ciramtis looked at the frail queen. The petite woman was extremely old, her face and neck, deeply lined, wrinkled and pale. The skin on her thin translucent arms was sagging at the elbows, and her hands were folded in her lap.

Motioning them to the carpet, the two sat opposite her, cross-legged, while remaining quiet. The queen looked very tired. "My child," she said in a soft wavering voice. "What is your name, and what would ever bring you to do such a despicable act like this. My great grandfather's tomb has lain untouched for hundreds of years.

Even King Magarus's vile men would not dare enter, and desecrate it after destroying it. Why would you?"

Cira calmed herself, answering in a smooth level tone of voice. "My name is Ciramtis. We were traveling on the road north of here, on our way to the Envarian border. The rockslide blocked our path. The only way to get by it was to move some of the loose stone. We had no idea it covered the entrance to your great grandfather's tomb."

Cystalen slapped her hand down hard against the side of her sitting stone. Her eyes widened with new energy and life. "That was no slide," she said emphatically! "Your King Magarus did that to punish us for not paying him tribute!"

Cira intertwined her fingers and placed her hands in her lap. "Your majesty, I am not a Worezian. I am from Iblac. None of the men with me are Worezian's either. King Mararus is our common enemy." Lavea poured out two cups of hot herbal tea, handing one to Cira. She took it and sipped while Cystalen thought.

"That still does not explain why one of your men, hacked a hole in the crypt door."

Cira set her cup and saucer down, refolding her hands. "You're right; the man you refer to was named Myritt. He was an impetuous youth and did not listen well. This sailor thought that the building was a dilapidated tollhouse, and wanted to see if there was still anything of value left inside. He didn't know it was a crypt, and he paid for that foolhardy mistake with his life. Do the rest of us have to pay for his stupidity and greed?"

Cystalen closed her eyes once more and rested while she thought. Lavea and Cira waited patiently, sipping from their cups. The old woman's eyes opened with slightly renewed energy. "That depends on you Ciramtis of Iblac. Will you drink of the tattla root?"

The white witch shifted her weight, letting some of her blood circulate in her legs. "I have heard, the root of the tattla, not only causes one to speak to truth, but it also causes death and madness."

A half smile curled the wrinkled lips of the aged queen for a zesta. "It is true," said the old queen. "But we know of other roots, that when given later, take away the madness and renew life."

Cira looked deeply into Cystalen's eyes, to see if she could catch any sign or hint of deceit or dishonesty. She found none. "Not that I doubt your majesties intentions or words," she said. "But how do I know if you're telling me the truth about the other herbs."

Again the wrinkled lips of the regal lady smoothed and curved. "You don't, my girl. If you refuse to take the tattle root, you must be guilty, and you will die. If you take the drug and admit your guilt, again you will die. On the other hand if you take the root and prove your innocents you will live. It is as simple as that."

Ciramtis knew she had no choice. "What about Captain Odelac and the rest of his crew?" The queen adjusted the wide brass bracelet on her arm and looked at her nonchalantly. "They will live or die, depending on your testimony."

Cira handed her cup to Lavea. "Alright, I will take your poison." The queen's daughter left the room momentarily, returning with two earthen crocks, and a wooden bowl. She sat next to Cira, crushing the gnarled root in a mortar with a pestle. When it was totally powdered, Lavea poured some boiling water from one crock into the wooden bowl, stirring the liquid slowly.

The last of the lumps dissolved darkening the hot water a deep rust color. Three pieces of honeycomb, a few mint leaves and a few mulberries were added to the bowl of heated medicine. The brewed concoction was again macerated and stirred before being passed to Cira. The sorceress looked timidly down into the inky black liquid, said a few prayers and took her first sip.

It was very hot and bitter, leaving a heavy almost metallic after taste in her mouth. The aroma was that of rotting vegetation. The smell immediately started to make her gag. Gathering all her courage, she took a deep breath and drank the remains of the liquid quickly.

"That is right dear, drink it all." Those were the last words Ciramtis remembered. The dirt floor seemed to move and her vision of the queen distorted and swayed along with the hypnotic wicks of the oil lamps. Numbness came over her like a cold blanket, leaving her in a paralyzed semi-comatose state. Her muscles began trembling uncontrollably.

The vourtre princess put her arms around Cira, and helped lower her to the carpet. Cira's head rested in Lavea's lap until the delirium tremors eased. The interrogation began as soon as Ciramtis's pupils dilated fully. She could not move anything but her eyelids and lips, as she answered each question in dull soft monotones.

Chapter # 16
Cystalen Queen of the Vourtre

Odelac paced about or stood in the doorway of their jail for over a zestar. With Ciramtis gone, he didn't know what to do, or what steps he should take. The men had already discussed the possibilities of escape after Myritt's burial. There did not appear to be many options and escape would only come if they were taken out of this village and sold into slavery. The captain was beginning to think that the vourtre had killed her anyway, in spite of their promise.

Watching out of the doorway, he saw two men turn the corner of a building down the street from where he stood. They carried a lifeless body on a stretcher between them and were walking slowly in his direction. A hard knot appeared and tightened in Odel's stomach the nearer they came. Cira was on it; her arms were folded over her abdomen. Her eyes were closed as she lay there rigid and motionless.

The captain's facial muscles tensed and hardened, as they carried her through the door. He couldn't see any wound, but there was no sign of life in her. Touching her hand, he found her skin stiff, cold, clammy and discolored. The bearers set her covered, near lifeless body on the ground near the rear wall. Both guards knew there was going to be trouble. They could see it in Odel's eyes and demeanor. The entrance guards cautiously backed out, while leveling their spears.

Odel stepped forward swatting the sharpened points aside, and cutting his hand. "She is not dead," said the guard! "She has only been drugged. Now back away before I have to stick this spear point clear through you." The other guard tossed a leather water bag into the room. "You are lucky she's strong. Not many survive the questioning, and fewer still prove their innocence." The two guards retreated slowly until they were outside. "When she wakes, you are free to leave."

Baradic jumped to his feet. "You mean all of us?"

The guard turned his spear point upward, leaning on the handle. "Yes, but the queen has asked that you spend the night and have food and drink before you do. She would also like to see the woman again when she regains some of her strength."

Three young vourtre women came up from behind the guard carrying trays of roasted fowl, fruit, assorted raw vegetables, and hot buttered bread. Karadis jumped up taking the first tray. He had half a bird devoured before anyone else could get to the door.

The men ate in silence while Odel tended to Cira. He poured water on a hand towel and washed her face and neck. Placing his ear to her chest gave him some reassurance. The captain could hear a slow steady heart beat. It was the only thing that convinced him, she was still alive.

Odelac could not eat until some color showed in Ciramtis's cheeks. The cloak that he laid over her helped, and some warmth could be felt returning to her hands and feet as he rubbed them.

"Captain." Odel looked up as the silence was broken. It was Vadeck that was speaking. "I still don't trust them," he said under his breath. "After all, they did kill poor Myritt without him ever having a chance to defend himself."

Baradic stepped over joining them. "I agree. We should leave this place now," he whispered. "That fool Myritt almost got the rest of us killed, and I do not want to give them a chance to change their minds."

Vadeck gave the deckhand a cold calculating glare. He didn't have to say anything more. Baradic closed his mouth and he sat back down out of the way. "Get me a piece of that fowl will you, and maybe a couple pieces of fruit," asked Odel?

Vadeck took his glaring eyes off Bara. "Right captain. I'll also set something aside for Cira. These athcas will not only pick that platter clean, they will slobber all over it and lick it." Karadis stood by the door eating and keeping a watchful eye on the movements outside. The sentries had left their post, but the Tarpenya's crew had decided to remain inside until the rest of the crowd dispersed.

"You two come over here." Karadis and Baradic walked over to Odel, Bara keeping Karadis between him and Vadeck. "I don't trust them either," Odelac said in a hushed tone. "If were supposed to be free, they should not stop us from leaving. I want the two of you to take a walk around the village. Find out what you can, and see if anyone tries to stop you from going any place in particular."

"If you are allowed to roam about freely, I want you to go and find our horses and wagon. If anyone questions you, tell them you want to fetch Ciramtis's medical bag. While you're there, get our weapons." Karadis wiped the picrican grease from his hands, and took a sip from the water bag. "You've got nothing to worry about captain. Come on Bara; let's go see if they kill us!" Baradic trembled, but he also knew if he stayed any longer inside the hut, he was going to have a fight with Vadeck.

Ciramtis opened her eyes a short time after they left. Her eyes rolled a bit and fluttered for a time, than they steadied as her vision cleared. She was sick to her stomach; after a sip of water she had to vomit. Odel and Vad helped walk her to the door. The fresh air helped, but did not stop the spasms. Her insides shook and all her muscles ached with cramps. No guard stopped them, and she looked about in wonderment. "What's a, where's a," she stammered?

Odel put his arm around her and helped her straighten up. "The guard said that we are free to go. I don't know what you told their queen, but what ever it was, she believed it."

Cira held on to him taking a few steps; her feet were still tingling and feeling a bit numb. "Captain, I can not remember the questions or the answers." She staggered a little, before her knees buckled. Odel tightened his grip around her waist steadying her.

"Thank you Odel! Where are Baradic and Karadis?"

Vadeck took a hold of her other arm. With her between the two the seamen, they walked her about until she felt like she could stand on her own. "They are out exploring the village. If you feel like it, we can take a walk and see if we can find the wagon. They are probably near it, or trying to locate our horses."

Cira's knotted muscles loosened as she walked and stretched. The wagon was not far from where they had been kept. It was two lanes over in a small clearing. "By the way Cira, I almost forgot to tell you. The queen would like to see you again before we leave."

She stopped a zesta and rubbed her temples. "I hope she does not have anything for me to eat or drink." They walked over and stood beneath a wide spreading tree for a few more zestas rest, after seeing how tired she was getting.

"I know that you're not feeling up to it right now, but I think you should see her as soon as possible. We have lost a man and a day, and we can't get back either. If we are to still have a chance of reaching the bridal party, we should start out before sunset."

Ciramtis took a few more steps, before turning to the captain. "That will only give us a little over two zestars. Why leave here now, just to find a campsite a few thastas down the road? It will probably take a zestar just to get an audience with Queen Cystalen. While we are waiting we can refill the water barrels and re-stack the provisions."

The captain nodded in agreement. "You're right Cira, but I still don't trust them, and would like to be out of here before my crew gets us into any more trouble."

She gave him a light pat on the forearm. "I can understand your apprehension, but that's my decision. I have decided to stay the night. If you wish to leave, I'll meet up with you and your shipmates further down the road tomorrow morning. I should be able to make it to your camp by first lunch."

Odel's face reddened. "No Cira. I promised Valadis that I would watch over you and keep you safe for him. I will stay right here, and so will the men."

She took a half step closer toward him, all the while watching his eyes. "What do you mean safe for him?"

Odel could not look at her and diverted his eyes. He looked down at his boots and stammered like a bashful teenager. "You know what I mean. You and he, you're his woman." His face reddened again this time a little deeper. Vadeck knew it was time for a hasty retreat. He knew his captain well enough to know how uncomfortable it was for him to be speaking with a member of the opposite sex.

"I will be over at the wagon;" he yelled back at them and ran on ahead.

Ciramtis did not move, and wouldn't speak until he looked up at her. "Valadis is just a good friend, nothing more, and nothing less," she said. Taking his hand, the two of them walked together the rest of the way to the wagon.

Baradic and Karadis were sitting up against the rear wagon wheel. Vadeck stood by talking with them, and looking more relaxed. The two sailors were drunk, as were the two vourtre warriors they were sitting with. The four of them had been passing around a skin of strong lusverus red wine and singing old tavern tunes.

At seeing them, Odelac became fuming mad; the veins on his neck were protruding. He nervously swept away Ciramtis's hand stomping toward his crewmen. Vadeck sidestepped blocking his way, before Odel could speak.

"Captain, their not as drunk as they appear," he whispered. "They know what their doing, and they have their swords."

Karadis staggered to his feet pretending that he had, tripped over one of the vourtre's legs. "Captain, have a drink, he said in a slurred voice." He handed the wineskin to Odel, all the while keeping his back to the vourtre warriors. Odel tipped it back and took a long pull. Karadis lifted the front of the captain's tunic and he slipped a nine-inch dagger into his belt.

"Is that all you can drink when greeting a new friends?" Kar tossed the bag to Vadeck. "Here Vad! Show em how a man drinks when greeting a new friend." Vadeck tipped it back, drinking for the longest time. The dark red vintage ran down the sides of his cheeks as he swallowed. Karadis slipped a knife into Vad's belt while everyone watched him drink.

Odel stepped forward, slapping Karadis on the back. "Men, we are going to camp here for the night. Don't get too drunk, I want the wagon unloaded and repacked before sundown. We will be ridding at first light tomorrow morning."

Kar dropped back to the ground and passed the wineskin back to the nearest vourtre warrior. "Aye, sir."

Odel stepped closer to Vadeck and spoke to him in a subdued voice. "Stay here with the men and see to our horses. I will take Cira back and see if I can find out what else is going on."

Princess Lavea was waiting for them when they returned to their holding cell. She had a tray with and an earthen crock on it and an amber glass filled with a clouded white chalky liquid. "Here, take a few more sips of this. The antidote for tattla root, will settle your stomach. We were only able to get you to take a little of it before." Cira held it to her lips taking small sips. It had a very honey sweet taste. Her stomach cramped up making a knotted spasm, but she clenched her teeth and forced the rest of the heated liquid down.

It was mostly goats' milk, mint, cinnamon and honey, but it also had an aftertaste of some other unidentifiable bitter herbs. "Are you feeling well enough to see my mother?" Cira handed back her glass and put her hands on her abdomen. The drink formed gas bubbles and made her insides roll and tremble giving her a fluttering feeling and the need to belch.

"Yes, she said swallowing hard. I will go with you right now. Why don't you wait for me here Odel? It should not take that long." The Captain sat down outside of the doorway. He didn't like the idea of returning to the inside of the smelly holding cell. The two women walked off slowly with Cira hanging on to Lavea's arm for support.

When they arrived at the queen's chamber, she was given a hot cup of herbal tea with a honeycomb in it. It helped fight off the nausea and tasted rather good. The old queen watched her sip the blended beverage while, saying very little.

"Tattla always makes you humans sick. It takes a few zestars for the antidote to work fully, and you're going to have a queasy upset stomach for a few days." Lavea fetched a tray of small honeyed rice cakes containing lus raisins and seated herself next to Cira. Eneas, the senior officer that had captured and led them to the village, entered the dimly lit room and walked over where the old queen was sitting. Then he knelt before her and spoke to her softly, before lowering his head.

Queen Cystalan replied to his questions in a very soft patient voice, as she ran her fingers threw his hair. He didn't speak, and did not raise his eyes. She reached next to her and lifted a small wooden box, with both of her hands. Around the top of hardened burkat wood were the Kaybeck runes of an ancient prayer carved in high relief and inlaid with polished eston whale bone.

She handed him the antique coffer, and from it he removed a ring. The square cut diamonds in the silver band sparkled in the light of the lamp oil. Slipping it on his index finger, he extended his hand to her. She kissed the ring and said a silent prayer. Eneas quietly moved to her side and sat cross-legged next to her. Still he had not raised his head or acknowledged the other women's presence while the queen whispered to him in soft tones.

Ciramtis had also watched the ceremony without speaking. She now turned to Lavea. "I thought that she was going to reprimand him for killing our friend Myritt," she whispered. "Instead the queen gives him a reward."

Lavea looked at her a little surprised and astonished. "Why would our mother reprimand my brother, for killing the desecrator of our great grandfather's tomb?" Ciramtis could not answer. She shamefully forced a smile, looked away and reached for her teacup. Thinking that it was about time for her to crawl under the small rug, she decided to remain silent instead.

From across the carpet, Eneas looked up after his mother finished speaking. He now noticed the human female for the first time. Glaring at the sorceress he got to his knees, bowed to his mother and left the room. The old queen did not speak for a few moments. She had closed her eyes and did not see or hear him leave. Lavea refilled the teacups and they ate chasom, crumb cake while waiting for the queen mother to once again open her eyes.

"My children, time grows short for me in this lifetime." Eneas has been given the ring of kingship. There is only one thing I have wished to see in my lifetime, and that was to see freedom for Am Hass and the people. "Lavea, I have taught you everything that I have learned in the past one hundred and thirty years. I know that you will take care of our people, after I am gone. I leave you the sacred scrolls of life, and all my love."

Lavea bowed her head, while the old woman sang a bird like soft chanting prayer, then she closed her eyes once again. Ciramtis started to rise. Lavea reached over and held on to her elbow. "The queen is not finished yet," she whispered.

Cystalen opened her eyes again, ever so slowly. "When I was a child, my great grand mother used to tell me stories of how our family served the lord of the horned red dragon. Great grandfather was even given one of his rings for valiant service. All my life I have dreamed that I would be fortunate enough to serve him. Now when my life is all but over, he returns. I have Eneas's promise that he will serve the new lord. We may not be able to help in the great war that is yet to come, but we will do all we can to aide him."

"You are fortunate to be his friend, and to be as young as you are. I can see that you posses an inner spiritual power. You are a descendant of the Goddess Esella, through her daughter Colinda. I am a direct descendant of her through her son Darius, the father of trees. The staff of Colinda was made from the wood of the first trees to grow on Palestus. We are therefore relatives, even though you are human and I be vourtre."

Cystalen raised her hand, and a warrior entered with Cira's staff. She had thought that she had lost it forever near the rockslide. The guards had taken it away when they were captured, and she had not seen it since. The sentry approached the queen, knelt, and placed the staff in her hands. Closing her eyes she clutched the staff tightly. It glowed brighter and brighter, coming to life.

Cystalen's face changed from the light green shaded color of the vourtres, to an ashen grey like the stone she sat upon. Her eyes flickered opened once more, her lips managing a smile. "That is all the power that I can give you, may it help you in times of difficulty."

The queen leaned back and slumped against the back rest of her throne, her voice now weak and shallow. "Lavea, help me to my bed. You will have to start preparing the feast in honor of Eneas, the new King of Am Hass."

Standing quickly Lavea went to her mother's side and helped support her. "Ciramtis, you should return to your shelter. Bedding will be sent for your comfort. Tonight your presence will be required at the feast and the crowning ceremonies. It is our custom to share our times of joy with honored guests. Being a distant relative you will give my brothers coronation an added prestige, a vourtre king has not had in many years."

Two servant women came in and helped the queen from her seat. "Thank you, I am honored that you have asked. May I bring my friends?"

Lavea hesitated for a zesta and thought about the question before answering. "Yes, but try to keep them out of trouble. There are some in the village that still want their blood."

Ciramtis left the audience chamber and went straight to the shelter that had been their cell. A rope latticed bed, blankets and a small sitting table had been added. On it rested a bowl of fruit plus a fresh water and wine skin along with several wooden cups. Odel sat at one of the stools eating a fresh semedia pear. He was relieved to see her. She told him of the coronation plans and asked him to join her.

"No thanks," he replied. "I have got to see to the men and horses. With the amount of wine at these celebrations, it is going to be difficult to keep them in line. If we are to leave at first light, I don't want anything delaying us. We are still leaving in the morning aren't we?"

Ciramtis smiled at the questioning look he gave her. "Of coarse we are. Now I would like to get some sleep. Why don't you go down to the wagon and check on what ever you need to." She could hear a relieved exhale come from him as he walked off.

Chapter # 17

Theisiah, Prince of Yoja

Traga's men worked themselves into a state of near exhaustion. They had slept little and had ten tarmegs of supplies to stow during a heavy rainstorm. The ships pitched bow to stern with the swell of the waves, but held steady to their moorings at the pier.

On occasion they would lose a gangway and some supplies but at least they were able to throw the men ropes and pull them from the water, before they were crushed between the ships hulls and the pier pylons. It was an unusually strong gale for the end of first summer. Most of the men not loading the vessels were thankful for the rain none the less.

Everro and Diezra the last two months of spring were extremely dry this year. This storm would fill the lowlands with the much-needed water before Vergus, the month of drought. The cursing and swearing was plentiful. No one liked being out in this weather but there were no choices.

The provisions had to be loaded as quickly as possible to prevent water damage, and spoilage. Agar had divided their wares and goods into equal parts, and had them delivered to the wharfs in front of each ship. They were carried aboard and loaded onto the holds as soon as they arrived.

While the cargo was being loaded, and stowed away Agar took two stratas of men with him back to the grand market. With the addition of Marshall Ebestar's warriors, more provisions had to be procured. Ebestar's men were already helping with the loading and stowing of freight for the cargo ship, Gleggas.

As each shop was bought out, carts laden to the top with supplies would race to the piers. The docks were starting to become overly congested. Kytos knew he had to acquire a third ship, and had been in negotiating sessions all morning with Captain Rom Ocsia of the Hesboth.

She was an aged Yojan war freighter that was in need of a lot of superficial repairs. There was nothing Kytos could do or say that would persuade owner into renting the ship at a fair price. The captain just would not agree to anything or make any concessions.

Rom Ocsia demanded a rental price of eighteen large gold pieces. Kytos did not have any choice but to break off the negotiations, saying that he had to get approval at such a high cost. Kytos left the smug captain standing at his own bridge. Rom Ocsia didn't mind waiting. He knew that his ship was the only one in the harbor that could meet the capacity and sailing schedules that had been asked.

Kytos rode as quickly as possible back to the command post staging area. The Oppowian Prince was ashamed and hated to admit his failure, but he had to inform Commander Traga. Explaining the circumstances and what had transpired during the negotiations brought Traga to the same conclusion as Kytos. They were being taken for fools, and there didn't seem to be any way around it.

The Hesboth had just been sold recently at auction for approximately thirty-two thousand coppers. This captain wanted over fourteen thousand coppers for the rental of his ship to make the ten to twelve day crossing to Zarhun. Kytos watched the older man rub his head, scratch his neck and rock back in his chair. Commander Traga leaned forward quickly planting the legs his seat squarely on the floor. "Get me pen and parchment."

Traga's aide ran off and returned quickly, with a wooden correspondence box. Taking out a new blank sheet of the heavily textured parchment, and the ink bottle, Traga began to write quickly with the quill and signing his name to it with a scrawling flare. "Read this then deliver it to Marshall Ebestar as quickly as you can." Traga got up from his table and chair and left before Kytos could finish reading it.

It was orders asking Marshall Ebestar to assemble his men and have them march to the western pier where the Hesboth was berthed. If Kytos had known the commander better he wouldn't have been so worried. The whole ride over to Ebestar's camp Kytos thought Traga was going to seize the ship by force, and hang Captain Rom Ocsia from the yardarm.

Ebestar unrolled the scroll and read it quickly. He asked no questions and made no comments. "Have all officers notified to form squares," he said to his aide. He then struck a flint and burned the letter. Kytos remained with Ebestar, and watched the small army assemble. Over seven hundred more recruits had arrived since the first call to arms. It was the first time that Kytos had ever seen a professional army form ranks. He was surprised at how efficiently and orderly it was.

Each santax had four stratas forming a perfect square. Five santaxes formed the front of the battle square. The second tadleta formed ranks behind the first, and the remaining four hundred men formed into two over strength sataxes bringing up the rear. The first tadleta began to move, after a thirty pace gap, the second tadleta began to move. Another thirty pace separation and the rest of the warriors and auxiliaries fell in behind following the main body.

There was no resistance as they moved out and onto the pier. Other than the normal amount of spectators, and people hanging out of windows waiving goodbye, everything seemed normal, almost too normal. From Ky's vantage point he could not quite see what was going on ahead of him. He was slightly behind and to the left of the first tadleta. The men appeared to be boarding the Hesboth and stowing their gear. There was no trouble, no complaining, and not even any shoving.

Ky nudged his mount forward riding up to the pier and stopping opposite the gangplank. This is where he found Marshal Ebestar speaking with Commander Traga. Captain Rom Ocsia was nowhere to be seen, nor where any of his shiftless seamen. The only crewmembers aboard the ship were sailors, marines and deckhands that had been selected from Traga's tadleta of the Red Dragon Army.

Ky dismounted, tied off his mount's reins and walked over where the other officers stood as they shouted out orders. "Commander what happened to Captain Rom Ocsia and his scurvy crew?" Traga motioned him to be quiet and to wait a zesta.

"As I was saying Ebes, she will hold your first two tadletas comfortably; the remaining troops and any additional recruits will have to sail on one of the other merchantmen, probably the Merimon. It will be the last ship to leave the harbor. The Gleggas has already been loaded and has provisions for twelve hundred men. You will find her on the tenth western dock. Captain Agar will be sending more supplies there as soon as he can procure them."

Marshal Ebestar gave Commander Traga a salute, even though he held a superior rank. "Thank you for the confidence and trust commander. I will see that our lord's standards are raised over both of his ships. I also want to thank you for the honor of commanding our lord's flagship in its first battle." They embraced briefly, both saying at the same moment, "Death to Helidon King of Envar."

Ebestar strode up the gangway calling out to Captain Psydak and Captain Azt. His most trusted officers where standing near the main mast. They finished giving the watch orders and last minute instructions to a group of seaman before joining him at the rail. They conferred briefly before Captain Psydak headed down the gangway leading in the direction of the Merimon's berth. Captain Azt and Marshal Ebestar gave a wave to Traga and strode toward the poop deck and ship's officers quarters.

"What's going on commander?" Traga smiled widely showing all of his teeth.

"Well after you told me of Captain Rom Ocsia's antics, I could see there was no sense in dealing with him. I went to the merchant's bank instead. I purchased Rom Ocsia's loan agreement from them for thirty-five thousand coppers. They were happy to sell it to me for a three thousand copper profit. As soon as they were able to write up the ownership papers, my first official act as holder of the loan was to demand payment in full from Captain Rom Ocsia.

He could not pay it of course and I was forced to take ownership. I then order him from the bridge and fired his crew." Ky's smile matched the one on Traga's face, and they both had a good laugh. Kytos now knew why Lord Jedaf had chosen this man to be his confidant and commander of his army. "Come on Ky, we should ride back to my house and see if we can get a hot meal. We will soon be living out of a sack, eating dried fruits, jerky and hardtack by a campfire. We should get at least one more good meal before sailing."

Thirty-five to forty guards from the royal Yojan Army of the Red were standing post outside of Traga's home. The commander put his finger to his lips. "No talking until were inside the house," he said softly. They dismounted and tied off their horse's reins on the steel ring set into the mortar wall at the courtyard entrance.

The sentries, standing post at the gate stood to attention while a second grade officer ran over to greet them. He blocked their way to the rear kitchen door and saluted. "This way commander," he said as he re-directed them around the house.

Traga did not comment; he just followed after the junior officer. They were escorted beneath the wide shade trees down the rear garden dividing path, toward Myra's secluded social gathering area. They ducked below the pergola truss uprights, past the family's tables and chairs and exited the gardens at a taller side gate which had a decorative transom.

The men walked around the side of the house where another four escorts fell in closely behind them. Kytos felt very uneasy as he nervously looked about. Traga could read his thoughts and see the apprehension on the young boy's face. "Don't worry about it," was all he said as they reached the front entrance. Lifting the latch the lieutenant stood off to the side allowing them to enter the hallway. The rear guards stood to attention blocking the exit while to officer quietly closed the door behind them.

Seated at the table in the dining area were all the members of Traga's family. Captain Agar sat at the far end of the table with his younger brother Trestan next to him. His face was rigidly tense, and his eyes denoted a fierce anger. He said nothing as did Traga's sister; neither Erthea, her daughter Sarasa nor Traga's wife Myra. They were all seated close together at one side; the chairs at the ends of the table had been removed. The seats on the opposite side had been occupied but were now empty.

Traga's trained eye had not only noticed the wet rings on the table from the missing ale mugs, he noticed that Agar's sword was not in its scabbard, nor was there a knife handle protruding from his weapons belt. Axeth; Lord Jedaf's twelve year old servant stood behind Myra as if protecting her from the rear. He also appeared to be unarmed standing with his hands at his side. All of the women kept silent with their eyes lowered, and with their chins down.

Traga suspected that they had been warned not to speak. Two fourth class guards stood near the fireplace, and a first grade officer stood near the table, slightly behind Agar. The three were all sipping ale when Traga and Kytos entered the room. The first grade officer acknowledged their presents by placing his hand on the hilt of his knife. "Sire, the commander has returned," shouted one of the other guards!

Axeth shifted his weight noticeably, allowing Traga to see a glint of sharp steel hidden in the folds of his cloak. Traga slowly shook his head, looking in the opposite direction.

"I am not deaf," yelled back a voice from the kitchen. Kicking the door open with his boot. The drunkard staggered out sloshing his ale and spilling half a mug on the floor. It was Second Officer Theisiah, King Vestrak's obnoxious youngest son.

The prince stood for a moment swaying from side to side and sneering at Traga. He was no longer dressed in the uniform of a second grade officer. His clothing was of the finest white silk with his leather trimmed tunic having the epaulets of a Grand Marshall in the Red Army of the Dragon. A silver ceremonial sword and dagger hung from his weapons belt. It looked like there were more precious stones on them, than braided leather grip.

About his neck and diagonal weapons belt support were chains of gold and ribbons of honor, as well as medals of commendation and broaches designating meritorious service. Traga gave the medallions a fleeting glance. Most of the campaign ribbons and medals were awards for battlefield engagements that had occurred long before Theisiah's birth.

"What is the meaning of this Theisiah? Are you and the Yojan Kingdom declaring war on the Lord of the Semedian Red Dragon and his army?" Theisiah stood his ground for a moment pondering the situation. He had not thought the commander would have taken his actions that seriously. After all he was a prince of the royal Yojan household and Traga was merely a lowly peasant warrior.

Taking another sip from his tankard he said in a slurred intoxicated voice, "Not at all my dear Traga. Who said anything about war?" Standing eye to eye with the commander he took another sip. "I just thought that since we are about to go off on a campaign against my fathers old enemy King Magarus and the Worezian people, that you should know who is really in command of these forces."

Reaching into his tunic, he removed an elaborately decorated folded parchment and handed it to Traga. It had a raised royal Yojan crested seal of silver arrows embossed into the fabric. The old warrior broke the wax seal and read the written decree out loud.

"Be it known, that on this second day of Asursa in the first year of Virros's sixth age. That I King Vestrak, Lord of the Yojan Kingdom, do here by take personal command of Lord Jedaf of Dolfi's Army in his absence. With the imprisonment of the Lord of the Red Dragon, I do here by designate and promote Prince Theisiah of Yoja to the rank of Grand Marshall, and charge him with the responsibilities of command. All Semedian, Yojan and Envarian Officers not willing to abide by these orders are to be beheaded along with all their family members."

The proclamation was signed; Vestrak, most high Lord and King of Yoja. A golden colored silken ribbon and large red wax seal was melted and attached at the bottom right, with the impressions of the Yojan Lord's crest of two crossed barbed arrows with white semedia pear blossoms at each side. Traga carefully folded the officer's commission and handed it to Kytos, to read for himself.

"Since you are now in charge and have taken command, Grand Marshal Theisiah, I suggest you let me fill you in on all orders, troop movements and the progress we have made this morning."

Theisiah hadn't expected Traga's response and was taken slightly aback. He knew that a soldier of Traga's age lived to take orders, and didn't question them. This loyalty and fortunate compliance was almost unbelievable, but before he could think the matter through, Traga was already giving directions.

Ordering his family from the room, he told Myra to fetch more ale for the Grand Marshal, Kytos, and himself. They moved quickly as Traga started filling in Theisiah about the armies provisioning and directing him toward a seat at the head of the table.

"We will be sailing with the morning tied, and of course you will have to sail with me. Most of the other senior officers will be sailing with the Merimon. It will be the last ship out, and rendezvous, later in the day with the other vessels just outside the harbor." Theisiah accepted another refill from Myra and relaxed a little. It was going to be easier than he thought.

"Very good, Commander Traga, I am glad to see there are no hard feelings about this matter. You have done well for a commoner, and for that you shall be promoted to the rank of marshal."

"We can not have an Envarian Marshal and not a Semedian Marshall." Traga said, "Thank you sire," over the rim of his tankard. Theisiah leaned far back in his chair rocking on the rear legs once more. By this time Traga thought it would be nice if this drunkard fell backward breaking his neck.

"Now that a member of the royal family has been placed in charge, I know that more intelligent and rational decisions will be made before we are engaged in any battle." Agar's face reddened once again and tightened noticeably at Theisiah's comment. Traga gave him a stern glare; it was enough of a warning.

"As you say sire," said Traga. "Will your guards of honor be accompanying you to the ship, or shall I send a strata of Semedian warrior escorts, for your personal protection? After all we hope to be sailing on or about the sixth zestar."

Theisiah staggered to his feet. "No Marshall Traga. Thank you for the offer, but my men will conduct me to the ship. We don't have to sail that early. The eighth or ninth zestar ought to be plenty early enough to start this war."

Traga gave him a salute, "As my lord commands. The ship will be awaiting your royal presents, and will be ready to sail by the eighth zestar." Theisiah nodded his consent and stumbled toward the hallway. His first officer moved quickly to the prince's side, giving him a little support. The two bodyguards stepped forward and followed closely behind the prince protecting his back. The other two junior officers paused a zesta, then left the house and closed the door quietly behind them.

"Father, how could you say?" Traga slammed his brass mug down with a bang, quieting Agar. It was hard enough to make them all jump and it bent the handle sloshing the ale out. He wiped the froth from his mouth, and swept the tankard from the table with the back of his hand. The mug hit the wall spraying the rest of its contents. All that remained was a deep smile embedded in the wooden table from the tankards edge.

They watched speechlessly as the anger left Traga's face. "Axeth, see to the door!" The boy sheathed the dagger that he had been hiding and ran off. From the threshold he could see that the stoop at the front portico, and the sidewalks were empty. The street was dark but he didn't see anyone within fifty paces. "They've gone master," yelled back Axeth!

"Good," said Traga. "Sit outside on the step and see that no one comes back to surprise us."

Agar waited until he heard the door shut before speaking. "What do you think Marshal Ebestar will do when he finds out that another royal dung pile is in command?"

Traga was only paying slight attention to Agar. His mind was elsewhere. He was watching his wife Myra on her hands and knees cleaning up the floor and wall. "Nothing," he said softly. "I do not plan on telling him anything before we anchor at North Point. By that time the problem will have gone away."

Agar leaned over toward his father a little closer lowering his own voice. "Have you come up with an answer?" Traga was not listening again. Myra walked by him with an arm load of wet towels. Traga hooked his arm around her waist and pulled her onto his lap, kissing her full on the lips.

"You old drunken fool," she managed to say, before he knocked the wet towels from her arms. Then he stood still holding her in his arms and he carried her away. "Leave the mess to remember me." She clung to his neck as they mounted the hallway stairs to the upper floors.

Agar looked at the others. "I guess that means lights out, I will see you in the morning."

Chapter # 18

The Fleet of the Dragon Lord

Traga gave Myra a last kiss and hug, holding her for a long time. The last time he had gone off to war on a campaign, he had come home without their youngest son. Closing his eyes he tried to picture Trestan's young face once more. Then felt all the worst for trying. The face that came into focus was the scared and weather beaten face of a malnourished slave that Lord Jedaf had returned to him and his wife.

His son was only sixteen the day before the last battle; they still did not know what he had gone through during his capture and imprisonment. Trestan had not told anyone about his experiences and they were too ashamed and afraid to ask him. Myra had been reading his thoughts while they hugged. A tear formed at the corner of her eye, and she quickly wiped it away. Traga whispered in her ear before they parted. "At least this time I will not be taking away Agar with me, and Trestan will remain home."

Myra shoved him away, the tears flowing more freely. She made no sound but she had to bite her lower lip a moment to keep it from trembling. "You would think this was the first time that you've gone off to war, the way you are squeezing the life out of me." Traga stepped closer taking her hands in his, then he leaned slightly forward kissing her lightly on the lips. She closed her eyes and let his hands go.

Traga left her standing there and walked over to his sister Erthea and this niece Sarasa. They were both crying quietly and he put his arms around the both of them at once, giving each a kiss on the forehead. He said his goodbyes and walked off toward the front door. They all knew he would not stop or turn to look back.

Kytos had spent the night in the guest room and he stood by while the family said their goodbyes. He thought of his own family, and all that had happened to him since leaving them. Not knowing just what he should do, he said timidly; "Thank you for all your hospitality," and turned to leave.

Myra ran over to him and kissed his cheek. "Take care of yourself son and come back to us soon." Erthea came over and also gave him a kiss. She did not say anything but took her sister-in-law's hand and led Myra from the room.

Sarasa stood her ground watching him, and he stood watching her. Neither made a move until they heard the door shut. Then Ky stepped closer as did she. They stood eye to eye not speaking. Ky's mouth was so dry he thought if he said something now, it was going to sound like a squeak. Sarasa closed her eyes and pointed her chin slightly upward, pursing her lips. Ky took a half step closer, wrapped his arms a round her giving her a long hard kiss.

Then he remembered Traga, let her go quickly and made a mad dash for the door. He did not look back either, he couldn't bear to see her tears. The commander had been waiting patiently holding the reins to their horses. He knew Kytos had become as close as anyone could, and still not be family. Goodbyes were hard on everybody.

They rode silently toward the docks, each lost in their own thoughts. Traga could not help but think, what will become of them. This war that he was hurrying to would probably be his last. He certainly was not getting any younger and, he expected to be out numbered ten to one in the up coming battle.

Officer's call was set for the fourth zestar at a small inn adjacent to the docks. Captain Drayus had rented all the rooms two days before the ships were to sail. The upper rooms were the officer's quarters, and the lower dining area had been turned into the war room. Window shutters had been closed and a guard posted outside of each. No one could come into or go from the inn without a written pass from Captain Drayus or Commander Traga.

The morning meeting was to be a very short one for security reasons. It was to be a good general get aquatinted meeting for most of the junior officers, followed by a quick strategy meeting for the senior officers. Each junior officer was introduced to the assemblage and given an envelope to be opened, after the ship they had been assigned had cleared the harbor. The senior officers were given a similar envelope, and an additional one to be opened in the event that their ship was separated from the other two vessels.

The first ship scheduled to leave the harbor was the Hesboth. The old Yojan war freighter was not as trim as the Gleggas, or the Merimon. Its four masts were all square rigged and she rode low in the water. It would be hard handling in the shallows of the harbor, and needed the tide at its highest to clear the far reef.

At its helm and in command of its armed forces was Commander Dimekon, a weather hardened mariner of more than forty years. He was the officer that had devised and carried out the evacuation of the surviving Envarian forces from North Point.

All troops of the third Green Army of the Envar owed him their life and would gladly fight to the death for him. This was going to be the flagship for the new Lord, and it would carry more than half the army and supplies. It took the contents of two warehouses to fill the lower holds with feed for the six stables of horses equipping the cavalry.

Two thousand men and at least two hundred horses were not going to be controlled easily. That was why Dimekon was put in charge. Captain Psydec would be subordinate to him and would be responsible for the ship's marines and the footmen at arms. Marshal Ebestar had been true to his word, at the topsail flew the flag of the Semedian Red Dragon. He would be sailing on the Hesboth and would be in charge of all three ships once they had cleared the harbor.

The cargo freighter Gleggas would be the next to set sail. They were to leave the docks shortly after the Hesboth. The Gleggas would be carrying about fifteen hundred cramped Envarian footmen. They along with the ship's marines would be under the command of Captain Azt. She was a wide beamed, four decked merchantmen with one bank of oars that would be manned in rotational shifts by the footmen.

The fore and aft castles gave her the appearance of being top heavy, but that was not her worst problem. She was square rigged fore and main, but lateen rigged on her mizzen. The top gallant of the main mast was in need of repair, and the inner and outer jibs had more repairs than virgin canvas. Her wide beam and rounded bottom was going to make her, the slowest of the three ships.

Extra canvas had been purchased to rig flying jibs, if the ships captain could manage it. They were also going to try to rig a topmast staysail and a topgallant staysail. Marshall Ebestar had chosen Captain Ramanan as the ships captain. He had also been one of the few officers that had helped in the North Point evacuation. For a sea captain he was soft spoken. He did not have to yell to get his men moving. There were others that could do that for him.

What he asked for was carried out at once and without question. None were respected more than he, and he had earned it. His right eye had been burned out because he had dared question Prince Quayot's decision to attack with all his forces. All his men knew this, and admired him for his courage. It was his thought to buy the additional canvas. She would need every inch of it just to run with the Hesboth.

The cargo ship and freighter, Merimon would be the last to sail. It would carry eight hundred Semedian warriors under the command of Captain Drayus, plus four hundred remaining Envarian warriors under the Command of First Officer Eggolis. The ships compliment and crew were to be under the command of sea Captain Cliedeous.

Commander Traga had chosen Cliedeous. Not because he was well liked, which he wasn't, nor because of his many crossings to Zarhun. It was because Traga knew that he had been, and still was, one of the best smugglers of the Eastern Sea of Tenolfo. If they were to be set upon by barbarians, pirates, or the Worezian battle fleet. There was no one who knew the shallows or the reefs better.

This was the ship Traga and the new Grand Marshall Theisiah would sail on. It was the fastest and most maneuverable of the three.

She was the same length as the Gleggas, but was narrower by a fifth of her beam. Having only three decks and no oars, she cut through the sea with hardly any effort. In case of trouble this vessel was to be the first to engage, giving the others time to run.

Traga had two additional catapults installed on her with twenty extra barrels of tarred cinder ball ammunition. With her speed she could cut across the front of any warship and pelt their bowsprit and foresails with enough fireballs to keep half a crew busy. She was to sail shortly after the sixth zestar, but Theisiah's interference had changed that. Commander Traga had given orders to Marshall Ebestar, that should the Merimon, fail to meet outside of the harbor by the tenth zestar; he was to sail for Envar along with the Gleggas.

Dismounting at the Red Dragon's Inn, which had been renamed by Captain Drayus, and the other officers, Traga handed the reins to Ledric his aide, and walked inside. The inn was empty except for Captain Drayus and four junior officers. They stood and saluted upon his entering. Everyone else had sailed, or had left for the pier. "Relax gentlemen, and finish your tea. We may have to wait a long time for Grand Marshall Theisiah."

All that remained were to sail on the Merimon. It was nearing the ninth zestar, and they still had not seen any sign of him. They would be loosing the tide in another zestar if he failed show. "Captain Drayus, get the men aboard. We will sail without him."

Drayus looked to the others before replying. "I am sorry sir. We can not do that! Marshall Theisiah has Yojan royal guards on the docks. They have orders not to let any officer board the ship until the Grand Marshal arrives." The jugulars on Traga's neck protruded once more, while his jaws and teeth clenched tighter.

"Very well, we will wait for him at the gangway." None of them dared speak while they walked to the wharf. They all felt that if one were to say something it would be like breaking a dike. All preparations had been made for sailing. Captain Cliedeous had been there since first light. He could not board, but no one said anything about yelling orders over to his crew. When Commander Traga arrived, he stood at his side and told his crew that the moment Theisiah sets foot on the deck; they were to cut the mooring lines. There wouldn't be time to haul in the hawsers.

A sailor high in the rigging yelled and pointed to the south. A great procession was coming toward them. Kettle drums and trumpets blared louder and louder. People came running from the shops and their homes to see what the fanfare was all about. Fifty guards of the royal cavalry dressed in their finest led and cleared the way. Crowds formed on both sides of the street straining their neck to be the first to see who was in the parade.

Following the mounted royal guard was King Vestrak's marching band, personal musicians, troubadours, jugglers and entertainers. At the end of the procession was the royal barouche. The decorated, double seated, white doeskin leather, carriage was drawn by four impeccably groomed, white steeds. Each horse had their manes braided with green and gold silken ribbons. They were skirted in bolts of embroydered and scalloped, yellow silks and having polished harnesses trimed in gold.

Prince Theisiah was standing and waiving to the downtrodden masses. This was what they were waiting for. It was not to honor a member of the pampered royal household. They were there simply to fetch a few coins that he would be throwing to the crowd. The commoners didn't have to wait long. The shouts and screams of the spectators scrambling for coppers announced his arrival at the docks. "Alright, he is finally here. Snap to attention when the carriage stops. We don't need any more problems."

After he had thrown his last handful of coppers, Theisiah's barouche slowed to a halt along with the loud cheers of the crowd. Inflated with pride, and his own importance, he gave one more sweeping waive and stepped from the carriages rear seat. His personal bodyguards flanked him quickly keeping the soiled fingers of the worthless from the prince's silks

If one of the rabble or urchins were able to touch him, the guard knew he would lose one of his hands. The Yojan prince approached the gangway as his bodyguards cleared the way. Four members of the royal family clustered about him, hanging on his every word. A retinue of ten personal servants brought up the rear, carrying a wagon full of trunks and personalized luggage.

The grand marshal gave Traga and the other officers a fleeting glance and a haughty nod, acknowledging their salute, but not returning one. The entire group of royals walked straight up the gangway, going immediately below deck to the main cabin.

It was exactly what Traga had hoped for. He and the other officers ran aboard going to their assigned tasks. Traga and Captain Cliedeous heard the axes fall and the ship swayed slightly as its mooring lines fell away and the pilot boats started towing the war ship from the docking facilities to deeper water.

It was nearing the tenth zestar with most of the tide gone. Captain Cliedeous knew that they were going to have to tack two to three times just to clear the harbor. He was thankful that he had been put in command of the Merimon. Neither of the other two ships could have cleared the reefs leaving this late.

Ebestar was true to his orders, for the topmen could see the two other ships setting their topgallants, heading for the open sea. It would take the Merimon at least two zestars more too clear the harbor, and another three to catch up with them. Traga and Cliedious stood at the bow, with the salty spray in their face. For awhile its coolness kept down Traga's anger. It was rising again with each tack of the ship.

For every three thastas they sailed east or west, they only made only one thasta forward. Traga did not like the sea and never would. He liked good solid dirt beneath his feet, it did not move every time he thought of taking a step. He knew it was the gods' way of playing a joke on him. Everyone else was able to move about without staggering.

In the far distance he could still see the top sails of the Hesboth. The Merimon came hard over to starboard and Traga had to grip the rail once more. Captain Cliedeous turned toward Traga giving him a smile. At first Traga thought he was going to laugh at him until, he realized why he was smiling. They had finally cleared the harbor and were heading east around the northern tip of the Dolfinian Continent. Traga smiled back at Captain Cliedious, he knew his time had come.

Turning around Traga gave second Officer Tymorat a wave of his arm.

The Second Officer had been standing at the entrance of the companionway door to the lower deck. With him he had ten hand picked mean and nasty looking convict warriors. They went below bringing up the ten servants and the luggage that had just arrived. The men as well as the travel bags were weighted with chains and tossed over the side. No one was spared. Their screams were not heard. Each sank quickly with the ballast at their feet. Some of the sailors were not happy about the decision. It was not right to let them die that way. Even some pirates sold their captives.

Traga did not like the orders he had given either, and he knew that he would have to live with this decision the rest of his life. He did not have any choice. Attendants for these royal households had been serving these monarchs and their immediate families for many generations. Like their fathers and their fathers before them, they had sworn an oath to give their lives protecting the members of the imperial family.

While these events were taking place, Prince Theisiah and his four friends had remained in the main cabin drinking, playing cards and gambling. They were left alone until Captain Cliedeous ordered the sails set and called the entire crew to stand amidships to witness punishment.

The trumpet call for assemblage brought the royals up from below. Theisiah was quite annoyed at first, and complained about the amount of the noise. Naturally he had been winning and his pockets were stuffed full of silver coins. His facial expressions changed to all smiles as he stepped out on deck. Seeing the assemblage he knew they had gathered to pay him homage, and pledge their allegiance to him.

He could not have been more wrong! The moment the gentry were all on deck, Officer Tymorat's men stepped forward and knifed the princes two personal bodyguards. The arms of all the others were held tightly preventing them from drawing their weapons. Theisiah yelled and screamed at Traga while the bodies were cleared from the deck.

His four friends stood as still as stone. They could not help anyone, and knew that they were about to die. Second Officer Tymorat tied Prince Theisiah's hands behind him, and striped him of his jewelry. Then the junior officer emptied all the coins from the prince's pockets. "No sense using silver for ballast," he joked until he saw the scowl on Traga's face.

The marshal was not amused and Tymorat knew it. Slipping off to the side he melted into the group of junior naval officers. He knew that Traga would be having a talk with him later. The coinage and valuables would be confiscated and added to the general seamen's fund.

Theisiah was raving mad, cursing everyone, and trying to kick anyone within his reach. Two of the deck hands stepped forward and grabbed the prince, while two others cut the clothing from him. Standing totally naked before the assemblage, Prince Theisiah froze. There was fear in his wide eyes, terror on his face and his lips were trembling. "Please, don't kill me. I will give you anything you want. I won't tell anyone."

Captain Drayus stepped forward, with his knife drawn. "I told you what was going to happen to you if you betrayed Master Jedaf."

"I did not betray him," screamed Theisiah! "It was my father, he made me do it!" The Prince of Yoja started whining and pleading for his life. It didn't do any good. Captain Drayus swept Theisiah's kicking leg aside stepping closer to him. A quick flash of the sharp blade put a six-inch long gash in Theisiah's upper chest. Drayus knew that he had made a good deep cut. He had felt the bones and cartilage of the young prince's ribs vibrate through the knife hilt.

Grand Marshal Theisiah screamed with the pain, and his legs started to wobble. The hot blood flowed freely; he could see it running down this chest. He was about to faint but another sailor stepped forward and stabbed him in the arm. The pain shot right through him, making his eyes bulge wider. "Stop, don't kill me!" He continued to scream again and again, as each member of the crew cut or stabbed him. Finally he fainted, thanking god for the end to his pain.

The Yojan Prince was wrong again! He was doused with salt water and kicked until he opened his eyes again. The cutting continued as well as the pain. No one sunk their knives in deep enough to damage a major organ. Some only cut an ear off, while others would stick their blades in his thigh giving it a good hard twist.

Theisiah finally stopped screaming, but jab after jab the blood letting continued. He did not have any feelings left; his body was deep in shock. Pleadingly he looked to Traga, he had suffered enough. In his eyes Traga could see he was begging for death.

The marshal unsheathed his sword placing its point upon Theisiah's sternum, "Death to traitors, and long live Semedia." Traga rammed home his point through the ribcage and heart. Theisiah didn't even move. His eyes stayed open, almost in defiance. The prince's regal friends had witnessed Theisiah's trial by Yara Zo.

The royal retinue had watched in horror, one of the cruelest forms of punishment and they knew that they were to follow. The Yojan flag of the green semedia pear tree in blossom was struck from the masthead. The royal banner was draped over the prince's body before it was weighted at the ankles and tossed overboard to the waiting serpents and sharks

Traga stepped before the prince's retainers, a wine bottle in his hand. "You men were not responsible for his actions and will not have to endure this type of punishment. I have here the drink of death." He held it out to them. "I give you each a choice. You can drink or go the headsman's axe." The first two reached for the bottle at the same time, drinking quickly. The third waited his turn with some dignity, drinking slowly, and passing the bottle to the last man.

The first two noble followers had fallen to the deck by the time the third had finished drinking. His eyes fluttered as he turned to Captain Drayus. "Death to peasant rabble," he said falling to his knees, then forward flat on his face. This middle aged snobbish aristocrat was lucky the poison had worked so quickly. Drayus pushed his knife back into his belt, looking at the last man standing.

This nobleman was a lot younger than the other three. The best guess Drayus could make about this bare faced youths age, was fifteen to sixteen years old. He had grown to full height but still had the gangly look of an adolescent. His silks were ill fitting and had the appearance that they had been made for an older teenager. Even this aristocrat's belt sash and sword scabbard were too big for him and extra holes had been added to cinch them snugly. It was a poor way for such a young man to die.

Tymorat stepped from the rear of the crowd. He had recognized the man before he had a chance to drink. "Wait, captain, this is my youngest brother." Captain Drayus stayed the man's arm, keeping him from drinking. "If Sinerat is to die, I must also." Traga knew Tymorat and had fought many years with this officer's father, Orantis. Orantis was the Duke of Western Tyne, and had been a friend and sponsor of Traga's family for many years.

Traga's father, Targen had served under the Duke as part of the Royal Guard of the Green, protecting the Villages of Tyne and the western provinces. His mother, Sahrasa was a hand maiden to the duchess. His parents had both been killed defending the royal coach from assassins. "Hold," said Traga. "Why is your brother amongst the scum of Theisiah?"

Tymorat turned and hugged his brother, speaking softly to him. Then he stepped before Traga and stood to attention. "Sir, my brother would like to speak for himself if it is permitted." Traga looked at Sinerat for the first time. This was no man. The boy could not have been over fifteen, but the teenager had more guts than most.

Traga gave his consent with a nod. "Sir I was ordered to go by our father. King Vestrak had asked each of the four western states to show their allegiance to him, by having each of them send a son to protect Prince Theisiah."

"My father could not offend the king, and all my other brothers were in Doretta on our fathers business. Knowing that the king was looking for any excuse to do away with my family and our estates, he had no choice but to ask me go." Traga knew that Simerat was telling the truth. That's how half of the noblest families of Yoja had lost their lands.

Traga turned to Tymorat. "Have your brother swear allegiance to our Lord Jedaf and enroll him into the army as a courier. Also inform him what will happen to him if he ever speaks of what he saw here today.

Turning about to the entire ships company, Traga addressed them as a whole. "Unfortunately the Worezian advanced forces were in the Village of Tenolfis at the North Point beachhead. We were ambushed upon landing. Each of us owes his life to Prince Theisiah and his retinue. It was a shame they had to sacrifice their lives to warn us. Isn't that right men?"

There were no further comments from the officers or crew members. The three bodies were stripped of their valuables before going over the side. Buckets of salt water washed away the pool of blood and the memories of their deaths from the deck. Everyone went about their assigned duties knowing they would be keelhauled if they ever mentioned a word concerning this punishment.

Chapter # 19

The Vellastran Pass

Ajoris gave Jedaf a light pat on the back as they rode up the valley. It was enough to arouse, but not startle him. Jedaf yawned, sat up straighter in the saddle and stretched. His back was aching from riding in a hunched over position, and his bladder felt like bursting. Ajor had ridden quietly at his side for the last few zestars and had kept the young man from falling off his saddle. A light misty rain started falling within moments of them breaking camp this morning and continued sporadically most of the day.

They only stopped to walk the horse in the midst of the heavier rains, and had to take cover beneath the trees during one torrential downpour. Neither of them had felt like stopping and they decided to ride or walk at a leisurely pace. They sipped wine and ate jerky and biscuits while on foot. It would have been nice to have a fire to warm them but everything about them was soaked, including their clothing.

Jedaf was so weary and bone tired that he had forgotten to thank Ajor for his help and advice. In addition to taking care of the horses, he had watched over the teenager and had made most of the decisions today. The Dragon Lord knew would never have made it this far if it had not been for the ambassador. For most of the day Jedaf had been in a depressed stupor, plodding along after the older man.

The clouds parted just long enough for them to see the suns finally nearing the edge of the horizon. Darkness was coming along with a cool crisp, blustery breeze from the east. Ajoris rode his horse between two large boulders that narrowed the muddy road, and dismounted.

To the side of the road was a deserted campsite that had been used by generations of travelers, but looked like it had not had a visitor for a long time. Rocks had been stacked around an abandoned fire circle that contained a few unburned chunks of coal but it was mostly filled with wet weeds. Nearby a few scraggily trees and part of a temporary stockade still stood. Its rails were covered with wild grape vine and a climbing thistle like plant.

Jedaf dismounted stiffly and walked into the bushes. Looking around the site as he relieved himself, he could see the remains of a lean-to and a half-buried refuse pit. Some wild animal had smelled it out long ago, and had dug it up looking for the scraps. "Ajor, how far have we come?" The Ambassador loosened the belly strap on his horse and pulled the saddle free. From where Jedaf stood he could see the salt streaks on Ajoris's wet horse.

"We have come a long way, lord." Ajor gave his mount a caressing stroke, on the side of its neck, and a few light pats. Easy girl, he removed the bridle bit, and tied a long leather lead to the ring below the horse's neck. "If you take a walk over that grassy rise, you should be able to see the fire lights of Adathe."

Ajor walked over and tied his mounts leader on the post of the old stockade, and went to take care of Jedaf's horse. "We should arrive at the west gate tomorrow evening, in time to get a good hot meal, and a bath." Jedaf walked up the hill. To the far northeast, he could see an immense black panorama just below the horizon. It had to be the Sea of Askalus.

A twinkling at its edge of the ocean was Adathe, the capital City of Cathon. It was the last great sea faring kingdom and the only one which had been able to remain neutral during the last three wars. Jedaf was surprised that Adathe, was not larger than the City of Joroca. It was nestled between two small rivers, on the delta. The end of the valley was void of shade trees, except for the fruit trees that the farmers had planted. The soil was rich and black from years of spring time flooding.

The main town had high stockade walls of fortified wood and stone, with a large deep port facility. The village surrounding the battlements could not be seen very well in the fading evening light, but Jedaf knew it was must be at least twice as large as the city proper. He watched the suns sink in the western most part of the Askalus Sea. It was peaceful and beautiful.

The last rays lit the western cliffs, and rocky shoals, that had protected this nation from the many wars. The sharp spires on the coast rose to a height of one hundred and fifty feet, and then extended inland blocking invaders and friends alike. The few minor passes to the west were narrow, steep, inhospitable and seldom used.

Jedaf turned his back on the panorama. He had to get back to camp and help Ajoris. It was his turn to rub the horses down. No matter how much they disliked him, they still liked the feel of currycomb and grooming brush. They certainly deserved it tonight.

It had been a long rocky road, mostly up hill. Tomorrow they would descend to the soft greenness of the valley. "Ajor, I told you that I would take care of the horses tonight." Jedaf had not realized how long he had been gone. The ambassador had already taken care of his horse, and was now working on Jedaf's.

"I know what you said, lord, but you're better at starting fires." Jedaf tossed his hands in the air and walked off gathering wood. He wished that he had started earlier. The ground in the area around the camp had been picked clean, of all loose timber. He had to walk up to fifty paces into the woods in the dark, trying to gather their fuel. It took over a half zestar, to gather enough to keep the nocturnal predators away for the whole night, and another zestar to weave a spell of protection over the camp.

The horses were much happier having Ajor care for them. He fed them the last of the oat sack and gave them a good portion of the water. Jedaf thought that, they liked him, because he had the patients of a stone, and seemed to know what they wanted all the time. Jedaf had the fire going in almost no time in spite of the fact that the wood was damp.

They fashioned and tied off a horizontal rope between two trees. It formed a make shift clothes line strong enough to hold all of their garments. Both men stripped to their underwear and paced about the fire while everything dried. The reddish-orange Kaybeckian runic spell that Jedaf had cast, hung over the pile of timber and clothing until they had given up their moisture.

The smaller twigs smoldered making a thick almost greenish smoke before bursting into flames. Steam hissed from the larger logs for the first ten zestas, and then they too started burning and spreading light and warmth throughout the camp. Jedaf sorted through the cook pans that had been unloaded and placed near the fire pit. They were ready for use, but there was not much left of their supplies. Ajor had given the majority of the provisions to Captain Odelac's crew. He knew to reach the frontier outposts of Jeupa they had a journey of over a week.

The ambassador had anticipated Jedaf and he would run short of food. It was his expectation to supplement their meals with some sort of wild game. One thing he knew about the hills and mountains surrounding the ancient City of Tabalis was that a variety of wild, sure footed, cloven hoofed goats were plentiful. It was unfortunate that they seldom roamed this far north. Other than a few long legged nestagin kangaroo rabbits, they had not seen any game.

After cooking a double portion of rena beans, he cut up the one remaining stale bread loaf. Mold was starting to grow on the bottom, and the top crumbled to the knife blade. Ajor sliced jerky stripes and added them to the boiling water after the beans where scooped from it. The thickly sliced smoky meat would still taste like a rawhide belt but at least it wouldn't be salty. The unappetizing meal was eaten slowly and quietly, being supplemented with their last bottle of wine.

Both of them were famished, and there were no leftovers. They had ridden most of the day and had stopped for only for a few moments of rest. The longest was during the midday cloudburst. One cold meal of dried measan meat strips, and corn cakes, covered with ly jam had been eaten. It was followed by a bottle of sweet red lusverus wine while they waited until the rain let up enough for them to leave the protection and shelter of the trees.

Ajoris sat staring at the flames and was lost in his thoughts relating to the daughter of the Cathonian noble, which he was supposed to be introduced to upon arrival. The duke's daughter was said to be a fine catch. She was in her thirtieth year, and in good health. Everyone that had met her found her to be lovely. He wondered what she looked like; if the nicest thing they could say about her was that she had a charm about her.

King Vestrak, of Yojan Empire, had personally asked him to call on the duke and his daughter. In addition he also strongly hinted, that Ajor ask for her hand in marriage. It would be a good first step in widening trade relations with the Kingdom of Cathon. What better way for a diplomat to ingratiate himself, then to marry a niece of the king.

The middle aged diplomat also thought of his old friend Kaimmus. He had been Ajor's Cathonian personal attendant and friend of many years. On the return trip to Joroca, last winter he had contracted a deep chest cough. After three agonizing weeks of wheezing for breathe and having a high fever, he died of pneumonia. All Kaimmus had talked about for months, was the birth of his god daughter. He was looking forward to attending his nieces' rite of inheritance this mursa.

Ajoris's servant had spoken of her often and of his brother Surmac. The family farm could not support both brothers, so Kaimmus gave the land to his younger brother and had moved to Adathe. They were so poor the family was barely able to scrape by. Surmac could not get any of his neighbors consent for him to court or marry any of their daughters.

In the end, Kaimmus's brother had married a pretty little vourtre, which lived in the mountains to the southeast. Her family had been killed, and she was left to fend for herself. Weveia was her name, and she was happy to marry Surmac. Their farm was ten thastas from the southern gate of Adathe. Kaimmus had never married and he had sent his brother and sister-in-law, all the money he earned doing back breaking labor and menial chores.

The much needed coins had been enough to keep them going, and gave them a little left over for extras. His dying request was that Ajoris attend the ceremony in Kaimmus's place. It would be a great honor, for his brother having such a distinguished guest. It also might make some of the neighbors friendlier. Not many visitors came to their home, unless they wanted to borrow something.

Jedaf thoughts drifted off to last nights dream. He could still see Elona's face; she was crying and holding the cut off hand of her brother Kytos. They were standing in the midst of a battlefield filled with rotting maggot filled corpses and the sounds of a laughing treskul. Maybe this evil specter was right. Why shouldn't he return to Joroca, and live out a safe comfortable life. Everywhere he had traveled, he caused death, destruction and misery.

He knew that he had fallen in love with her and was afraid that he would never see her again. The Gods of Palestus must still be laughing at them. His gaze went beyond the fire, and into the trees. There was a flickering light on the hillside to the far north. Standing quickly, he banked their fire. "We have got company Ajor!" Jedaf pointed at the small blaze in the nearby camp. "Do you think that they have seen our fire?"

"I don't know," said the ambassador.

Jedaf stood and drove two long stakes into the ground, three feet apart in front of their rock circle. Then he stretched his blanket over them, and sat back down on the opposite side. The sightscreen worked well enough for him to relax and not consider running a cold camp. "Are they on one of the old trade roads," he asked?

"Yes, it's one that is seldom used by most of the merchants gathering in this area. The road forks north to the western and southern gates. The one off in the distance is used less but is a little wider. Merchants, from all over the Worezian Kingdom, camp there and set up bazaar tents. Buyers come from all over the distant Cathonian territories, come to inspect the goods and ensure their quality before shipping them on to the other cities."

Jedaf took a charred stick from the fire and began using the carbon to darken his face. Ajoris sat quietly amused while watching. He had seen the young lord do some strange things, since they had met. It also occurred to him that if he watched long enough, he would find out the answer for his strange behavior, without having to ask so many questions. Jedaf's face was now blacker than a Kelleskarian cave bat, and he went to work on his arms and legs. "I am going over to their camp, for a little visit. You stay here and arm yourself. They may have already seen our fire."

Unbuckling his scabbard harness, he set his sword and purse aside as he stuck the knife into his waist belt. "In three zestars, take the sight screen down and build up the fire. I'll use it to find my way back here. If there is any trouble while I am gone, I want you to clear out; I will meet back up with you in Adathe." Before the ambassador could object, Jedaf was trotting off into the darkness between two bushes toward the distant flickering.

A hundred yards from the neighboring campfire, Jedaf dropped to his hands and knees. Through the sparse smooth barked trees and undergrowth, he could see three covered two wheeled carts, and as many as eight men. They were dressed in the brown and yellow clothing of the mercantile guild, and had an emblem of a loom, embroidered on the side of their wagons. They may have been dressed like merchants, but from their stance and mannerisms, they were definitely warriors. One of them was more obvious than the others and stood out like a rooster in a hen house.

This man was standing near one side of the fire and all the others were on the opposite side listening to him speak. Jedaf took him to be their commander. He confidently strutted about, giving directions and pounding his left palm with his right fist. It was some sort of peptalk, or rally Jedaf thought.

Crawling slowly forward, the young lord looked about the camp for the perimeter guards. He knew there must be at least one, but Jedaf could not locate him. Low crawling behind and below a wide bush, he was able to get within twenty feet of the campfire.

These men were not only warriors, they were Worezian Royal Guardsmen. Jedaf could see the officer's signet ring glistening in the firelight as he removed his leather forearm guards, metallic epaulets and weapons belt. The wagons were full of mercantile goods, especially carpets, blankets, and bedding.

A sentry stepped out from behind the tree left of Jedaf's position. He was very close. Another step and his boot would have landed on the Dragon Lord's fingers. Holding his breath, Jedaf inched foreword on his stomach, slipping closer to the center of the bush. He laid flat at the side of the trunk, with the knife blade in his hand ready for throwing.

"Now that everyone understands why we were sent here and why our mission is so critical. I want each of you to repeat back to me, what you're responsible for and what you're supposed to do?" He stepped toward the seated men pointing at a bearded, hard faced individual, with an angular jaw.

"We will start with Ukam and Dorat." The two men stood. The stocky one remained silent while the taller one, Ukam did the speaking. "Lord Tavay, our part is the easiest. All we have to do is set up the shop in the market square to sell the goods. It will give us a central meeting place where no one will become suspicious." Dorat stood next to him with a satisfied but dumb look on his face.

"Is that all?"

"No, my lord. We will also rent lodgings large enough to feed and accommodate the ten of us and the ten warriors in First Officer Futhey's party."

The officer stepped in front of them looking directly at Dorat. "How will you know Futhey or his warrior's? You know they're from one of the eastern border troops?"

The dimwitted warrior looked to his feet, stammering and tryied to think of an answer. "Sir, he will come to our stand, asking if the festival is going to be on the fifth of Asursa. My reply to him will be, no the fires will all be out by then."

Ukam answered the question for his comrade, which did not please Tavay. The officer eyed them coldly for a moment, not knowing if he should make an example of them, but let it pass. "Good enough," he said peevishly. "See that the two of you memories that reply. If you change one word, he might stick a dagger into your belly."

The regal officer turned to his left. "Now let's hear from Hasto and Learic." The two warriors seated themselves as the other men stood.

"We are to scout the city, locating all the largest supply buildings and warehouses. On the third of Asursa during the festival, Learic and I along with half of First Officer Futhey's men will set them on fire. No war supplies will be reaching Jeupa from here."

"Very good answer," said Lord Tavay. "Oryel and Sindo you're next, what are you going to be doing?"

A dark curry haired man with large bulging muscles stood. He looked more like a horseshoe fitter than a man at arms. Next him stood his equal in strength, but a little shorter in stature. "Lord, it is our duty to scout the docks and shipyards. On the night of the feast, we along with the other half of Futhey's party will set fire to as many ships in the harbor as we can." The officer gave them an approving nod and wave, turning toward the two men at arms leaning against the carts.

"Renya and Bothar you're last," said Tavey.

"Lord, we are to kill two guards, dress in their Cathonian warriors uniforms, and after all our men have crossed the rivers we are to set the bridges from the city on fire. Ukam and Dorat will be buying our fuel oil. We will be storing it near each bridge, the day before the celebration."

Tavay tossed another log into the fire and watched as the embers and sparks flue above him. "It will be my job, along with Gentuc and First Officer Futhey, to set fire to the royal guardhouse and armory. We will all meet back here, before returning to Woreza."

Gentuc, the sentry stepped into the firelight from the outer perimeter. "Lord. There is a large campfire, to the south of us," he said. All the men stood looking at the tall blaze. Ajor must have put all their wood on it.

"Dorat, take up a guard post on our wagons and Oryel take up a position on the east side of camp. Gentuc will remain on the south side. We will leave are neighbors there for the night, but by first light, I want to be standing in their camp. Sindo, see to it that the men are relieved in two zestar shifts. I am turning in for the night. Wake me a zestar before Horastus rises." The warriors that were called out jumped in response to the orders, while the others unrolled their bedding.

Jedaf returned to his camp, as quickly as he could. With the additional guards posted, he could not return the way he had come. He had to crawl around the merchant's camp, in a more westerly direction. There were more trees and in the moonlight, there was less of a chance of him being seen.

Jedaf sat with Ajor for the next half zestar filling him in on what he had heard. They decided that the best thing for them to do was to get a few zestars rest. Then they would pack, and head for Adathe while it was still dark.

The ambassador's first duty was to introduce Lord Jedaf to the king. Not only did they need to stop the sabotage effort, they needed to get the kings permission to rent a few fast ships. They would also like to hire at least two santaxes of Cathonion warriors to accompany them to the Kingdom of Bintar.

Ajoris had warned him that King Samalis did not like getting involved in other kingdoms disputes, unless there was a profit in it for him. Usually he urged his countrymen to sell arms and supplies to both sides. Jedaf had been trying to think of a way of persuading King Samalis into joining their cause.

There was a dispute known to exist between the Kingdom of Bintar and the Kingdom of Cathon. This was over the ownership and allegiance to some of the islands south and west of the Histajonies Archipelago.

King Samalis also did not have any alliances with the Kingdoms of Jeupa or Amrig because they were on the opposite end of the Zarhunian Continent. They were known to have continual disputes with the Kingdom of Envar and Worez. His merchants and nobles made a lot of profit supplying both of them with much needed goods.

Now Jedaf did not have to worry about finding an excuse to get Cathonian support.

If Worezian spies or mercenaries set fire to Samalis's capital city during his jubilee and twentieth anniversary of his coronation, it would be the end of his reign. The other members of the royal households would turn on him and hold him personally responsible for the burning of their homes and have him beheaded.

Chapter # 20
King Eneas of Eastern Semedia

Vadeck crawled into the back of the wagon and had finally fallen asleep. He was totally exhausted and had been awake now for nearly two days. In the meantime, Karadis and Baradic had pretended not to get drunk for such a long time that they had passed out along with their two vourtre warrior companions. Captain Odelac remained standing on guard over the men the rest of the night.

The horses were brought over and staked out closer to the wagon. This way he could keep a better watch over them. Then Odel lit a small campfire to warm himself and the men. The village became more and more crowded, as the evening progressed. The commotion made him all the more uneasy and watchful.

At the twenty-third zestar, two honor guards arrived at Cira's quarters. They were dressed in their finest uniforms, with ancestral swords and polished armor. The elder of the two wore a wide necklace of dark cobalt blue rectangular stones. From the braided chain a six pointed silver star hung. His scabbard was also decorated with the same blue gemstones, as was the pommel of his Theodian steel sword.

There was no doubt; this man was of royal lineage. He walked with an air of authority and from his countenance, he expected obedience. The other officer was also dressed well, but did not have a coat of arms embroidered on his tunic. He walked a little behind and to the right side of the more senior ranked warrior.

"I am Prince Pfitas, and this is my aide, First Officer Ush Tyan." We have been sent here to be your escorts for the evening. Snapping his fingers, the younger man stepped forward. He handed Ciramtis a deep green full length, laced dress with golden piping, a matching cape, and a pair of soft leather slippers with a threaded golden trim. "Princess Lavea thought you would like to wash and have more appropriate attire for the ceremony. Our princess said the clothing is yours to keep in remembrance of this night."

Two young women came into the light of the doorway carrying large buckets of hot water in each hand, along with fresh towels. They were followed by a male servant with a copper wash tub, and two other women with boxes of scented powders, perfumes, sponges, combs, brushes, laced trimmed cloths, undergarments and ribbons. They ducked passed the guards and entered. "We will wait for you outside," said Prince Pfitas.

The women stripped Ciramtis, and had her half rubbed down with soap and scented oils before she could object. A zestar and a half later she stood at the threshold. The gown fit like it had been made for her, and its material formed to her every curve. It was the richest clothing that she had ever worn.

First Officer Ush Tyan stepped forward, a thin square gold link necklace in his hands. "You would do me a great honor, if you would wear my mothers crest." She took it from him and fastened the clasp behind her neck. Smoothing down and flattening the small silver stars and crested moons that hung from it, she thanked him.

A large circle of campfires had been lit in the clearing beyond the wagons, and the streets started to fill with quests. They walked over to where the crowd was starting to gather. In the center of the clearing, eight man high stone cubes stood. Each had different markings carved deeply into them. The center two stone stood a little higher than the others.

Eneas was dressed in silver blue iridescent silks and silver armor. She could see him standing near the dais constructed of stone blocks.

The torch light reflected off his armor spraying the assemblage in a dancing radiance. Ciramtis had never seen such fine clothing in all her life.

All the lords and ladies wore silks of every color in the rainbow. Everyone had donned gold and silver jewelry studded with precious stones. These unique bobbles and lavish trinkets had been created and designed by the finest craftsmen in the entire world. The glade was filling quickly and becoming overcrowded as the assemblage sighted Eneas.

Ciramtis guessed there were eight hundred in attendance. It was obvious from the number that most did not live in this village. Many different tribal pennants were prevalently displayed among the various royal families coat of arms. Vourtre from all over Zarhun were in attendance.

"Pfitus! How did so many people get here on such short notice, she asked?" Her escorts didn't know all the details, but Queen Cystalen had sent runners out over two mursas ago. "My mother has made most of the arrangements," said Pfitus. "I know the ceremony has been in the planning stages for over a year. Your being here at this moment in time, is just a coincidence."

Prince Eneas waived to a few passing guests and shouted out greetings to them. Glancing in Ciramtis's direction he cut his conversation short with the friend that he had been walking with and took a few steps closer toward his youngest brother. "Thank you for escorting mother's special guest, Pfitus. See to it that she is led to a seat of honor." They did not have time to speak to him. He turned about, picked up a lighted torch, and ascended the marble steps to the highest cubic stone.

The gathering in the glade quieted down as they watched him touch the torch to a large bronze oil filled urn. The ornamental casting had been formed in the shape of a sharp, tusked warthogs head and the base was forged as a short twisted tree stump with wide leafed ivy engulfing the trunk. The ceremonial lighting vessel stood at the right side of the delmet dais. A high blue flame shot up in the air rising to a height of about four feet before the combustible gases burned off.

Then the flame lowered turning to a soft reddish orange, lighting the immediate area.

For a few zestas all was quiet. The two elaborately dressed vourtre warriors that Eneas had been speaking with earlier ascended the stone blocks. They carried with them, a large inlaid wooden chest with blackened steel bands. After setting the trunk down, one of the men descended to the lower level stone blocks and knelt down. From the strong box the other regal vourtre removed a thin, elaborately designed, yet delicate crown.

Holding the vourtre symbol of kingship aloft, he moved to Eneas's right side. The torchlight gave the woven crown of gold a life all its own, sending its rays out to the crowd. It had been created by braiding many individual fine strands of gold wire into the shape of an ivy vine wreath with burkat leaves. Intertwined in the pseudo foliage were large pine cone shaped emeralds. A large tree like symbol was formed at the front of the crown. This was the coat of arms and symbol for the Goddess Esella.

"Citizens of Am Hass, I am Ada Hon, the protector of the vourtre of Jeupa, and of southern Envar. I am also Eneas's first cousin." The crowd cheered waiving their banners and banging on their armor. "On my right is Cul Tarac, Eneas's younger brother, the protector of the vourtre of Amrig and Wurda!"

Cul Tarac stood briefly, bowed to the cheering crowd and knelt back down. "Eneas my oldest friend, and companion of many campaigns, has given me the honor tonight of crowning him." Holding the golden band aloft, he turned in all directions, as the assemblage erupted in a thunder of cheers and shouts. Eneas raised his hands, and waited for the noise to subside while Ada Hon stepped to his cousin's side.

"Before crowning our new king, Queen Cystalen has asked an outsider to say a few words to our people. I give you Ciramtis of Iblac." The glade became as quiet as the stones. Ada Hon pointed out the human female standing at the front of the crowd. The sorceress was embarrassed; she had no idea that she was going to be called on to speak at the coronation.

The white witch nervously ascended the stone blocks of the dais. Eneas's scowling expression showed that he was not pleased. Obviously he had not been told the human female was going to speak either. The vourtre prince did not want her there at all, but it had been a request of his mothers and he would honor it.

Stepping timidly to his left she clutched her staff tightly. The stave gave her the support and courage that she needed to continue. "Good people of Am Hass, and honored quests. I am Ciramtis of Iblac, great grand daughter of Minatis of Naros, great grand daughter of Colinda, the daughter of our Goddess Esella." A hushed murmur went through the crowd.

Eneas turned a surprised face toward her then extended his hands quieting the gathering. "Thank you your majesty. My companions and I are traveling west to the Envarian border. We will try to intercept the marriage caravan of King Magarus's daughter, and break the proposed peace treaty with the Kingdom of Envar. If we fail, Envar and Worez will unite, forming one empire. They intend on invading the lands of western Jeupa and laying siege the fiefdoms and kingdoms of south central Zarhun."

Swords banged angrily against the armor and shields. "I know that war is about to be thrust upon you. In times like these, the only gift I can give to your king, and my distant cousin, is wisdom and the knowledge that patience brings."

Ciramtis raised her staff high above her head with both of her hands, as she said a soft prayer in the ancient language of Kaybeck. Her staff glowed white hot, lighting the whole dais. The gathering quieted half in fear and half in amazement. Walking over to Ada Hon, the white witch touched the crown with the pointed end.

The golden band and jewels also began to glow brightly. The vourtre lord held the crown aloft again for the crowd to see. Its beams seemed to reach even the farthest in the gathering. The vourtre people were dead silent. No one had moved a muscle until Ciramtis said, "Long live the King!"

Ada Hon pivoted slightly and placed the still shimmering crown upon Eneas's head. A gentile raping on the shields started in the rear of the assemblage. It gathered momentum as others drew their swords. Soon the whole glade sounded as if thunder was moving down the valley. Eneas swelled with pride as he turned to the four sides of the stone platform bowing to his subjects and friends.

Ciramtis slipped away during the frenzy and shouts, descending to where her escorts were waiting. Upon her return Prince Pfitas knelt, took her hand and kissed it. "I am sorry. Had I known who you were, I would have been more respectful. Please forgive my ignorance." Ush Tyan knelt next to him, keeping silent.

His chin was lowered and face hidden. The young warrior was ashamed of himself for having allowed her to wear an inexpensive necklace, and for not offering her a scarf to cover her hair. "There is nothing to forgive," said Cira. "Now please stand up. The king is about to speak." Eneas took his last bow and held his palms up and out to his people.

"My friends, I have already been told of this treaty and of its consequences. Already the borders of many nations have been closed. Because of it, many of my friends and relatives were not able to attend this ceremony. King Magarus has our friend Prince Sesmak of Envar trapped on the Zarhunian Plain. Shortly a war will begin, and the Worezians will drive the last of Sesmak's survivors across our land and into Jeupa."

"The gods have sent us a new lord of the horned Semedian Red Dragon. He supports Prince Sesmak, and so do I." A loud rumble of disgust and jeers for the Worezians went through the assemblage. "For generations humans have killed or hunted vourtre for sport. The last lord of the dragon gave us our lands on Zarhun, and made it a law punishable by death for any human to settle here."

"King Magarus destroyed the tomb of my great grandfather last year. He was one of our greatest kings and one of the few that has ever allowed humans to travel through our lands. Dracar's resting place is now nothing but rubble. Magarus is again trying to take our land. The Worezians have been expecting us, to spend all our energy and resources repairing the tomb. They were wrong! We have been using this time to make weapons."

"Tonight, you have not only come to a coronation, you have come here to declare war!" He raised his ringed fist high into the air. "By the ring of the Dragon Lord, I order the standards of ancient Semedia be raised along with our standard of the woodsman's axe." The thundering clatter and banging on armor rose to a deafening clamor. "Send messengers to all the royal vourtre households. We will unite with Ciramtis, and the Lord of the Dragon." Eneas drew his sword and pointed the sharpened blade skyward. "Death to Magarus, and death to all Worezians," he shouted!

The gathering was near to rioting. Everyone was yelling death to the Worezians. The chant becoming louder each time it was yelled. Ada Hon stepped up next to the king, waving his arms for them to listen to him, and waited until he could be heard. "Tomorrow there will be death for the Worezians! Tonight go to the banquet tables, and eat and drink to our new king."

The feasting and merrymaking would go on all night. Ciramtis was given the seat to Eneas's left at the banquet table. Ada Hon and Cul Tarac were seated to the king's right. King Eneas's youngest brother, Prince Pfitas was seated on Ciramtis's left, with Ush Tyan next to him. It was a great honor for both of them, and the story of this coronation would be told for generations. Queen Cystalen and Princess Lavea were seated at the opposite end of the table, with the majority of the other royal ladies, and dignitaries representing vourtre from all over Zarhun.

During the dinner, Cira told Eneas all that she knew of the situation. He sat quietly amused, at the way she seem to take charge. She made many suggestions, hardly giving him a chance to respond. Eneas agreed with a few of her ideas, promising to send messengers to Sesmak and to King Galthadon of Jeupa. The king would also send his cousin Ada Hon back to Jeupa to gather more warriors and to help strengthen the frontier outposts. A scouting party would be sent northeast to Tabalis to locate and aide Lord Jedaf.

Cira stopped talking long enough to take a few bites of the roasted redolga boar and bread, giving Eneas his opening. "Now may I say a word," she looked a little surprised at first, and then reddened while

Ada Hon laughed. It had just occurred to her that she had monopolized the conversation for over a zestar.

"Tomorrow I will send an escort of about thirty warriors with you. If they can not intercept the bridle caravan, they will stay with you until you reach north point. Each of them has been given orders to give their life in your protection. Don't try changing that. These men will take their own life, before returning here in disgrace."

The conversation turned to happier times and the minstrel's music turned a little livelier. Cira could not remember when she had a better time. Finishing the food that had been placed in front of her she thanked Pfitas, and returned the necklace to Ush Tyan. She told them it would not be necessary for them to escort her back to her quarters. They were to stay and enjoy the festivities. Bowing to Eneas, she said, "Thank you for the honor of being able to eat at your side. Please thank your sister and mother for me. I would like to stay up all night, but I must get some sleep."

The king reached over took her hand and put it to his lips. "The honor was all mine, you are always welcome at my table, cousin." Ciramtis gave him a smile as a reply and waived goodbye to Ada Hon. There were only about three zestars left until sunrise. She thought about what plans still needed to be worked out as she looked at the clear sky and walked beneath the twinkling stars.

Captain Odelac pulled up on the four horses reins. The vourtre warriors were blocking the road ahead and motioning for him to stop. Ciramtis dismounted, tied off her horse and climbed into the supply wagon from the rear. Stepping over and around the crated supplies, she moved to the front of the wagon. There was just enough room for her to sit between Odelac and Vadeck. "What is the hold up captain?"

Odelac scuffled over a little giving her some more elbowroom. "I don't know. Could be that they are finally beginning to tire." Ciramtis looked down the side of the wagon. Heyo Zon stood there; he was one of the third grade warriors in the vourtre strata.

They had been running along side the wagon since it had left the Village of Am Hass early this morning. This warrior was very muscular, with straight jet black hair and forest green eyes. Cira thought that he looked about fifty years old, which meant in human terms he would be in his mid sixties. Sweat ran from his forehead and sides, but he was not breathing hard. "I doubt it," she said.

Odel looked at her than to Heyo Zon. "Vourtre warriors seldom ride," Cira said. "They are used to running twenty thastas a day. Come on let's climb down and find out what the problem is."

Odelac handed the trace lines to Vadeck, and jumped to the ground. Cira followed, turning about, placing her foot on the top of the front wagon wheel. Her dress caught in the spring guard of the wagon seat. Holding on the front canvas support, she tugged at it. Heyo Zon walked over to her. "Can I be of any help, my lady?"

"No thank you," she said with her back to him. "I've almost got it." Vadeck stood up suddenly relieving the spring tension. Ciramtis fell backwards into Odelac's arms. The captain set her down and she straightened her dress. "Thanks Vad," she said sarcastically. He looked down, seeing that she was all right, and gave her a toothy grin.

Quay Thauk with his advanced guard had returned. Reporting to Prince Pfitas and Ush Tyan, he caught his breath, and waited for Ciramtis to step nearer before continuing. "As I was saying, Gat Hyados's men have located the wedding caravan. He and a taxt of his men will remain with them, keeping us informed."

"The enemy's camp is half a day's march, from here. There are six to eight wagons, a retinue of about fifteen men and women, and two over strength stratas at the site. The entire entourage probably totals about eighty warriors."

"Thank you Quay," said Cira. "Odel, have your men get out of the wagon and have them use their legs. We will need the extra room to sit back there and plan our attack."

The muscular ships officer did not comment. He now knew in his heart, who was in charge. He ran back to the wagon, and stuck his head threw the rear flap. "Karadis and Baradic you lazy sea slugs, are you going to sit here the whole day, and do nothing?"

The two looked at each other. "But captain, we haven't done anything. Why are you yelling at us?"

Odel threw back the flap. "That is right you haven't done anything. The vourtre are laughing at you behind your backs, for being so soft. Now get out of the wagon, and report to fourth class Quay Thauk. I'm sure he can find something for you to do."

Karadis jumped down. "Who is he?" Odel pointed ahead to the front of the column.

"Kar said, "He is the ugly one with the sparse moustache and bowed legs."

Bara jumped down into the soft silt mumbling; "Damn green sons of bitches are all ugly." Odel stepped next to him, and grabbed the collar of Baradic's tunic. "I didn't quite hear that." Baradic swept the tightly clasped hand away. "Nothin captain, we will be glad to do anything. Come on Kar, let's go lick their boots."

Pfitas, Ush Tyan, Odelac and Ciramtis sat in the back of the wagon. For another zestar they planed while the troop pressed on. Ush knew the terrain like the back of his hand. There were no places in this part of the country where an ambush could be staged. They had thirty warriors with them, but how does thirty surround ninety. Pfitas suggested that, they pick off enough of the out-riders with arrows until the odds were better.

Cira rejected the plan, because she thought that it would make them run all the faster for the safety of Zarhun City. If that happened, they would never have another opportunity to rescue Princess Elona and Diara. There're best chance of rescuing anyone would be to strike once and ambush them quickly, without any warning. They also reluctantly agreed that they had to kill all the guards that remained un-drugged. After the attack, they would have to make their escape taking away the captives and running like the demons of Dedeok were after them.

"I still feel that Cira's original plan was the best," said Odelac.

"So do I," agreed Ush. "But after drugging the water supply we can't just leave them. We should go about the camp cutting their throats."

"No, Ush! I don't mind killing someone in combat, they have as good a chance at living as I, but I am not a throat cutting butcher."

"Your ethics are commendable Captain Odelac, but with the amount of men that they have, we can't be too squeamish. The survivors will be after us in hot pursuit, and they won't be worrying about how many vourtre throats that they cut. I do not even like the thought of them coming after us. They will chase us from here right into the arms of the Envarian Army."

"Wait a zesta," said Ciramtis. "We have forgotten one very important detail. The whole purpose of this caravan is to take the Princess Shayla and the written treaty to Envar. If we free the concubine woman, and burn the treaty, it might delay the war long enough for us to gather more forces. The more troops that we have at our command, the more likely King Magarus will have to change his plan." The rest grudgingly nodded in agreement. "Now, after they are drugged, we can scatter their horses. By morning, they will be over half the countryside, and we will be long gone."

"The Worezians would not know who or what had happened, and would have no means of tracking us." The plan seemed to be a good one. What was most convincing about it was the fact that it didn't have any major flaws. There was little risk and it seemed easily executable. Ush wiped the sweat from his face. It was starting to get hot under the canvas. He did not like being cooped up, no vourtre did.

"I think we all agree," said Pfitas. "I especially like it, because of Princess Shayla. After they wake and find out what has happened, they will only have one mission. Find their horses as fast as possible and get the princess back to safety. I would also like to make sure that we cause enough damage to the caravan, to make the princess fear for her life."

"We will leave that to Captain Odelac," said Ush. "If the princess sees any vourtre, she will think that our people have her captives. Their armies will invade the woodlands seeking revenge."

Odelac and Ciramtis knew he was right. It wouldn't be right for hundreds of vourtre to die, for saving the lives of two humans. "After the raid, we will split up into four separate parties, and head in different directions. That will prevent them from following us."

Ciramtis stood holding onto the top canvas slat, for stability. "I think that is a good idea, Pfitas. Tomorrow evening I will enter the camp just before kreb is cooked. It won't take long to drug the water or food. But it will take some time for them to digest their meal. Nefren usually takes a few zestars to get into their systems before it takes effect."

Chapter # 21

The Road to Envar

Elona and Diara were uncomfortable and having a very bad nights rest. They were cold and the ground beneath the wagon was rocky and uneven. Normally for first summer one blanket would have been sufficient to keep the cool air and early morning dew off of them. This summer was different. They had used Elona's blanket to cover the coarse stubby grass stalks, and Diara's to cover the two them. Shivering Elona rolled over. The grass stems crunched beneath her weight. "Are you still awake?"

Diara rolled over facing her. "Yes. I am so tired that every time I close my eyes, I dream of carrying those water kettles." She could barely make out Elona's silhouette in the moonlight.

"How are your blisters?" Diara held up her right hand, rubbing the spongy bumps. "There still soar, but the axle grease that I put on them, has helped. How about yours?"

"Sh, the guard is coming."

The sentry walked over leaning against the rear wagon wheel. He readjusted the straps on his sandals, tapping out some of the loose soil. Continuing on his rounds they watched until he stopped at the burned out remains of the dowry wagon. Then he turned and walked off out of hearing range. "I hope your princess had all her favorite possessions in that wagon," said Elona quietly.

Diara inched over clamping her hand over Elona's mouth. "You better not say anything about that again. If they even hear you joking about it, you could be dragged behind the wagon until most of your skin is scraped off." She let go of Elona's mouth while she whispered.

"Now let's try to get some sleep. No telling what time we're going have to get up, or whose chores we are going to have to do." She pulled her half of the blanket over her legs. Wiggling she flattened the stalks, making herself a little more comfortable.

"I guess your right," said Elona. She pulled the blanket over her and turned facing the compound. The guard fires had been banked to a low warm glow. She watched the red swaying motion of the flames for awhile then drifted off to a restless dream filled sleep.

Bang, bang, bang. Diara jumped to a sitting position, hitting her head on the bottom of the wagon's rear axle. Elona rolled over springing to her hands and knees. She looked like a frightened cat seeking a tall tree. "Come on, you lazy slaves. Let's get the food on. The princess is going to be hungry this morning."

It was Atus, a large dented pan in one hand and a wooden ladle in the other. "I said; get out from under there, it's time to get to work." Nudging Elona with the toe of his sandal got her attention. "You go fetch the firewood and bring it to the cook area." Diara sat rubbing the knot from her forehead.

"I said let's go!" He reached down, took hold of Diara's ankle, and pulled. She flopped backwards as he dragged her.

"Let me go," she screamed. It did not do any good. He didn't stop until she was free of the underside of the wagon. Then he took her by the arm, pulling her to her feet. Elona crawled out, slowly. The broken blisters on her hands hurt terribly.

"Are you going to get that wood today, or am I going to have to give you a beating?" He gave Diara a shove toward the main campfire. She turned around at the same time that Atus gave Elona a hard kick in the ribs. It knocked the wind out of her. Holding her stomach, she tried to get her breath. The young woman was also tired of being kicked. Her ribcage was still sore from yesterdays kick and it was starting to bruise. He pulled her up by the hair, shaking her head. "Next time I tell you to move you had better do it quickly."

Elona glared at him a moment, but kept her mouth shut and shuffled off toward the wood line. She mumbled a few expletives under her breath and stopped only long enough to pick up a few branches. Diara scurried off ahead toward the main campfire.

Two of the younger guards were doing punishment duty cutting up logs, and stacking firewood. Diara picked up two of the smaller branches and set them on the low fire. A large black iron pot with boiling water in it, hung over the coals on the spit. Taking the ladle she filled the wash basins and carried them to the long tables that had been set up near the guard area.

The royal guards had been waiting for some time. Fifteen men stood by in the line with their tunics already removed. Diara disregarded the heckling and arm gestures. Then she fetched a couple of clean towels, and four buckets of cold rinse water.

Meanwhile Elona stumbled back into camp. Dirt and loose bark were stuck to her cheek. Diara stood near her refilling the iron kettle; her face was a sickly white. Elona dropped her first load of firewood. "You look worse than I feel! Elona knelt down and began stacking the wood, as she looked at her friend.

"It's Hyeasan, the supply officer, and the dowry guard. Their bodies are in the bushes behind the wagon. I saw them when I went to get more water. Their heads are missing, but I still knew it was them." She gathered some of Elona's smaller branches and dropped them into the ashes of the other cook fires. The two blew on the remains of the hot charcoal embers, rekindling them to a small smoky blaze.

"Hey skinny take this!" Elona saw Atus standing at the back of the cook wagon struggling with a cereal grain sack in his arms. He tossed the burlap bag to her when she was within an arms distance of the wagon. It landed full on her knocking her to the ground. "You pig! You filthy redolga pig! Don't you use your head for anything? You knew that meal sack was too heavy for me to carry." Atus wiped the sweet from his brow with the back of his hand. Then he sat down at the wagon tailgate, breathing hard and dangling his legs over the edge.

He laughed deeply while she continued yelling. "If I were five or six tarmets heavier, I'd pound you into the ground. You're an idiot." She glared at him with all the hate she could muster.

"Bitch, if you were five or six tarmets heavier, you might have been able to tempt me into dragging you off into the bushes. But as things stand now I am not sure you're a woman." She staggered to her feet as he jumped down. Before she could say another word he reached into the ripped seam of her dress, and gave her breast a squeeze. "Like I said, I am still not sure you're a woman."

She slapped his face as hard as she could. "You animal, keep your filthy hands off of me."

Atus pushed her backward over the grain sack and continued laughing. "Dump that meal sack into the water, and fetch the bowls. I have got to get the fruit pealed and cut up." He walked off leaving her on he ground. She was fuming mad but knew she could do nothing about it.

Princess Shayla came out of her wagon in a huff and went straight over to where her breakfast table and awning had been set up. She didn't say a word to anyone. The disgusted look on her face showed she was looking for an excuse to punish someone. She was still upset over yesterday's tragic loss of her dowry. Elona and Diara sat behind her trying to stay out of her sight.

A new male slave had been selected to wait on and attend to the princesses needs. His most qualifying attribute, was the fact that his tongue had been cut out. Setting down the large bowl of oatmeal in front of her, he stepped to the side lowered his head and knelt. She shoved a large spoonful in her mouth and grudgingly approved. Licking the honey off the back of the spoon she looked around at all of the other retainers. She was hopping someone would speak out of turn. Even Gietra, her most trusted female attendant knew she was looking for an excuse to have someone flogged.

"Captain," she said crisply to the middle aged warrior standing off to one side!

"Yes princess," the officer stepped forward and knelt, bowing his head.

"Have you removed the heads of the traitors yet?"

The captain answered her without raising his chin. "Yes princess. We have their heads in a sack. Would you care to see them?"

Shayla shoveled in three large spoonfuls of cereal into her mouth. "No, just stick them on a pole and have it driven into the ground at the roadside ahead of us. I want the rest of your incompetent men see the athcas eating their faces when we ride by them later."

One of the other male servants that had been assigned the duty of setting up the tented shelter brought Diara and Elona a cereal bowl. They were hungry enough to finish it without any coaxing. Shayla didn't say another word to anyone while eating the next three courses. She finished her breakfast and was escorted to her wagon. Everyone was thankful that no one was punished this morning. Atus had already been told that they would get a late start this morning.

Almost the entire wardrobe that the princess owned had burned in the dowry wagon. The only exceptions being; two large double handled trunks which had been stored in the servant's wagon and three smaller ones that had been placed in the wagon with Diara and Elona. The only other good full length dress that she owned was dirty and covered with food. It had to be washed and rinsed a second time this morning before the stains started to set

The captain motioned for Atus to step forward. "After the princess retires to her wagon, have those two female slaves wash and rinse this, and they better not ruin it."

Atus immediately went over where Elona and Diara were sitting "Alright breakfast is over, for the two of you." He pointed the ladle at Diara. "You clean the princess's dress this morning while the mouth and I finish feeding the men." He looked at Elona and said, "Let's go mouth."

It took a zestar to rinse and re-rinse the food from Princess Shayla's dress. First Diara soaked it in the cold stream, and then washed it in the largest iron kettle that Atus had brought. The stream was not far from camp but two guards were sent along to watch her and keep the animals away.

It was not that they were worried about loosing a slave to the roaming carnivores. It was the fact that, if the princess's bright yellow dress was not returned in good condition; more of the royal guardsmen would loose their heads. It took the strength of both Diara and the slave boy Caysa to wring it out and hang it to dry. At the clothes line, a young second officer was posted to protect it.

The sight of the yellow fabric billowing in the wind made the preteen laugh. Pointing over his shoulder with his thumb, he said; "Look at that dress Diara. With the guard standing near it and its size, it looks like a two man tent." She also laughed as they hurried back to the main cook area. Elona had served all the warriors by this time, and had burned one hand on a hot kettle.

Diara helped scrape the burnt on left-overs from the last serving kettle and they buried the remains. The two women felt like they had put in a full day's work and it was just the beginning. Pouring in some hot water into the last kettle, they let it soak, while they sat on the ground. "If this is what we are going to be doing the rest of our lives, escape is starting to look better and better."

"Escape to where Elona, the woods or the snake infested marshlands?" The Oppowian princess sat hunched over scribbling in the dirt with a stick. "I don't care Di. Anything is better than this."

"You wouldn't be saying that if the animals were to get you!"

Elona looked off into the distance, at the far end of camp. "Speaking of animals, here comes that beast Atus." He was sweating profusely and kicking the dirt as he walked. One of the officers had ordered him to unload one of the supply wagons and had him repacking some of the princess's trunks. He complained about the amount of work he had to do, and he received a black eye in response.

Stopping at the kettle of hot water he washed off his hands and splashed some of it on his face. Then he wrung out the wash cloth and held it against his swollen eye. "We will be leaving shortly," he yelled over at them. Dumping the remaining water over the hot coals of the fire and tossed the rinse bucket near the wagon. Elona and Diara stood brushing the loose dirt from their dirty and tattered dresses.

Atus hefted the large empty kettle on his shoulder, and left for the cook wagon. Nothing further had to be said. The women ran as fast as they could for their wagon. At least now they could sit and get some rest. The rear guard was waiting for them and secured the canvas as soon as they crawled into the back. It was going to be another long arduous day of sore muscles, blisters, and bruises.

Caysa stood in the bed of the open buckboard supply wagon while tipping the heavy water barrel over the side rail. It had been a hot, dusty day and they had used up most of the fresh drinking water. The three of them were thankful that the day was almost over.

It was nearing the twenty-first zestar, and time to start fixing the evening meal. Elona and Diara stood at the side of the wagon filling the iron cook pots. Atus had told them that they were his to do with as he sought fit, and he had been on their backs for nearly a two and a half zestars.

Both of the women had soot smudged faces. There was silt and grease in their hair, and both had splinters in their hands from gathering and stacking firewood. Their backs ached, and their dresses were ragged and filthy. They had been warring the same clothing now, for three days. Earlier Elona had joked about them smelling so badly, that they now could keep the bantas away.

"Who is she?" Elona looked across the compound, to where Caysa was staring. A twenty-five year old woman with light brown hair and a slim figure was approaching them. She wore a very small frayed orange dress with the bodice partially unlaced. Her hips swayed as she walked. The tart's breasts were half exposed, and bounced as she carried an iron cooking pot in each of her hands. She stepped over to where they were standing and gave everyone a big smile.

Atus had also been watching her intently as she approached the cook wagon. He trotted over to them, shoving Elona off to the side as he stepped infront of the sexy female slave. "Who are you," he bellowed? "And what do you think you're doing?" Taking her by the arm, he spun her around toward him and away from the water barrel. She fell to the ground, dropping her lidded pots and the serving ladle.

"I am sorry master, I was told that this was the common water wagon and I came to fill our pots." She flashed and batted her eyelashes at him. "I thought that this was the filling line," she said apologetically. Brushing the dirt from her dress she reached down and retrieved one pot, putting the cover back on it.

"Where did you come from? I haven't seen you before today!"

She pointed to herself, and smiled. "Who me," she replied in a soft coy voice? "Why I am the third strata's woman." She adjusted the top of her dress, reducing his ogling view. "They sent me to fetch some fresh drinking water, and then I am supposed to come back with the some bread and vittles."

Atus scowled. "How come I haven't seen you since leaving Woreza?"

She smiled at him provocatively, and replied in a low alluring voice. "Well master, there are an awful lot of warriors on the other side of the camp, and I am the only woman. They barely give me time to eat and wash. When I'm not flat on my back, I have to fetch water for the horses."

The cook held her by the triceps, giving her muscles a squeeze. "You are stronger than you look! I'm glad you came over here; it gives me a good idea about how lax I've been." He turned back toward Diara and Elona. "If she has time to water the horses and take care of all of those men, you two will have to start doing more work around here. Tonight, after you clean up the cook kettles. You can start watering and tending our horses. Caysa can help you; he doesn't need all that sleep."

Atus reached down and picked up the other kettle that the woman had dropped. "Thank you again for coming over here," he said. Looking beneath the lid he notices the kettle was half full of finely chopped, fresh, light brown leaves. Handing it to her he said, "By the way, I didn't catch your name."

"It is Ciramtis master. I should be free tomorrow, just after first lunch, if you should want me for anything. I'm in the tent usually set up at the end of the second row."

Atus's face glowed at the tempting invitation. "Will you be making the soup for the third strata tonight," he asked?

She smiled back at him. "No, we've heard the princess has brought along a royal chef with her. He does all the cooking. Why if it wasn't for his cooking and keeping the men at the food pots, I'd never even have time to change my clothes."

Atus laughed deeply, shaking his fat rolls. "Well then, what are the chopped herbs for?"

She took the cover off and shook the diced leaves to the side. "Why master, they take the stagnant taste of the barrels from the drinking water. All you have to do is stir in a half cup of nefren while the waters boiling. The leaves melt away, and improve the flavor of any soup or stew."

Elona stood off to the side with her friend mimicking and miming the new woman's stance and hand movements until Diara poked her in the ribs.

"Ciramtis, I'm chef Atus and I have never heard of nefren."

She set her kettles down looking surprised. "You can't be the camp cook," she said stepping closer to him and running her fingers threw the hair at the side of his head. "All cooks are fat and ugly; why you're better looking than half of the strata."

Atus pulled her close, kissing her full on the mouth. She did not resist, and seemed to melt in his arms. It was a long zesta in Ciramtis's mind, but finally he gave her some air. He squeezed her tighter and tried to give her another kiss. She placed her hand between their faces, touching his lips gently with her fingertips.

"It's too bad you're the cook," she said as she stroked his cheek and gave his earlobe a little tug. "You have to start preparing the meal now, and I have got to bring the strata some drinking water." As she spoke, Atus immediately looked toward the princess's wagon, and thanked the gods her servants had not finished setting up her tables and dining area. If the meal was late this evening he would be lashed, or worse.

"Maybe," she said softly with a little shrug of her shoulders. "If I tell the warriors that you need my help preparing the dinner, we could slip off behind the wagon after the food's been cooked." Atus gave her a light kiss and another squeeze. "That sounds pretty good to me and tonight I can have Elona and Diara carry the water for your horses. It will give us a few more zestars to be alone."

Ciramtis dumped all her leaves into one kettle, and tossed the other one over at Elona's feet. "Fill that one too, and bring it over to the warriors for me, I've got to help with the soup." The brassy wench took a hold of Atus's chubby arm and the two of them strolled off toward the main cook fire.

"I'll be hung before I lug water for that wenches horses." The two women looked up and over at Caysa. The twelve year old boy stood there shaking his fist at Atus's back.

"Come on Caysa; let's get these damn pots filled. My arms are starting to ache." The grubby slave boy looked back at Elona.

"Didn't you hear what they said? We're going to start doing her work now too!"

Elona set the kettles downs and whispered in his ear. "Yes we did hear what she said, and we heard how Atus is more handsome than half the strata. And I will bet she knows that from first hand experience too. If she starts passing on her jobs to us, we will work extra hard one day, and then toss a bar of pligolg soap into the princess soup. When they question us, we can tell them that Atus dropped it in there after washing her sweat from his hands."

Diara's face whitened, "What are you plotting now?" The boy laughed so hard he lost his grip on the heavy barrel. It tipped too much and soaked Elona to the skin.

"I'm sorry Elona," he said in a quivering, frightened voice.

"That's okay Caysa," said Diara. "She deserves it, and needed a bath anyway."

The two large main cooking cauldrons were boiling away Ciramtis's leaves, when Diara dumped the rena pinto bean sacks into them. They weighed seven tarmets each and if it weren't for Caysa's help she would not have been able to lift and empty them.

Elona stacked the wood near the fires, and carried all the drinking water to the warriors. Caysa ran continuously between the cook kettles stirring them and preventing them from boiling over. Atus sat at the rear tailgate of the supply wagon all the while, kissing Ciramtis's neck and barking out an occasional order.

Chapter # 22

The Third Strata's Woman

Captain Alament, the military's commanding officer had been visiting the princess wagon. He had been trying to assure her that they making good progress and that they would arrive at the City of Zarhun on schedule. After consulting with her; he walked over to the cooking and food preparation area. "Where is that miserable excuse for a cook," he yelled?

Atus jumped down from the chuck wagon before he was found, and ran over to the captain. Ciramtis hid herself from view in the back of wagon as soon as she heard the officer's booming voice. "The men are extra hungry tonight. It was pretty a rotten lunch you put out for them. The one's that were able to eat that slop, had indigestion for zestars. It tasted so bad that half of them couldn't get it down." Atus stayed out of striking range, as the captain continued to yell at him.

"Now all you've got on the fire for them to eat tonight is a thin celban soup, dried jerky meat strips and a few loaves of hard moldy bread." The captain tried to grab him, but Atus was too wily and stayed on the opposite side of the fire.

The captain took a thick log from the woodpile. He smacked the palm of his hand with it a few times. "The men haven't had a decent piece of meat since we left Woreza. If they don't get some good meat tonight, along with a piece of fresh bread, I am coming back here with a few of them and we're going to put you on one of those spits."

He threw the log at Atus, and stormed away into the darkness. The cook ducked quickly and ran away from the stirring kettles and preparation area. A few zestas later he returned with two muscular, male slaves following him. They were barefoot and wearing only loincloths. One carried long curved knives and several one inch diameter steel rods with the ends ground to a sharpened point. The other bearer had the better part of a bloody hindquarter slung over his shoulder. Two butchered measan steers had been salted and brought along, but Atus had intended on saving the meat until they reached the outskirts of Zarhun City.

The bloody hindquarters were carried over to the wagon tailgate where the three of them pride and hacked away the few sections of remaining ribs. Then they started slicing the meat off of the leg bone. If would have been better, had it been roasted as one piece of meat, but he needed to have it cooked a lot quicker if he was going to avoid a beating.

The women stayed out of sight not wishing to see the butchering. They also did not want to be handling or carrying the large bloody chucks of meat. Before the zestar was over, both cook fires had a rack of sizzling rump roasts on them, and one had the remains of the ribs and other bloody bones. Once these were brazed, the bones and meat scrapes were going to be thrown into the vegetable soup kettles.

During the carving Ciramtis had taken charge, and had ordered all the smaller crocks filled with soup. Elona, Diara, and Caysa along two other slave attendants distributed the cooked vegetables and broth throughout the camp. Very little of it was left by the time Atus returned. Ciramtis poured out the rest from the one large remaining kettle, scraping it with the ladle, and setting some of it aside for the roving guards.

The majority of this kettle was to go to the princess and her retinue. Atus walked over and watched the slave women working a zesta. Cira covered the last serving kettle with a lid to keep it warm. Then she slipped the carrying pole threw the two ring handles, and waved over the two men standing at the rear of the wagon. The two kitchen household slaves ran over immediately and picked up the poles, letting the pot swing a zesta. Then they proceeded to the princess's table and dining area.

"Who told you to dish out and serve that soup?"

Atus glared at Ciramtis. "No one," she yelled back at him, throwing the ladle into the empty kettle in a disgusted manor! "I heard what that loud mouthed captain told you. If we are ever going to have some time together, I thought that I should get the soup dished out. It will give you time to get some of that roasted meat served."

"I also told those two worthless scullery maids to mix up the bread dough and set up the baking ovens." Pulling off her apron, she tossed it into his face, and started to leave for her tent. He snatched up her wrist and held it tightly while looking about the cooking area.

Diara and Elona were up to their elbows in soo bread dough. Their faces and arms were now smudged with flour. The folding table near the wagon was stacked high with unbaked locis loaves. Off in the distant shadows he could see the warriors standing about with soup bowls, eating and laughing. Atus walked over to where the bread was being mixed. Ciramtis's wrist was still in his grasp. The dough looked good and smelled even better. Pulling off a piece, he tasted it. It was good, perhaps even better than his own.

"Who mixed up the ingredients for you?"

Diara tried to scratch her nose without leaving more flour. "It was the army's new servant woman, camp follower!" She pulled off a large section of the sticky dough from the mixing table and rolled it into a wheel shape and made three long slices on top. Then she carried it over to Elona. Elona had the flat metal baking sheets staked with more unbaked wheels.

The small metal baking tents, had already been set up, and were just about ready to have the last of the loaves shoved into them. Atus looked really pleased. His face glowed with pride and enthusiasm. "What a woman!" He gave Ciramtis a hard pat on the rump, while leaving his hand. With a woman like this he could set up a food stand in any market place.

"You there boy," Ciramtis yelled at Caysa! "I need some more hot coals for these oven racks."

Caysa gripped the small metal shovel tightly and wiped the soot from his cheek. He was about to step in front of her and give her an argument. He did not have a chance to speak. Atus hit him on the side of the face knocking the boy to the ground.

"You heard her. Pick up that shovel and fetch another load of hot coals. Then fetch some more branches and bank that fire, the woods burning too fast."

Ciramtis took the lowest tray from the oven and poured hot melted butter over the crust. Atus took the large flat knife and cut each of the hot bread wheels into six pieces. Each dakalug loaf smelled delicious. Selecting the two loaves that had a light golden appearance, he set them aside for Princess Shayla's table. Then he went to the meat spit and chose four of the best and leanest pieces of roasted measan. The princess will surely not forget this meal. He carried the bread and platter over to her table personally.

Captain Alament was dining with the princess tonight. Atus knew that this officer was a distant cousin of the princess's. Alament sipped his soup and was surprised at how good it tasted. Eyeing Atus contemptuously, he remained quiet while the cook stood in front of the head table. Not even he was allowed to speak at the princess's table unless spoken to first. Atus stood balancing the tray and platters in his hands, waiting patiently. The princess finished her soup, licking off both sides of the spoon, before seeing the cook.

Princess Shayla waved him closer, smelling the cooked meat and seeing the tray full of thick strip steaks. "That was one of your finest soups, and the meat and bread look fabulous." Licking her lips like a starving lioness, she stuck her fork tines through two ten ounce pieces of meat, and hefted them to her platter. Then she took two wedges of hot buttered bread.

"I thank the princess for the compliment but I came here to beg your forgiveness."

She gave him a cold fish eyed expression as she chewed. If it wasn't for the captain's presence at the table, speaking could have cost him his tongue. Atus had risked the princess would not want to make his ill reverence into a spectacle, while in front of another member of the royal household. His gamble had paid off; Shayla looked over at her cousin. Then she smiled in an amused yet haughty arrogant mannerism, and finished chewing.

"Why is it that you are asking for my forgiveness?" Atus lowered his head. His voice took on a timid and apologetic sound, wavering slightly. "My princess, it's because I've timed the meal poorly. It's almost the twenty fourth zestar and I am still using your lady servants to distribute the meal for the rest of the men. I'm afraid they will not be able finish until after you are done eating." He bowed even lower, awaiting her response. She laughed as she cut her roasted meat into large cubes.

"The skinny ones? The way those witches have behaved, I wouldn't care if you keep them until we arrive in Renvas. But mind you, I want no bruises on them. They better be unharmed and in good shape when we arrive!"

Atus's gleamed, "Thank you princess I will take especially good care of them. A little hard work will do them good, and make them a little more respectful." He bowed again, backing away from her presence. This was perfect, now they could do most of his work and he could spend more time with Ciramtis. He hummed a tavern tune as he walked away thinking of this sexy woman and the sumptuous meal that she had prepared.

The last tray of baked loafs, was pulled from the oven racks. Ciramtis set them aside to cool. Caysa was so exhausted by this time; he had fallen asleep on the ground near the wood pile. Elona and Diara were sitting down with their backs to the wagon wheel. Their eyelids were getting heavy; their muscles were stiff and aching. The ground around them swayed, but they could not fall asleep.

Ciramtis cut some of the meat into smaller pieces, and placed the diced cubes on a plate. Then she sliced two pieces of bread, and filled two mugs with wine. She walked over to them and knelt down. Elona gave her a blank almost lifeless stare. "I suppose now you want us to serve the princess?" Her voice was weak, drained of its energy and just above a whisper.

Ciramtis watched Elona's drugged eyes as she spoke. They were glossed over, with dilated pupils and tearing at the corners. "No Elona this is for you and Diara." Ciramtis placed the plate on Elona's lap, and set down the wine cups. "Eat if you can. Tomorrow will be a better day." Diara couldn't speak. She reached over and took a small piece of meat from the plate but she couldn't eat it.

They both watched as Ciramtis walked off to look after Caysa. After shaking him several times, he hadn't awakened. Reaching down the buxom slave scooped him up in her arms and carried him to the wagon. They did not know what to think.

"Where does he sleep," asked Cira?

Elona pointed her thumb at the rear of the wagon. A dirty pile of rags were just underneath the rear axle. She laid him down and tried to cover him as best she could. They could hear Atus returning. He came around the wagon, a broad smile on his face and still humming his rhythmic ditty.

It was a grand day and now Ciramtis was going to make it an even grander evening. Taking a sizzling piece of meat from the cook fire, he looked about the camp while it cooled. Everything was quiet and peaceful. Almost too peaceful, he thought as he nibbled on the steak. The male kitchen slaves were asleep on the ground near the supply wagon. Only three guards could be seen walking their posts. No one had cleaned the empty cook pots, or utensils. He picked up his ladle and kettle, with his intension to start banging on them, when Ciramtis ran over to him.

"There you are," she said as she stepped closer putting her arms about his neck.

Atus pointed at the sleeping slaves with his ladle. "Who's going to clean up all this mess, and repack the supply wagon?"

She kissed him. "I told those miserable scullery maids to get some rest and I would wake them early tomorrow." She pointed at the bottle of lusverus wine on the mixing table. "Let's go off into the woods and finish it off." Atus picked up the deep red grape alcohol as they sauntered by the table. They hugged briefly, then walked past the wagon and headed in the direction of the darkening shadows beneath some overhanging boughs.

Diara was slumped over and sleeping but Elona's eyes were still open and blinking. "As long as you are not tired, you can clean the pots while were gone." Elona looked up at Atus a little bewildered; she knew he had said something to her. She had even seen his lips move. There was no sound, only a buzzing noise in her brain. Her head began swimming then cleared again. She looked to her side in the direction of their laughter. Atus took a long drink from the wine bottle, and handed it to Ciramtis. They walked off into the darkness, arm and arm.

"Diara, Diara, now's our chance," said Elona with an emotionless tone to her voice. "They forgot to send over the night guard. We can escape now." She reached over and pulled on the sleeve of Diara's grimy blouse, she wouldn't wake up. Instead she rolled to the side and curled up on the ground. "Come on, wake up, we'll never have another chance like this to escape."

"Escape? Is that what you're thinking about?" Elona looked up out of the corner of her eye. Striding in their direction was one of the roving guards. "Where's the sentry for this post," he asked? She let her head fall backward against the wagon wheel spokes. Their last chance had vanished. Tears filled her eyes, but she couldn't cry.

"I asked? Where is the sentry?" She swept the fallen hair away from her eyes and stared at him a zesta, trying to recall something. Now she knew what it was. She recognized him. He was the contemptible ogre of a guard that had left them cooped up in the sweltering heat in the back of the wagon.

"I don't know where he is," she said in an almost lifeless disparaging voice. "And I don't care! If he is as smart as you are, he probably got lost in the dark." The guard reached down and grabbed her face by the chin. She tried to pry his hand away but he was too strong.

"You there guard." He stood up straight until he noticed that it was not a sentry that was coming his way, it was just another slave woman. She walked out of the dark shadows and into the firelight.

Elona looked at her. It was Ciramtis. She must have given Atus a heart attack to have finished with him already. It had been less than ten zestas.

Ciramtis swayed her hips and walked over to the guard. Her right arm was behind her back, and there was a big smile on her face. Elona thought she had the wine bottle behind her back, and had returned to fill it. The guard was sure to take it away from her. "What have you got there sweat cheeks?"

She stood before him, swaying her shoulders and modestly teasing him. "I am not telling."

Elona cleared her throat. "Go on Cira. Give him the wine bottle," she said. "It's not worth the beating."

The guard extended his hand. "You heard her, give it to me."

Ciramtis took a bashful step closer. "Alright," she said sweetly. Her hand swung out quickly from behind her back. The guard jerked erect turning toward Elona, his eyes were wide but he couldn't speak. The handle of a sharp bread knife was sticking out from below his ribcage.

Elona could not believe what she had just seen. The guard was dead, Ciramtis had killed him. She watched as Cira lowered the guard to the ground. Then the wench pulled out the bloody knife and covered the guard with a blanket. He looked like any other tired warrior, except that his eyes were still open.

Quickly Ciramtis moved to Elona's side. "Just sit still and be quiet. I am a friend of Lord Jedaf's and we came to rescue the both of you."

Elona was befuddled, and was loosing her hearing again. "Where is Atus," asked Elona?

"Shayla's cook is in the bushes where he will never bother anyone again." Ciramtis held her by the shoulders, and tipped Elona over on her side. She was too exhausted to resist or move. Her eyes closed and the tears flowed freely below her lids. The buzzing sound had come back louder than before. She kept her eyes closed and tried to think of what the wench had just said, but she could not remember.

Chapter # 23

The Green Envarian Army

The sunlight came streaking into the back of the wagon through the crack in the rear flap. It had been shinning on Elona's face for quite some time. It was annoying, but she was too tired and sore to move. Pulling the blanket over face, she shielded her eyes. It felt so good to just lie there, she thought. The wagon hit another bump jostling her head about. The swaying movement gave her a queasy sensation in her stomach.

Elona's temples started to throb, as she sat up to see Diara sleeping next to her and Caysa sleeping at their feet. The wagon was almost empty compared to what it had been yesterday. One large clothing trunk and an assortment of food supplies had been stacked and lashed together at the sides. This left the entire center of the wagon clear for them to lie down.

There were six stacked crates of either green or yellow leafy vegetables, three large burlap bags of raw tubers and two barrels of dry goods on her side of the wagon. On the other side were stacks of blankets, towels, large oily canvas tarps, along with coils of ropes, most of the cooking kettles, utensils and the baking equipment. Shaking Diara awake she asked, "Where are the rest of the princess's clothing wardrobes and her other possessions?"

Diara sat up. Her head felt like she had downed two bottles of strong wine the night before. "Maybe Atus put them in another wagon," she said groggily. Then she noticed Caysa sleeping at their feet. Diara crawled over him, and tossed back the rear flap. It was not tied. The air and sunshine made her head hurt worse. She closed her eyes, and rubbed her temples with her fingertips. "Oh does my head hurt," she said and crawled back to where Elona was sitting. "There's no rear guard or outriders, back there. Elona, are you sure this is our wagon?"

Elona leaned against the rough wooden barrels on her side of the wagon and closed her eyes. She tried to remember what had happened last night. "I don't even know how we got into the wagon. Everything seems to be jumbled up in my head." She remembered very little of lunch and second lunch. Kreb, the evening meal was half dream world and half-sketchy drug induced memories. She remembered kneading and baking bread. Opening her eyes she looked at her hands. They still had flour on them and under her fingernails.

A wave of nausea came over her; holding her stomach she crawled over Caysa to the rear flap. She vomited out the remains of yesterday's soup. It was acidic and the sour taste made her gag all the more. She reached over and took the water skin bag. She was thankful it was so close. Pulling the cork she rinsed her mouth and took two small swallows. "Diara do you feel as sick as I do?" Elona turned around to see her. Diara had curled up, and fallen asleep again.

Laughter was coming from the front of the wagon. Elona crawled over where she had been sitting and looked at the drivers. There were three individuals, sitting on the bench seat. Two men dressed in the yellow, brown and white colored clothing of the seamen's guild, with a slave woman seated between them. The men's backs were muscular, and they were laughing deeply as they joked with the woman.

A cold chill ran down Elona's spine. She grabbed her blanket tossing it over her shoulders. Leaning to the side, she stared at the back of the female's head. While the woman was speaking to the wagon driver, Elona recognized the sound of this slave's voice and its tone started to bring back some memories.

Elona knew her, but from where? The woman's head turned to the brakeman, making some inaudible comment. "Ciramtis," she said slowly to herself. It's the third strata's woman that came to their wagon yesterday. She recognised her profile.

Pulling the blanket up over her head, she crept up a little closer to them. "Diara was probably right, this was not their wagon. It had to be the army's and the wench had convinced Atus into having them do some of her work." She was talking to herself in a very low hushed voice as she watched them. Lying down behind the bench seat; she quietly listened to their conversation. They did not look behind them and did not know that she was awake.

"You should have seen her Vadeck. Her purple and lavender robes made her look like a pregnant sea cow." Ciramtis laughed as the hunched over brakeman spoke.

"I did see her. I heard her screams from the other side of the camp, and ran over to see if I could shut her mouth. We were lucky that most of the warriors were already drugged and that the roving guards had been killed. When I stepped threw the shrubs, I could see Karadis tying her hands and feet, while you were stuffing a rag in her mouth."

The man called Vadeck flicked the reins picking up the speed. The old sailor laughed making a whistling sound threw his broken nose.

"That is nothing; you should have seen us trying to get her out of the wagon. No matter where you grabbed her you lost your hand in the blubber. Finally we were able to pin her down but she was too heavy for us to lift."

"Then how did you get her out of the wagon captain?"

The man on the break side laughed again. "That was easy we rolled her out and let her bounce on the ground." I never thought her flab would stop shaking.

Vadeck's voice changed to a more serious tone. "Do you think you scared her enough to make her flee to Zarhun City?"

"Sure do, Vad," Odel took the whip from the side of the seat and gave it a couple of cracks. "You're starting to fall too far behind Bara, and Kar." The wagon jumped ahead a little faster, until the horses adjusted to the new quicker stride. "When we rolled her out, I told her that we were going to sell her to the man eaters of Mokan."

"Bara did kind of talk me out of it; he said that tonight's raid we'd take only the skinner women because they would sell quicker. Then we will come back tomorrow morning and take the fat one for the cook pots. What bothers me more was the fact that the nefren leaves did not put her to sleep and she almost had enough time to warn the guards."

"I suspect that it must have something to do with her muscle to fat ratio," interjected Ciramtis before Odelac could continue.

"While the wagons burned we turned our backs just long enough to make sure she was able to crawl off into the dark and under the bushes. She was still there cowering in the foliage and hiding when we rode out."

Ciramtis reached behind the seat, fetching her cloak. She still had on a very skimpy and soiled slave woman's dress. Her back and bare arms were getting cold. "Do you think they saw any of the vourtre," she asked?

"No! I don't think so," replied Odel. "Most of them had already pulled out before we took the princess's wagon."

Vadeck slowed their small freight wagon; it took a few hard jostling bumps in the road ruts. Then he flicked the reins, and the team picked up speed once more. "I think he's right about that," said Vadeck. "Prince Pfitas, Ush Tyan, and the rest of his men rode out for Jeupa, as soon as the last sentry had been killed."

"Heyo Zon and Quay Thauk decided at the last zesta that they would not scatter the horses. They would drive them south and sell them to the Jeupan border guards. Why let the Worezians find them at all? Gat Hyados's men gathered all the swords and weapons, and took them into the Eastern Semedian highlands. He said this people will re-forge them to better fit vourtre hands, and use them against the Worezians."

Odel leaned forward in front of Ciramtis to see Vad, better. "Do you think he will live to see that?" Vadeck shook his head in reply.

"Why do you say that Odel," asked Cira. "Was he wounded? I had not heard anything about it."

"Yes. The last time I saw him, I thought that he was already dead. He was with Vad, when he was wounded. Why don't you tell us what happened."

Vadeck shifted nervously, looking straight ahead at the trotting team. "I don't think it's for me to say anymore."

Odel reached over in front of Cira, pulling the reins from Vad's hands. "What do you mean by that remark?" Vadeck lowered his head a zesta feeling a little self-conscious. "I have known you a long time," said Odelac. "This is the first time that I have ever asked you a question, and you've avoided giving me the answer. Now out with it! I want the truth, and I don't want to hear it from someone else."

The old taskmaster looked over at the two of them. The captain was angrier than, Vad had seen in a long time. Cira's face had a curious look but her eyes were certainly more sympathetic. "Okay captain. I guess that I owe you, at least that much."

"Gat ordered Karadis, Baradic, and myself to help him take out the two sentries at the lead wagon. It was supposed to be a simple job. The four of us were to come around the camp from the south, crawl up to the hedgerow, and wait on the side of the wagon for the signal."

"Karadis and I were to take the sentry, near the wagon tongue, and Gat and Baradis were to take the one standing by the fire. We all made it to the wagon without being seen and waited quietly. Kar and I were given the signal and we moved forward quickly. We took the sentry without a sound, and dragged him off into the bushes."

"Baradic and Gat made it to the front of wagon without being seen. We moved closer in case they needed help, but we stayed far enough back, as not to interfere. Gat crept around the end of the wagon with his sword drawn, and trotted toward the guard."

"He was ten paces from the guard when a cup fell into a metal pot in the back of the wagon. It alerted the sentry. He turned quickly and seeing Gat. He threw his lance at him. He would have warned all the rest of the other guards if it weren't for a fantastic knife throw by Karadis."

"Gat's left lung might have been pierced. We pulled the lance from him, and put a compress on the wound." It did not look good. "He was coughing up blood, when his men carried him off on a stretcher."

Odel looked to Cira, then back to his taskmaster Vadeck. "So what about that, didn't you want us to know? It was no ones fault. The guard just had sharper ears than most."

Vadeck turned his face away, and spoke without looking at him. "The cup fell into the wagon, because Baradic reached over tailgate, and tried to pull a wine bottle free. In the dark, he couldn't see the cup had a string around it that was tied to the bottleneck. When he pulled the bottle out, the cup fell into a kettle."

"As soon as it dropped he knew he had alerted the guard. He stayed in the dark at the side of the wagon holding his knife, but he did nothing. While Gat's men were loading him on the litter, I questioned Bara. He denied it until I told him that I had seen it myself. His answer was, and I quote, so what, another green dies. It's not like he was human."

Odelac flicked the reins. "You don't have to worry about it Vad. I will take care of it."

Vadeck reached over and re-took the reins. Then he separated the leather straps between each of his finger again, before looking at the captain. "You don't have to worry about it either Odel! I heard Gat speaking to his men before they took him away. They will take care of the problem."

Elona had been silent during the whole conversation. She crawled back to Diara and gave her a shove. Her friend rolled over moaning and pulling the blanket over her head. Elona sat back against the wagon, thinking about what she had heard. So they were raiders, working with the vourtre. If they take her to a slave market of a large city, she would have the chance of buying back her freedom. She knew her father would pay any price to get her back. She closed her eyes and dreamed out her fantasy.

Diara opened her eyes and watched the canvas top, sway to the jostling wagon. The queasy feeling in her stomach was somewhat better, but she was still cold. She pulled her blanket up around her. Elona was lying awake next to her. Diara could see her eyes, as Elona watched the drivers. "What time is it," Diara whispered?

Elona put her finger to her lips, and replied with a shhh sound. The big man on the right side of the bench seat had just asked Ciramtis the same question. They watched as she took a small sundial from her leather pouch. She held it as steady as she could, watching the central levelling bubble, and moved the two outer brass rings, aligning them with the two suns. "It's about the ninth zestar Odel."

Vadeck gave a loud whistle to the driver of the large Conestoga ahead of them. The mid-sized wagon that they were riding in had been stolen from the Worezian princess's caravan. It was one of Atus's cook house utensils and equipment wagons. Vadeck transferred their vegetables and some of their other food supplies to this vehicle. He needed to make room for the side of measan and the flour barrels that he had appropriated from the other wagons.

The two wagons slowed to a halt. "We have been riding off and on now, for nearly twelve zestars," said the Captain. "It is time we rested for awhile and I don't mean just a short break. I am sure if we had any followers, we lost them long ago. Vadeck hop down and tell Karadis that will take a few zestars rest, and give these teams a break."

The lead wagon moved ahead slowly for a short time with Vadeck hanging on the side. The countryside that they had just come through had been nothing but scrub brush, thickets and thorn trees. It was nice to see soft green pines and ferns ahead of them.

Karadis led his team into the tall grass of a clearing and dismounted. Vadeck jumped off and unhitched the team, while Baradic tended to Odelac's horse. The south central Zarhun Plain was ahead of them and stretched out before them as far as they could see. It was dotted with tall straight conifers. The ground was covered with knee high waving wild wheat and a multitude of tall wild flowers. The soft pastel colors made the distances hard to judge. It was an endless sea of swaying golden brown and yellow-green undergrowth.

Ciramtis stood in the jostling wagon looking to the west. The wind was at her back, blowing her hair up and over her head. She smoothed it back down with one hand and tied a soft yellow cloth strip around it with her other hand. The air was scented and clean. It was easy for her to see why the ancients had named the second month of first summer after Asursa the Goddess of Flowers.

Vadeck arranged the two wagons in a vee, with the tongues pointing to the east. Baradic unhitched the teams and removed the harnesses and bridles. He gave all of them a well-deserved rub down before lighting a small fire, sheltered from the wind. Karadis set up the spit, fire irons and a grated meat rack at the fire circle. He turned the meat strips on the racks while Baradic gathered some additional firewood.

At the far side of the campfire was a small metal stand with a fancy decorative porcelain tea crock. The crockery was colored and shaped like a pumpkin gourd. Leaves and vines decorated the bottom and sides, with the stem being fashioned into the pouring spot. The battle hardened old seaman had seen it in Princess Shayla's wagon along with a set of ten cups. He had immediately had taken a liking to it and decided to steel it for himself.

While Vadeck set up his dainty tea cups and inlaid wooden serving tray, Ciramtis chuckled. The sight of this boisterous muscular marine handling this fine translucent porcelain was so incongruous. His large finger joints would not even fit through the vine shaped loops in the cup handles and he looked like he was handling delicate plicrican eggs.

Odel and Cira decided that they would do a bit of exploring and walked out onto the plain. Twenty paces from their wagons, was a large raised mound with two trees growing at the summit. From the hilltop they could see in every direction.

The foundations of an old farmhouse, one hundred paces to the north were the only visible man made landmarks. Odel decided after seeing the surrounding countryside, they should spend at least half a day here resting. He returned to camp to help Vadeck gather wood from the edge of the timberline. Further out on the grasslands, they would find it difficult to keep the predators away.

Ciramtis continued her walk, resting at the remains of the old farm house. A small, cold spring fed stream was nearby, what had been a fenced stockyard. Two or three dry rot sections still remained. She removed her clothing and sat at the low bank. The cold water felt good and was refreshing. She washed thoroughly, rinsed her long hair a second time, and braided wild flowers in the soft curls.

Sitting for a few restful zestas, she dangled her feet over the edge and splashed water at a brown and yellow speckled frog sitting on the opposite side. It was a good relaxing moment while it lasted, but she was starting to have a creepy feeling that someone or something was watching her.

Ceratuses and packs of speckled dujiaks were known to roam these plains. The thought of being eaten by one of these large puma's or a pack of wild dogs didn't help. She dressed quickly and ran back to the camp.

Odel and Vad had carried in three loads of wood and had gone back for the remains of a fallen tree. Karadis had a sizeable amount of fresh meat cooked. At the edge of the fire where the flames had left only hot glowing coals, he had tossed ten large oolets and a dozen or so nestabs.

The potato like oolet vegetables grew to the size of two men's fists, and had a thick deep reddish skin. They were starting to sizzle and pop open, revealing their soft, snowy white insides. The baked tubers would soon be ready, to peal and eat. The harder, three inch diameter, round maroon colored nestab beets would take longer to roast.

Ciramtis climbed into the lead wagon and changed her dress. She donned a long brown dress, a robe with hooded cape and a pair of high soft leather boots. She no longer needed the skimpy slave dress, or open toed sandals. Walking by the fire, she dropped the tattered rags onto the hot coals before giving Kar a hand at taking the roasted meat from the spit. "I wonder were Baradic is," she asked as she looked about?

"I sent him to find that stream that Odel told us about, and I haven't seen him since." Ciramtis stood and looked in all directions. Karadis was the only one in the camp when she came back. She had seen the captain and Vadeck at the edge of the woods, but she hadn't thought about Baradic or noticed him missing. She did not like him and if someone mentioned his name, all she could picture in her mind was the cowardly way he had acted around the vourtre. Baradic was also the quiet, devious type of a man that you didn't notice, even when he sat next to you.

Both of the captive women had been awake for zestars, but they had decided to stay inside and watch the highwaymen set up their camp. Elona had told Diara and Caysa what she had overheard earlier this morning. The boy couldn't understand their fearful apprehensive attitude. He would rather be anyone's slave, than be Shayla's. How much harsher could he be treated than what he had already been subjected to?

The twelve year old could barely remember anything of the previous day. He had no idea what had happened, or who had carried him to the women's wagon. The only one he recognized walking about the camp was Ciramtis the third strata's woman. She certainly looked much different than the last time he had seen her. Caysa tossed the canvas flap back and jumped down from the back of the wagon.

Ciramtis walked over to him and handed him a piece of roasted meat on a stick and a hot baked oolet. "Caysa, I am Ciramtis, of the Order of Esella. I'm sorry for the way I treated you yesterday, but I promise to make up for it today. Won't you join us at the fire? Elona and Diara," she called out. "You've been in there long enough. You can also come out and join us." They both knew that they would have to come out sooner or later.

Elona's fear had made her stomach knot up as hard as a rock. Her hope was that they would not molest them and sell them quickly as planned, but how was she to trust anything they said. Diara was just as worried as she timidly climbed from the wagon. Her hands trembled while waiting for Elona to jump to the ground. The two stood in the matted grass and looked about nervously until they gathered enough courage to walk over to the campfire.

Vadeck and Odelac came out of the woods dragging a ten-inch diameter log with a forked end. The dead tree was as least six paces long and weighed as much as the captain himself. They dropped it and walked over next to Karadis and Ciramtis while dusting off the crumbling bark from their hands. It was about time for them to meet the women that they had risked their lives for, in seeing to their freedom.

Ciramtis stepped forward and extended her hand palm upward in welcome. "I am Ciramtis of Iblac. Don't be afraid, we are friends and servants of Lord Jedaf of Dolfi." The two women both looked a little bewildered and confused. Dressed in her normal attire, they had not recognized her at first. Diara hung onto Elona's arm, and her face looked questioningly back, in a totally perplexed manner. How could this be? Elona thought to herself. Why would a youthful bond slave have such powerful friends?

Taking a cleansing breath, she stood taller with her shoulders back and her head held high. It was the first time, in what seemed like years, that she felt some of her dignity returning. Twisting a little nervously at the dragon headed steel band on her finger; she felt the high raised edge of its horns. The sudden thought of him made her feel sad, and uneasy. "Did the ambassador give that slave permission, for you to come and rescue us?"

Ciramtis was surprised at Elona's question, and she looked to the others for an answer. They were just as confused, all of them except for Captain Odelac. "I asked, whether the Yojan Ambassador gave his approval?"

Ciramtis shrugged her shoulders. "Why would our lord have to ask permission from Ambassador Ajoris to do anything?"

Odel smiled at first, than started a subdued chuckle. Everyone looked at him. They couldn't see anything funny in what had been said. He must have thought of an un-spoken joke as he stood by. "Don't you see Cira; both of the princesses still think that Lord Jedaf is Ajor's servant and bond slave. They have never been told anything different." Elona watched as he held his sides, and continued to laugh quietly while he spoke.

"You mean he is not a slave," replied Elona and Diara, in unison? Ciramtis waved her arm in the direction of the campfire. "Let's sit down and talk for awhile. You need to be set straight on a few things, and there is some information that you should be given." The group returned to the campfire and sat around it as Karadis served the meal he had prepared.

Baradic stepped out from behind a short stand of pine trees. He had been standing there listening, since following Ciramtis back to camp. He liked watching everyone without them knowing it. Setting the water kettles down near a meal bag, he walked over to the fire circle. Pouring himself a cup of tea, he took a piece of roasted meat as he watched them out of the corner of his eye. He did not look up at them, or say anything. Instead he walked over to the wagon and sat by himself on the ground with his back to the wheel hub.

Caysa remained sitting near the fire, eating his second oolet. He did not know who or what, they were talking about, and he really didn't care. The longer they talked the more he had to eat. After the introductions, Ciramtis told them that it had been the captain's idea, to make it appear to the pirates, that Jedaf was the ambassador's slave. Had the brigands known who he was, it might have cost Jedaf his life, or a very great ransom.

They continued sitting around the fire for more than two zestars. Vadeck passed out the roasted meat strips, while Kar handed out the vegetables and poured the tea. Captain Odelac told the women all that had transpired since the pirate ship Culba, had docked in Woreza. At the conclusion of his narrative he informed them; about Jedaf of Dolfi being the Lord of the Dragon, Protector of the Dead and the rightful King of Ancient Semedia. "We are all his servants including Ambassador Ajoris. The five of us are riding to North Point, to meet up with his army and to give them their orders."

Diara ate hungrily, while Ciramtis spoke, but not Elona. She sat holding a teacup in one hand, and meat on a stick, in the other. She hadn't tasted either. She stared into the flames of the fire thinking of Jedaf. She had been a fool, and had treated him worse than she had treated anyone, slave or nobleman. She listened quietly, while tears formed in the corners of her eyes. Would he ever forgive me, she thought?

It was good to be among friends once again, and what was better still was the chance to wash and throw their clothing away. Ciramtis had thrown a trunk of Shayla's clothing into the cook wagon before Odel burned everything else. The women carried it to the stream with them, along with towels and two bars of pligolg soap each. Before leaving the camp Cira had a whispered chat with Odel. The captain was going to see to it that Baradic was kept busy while the women were away.

The pleated floral skirt that Diara chose, rapped around her three full times. The rose colored tunic top looked like a parka on her, except for the fact that she kept slipping through the neck hole. Elona rummaged through and tried on everything in the trunk. Nothing she chose fit her any better. Ciramtis returned to the wagon and fetched her travel bag. It had a good sharp surgical scissors, thimble, needles, thread and a stitching pad for the palm of her hand.

The three sat at the stream bank, cutting, tucking, and re-sewing enough of Shayla's wardrobe, for each of them to make two partial ill fitting outfits. The rest of the clothing scrapes were tossed back into the trunk, for another time. They had been away from the camp for nearly three and a half zestars, and it was the best time that Elona and Diara had spent since leaving their Kelleskarian homelands.

Upon returning to camp, the women found Karadis and Baradic had left. The captain had sent the out on a scouting party, two zestars ago. Neither had liked the idea of a ten thasta ride, but the captain wanted to know what was ahead of them out on the plain. Elona and Diara were both glad that they were gone. Diara felt that Karadis was trying to make advances on her before they left for the stream, and Elona didn't like the way Baradic was acting.

When they sat down to eat. Baradic had returned to the fire and squeezed between her and Vadeck sitting down next to her. Every time she moved to the side a little, he would also move. Finally he had moved so close to her that she was hitting his elbow while she pealed her oolet. She stood, fetched a piece of meat and sat on the other side of the fire while Ciramtis and Odelac spoke.

As long as the two of them were in front of her she felt better. Ciramtis had another private whispering session with the captain, while they chatted with Caysa, and Vadeck. Both women knew what

Cira was talking about even though she had not told them. Each had thought that they had seen some rustling in the tall grass, as they washed in the stream. Cira was furious, and even though she whispered they could see the anger on her face.

It was very difficult for the women to understand Vadeck. He felt uncomfortable speaking to women and spoke very softly. His heavy nasal and timid speech had a whistling sound which made it even worse. Even though he was disfigured, quite ugly, and almost twice Diara's age, she took a liking to him and sat at his side talking quietly. How this fifteen year old princess could find this uncouth, hardened old marine warrior of any interest was beyond Elona's understanding until she pondered her own circumstances.

The Oppowian Princess kept her thoughts and comments to herself thinking of how she had fallen in love with a common slave. Sitting next to the gangly slave boy, she occasionally spoke with and responded to Caysa's questions. Elona wasn't really listening or interested in what he was saying. She remained politely quiet most of the time while thinking of Jedaf.

Elona pulled her knees up and hugged them tightly as she sat with the boy near the supply wagon. Will I ever feel his arms around me again, she thought? She put her chin down, lowered her eyes, and let the tears flow. She didn't say anything for long periods of time.

Occasionally she would nod in agreement with Caysa, but she did not know what he was talking about. She also thought how odd it was for her not wanting to be rude to this waif. Two mursas earlier, she would not have ever considered that slaves are humans let alone have feelings.

Hoof beats off in the distance didn't raise her curiosity. She already knew that it must be that letret worm Baradic. She was wrong it was Karadis and he had been riding hard. Tying his mount's reins to the wheel of the supply wagon, he ran over to Odelac.

"Captain, there's a large body of men moving this way! They're over twenty thousand strong, and have at least two tantaxes, plus auxiliaries. These warriors are moving very slowly trying to keep their dust down, but their cloud was a thasta wide."

Odel waived Ciramtis over to him and Karadis. The white witch had been picking herbs at the forest edge. He filled her in on what Kar had reported and asked for her advice. "Kar did you see any of the banners," she asked?

"Yes, but they were too far away to make out what was on them. I told Baradic to hang back, until he could tell whose army it is." Vadeck and Diara came over to hear what was going on. "I don't think that we can wait to find out. We should break camp now, and move the wagons back into the forest. Their scouts were about five thastas behind me."

"I think your right Kar," said the captain. "Cira have the women help pack up the wagons. Vadeck, load the cut timber and logs into the supply wagon, we will need it anyway. Caysa put out the fire. Make sure that you burry it and then douse it good. Kar get the teams into the harnesses."

There were no questions, everyone went to work. Odelac had found a secluded and rocky area north of their position, while gathering wood with Vadeck. They decided to drive the wagons into the forest near the large rocks. The high stones would block the sight of the army from one side, and still allow them a clear view of the open plain.

Odel cut down some brush, and with Vadeck's help they swept away most of their tracks. Ciramtis and Elona cut down some small saplings and lower branches from the taller trees. They placed the foliage barrier in front of the rocky opening in the woods. After they were through camouflaging the site, no one would ever suspect that there were two wagons there, unless they rode right at the edge of the forest.

Karadis rode out to find Baradic, and to let him know where they had moved the camp. Odel also gave him instructions concerning the enemy. If these warriors turned out to be part of the Worezian Army, the captain would abandon the wagons. They would evade pursuit by moving northwest at the forest edge until the area was clear. Odel's sailors could meet up with them later if they were separated.

Two zestars after Karadis had ridden out; there had been no word from either of the crewmen. Everyone was a little nervous and on edge, but at least the campsite that Odel had selected, was dry and comfortable. They were secluded and had a good view of the plain.

The large dust cloud approached them, but there were no out-riders visible. Vadeck stayed with the horses another fifty feet further into the forest. The mounts were saddled, and had bags filled with the food and other necessary supplies taken from the wagon. If they had to make a fast get away, they were as best prepared as they could be. Caysa stayed near the captain's side the whole time. Odel had taken the lad under his wing, and had given him a short thrusting dagger to protect himself.

Ciramtis, Elona, and Diara, had also armed themselves. Each had a long thrusting dagger and a good sharp throwing knife. They squatted on the ground near the wagon while looking threw the brush. Finer details on the point men were starting to become recognizable.

The warriors were dressed in grey and green woolen kilts, with light grey leather tunics and brown boots or sandals. They could belong to any army. Elona clutched her knife tightly. She had decided to take her own life before being captured again. "There Ciramtis! A flag over on the far right of the column, can you make out the insignia?"

Diara was right. Cira shaded her eyes, looking off through the holes in the dust cloud. Elona stooped down on her knee caps, looking where Diara was pointing. "I can see the flag too. It is some kind of a bird on a green field. There is another not too far behind it that looks like a stack of harvested wheat with a large eye over it." They looked at Cira; she had turned around leaning her back against the wagon wheel and breathing a sigh of relief.

The army stopped and appeared to be preparing to camp for the rest of the day. They were less than a thasta from Odel's original campsite. Karadis was right about one thing, there were thousands of them. "Well Cira, who are they?"

"They're Lord Sesmak's Envarian rebels," she replied. "Diara, go tell Odel that we can start uncovering the wagons. Elona run down and tell Vadeck he can bring the horses back up here."

"Are you sure that they are friendly, Cira?"

"Yes, you see that banner on the center left. Its light green is for Envar. The sword in the center with the crown over it is the coat of arms of Prince Sesmak and the ancient City of Zarhun. Now go tell Vadeck before he bursts."

Elona ran off without another word. Caysa and Odel pulled all the branches out of their path, and mounted the first wagon. Elona sat between them. They thought about waiting for Karadis and Baradic but there was no telling where they had gone. Vadeck drove the other wagon with Diara seated next to him. Ciramtis rode one of the remaining saddle horse, parallel with Odelac's side of the wagon.

They were less than a hundred paces from the forest edge, when the scouts saw them and reported back to the main column. A strata of warrior's were sent to investigate, and to bring them in. They asked no questions of the drivers as they approached. The troop split in two columns and followed along on both sides. They escorted the two wagons and the single female rider back to their camp.

Chapter # 24

The Ancient City State of Zarhun

Horastus, the larger of the two suns rose hot and bright to a cloudless sky. For the first day of Asursa, second mursa of first summer, it appeared to be one of the few days this year that the temperature was going to be near normal. The entire weather this year had been unseasonably cold and wet. Each of the pervious mursas had been ten to fifteen degrees cooler than normal. Spring was so wet and cold that new shoots had either frozen or rotted in the muddy fields.

Now first summer was half over and the vegetables were stunted, shrivelled and hard. In another sixteen horamyas or days, Vergus the month of drought would start. If this season's temperature and weather patterns had been normal, thousands of peasants around the planet would not be expected to die of starvation.

Last night a large band of highwaymen had raided Princess Shayla's dowry caravan. In the night blackness they had crept into the camp apparently killing many in their sleep. Her evening cloak and shoes were still in the wagon when she was dragged from it.

Shayla's maid servants had been captured and taken hostage during the raid. These captive were to be sold in the eastern slave markets. She had heard them talking of returning at dawn to roundup the stragglers They planed on shipping them to the cannibals on the eastern Zureathion Continent where they would get the best price for the meat.

Princess Shayla had escaped capture but was still bound hand and foot. A sword fight had broken out near her wagon. In the dark the brigands turned their backs on her, and while their attention was diverted, she had rolled into the shrubs and down an embankment.

The Worezian Princess lay beneath a hedgerow of dense black thorns. She was gagged, bound hand and foot, and shivering from a night of exposure. Wearing only a thin cotton dress, purple knee length stockings and a coating of dried mud, she had cursed the bandits throughout the night. Dastus the God of Fate was with her and had saved her from a fate worse than death.

Now in the early morning light she could see the silhouettes of men moving about searching for her. She thought that the highwaymen had returned. She was frightened, whimpering and unable to call for help. She suspected most of her worthless guards had deserted her and had run for the cover of the woods. Lying on her stomach, she decided not to make any further sounds. Then she recognized the stout legs of her servant Gietra. She was Princess Shayla's oldest slave and personal attendant.

Crying out to her, Gietra heard the muffled sounds of her mistress's distress and got down on her hands and knees. Looking under the thick prickly bushes she located the princess. Geitra yelled to the captain of the wedding caravan and he, along with two of the strongest warriors ran to her assistance. The three of them untied the princess and helped her up the muddy hill to the remains of the campground.

Captain Alament, Princess Shayla's distant cousin thanked the gods for her safety. The princess did not show any appreciation, nor was she thankful as he wrapped a warm cloak about her. She was still quite shaken and scared as she told him in a panicked voice, that the highwaymen were going to be returning shortly. They must break camp immediately and make a run for Zarhun City.

Among the anxious guards, Shayla stood shivering and looking around at what was left of her bridal caravan. Her wagons had been burned and all the horses were either scattered or stolen. Most of her royal retinue and handmaid servants were missing. Those that had survived the attack had made their own escape into the woodlands. The remainder of the escort warriors were huddled around campfires. They were vomiting and sick with cramps. Very few of the men were armed.

There were two rows of ten bodies lying near the roadside. Shayla walked over and noticed that her cook Atus and her personal body attendant were amongst the dead. It was only than the realization came to her that the cook house chuck wagon had also been stolen and that she was not going to be fed today. She almost collapsed from the thought and four men had to help her to a fallen tree log that had been placed near one of the warming fires.

Captain Alament posted these four guards around her and Geitra for their personal protection. One of the men had found a cook pot and had fetched washing and fresh drinking water for them. The other warriors that were well enough to move about were ordered to search for the horses, fetch firewood, and anything they could find to make weapons.

Six warriors where assigned the task of scavenging enough planking, banding metals, fittings and wheel parts, to construct a make shift cart for the prince to ride on. It was going to be the only way they would be able to get her to Zarhun City. She certainly did not have the stamina or physical endurance to walk that far. The captain also knew that if the highwaymen returned, there was no way he could defend her. The entire entourage had less than ten swords and half a dozen knives.

Princess Shayla screamed at them for the first two zestars of the morning. She kept yelling, "They're coming back to get me! Hurry! Hurry or all of you are going to die!" This did not encourage or help the men work any faster. Most of the seventy or so survivors knew their lives were forfeit, even it they were to make it to Zarhun City.

Punishment for this unit's disgraceful actions would include Captain Alament. King Magarus would be making an example of him for this failure. This officer was also responsible for losing the royal dispatch pouch that the king had personally given him in Woreza.

It contained the finalized marriage contract as well as orders for the western armies and personalized letters addressed to King Helidon and Prince Quayot of Envar.

Alament had placed the dispatch pouch in the supply wagon last night for safe keeping while he made his rounds. At the far end of the camp, he had been jumped and knocked unconscious. The wagon was the one that the highwaymen had taken with them. Now he wished that it too had been burned. Being part of the royal family had its one consolation; his failure would not cost him a prolonged and painful death like it would for the one in ten that would be executed in this decimation.

The surviving warriors were ready to move out within three zestars of locating the princess. One strata of thirty would lead, one strata of thirty would follow, and the remainder would stay in the middle guarding the princess. They would be pulling her cart and alternating in shifts. The flatbed was just large enough to load their liege's daughter in the front and still have enough room for Gietra to sit with her legs dangling out the back.

Most of the royal guards had made crude weapons of sharpened sticks or carried rock clubs. They were poorly armed but better than having nothing at all. Clubs and pointed stakes were going to be their only means of defense. The Worezians would be running all day, and only stopping for water and short rests.

Captain Alament estimated their location to be, just northeast of Zarhun City. If they continued at a forced march pace, the troop could be there in two days. Before the day was half over, Shayla was yelling at him. "I am starving to death. You have to stop and find me something to eat." His patience had run out, and his anger got the better of him.

What could she do he thought, have me killed? It gave him his one and only gratifying moment of the day. He reminded her that if they stopped and were attached, the only food around was going to be her. His satirical comment stopped her complaints. She rode quietly the rest of the day, while holding her stomach as the cart bounced in the ruts.

THE ZARHUNIAN CONFLICT

A zestar after the suns set; the survivors of the bridal party could see the flickering of a line of fires along the far crest of the eastern ridge. The captain ordered two strata's to guard the princess while he scouted the area. The exhausted warriors sat around her three deep facing outward. If attacked they would sacrifice their lives in her defense. Captain Alament along with a taxt of ten other warriors ran through the trees and scaled the hillside. There were a lot more campfires than what would have been lit if they had been the highwaymen.

In the firelight Alament could see the banners with the three silver horizontal arrows beneath a crown on a checkered field of light green and tan. As luck would have it, the banners belonged to the main body of the Worizian Army of the Tan. He was escorted to the command tent where after a fifteen zesta narrative, the commander of the day sent word to Marshal Malenum. Immediately an order was given for a santax of one hundred seventy five warriors be dispatched to rescue Princess Shayla and to escort her safely back to the armies base camp.

Upon arrival the princess and her servant were taken to and given the commanders personal tent for their use. Enough cooked meats, roasted vegetables, and fresh fruit was brought to feed ten men. After being forced to dig a trench, a tenth of the royal guards at Shayla's camp were put to a gruesome and painful death. Captain Alament was excluded from this ritual punishment. It was his duty to write a report outlining the events and circumstances of the past few days. He formally accepted the blame for the loss of Princess Shayla's belongings before being allowed to take his own life.

Marshal Malenum ordered one santax back to Shayla's last campsite to track and kill all the highwaymen. He sent another off to Zarhun City to warn the Worezian Army of the Blue. A taxt of couriers rode to Prince Quayot and the Envarian Red Army's camp, notifying them of the princess's rescue, and requesting a delay in their meeting. Lastly he sent couriers back to King Magarus with Captain Alament's report and his head. A new copy of the wedding contract was urgently needed as was a second copy of the orders that they were supposed to receive from Alament.

Princess Shayla was so shaken by the experience that she could not be moved for two day and had to be under the continual care of a healer and cooking staff. The third of Asursa, she was well enough for them to continue their journey south to Zarhun City. They should have reached it in one long day of traveling, but the princess insisted she had lost so much weight from the stress that she had eaten eight meals instead of six, and had to bathe twice before she could make an appearance in the city.

Marshal Malenum had written a letter to his friend Marshal Bythemum of the Blue Army not to spare any expense in welcoming the princess. He also notified Bythenum of his first cousin Alament's death. The Tan Army of Worez was camped outside the northern gates of Zarhun City. The princess's caravan would enter the city at the rising of Myastus. This way all the residents of the regional capital could see a true royal princess in the light of both suns.

It was a grand entrance, Marshal Malenum had taken one of his best wagons and had it richly painted and decorated during her illness. The canvas top had been removed and dyed a mint green and fashioned into a shaded awning. The surrey was then garlanded with white roses. A scalloped red and gold satin trim was added at the edge of the canopy. In front, a large and curved, raised bench seat had been constructed with a smaller one behind for her handmaid. The red velour seats were deeply cushioned and padded. Six white horses pulled the carriage through the streets, while her servant Gietra tossed handfuls of copper coins to the cheering crowd.

The populous was actually glad to see her. The Zarhunian's had been under occupation of Worez for the second year, and living in this ancient city was not getting any easier. Perhaps the merging of their two kingdoms would change attitudes and these citizens would be treated as one people. King Zagarus of ancient Tarot constructed this magnificent city over two thousand years ago. It had been build in memory of his father's victory over the Eastern Semedian Empire. After the king's death his son signed "The Great Treaty of Megath" in the year two hundred and sixty K.C. The Continent of Megath was renamed Zarhun as a tribute to the Tarotian King.

THE ZARHUNIAN CONFLICT

This city and its populous had seen many wars since its construction and there were many monuments to new and old rulers scattered throughout the wide paved avenues. The greatest being the mausoleum and gardens of King Zarhun. It was the central theme in the construction of this city.

Royal houses, estates and gardens surrounded the central square at a distance of one thasta. The second circle of the inner city was for governmental buildings and houses for the magistrates and city officials. These buildings as well as many of the Royal Envarian households had been confiscated by the Worizian Blue Army during the occupation.

Marshal Bythenm had Princess Shayla moved to the estates that had once belonged to Prince Sesmak's in-laws. This is where she could rest and recover in comfort from her resent ordeal. She could also receive gifts and congratulations from all the Envarian Royalty loyal to King Helidon and Prince Quayot. Following the entrance procession, the princess decreed several days of calibration and feasting. Meat and vegetable markets, bakeries, and wine houses, were raided and looted.

The Army of the Tan and Blue would feast for the next three days. It did not matter that there was not going to be any food left in the city for the next month if not longer. Shayla was pleased with the festival and knew in her heart, the royal families would speak of her for generations.

Marshal Malenum and Marshal Bythenum were to be awarded the "Star of Worez" for gallantry. Their warriors emptied most of the warehouses and shops replenishing the supply wagons before marching out of the city toward the south eastern plains.

The santax that Malenum sent out after the highwaymen returned informing him that the horses had been driven to the south across the plains and most likely sold to Prince Sesmak's rebel army. Princess Shayla once again proceeded to her rendezvous with Prince Quayot.

Along with her retinue was a new dowry wagon. It had been filled with trunks of gowns designed and hand stitched by the best clothiers of Zarhun. This time she had a tantax of ten thousand warriors as an escort. The other nine tantaxes of the Tan Army marched out and took up strategic positions southwest of the city on the great Zarhun grassland plain.

The following day, the Blue Army's ten tantaxes of approximately eighty thousand warriors were to march due south. They would construct a fortified stockade and remain there until the war horns sounded. During the celebration, a courier arrived with a new copy of the treaty and orders for the battle preparations.

Marshal Pallegon of the Violet Army of Worez sent couriers to the other two Marshals notifying them that his army had crossed the north eastern Worez — Envarian border. They were now camped five thastas southeast of the coastal City of Tespaden. His army had also received word that King Zaghar of the Sylakian Empire was sending them additional war supplies. In addition to this military hardware, the dark lord would be sending seasoned warrior advisers with auxiliary troops fresh from the "Kelleskarian" and "Agorthan Continental Wars."

These two santaxes of Sylakians and two santaxes of Onondonians would be led by a representative of the dark lord. This evil female's orders were to be obeyed without question. Arrival of these allied kingdom's transport and supply vessels were expected on the fifth or sixth day of Asursa.

These foreign mercenary warriors would start marching west to North Point and then march due south, driving Sesmak's troops in the area toward the Zarhun Plain. The battle line of the Tan Army would extend from the Forests of Envarac to within fifty thastas southwest of Zarhun City.

Chapter # 25

Tenolfis North Point of Envar

The weather finally calmed and become more seasonal by the middle of the mursa of Asursa. The three ships which made up the small flotilla of the red dragon fought head winds most of the way since sailing from the Yojan City of Joroca. Ships Captain Cliedeous of the Merimon had plotted the course for the fleet before embarking. They would sail slightly south of the normal shipping lanes for vessels navigating the northern seas of the Continent of Zarhun.

Commander Traga grudgingly accepted the rank of Marshal of the Dragon Army to make it easier on the command structure. It was the one good idea, Second Officer Theisiah had made. It was too bad the Yojan Prince had to be executed in order to maintain discipline. Marshal Traga stressed the importance of speed and time in getting this fleet to "North Point."

It was a small spit of land on the western bay of the Village Tenolfis, Envar. The main purpose of this expedition was to rescue Princess Elona and Princess Diara from being made part of the wedding concubine for the treaty. Once the fleet rounded the land of the northern Continent of Semedia, they tacked southeast as if they were sailing directly for Renvas, Envar. After six days at sea they shifted sails and tacked back to the northeast and rounded the rocky shores of the Continent of Zarhun, at the inlet to Tenolfis, North Point.

On the eight day, shortly after sunrise a seaman in the Hesboth's crow's-nest noted a large fleet of ships northwest of their location. He was able to count twelve vessels in this squadron by the time Captain Dimekon notified Marshal Ebestar. Everyone knew this was not a mercantile fleet. Semaphore flags, were raised notifying the cargo ship Gleggas and the coastal runner Merimon to close up formation for message arrows to be shot.

The course of this fleet was too far north to be sailing for ports of Envar. They were most likely making for ports in the Worezian Kingdom. Ebestar also knew that once they sighted his ships they would be altering their course. Marshal Ebestar ordered Captain Cleideous to make all possible speed for North Point. Once inside the small inlet bay of Tenolfis, they were to unload as quickly as possible and to put back to sea.

The Merimon was the fastest ship in his fleet, and she had been fitted with two additional catapults amidships. Each of the ships four catapults was capable of shooting burlap bags weighing as much as six tarmets. The sacks were filled with cinder packed tar spheres surrounding ceramic jugs. The crocks contained lamp oil that had been thinned with alcohol. It would be her duty to protect the other two ships while they were unloaded and able to put back to sea.

Marshal Ebestar and Marshal Traga stood on the far end of the docks. Their ships would take at least one more day to unload. Everyone on board and everyone in the village had been working day and night getting the cargo and equipment off of the docks and central wharf. Base camp had been set up at the southern outskirts of the Village of Tenolfis, and two continual streams of supplies flowed from the docking berths.

Ebestar and Traga knew they would make their deadline for unloading, but were worried about the Gleggas and Hesboth. Even empty these ships were slow at sea. As they stood on the docks watching their men work franticly, they could see three dark plumes of smoke rising from the waters edge far north of their position.

"What do you think Ebes," asked Traga?

"I don't know," the Envarian Marshal replied somberly. "There was nothing in Lord Jedaf's letters saying anything about this fleet. It also looks like they were not pleased to see us either." The two old war veterans shaded their eyes and watched the horizon of the northern seas.

The smoke clouds in the distance had cleared to thin greying wisps. From the size and color of the dark black curling masses, they had been large fires. The ships had burned and sunk quickly. They both hoped that one of these wispy grey vertical lines did not belong to their ship the Merimon.

It was their only indication that Captain Cliedeous had engaged the enemy. His orders were to protect the unloading at all cost, and it looked like he had done just that. The ships Gleggas and the Hesboth would now be able to catch the last of the high tide before leaving the harbor and set a coarse to the southwest.

It had been Clieduous's plan for them to make their getaway to the west with the winds at their stern, while he would sail and engage the enemy further to the northeast. If he was able to out run the other fleet, he would rendezvous with them half way back to the Continent of Dolfinia. Once off the coast of the Kingdom of Azzon the small dragon fleet would head back to the Yojan Port of Joroca. They would sail there together and wait for further orders.

"Have your men finished assembling the wagons?"

"Yes," answered Traga. "Dragon Captain Drayus had the ten vehicles filled and moved to base camp about mid afternoon. He and Second Officer Kytos will also be setting up the standards for the battle groups. The men marching south would gather at their unit flag until everyone has assembled. As soon as these warriors disembarked from the Gleggas, First Officer Eggolis marched off to an area southeast of the base camp with four hundred of your men."

It took the rest of the day for the supplies that were stacked on the wharf to be delivered to the camp. It was an excited and hurried pace which brought back a lot of bad memories for Marshal Ebestar. A little over three years had passed since he had been in this village. He was surprised at the warm welcome these people gave him as he stepped from the gangplank. These villagers, fisherman and farmers were responsible for burying his dead after his last evacuation.

Four thousand of his warriors sacrificed their lives in the Valley of Volendale protecting his retreat, while the fishing ships could return for a second group to be rescued. The Worezians killed many of the villagers before burning the wharfs, piers, and pylons in retaliation for their help in evacuating Ebestars warriors from the village and coastal port.

Captain Psydek rode up to the dock, saluted and dismounted. "Sir," he said. "The cavalry have gathered all their equipment and horses. They will be riding from the village in about a zestar. I have ordered half of the men to the south and the other half to the east. They will ride on our flanks at a thastas distance from the main body."

"Very good captain," said Ebestar. "See to the cook fires and make sure a large supper is prepared at the campsite. We can't afford to stop and be caught here on the shore. We have to get these men to the staging area, feed them and with any luck march south a few thastas inland."

"The base camp can remain behind and start cooking for tomorrow's forced march. The cook house detail can catch up with the cavalry's protection. We can't have this army strung out from the shores of Tenolfis for very long." The Captain saluted, mounted and galloped off quickly.

Traga's warriors were the first to disembark from the Merimon. After closing the roads to prevent Worezian spies from leaving the village, his men secured the waterfront and docks with the help of the Envarians that were on board ship with them.

They marched to the old south ramparts where Ebestar's warriors had made their last stand three years ago. Most of the earthen mounts and timber fortifications were still intact. There were still stacks of timber, a good spring fed well and a large cleared deforested area for Kytos to set up a camp large enough that would accommodate the majority of the army.

Another half thasta due south was a krastant wheat field which had over half of the first summer crop harvested. This is where Captain

Bygin of the Dragon Army's first tadleta set to work clearing the rest of the land setting up the battle formations. He also sent the second and third dragon tadleta one thasta further south to the edge of the wood line, setting up a secondary base camp as the advanced guard.

By the end of the second day most of the equipment and warriors had been moved to the encampment under Prince Kytos's command. Although he did not have formal military training, the young prince did have a knack for organization. Last year the Prince of Therda had paid a state visit to Kytos's Kingdom.

It had been a major event for Oppow, and one of the most impressive and lavish ceremonies had been laid out for a dignitary of this small southern regional kingdom. It was one of the few times that Kytos had defied this father King Desactus, and helped with organizing and setting up the cooking and feasting areas.

Captain Bygin organized the men into their battle formations and set up a schedule for each strata unit to be fed. After giving the men a short rest; the marshals gave the orders to move out. They would not march very far beyond the southern edge of the wood line the first day. After sitting for more than a week on ships, they had lost some of their stamina. Traga decided that this camp would be the last one in which the army would get a totally hot meal before reaching the northern part of the Zarhun Plain.

This site was where they were camped when they received word from one of the cavalry couriers that a large enemy force was located to their east. The best guesses at the size of these enemy troops were, three to four tantaxes totalling about thirty-five thousand warriors. The advanced scout had identified orange battle flags with three black stars and white regimental flags with a red redolga boars head on them.

The dark lords southern commander sat mounted on a hilltop west of Tespaden overlooking the remnants to his fleet during the unloading efforts. Indwok the evil female treskul of war, like her master King Zaghar of Sylak did not forgive mistakes. The head of the Onandonian commanding officer had been placed on a stake in the center of the road. It had been his decision to split the fleet at the sight of the flotilla to their south.

Much to the surprise of Commander Furogus, and his ship fleet captains, a single vessel came straight at them from out of the morning eastern fog bank. This fast coastal runner was at full sail with a strong wind at her stern.

No sooner had shouts for action been yelled when the on coming frigate swung hard to starboard crossing the bow of the leading Ayesan galley. As they came about a double bag volley of lamp oil, naphtha and flaming tar coated cinders was fired into the jibs. The flames quickly spread to the mast, foresails and deck cargo.

The sleek coastal runner, shifted sails and tacked hard over to port negotiating between the burning ship and the next Kaybeckian ship of the line. It came within twenty paces when it pelted this galley with two strikes amidships and a flaming volley of naphtha to the stern castle before cutting hard to starboard once again.

Sailing between the stern of the burning man of war and between the next two merchantman ships, the midsized adversary was able to shift sails once more to port. Cutting its wheel close enough for the bow to almost hit the last ship in the convoy before letting loose a double incendiary volley to the port aft castle. The last merchantman was immediately engulfed in flames before the deckhands could get to their stations. The enemy sailed away from the fleet due southwest. The frigate's canvas stretched to the limits.

Two of the allied man-of-wars were out of the Port of Adros. They had a compliment of over four thousand warriors. The foremost Ayesan vessel was one of the largest sea going ships and carried a compliment of over five thousand cramped warriors. Most never knew what happened.

There were such intense flames on deck; that few made it to the rails. Burning canvas blanketed the decks covering the holds. The men did not have a chance, most died of smoke inhalation. The cargo ship that had been last to be hit by the enemy catapults, carried rations of mostly grains, dried fruits and meats along with most of the army's equipment wagons.

Decking cargo consisted mostly of pallets of grain bags covered with canvas tarpaulins. These soaked up the flaming oil and spread the fire quickly. The deckhands that were on watch were able to jump overboard, but they knew the rest of the fleet would not be coming back for them. Most of the warrior contingents died below deck as the flaming grains poured down through the cargo hold grates.

Indwok ordered all the villagers of Trespaden to work day and night without stopping. Men, women and children were conscripted and sent to the docks. This is where they were whipped and beaten until the last ship had been unloaded. It did not matter how many died of exhaustion. It was not her problem.

Her warriors unloaded the horses and the cavalry equipment first. They rode to the west toward the north woodland Hills of Roomaris without a rest or a meal. The remainder of her forces marched out after looting the town, replenishing the supplies that they had lost.

The main body of the enemy army consisted of sixteen thousand Sylakian's, four thousand Onandonian's, and four thousand Otaskan slave warriors. The remainder of the force was made up of five thousand auxiliary Ayesan's alongside twelve thousand Kaybeckian warriors fresh from the "Agorthian Wars." They also marched off without a meal, slowing their paces only long enough to go around the stake with Commander Furogus's head on it.

Indwok would have her captains march the warriors the rest of the day and into the night before a camp would be set up. Her cavalry rode twenty thastas south stopping at the fork in the road leading to the wooded southwest pass to the Splindia Valley. Commander Jetanous of the Kingdom of Estron had been put in charge of the Otaskans and Onandonians. He marched the men unmercifully until they dropped. All the Sylakian and Onandonian warriors would be fed, but only hard tack, jerky and beer looted from Trespaden.

The dark demon of the underworld would not be accompanying them. She would spend a full day near the beachhead. Indwok needed to communicate with the dead, the spirits of her brother treskuls and of her lord and master King Zaghar of Sylak. There were incantations to write and spells to evoke. Many blood thirsty beings still needed to be created before she would be able to rendezvous with the bulk of her army at the northern edge of the Zarhun Plain.

Late in the evening, Jetanous received a report from his scouts. A small contingent of warriors had been sighted heading for the Great Plains. The report speculated the warriors numbered no more than five thousand. These men were currently bivouacked to his southwest at the northern end of the Volendale Valley. The commander ordered his men to full alert but decided that since Lord Indwok was not in the camp, that he would let his men rest for the night. His subordinates could make plans in the evening and they would engage the enemy tomorrow before the suns set.

The units comprising the four thousand Onandonian and four thousand Otaskan slave warriors were chosen to make the first encounter. The "Agorthian War" veterans would enter the western end of the gorge, and march through the narrow Splindia Valley at sunrise. By the end of Mya, the Sylakian allies would exit the narrow chasm. They would enter the more open flat lands of Volendale. This was where the commander expected to engage this unexpected militia of raw recruits and new conscripts.

The eight thousand Sylakian warriors under Commander Quaduk of the Kingdom of Wyloth would continue their trek to the southwest and hold the field until relieved by the Worezian Violet Army. This army was on the march and had just crossed the Worezian — Envarian border.

Marshal Traga and Marshal Ebestar knew that they were in trouble. They could not be caught on the Volendale Plain only to die like the men that had given their lives allowing them to escape. They would break camp three zestars before sunrise. Marshal Ebestar would march most of his Envarian warriors and all the wagons through the valley along the Gothom west woodlands and onto the northwest Zarhun Plain. This is where he expected to rendezvous with Prince Sesmak's rebel army.

Traga's seven hundred warriors plus two hundred of Marshal Envarian Ebestar's archers would march down the eastern side of the Volendale Valley and enter the east-west perpendicular pass of the Splindia Valley. They were to take up defensive positions at the abandoned pligma mining Town of Zongra.

These warriors would fight a holding and delaying action until Ebestar's Army reached the southern end of the valley. Both marshals expected the enemy tantaxes to reach the west end of Splindia by midday. Traga's warriors would be out numbered four to one. That is why the two hundred Envarian archers were sent in support of the under strength Red Dragon Army.

Marshal Traga stood on the slopping flat roof top of a dilapidated soap factory. It was one of the few ramshackle buildings still standing after the war. Zongra was once a mining town for pligma; a stone rich in lye. It had been one of the largest producers of soap and cement crusted lye ash in all of western Zarhun. Now all that was left were decrepit and rundown one story buildings that the paint and wood had been eaten away by the wind and caustic dust.

Marshal Traga had never been on the Continent of Zarhun and thought this valley was the most incongruous place he had ever seen. The mountains at each side of the gorge were quite sheer and looked like they had been cleaved during an ancient quake.

Each of the differing layers of stone that formed the lower two thirds of the colorful escarpment could be identified at a far distance. The upper third of these mountains were mostly bare of vegetation. The dark grey sediment was made of a fractured slate. The Splindia Valley floor was narrow but fertile and very beautiful. As far as the old warrior could see there was nothing other than thousands of full bloom splindia plants intertwined with flowering arisdi vines.

These one foot tall flowers had bloomes with dark brown centers, surrounded by two rows of large white peddles. The flowers were mixed with and grew between the blanketing yellow buttercup arisdi vines. High above the fields of flowers flew hyleren meadow birds. These small pigeons had brown wings, white speckled breasts and long yellow-white tail feathers. They were chasing swarms of fat, golden tessa honey bees. It was quite, a peaceful and serene visage.

This was the imagined panorama of the Splindia Valley. In reality the thousands of flowers hid the real dangers. Hundreds of years of open strip mining had made the western end of the valley look more like the pockmarked craters of the moon. These thirty foot diameter excavation pits where six men deep and spaced forty feet edge to edge. This gave enough surface room for wagon traffic in both direction and still left edge room to prevent a slide or rim collapse.

Between most of the shear walls to the open pit mines were broken slabs and sharp edged limestone rubble piles. The vines and flowers had overtaken most of these spaces providing a nice moist shaded area that was perfect for the breading of rodents and meadow stamuses. These vipers were the smaller but more venomous of the two breeds of these brown and green striped snakes. Luckily the local farmers of Volendale had warned Traga and his men about these poisonous sidewinders.

The marshal's warriors cleared only enough space between the open pit mines for the pike and swordsmen to stand protecting the archers. Walking through the vines and flowers, you could not see the pit mines until you stood right at their very edge. Half of Traga's warriors and archers filled the spaces between these circular mine shafts.

The other three hundred Semedian's cleared four areas one third of the way down the valley. This was to be their first line of defense. The swordsmen and archers at the forward possition would be under the leadership of Commander Drayus. After all arrows were spent or if they were about to be over run; these men would fall back retreating to the pit mine defenses.

It was nearing the thirteenth zestar. Marshal Traga was anxious but thankful for two unexpected events. First his warriors were given enough time to prepare for battle and still were able to eat a light first lunch. Even if it where only bread, cheese, wine and chavna, it was still better than nothing. The leathery rolled chavnas usually had a lot of dried fruit in them, and the brown sugars gave you a lot of fast energy.

The other event was the rising of the second sun Myastus. The additional heat finally sent the snakes into or under the cover of rocks. There were so many of them out sunning themselves when they marched into the valley, that Traga had to assign a third of his warriors the duty of keeping the vipers out of the clearings. They could not fight off serpents and the enemy at the same time.

The sunrise could not have been timed any better for them, because Marshal Traga could finally see his adversary's pennants advancing down the valley. The Dragon Army's greatest disadvantage was the fact that they were facing east into the suns light. The marshal didn't think the glaring problem would make that much of a difference. His warriors would not be standing and fighting.

The Dragon Army would confront the enemy and hold each of the positions just long enough to enable the majority of the army time to retreat to the safety of Volendale. The banners of the rival armed forces advanced slowly. Their foreward santax units covered a half thasta in width and as far to the east as he could see. Traga knew that shortly Commander Drayus would give the orders for the archers to engage. As soon as Onandonian warriors reached the halfway point in the valley, the battle would begin.

Traga did not have to wait long. As he thought about his tactical situation, he could see a commotion and than hear the sounds of battle developing ahead of him. Drayus had let the Onandonians close within one hundred yards of his position. Then his hidden warriors that had been lying in wait stood and fired their arrows. The commander had set up his formation so one hundred arrows fell at a volley. While fifty shafts were being fitted to cord, fifty were flying overhead. After five volleys for each archer, a cease fire was ordered.

The enemy forces had scattered and broken ranks. A third of the arrows had hit their mark leaving hundreds of bodies lying in the flowers, and at least another hundred wounded were stumbling about. Another third of the surviving phalanx had to carry their injured comrades back to the rear formations. This left the forward santaxes decimated, in disarray and causing a halt to the main body's advancement.

Commander Jetanous retreated and reorganized his Onandonian warriors. It was bad enough to have over sixty down with snake bites. Now, he just lost another three hundred of his best swordsmen. In the routing confusion, his own archers could not see the enemy. The bowmen were another fifty paces back in the ranks to do much good. He immediately halted his seasoned troops and ordered Commander Sorjen of the Otaskan slave and convict warriors into action.

Most of these men were either farmers or shop keepers prior to their homelands being invaded by the Sylakian Empire. The male members of whole towns were pressed into the army. The females were taken away to harvest crops or to work in the military trade goods warehouses. These poorly trained and inept warriors could take the majority of the losses and he would not be punished for it.

Commander Sorjen marched to the front lines at his standards. The Sylakian occupation flag of white with red redolga's head and black stars on it, fluttered in the wind while he waited for his Otaskan officers to move up to the front. As soon as their battle lines were formed, Sorjen gave a nod. The red and black checkered, attack banner was vigorously waved to the sides and then pointed toward the entrenched enemy.

The conscripts marched forward to the thumping beat of the kettle drums and the blare of trumpets. Once the Otaskans reached a distance just forward of the bodies of the dead Onandonian advanced guards, Commander Drayus of the Dragon Army let loose his second set of five arrow volleys. Commander Sorjen was one of the first warriors to fall. The inexperienced swordsmen behind him, paniced as the arrows hit their mark. They tried to retreat by climbing over the pile of dead bodies. Another three hundred plus warriors had fallen into the crushed flowers of Splindia.

Commander Jetanous ordered his swordsmen to prevent the slaves from retreating and drove the Otaskan regimental battalions back toward the enemy. This time Commander Drayus let them march within fifty yards when he ordered his archers to pick individual targets, each using their last ten shafts. After they had killed as many as they could, his archers and swordsmen retreated to where Marshal Traga had set up his second line of defense.

Drayus's swordsmen protected the retreat until the last possible moment. Jetanous thinking that his men had finally routed the enemy ordered a full forced advance. As the major attack began Drayus and his men trotted back following the main evacuation path that they had laid out. He waived to Traga as his warriors came through the second line of their fortifications and continued marching and evacuating his warriors with their wounded to Valley of Volendale.

Traga had ordered his bowmen to let loose their first volley as soon as Drayus's warriors were safely behind their lines. This meant that the enemy was less than thirty yards behind. The first volley found more than half their marks, and the advancing enemy slowed, but it could not stop. The Onandonian lance and sword pressed the Otaskan civilians forward on themselves.

They walked in lockstep formation pressed from behind by the points of leveled spears. Turning toward the enemy once again, the Otaskans found that many were now standing at the leading edge to the pit mines. They tried to turn; they tried to stop; they screamed; and were pushed into the pits from the warriors stacked up behind them.

Traga had positioned his archers only between the open spaces to the mine shaft pits. Each void was quickly filled with the bodies of the dead and wounded. When there did not appear to be any more space to manoeuvre, Traga's warriors would retreat to the next row of pit mines. Each of Traga's two hundred archers carried thirty five Theodian hardened steel pointed arrows with plicarren feathered shafts. They were the best ones that money could buy and they didn't miss their marks very often.

Thousands died, by falling into the deep pit mines, arrows or by being pierced with lances. Commander Jetanous did not know there was a problem until he saw the banners of his Onandonian warriors at the leading edge of the battle formation. This is when he sent runners to the forward positions ordering a halt. He could no longer see the Otaskan battle flags, banners or regimental unit pennants anywhere.

The moment the Onandonians stopped advancing, Traga ordered a full retreat. All of his bowmen had pulled back to the Volendale carrying his wounded. They continued marching south catching up with Commander Drayus's first line defenders. This left two hundred men with Traga, and they were beginning to tier and lose more and more warriors as they fell back to the last row of mine shafts.

For the last zestar it was man to man sword to sword hard fighting. The last of the Otaskans fell quickly but the Onandonians were all battle hardened warriors fresh from the "Northern Kelleskarian Wars." They gave as good as they got and killed more than had been expected.

Marshal Traga led the last of the evacuation thanking his men for putting up a good fight. None wanted to run away, from this battle and many said if they stayed they could win. Traga was firm and made sure that none stayed behind. He had lost over fifty men and had over a hundred wounded or missing. This was enough on his conscience, as they retreated through the pass to Volendale and south toward the Zarhun Plain.

Chapter # 26

The Red Dragon and Silver Sword

Ciramtis rode into Prince Sesmak's northern encampment. She was followed by Captain Odelac's wagon and the cook house supply wagon that had been Princess Shayla's. The captain renamed this wagon Caysa's wagon, so no one had to hear the name Shalya or Atus again. This made Caysa very proud. The strata that escorted them to the camp rode off leaving them at the command center.

The central tented area had a large garrison style banner outside the entrance. The silver sword and crown were in the center of a mint green field, which had a forest green border and a trim of silver tassels entirely around it. This was the flag that Ciramtis had been able to identify from the edge of the woods, as the royal Envarian flag of Zarhun City.

Ciramtis dismounted. Then she walked her horse over to Captain Odelac's wagon and tied off its reins off at the rear warkmeg cleat. "Captain, the sentry said we are to wait here. Prince Sesmak is at the southern encampment interrogating some Worezian spies." Odelac, Princess Elona, and Caysa climbed down stretching their back muscles. Taskmaster Vadeck and Princess Diara climbed down from the wagon and joined them. There was nothing for them to do now but sit down near the wagons and rest.

Odelac poured Ciramtis a glass of wine and as they sat down he handed her a bound green leather dispatch pouch. He had found the correspondence valise tucked behind one of the oatmeal grain sacks. "Cira, I think you should read this," he said. She untied the leather strap and pulled four folded sheets of parchment from it. Each sheet had been sealed and having the signet ring of Worez's king imbedded in the red wax. Odelac had already broken all the seals and had previously read each of the letters.

The first document was addressed to King Helidon of Envar. It was a revised copy of the wedding contract between Princess Shayla of the Worezian Kingdom and Prince Quayot of the Envarian Kingdom. She read it quickly, and refolded it. There was nothing in it that she had not already known. The second was a personal letter to Prince Quayot apologizing for the delay of the wedding caravan. It also listed all the items in Princess Shayla's dowry, including the two slaves Princesses Diara of Eurkus and Princess Elona of Oppow.

The third was also addressed to Prince Quayot, Commander of the Host of the Envarian Red Army. It was instructions for him to proceed with the plan of driving Prince Sesmak's rebel army southeast toward the Jeupan Kingdom's border. Upon receiving this letter he was to march his army north to the Village of Moland. It was a small farming community on the Zarhun Plain, located at the northwest central edge of the woodlands of Moland and the City of Aruntis.

Prince Quayot was to take no action or move his troops any further east until the Worezian Army of Violet's banners were seen to his north. This midsized army of six tantaxes, along with the Sylakian allies would be the driving force that his Envarian armed forces would be supporting. The Royal Red Envarian Army would remain on the western side of the "Great Divide" and prevent the rebels from escaping to the western portion of the Zarhun Plain.

The last document was addressed to Marshal Malenum of the Worezian Army of the Tan, and Marshal Bythenum of the Worezian Army of the Blue. It was their orders to form battles formations east and south of the ancient City State of Zarhun. Marshal Malenum's army was to the form a single line of ten tadletas east to west of the farming Village of Rotanis. It would be his army's responsibility to prevent Sesmak's Army from escaping to the east taking refuge in Zarhun City.

Marshal Bythenum's Army was to form a single line of ten tadletas east to west of the Village of Rotanis. It would be his army's responsibility to hold the line preventing Sesmak's Army from swinging around Malenum's Army and once again escaping north. They would also hold their positions until they could see the banners of Worezian Marshal Pallegon's Army of Violet.

Ciramtis refolded these letters and put them all back into the leather pouch. Retying the strap she held it out for Odelac to take. He waved it off. "No Cira," he said. "I think you should keep the dispatch, until you can give these letters to Prince Sesmak." After all it would look better coming from you, than an old Yojan sea captain. She reluctantly nodded acceptance, then placed them in her own satchel.

"I wonder how long we are supposed to hang around here waiting," asked Elona? She couldn't sit any more and stood pacing about. There was a commotion, some noise of hoof beats and the beat of drums south of them. Climbing up on the wagon seat she could see a procession, with riders four abreast coming toward them.

"Looks like Prince Sesmak and his escorts are back. It also looks like the army is starting to break camp. I thought we would be here at least until tomorrow morning." It was getting late and nearing the nineteenth zestar. By the time they struck camp, the suns would have merged and set.

The Envarian Prince rode by them giving them a fleeting glance, before nudging his mount forward. Leading a party of twenty lancers he sat tall in the saddle. He was dressed in white and green silks, and wearing a silver sword with highly polished armor. His green colored forearm guards, breast work and boots were of finely stitched leather. Sesmak's horse had the same quality green leather work, a mint green saddle blanket and a silken scalloped edging on his horses reins.

The honor guard riders directly behind him carried his banner. The rider to the guidon's left carried a green banner with a quayga ja in the center. The black hawk with red tipped wing and tail feathers was the crest for the grassland Villages of Blineva and Aruntis. They were two of the north central Zarhun cities that had been feeding and supporting Sesmak's Army during the war years.

The banner to the guidon's right was Envarian mint green with a golden haystack in the center. Over the haystack was a large eye with a tear at the corner. This was the crested banner of the Valley of Volendale; the tear had been added two years ago, it was in remembrance of the forty thousand warriors of the Green Army that had been captured or killed because of Prince Quayot's incompetence.

Ten zestas passed before a runner was sent over to the guards that were watching Odelac's and Ciramtis's party. They closed ranks on the group with drawn weapons, leading them toward the main command and war strategies tent. Odelac and Vadeck did not like the looks of it. They had been disarmed, and there was nothing they could say or do. Ciramtis notice their concern. "Don't worry," she said. "It is just a precaution. As soon as we see Prince Sesmak, things will be back to normal."

The command tent was quite large with one large rectangular folding table at each side. The table to the left had a large map in the center. Wooden game shaped pieces were scattered about with small colored flags and rectangular name plates. An aide was penning and transferring the resent locations of the battlefield pieces to the chart, and noting tantax division strengths.

At the other side of the tent, a long table had four officers seated at one side. There was one captain and one commander for each of the green and blue army. Odelac and Ciramtis were pushed in front of the table. The commander of the blue demanded their names and for them to state their business. Ciramtis was speechless at first, as she stepped forward.

"We prefer that your master does the speaking," the commander said. Odelac put his hand on her shoulder and spoke before she could start swearing at them. "My name is Odelac; I was the captain of the merchantmen Tarpenya, out of Joroca, Yoja. This is my taskmaster, mister Vadeck. This is Princess Elona of Oppow, and this is Princess Diara of Eurkus." He put his other hand on the boys shoulder. "This is my aide Caysa and the woman that you have been so rude to is Ciramtis of Iblac, the great granddaughter of Colinda, daughter of our Goddess Esella."

The Commander stood and walked out of the tent. He returned a short time later with two guards dragging Karadis and Baradic behind him. Both of Odelac's men were gagged and their hands were tightly bound behind them. They had bruised faces and bleeding noses.

The Commander took his seat again. "I am Commander Ebeston, of Lord Sesmak's Army of the Green. We have questioned your servants, and that's not who they say you are."

Odelac glared at the officer, then walked over to his men and untied the rawhide thong that held the gage in their mouths. The guard started to stop him, but Ebeston waived him away. "What in the name of Krebolus have the two of you been saying?"

Karadis spit on Baradic, as soon as the binding and dirty rage was pulled from his mouth. "Captain, this fool was told; they would let him go if he told them who we really are. I don't know what he told them, but I got a good beating for it, and as soon as my hands are free, I going to cut him from groin to gullet."

The captain stepped in front of Baradic and untied his wrist while the sailor stammered. The shifty eyed seaman said, "I didn't think they were going to let us go, so I told them we were Envarian warriors from the northlands. How was I to know they were the Envarians?"

As soon as he finished speaking Odelac gave him a hard knee between the legs. The sailor dropped to the dirt and curled into a ball holding his grown. "Ciramtis give Commander Ebeston the courier pouch." She had pulled it from her travel bag and handed it to the commander while Baradic was gowning.

"This should be given to Prince Sesmak immediately," she said!

The officer took the pouch opened it, and saw the red wax seals on the letters. "I will be right back," he said. Standing quickly, he gave her a slight bow before leaving the tent.

Baradic was lying on the ground behind Odel and the others. He was trying to sit up or get to his knees. Odel saw him out of the corner of his eye, and kicked him in the face breaking the sailor's nose. Bara's eyes rolled back and he fell silently to his side.

Commander Ebeston came back into the tent. "Release them at once, and get them food and refreshments. Prince Sesmak would like to see you now sorceress. I'm sorry I thought so ill of you." Ciramtis didn't speak; she just followed him from the tent.

Out in the twilight she could see that they were indeed breaking camp, and starting to form ranks. Some had already started marching north. Ducking through the flap of Prince Sesmak's personal tent, she could see he had already poured two glasses of red wine. He motioned her to the glass and chair while he continued reading.

Watching his lips move between the curses, gave her some insight to his soul. Finally he finished reading and looked up at her. Ciramtis had emptied her glass and he refilled it for her. "I am sorry for the ill treatment; I don't know what your men were thinking." She did not reply she just set her glass down.

"I see you're breaking camp and moving out to the north. I would have thought that after reading those letters you would have been marching south as fast as you could. I have not had a chance to tell you why we were seeking you out, other than bringing you these dispatches of King Magarus."

Sesmak folded the letters. "We questioned your two men. The one named Karadis told us why you were looking for our camp. If the other one hadn't contradicted him, and told us they were both Envarian warriors escaping south, we could have saved a lot of time and them a lot of pain."

He poured himself another glass of wine. "Do you know how many of your Lord Jedaf's warriors will be sailing from the Yojan Kingdom?"

"No. He didn't say, and I am not sure he knew how many either. The only instructions that I was given by my lord was to get to North Point as fast as possible. I was to give his Commander Traga, and a Marshal Ebestar a letter of warning, and new orders. My delivery is going to be a lot later than I had hoped for."

"The good news is Captain Odelac and his men were able to rescue Princess Elona, and Diara, before Princess Shayla reached the safety of Zarhun City. But now I'm afraid getting to North Point is going to be impossible." A smile crossed the prince's face as she spoke.

"You said, a Marshal Ebestar, didn't you?"

"Yes," she said. "I think he is an old officer that knows Envar."

Sesmak choked on his wine. "Knows Envar? I will tell you that there is no one that knows it better. He is one of my oldest and most trusted officers in the army. As a matter of fact, Commander Ebeston is his son. He will be glad to hear the news."

Standing and walking over to her he extended his hand. "Thank you, Ciramtis of Iblac! This information could not have come at a more opportune time. We had just finished completing our plan to retake Zarhun City. With three Worezian Armies stationed on the northern outskirts we would have been slaughtered." She took his wrist, clasped it in formal greeting and smiled. She was satisfied in the knowledge that at least some of her objectives had been accomplished.

A courier stepped through the flap and handed Sesmak a dispatch. He quickly read it, and yelled out to his aide to have the officers assembled in the command tent. "I am sorry I have some bad news; you had better head back to your friends. You will find them at your wagons. I will send some word to you after I speak with my officers." Prince Sesmak ran off leaving her with two warrior escorts to lead her back through the maze of tents to where their wagons were located.

The officers that were still in the base camp stopped the other warriors from advancing north. They walked to the command tent where Prince Sesmak was waiting for them. With a quick head count, he could see all but six were present. "I have just received a dispatch from our post located in the eastern woods of Mount Vlatok. Sixteen tadletas of Sylakian warriors and foreign auxiliaries have marched onto the northern Plains of Zarhun."

"They have set up defensive positions, and are building fortifications for a longer stay. My guess is they will be meeting with the Worezian Violet Army which crossed the border two days ago. From the dispatches I have just received. The armies of Worez and

Envar are going to box us in and drive us south toward the Kingdom of Jeupa."

"They have three full armies to the east and one full army to the southwest. We have no choice but to gather our men and do as they have planned. With this disheartening information, there is some good news. I have just received word that our Marshal Ebestar has returned and he has brought home some of our friends and relatives from Dolfinia."

"There are not enough warriors to make up the differences in our strength, but they are now trapped in the Volendale Valley as we once were. I have ordered advanced guards and the two tadletas of the green to their rescue. Hopefully our men will reach the southern end of the valley to see that they are brought to the safety of our camp. For now there is little we can do. One way or the other, we still need to pack up our camp."

"I have sent word to Commander Quenelyn of the southern encampment to march due southeast. They are not to stop until two hours before daylight. After a two zestar rest they are to continue with the march southwest until they are ten thastas south of the Village of Rotanis. This is where the Worezian Tan Army has set up their defense. Commander Quenelyn will keep the space between the Envarian Army and the Worezian Army open until we get through."

Prince Sesmak assigned two stratas of warriors to stay with Captain Odelac and Ciramtis. One strata was dedicated to the safety of Princess Elona and Princess Diara. They were ordered to not let them out of eye sight, and to see to their every need and comfort. It was a welcome feeling for both of them; except now they didn't know what to do with their time.

As soon as one of them stood up a warrior would run over asking what they would like. Caysa thought this very amusing. He sat with Elona asking the warriors to fetch water, wine, fruit and bread. He would have had them running the rest of the evening until she reminded him that he was still a slave himself, and that he was acting like the cook Atus.

Their wagons were given some additional supplies and amenities for their comfort. They were also given an assortment of better fitting clothing. It was unfortunate, but there was not much of a selection of women's clothing. The two princesses elected to don men's attire than the ill fitting gowns that had scrounged.

Captain Odelac was asked to follow the last supply wagons heading south. Ciramtis convinced Prince Sesmak that she be allowed to ride north to meet with Commander Traga. It was a request he could not deny. Karadis volunteered to accompany her and Odelac thanked him for doing so.

The seamen Baradic was nowhere to be found. They had left him alone and unconscious in the command tent. Vadeck looked throughout the camp for him; but neither he nor any of Prince Sesmak's warriors knew of his whereabouts'.

Two and a half zestars of hard ridding brought Sesmak's advanced party of the Green Army's cavalry to the southern entrance of the Volendale Valley. They reined up at the sight of warriors emerging from the valley. It was dusk and in the poor light, neither could see which army they had confronted.

Ebestar ordered a full alert sending pikemen to the front. He had just been told of the army at the end of the valley blocking their egress. They were not going to be trapped again, especially by cavalry. He expected the pikemen would take care of that problem quickly enough, but he had to follow up with an immediate counter attack with his sword and axmen opening a breach in the enemy's lines.

Zestarius the God of Time had intervened once again of behalf of the humans as the two groups of warriors closed upon one another in the dark. Ebestar's front line charged forward with halberds leveled. The enemy horsemen reined up in the dimming twilight and closed ranks. They were just about to use their spurs when they suddenly pulled up and dismounted. They recognized old friends advancing toward them, that they had thought long dead.

Marshal Ebestar could not see what was happening. In the semi-darkness the men shouted loudly and clashed hard into each other but no one was falling. He almost fell from his saddle at the sight of them embracing each other. These warriors were the last survivors of his old army unit.

Covering the tears in his eyes, he stayed in the saddle. It was all he could do to hide his joy. Forty two hundred men had finally come home. The marshal let them mingle and find old friends and comrades while he ordered others to unload Traga's wagons. The vehicles would be sent back to the Splindia Valley without delay. They were urgently needed to help evacuate Traga's wounded and exhausted rear guard warriors.

No fires would be lit at this temporary campsite. Prince Sesmak had sent word that a Sylakian Army of sixteen thousand were camped to their east at the base of the Vlatok Mountains no further than five thastas from their position. Sesmak's warriors made their own night fortifications in the burned out remains of Vlatok. This village had once been a thriving community on the west side of the mountain at the headlands to the Volendale Valley and the Zarhun Plains.

The only inhabited building in the town had already been taken by Captain Surhaas of the first tadleta. This was one of the active Envarian courier stations. It was manned by a typical ten man taxt unit, with six of the fastest horses in the kingdom.

The captain ordered his men to ride to these buildings and surround them as soon as the town came into view. They did not want these couriers warning any Envarians loyal to King Helidon. Each messenger met death quickly and their mounts were confiscated for Sesmak's own dispatch units.

Ciramtis and Karadis wanted to ride further into the Splindia Valley but Captain Surhaas asked them to wait. It was now pitch black and in the darkness, one could not tell friend from foe. There were too many stragglers still coming into camp that had not known that they were among friends.

Marshal Traga's remaining warriors had not been notified that the main body of his army had reached Prince Sesmak's northern outpost. These men at arms would be dog-tiered and have their hands full of any non survivors gear. With the marshal would be the walking wounded and the warrior's lagging behind that had stayed to fight the last delaying action. The marshal did not need to take care of two more people that he did not know or trust, during his retreat.

Traga's warriors moved slowly in the dark, guided only by the southern star of Sestra, Goddess of the Sky and Planets. His warriors slogged forwards, holding onto each others arms, supporting comrades who were too tired to walk on their own. Commander Drayus had been ordered not to wait for the men of the second defensive line. He was to march his two hundred swordsmen and Ebestars two hundred archers south as soon as they retreated from their forward positions.

Traga's remaining warriors held out for four zestars giving them a good head start. He figured the survivors of the first two defensive lines would be less than two thastas from the end of Volendale when darkness fell. On the other hand, his last delaying action had caused a lot more casualties than expected. The marshal had lost over fifty warriors and another seventy to eighty of his Semedian Dragon warriors were wounded. He was unaware of how many were unaccounted for; some were lost in the dark and still missing.

A warrior at his side stumbled and fell, unable to stand. The marshal offered him an arm up. Shaking his head he said, "No sir, I can not go on. Leave me here with the other walking wounded and the men on stretchers. All we are doing is slowing down and tiring the rest of the men in our santax."

Traga ordered an immediate halt. He knew the best of them would last no more than another zestar. One hundred of the strongest warriors would remain behind protecting the wounded; the remainder of the force would continue marching south. Traga would remain behind until the enemy caught up with them or until he could find a means of protecting them from slaughter.

Most of the warriors had very little stamina left in them, and were lying as still as death on the cold ground. Even the sound of horses' hoofs did not rouse them. The wagon teams rode amongst the men in the moonlight, until locating and stopping in front of Marshal Traga. Captain Urmos of the Red Dragon Army's first sword jumped down and ran over supporting him. "Sir we have made contact with Prince Sesmak's Army, and they are keeping the pass at the end of the Volendale open."

Traga looked at him. The haggard young captain looked as tired as he felt. "Did Drayus's men meet up with them yet," asked Traga. Captain Urmos draped the marshal's arm over his own shoulder and led him toward the wagons. "Yes, we picked up all of Ebestar's archers the first trip, and then we went back and picked up Drayus's men for the second trip."

They stopped at the rear of the lead wagon and sat at the tailgate. How many men have we got left, asked the captain? Traga tried to think, but he was having a hard time concentrating. Captain Urmos handed him a wine skin. It contained krasta en, the strong whiskey made from the brown wheat they had been trudging through. The one hundred and twenty proof alcohol burned his throat, but he tipped it back taking a long second pull on it, before handing it back. "How many can we get in a wagon," asked Traga?

"Twenty-five at best, with the tailgate down, including the two or three on the bench seat," he answered.

Traga rubbed the stubble of a beard that was growing on his chin. "Marshal Ebestar told me that there is a small village on the other side of the valley almost opposite the Splindia pass. He said it was called Gothom. We have a lot of wounded that can make it no further. I want you to load all the wagons with them and take them to the village. Those that can still stand will continue with our march south. We may need to make another two trips to get the rest of the men to the end of the valley, but I think we should be able to do this by daybreak."

Horastus the larger of the two Palestus suns had already risen before the last wagon of the Red Dragon Army rolled into the Marshal Ebestar's north base camp at Vlatok. Traga was asleep hunched over on the bench seat with a blanket draped over his shoulders. His driver had been continually catching a hold of his arm so he would not fall out.

Ebestar could see that the Dragon Army was unfit for duty. There was no way these men could march and catch up with the rest of Sesmak's warriors. He ordered the drivers and horses changed, but had the wagons continue their journey south for another half day.

The beleaguered warriors would get additional wagons and help from the Village of Blineva. This is where he had moved his second campsite. It was the same temporary bivouac location that Sesmak had been occupying for the last mursa. The prince's Envarian rebel army was still fresh. They would protect the retreat, bringing up the rear.

Traga's spent warriors would ride in shifts from the waylay stations until everyone was moved onto the Zarhun Plain. Prince Kytos marched off with the supplies being carried on the backs of Sesmak's warriors. If the young lieutenant could not light cook fires, he could at least set up water, jerky and journey bread stops along their evacuation route.

Chapter # 27

The Worezian Army Pincer

Prince Quayot sat in the luxurious lounging area of the command tents. The brightly colored green and gold Envarian canvas tents were set up in a tee shaped arrangement and were very elaborately furnished. One side of the tee was a twelve foot square, used as a personalized quarters. The royal sleeping area had a thick, plush carpet on the floor. The central lounging area was covered with overstuffed silken cushions and aromatically scented sleeping furs.

The other side of the command tent's tee was set-up for formal dining. The banquet area was of the same dimensions as the sleeping area. It was also as richly decorated and furnished as the other half of the tented structure.

In the center was a low, wide, horseshoe shaped table. The short fluted legs were bound with glossy brass rings. The table top was constructed of red oak and having irony inlays. Surrounding the table were green and gold silken seating cushions with the royal crest embroidered on them. At the three side walls away from the entrance were low sideboards matching the stained woods of the central dining table.

To one side of the dining area, trays of roasted, spiced meats, fish, game birds and steaming vegetables were on top of the serving table. The vanity on the opposite side of the tent had washing basins, pitchers of water, and stacks of clean linen towels and hand wipes. One of the low cupboards at the rear of the tent had bread wheels, cheese, pastries and pies of many varieties. The other had dozens of bottles of white, pink, red and purple wines with wooden boxes containing silver serving utensils, knives, drinking cups, and crystal glassware.

In the front half of the twelve foot by twenty four foot main tent area, was a six foot square command table with twelve chairs surrounding it. A large scale leather topographical map of western Zarhun was stretched out in its center. There were many movable, painted and carved, small wooden game board sized pieces. The miniatures depicted flags, warriors, horses, wagons, tents, catapults, and various pieces of siege equipment. They were scattered about the canvas chart depicting the current logistical positions.

At the rear of the main tent, between the two personal accommodations; was a centrally located receiving space for visiting dignitaries and patronizing members of the monarchy. This regal lounging area was where the crown prince conferred and entertained his senior officers and other guests.

The tarpaulin floor of this area was covered with a ten foot diameter carpet with interwoven wires of silver and gold. At the borders of this thickly braided fabric, the twelve major gods were depicted. These ancient deities were surrounding and pointing to a centrally located crystal ball. The image depicted in the quartz globe, was a panorama of the Envarian capital City of Renvas as the center of the world.

On top of this carpet were thirty to forty, three foot square overstuffed silken cushions. They were scattered about in a semicircular seating arrangement. Located at the outside edges and dispersed throughout this pillowed area were short, small round pedestal stands. Trays of assorted cheeses, fruits, or nuts were on most of them. Others had multi-flamed oil lamps or incense burners on them.

The lounging area was always rowdy, smoky and overcrowded. Ten to twenty individuals were forced to wait outside until one of the privileged guests exited the tent. No less than half a dozen courtesans mingled with the dukes or lesser earls, while they sat around discussing the affairs of state.

The kingdoms industries were controlled by the heraldic households. To stay in the good graces of the crown, they made sure the king and his son received a sizable share of each guilds profits. Among the many diplomats seeking ambassadorial positions, were rich tradesmen attempting to peddle their wears or merchandise to the royal estates. Most visitors came from Renvas or Palensa. Each of them was seeking some sort of special consideration for promoting or for funding a ludicrous enterprise.

During their stays, they never failed to praise the prince for the marvelous job he was doing in commanding the army, or his miraculous war efforts. Today as most days, the crown prince was inebriated almost to the point where he could not stand. His boisterous laughter could be heard throughout the campsite.

This afternoon Prince Quayot was joking and drinking with the two vintners who managed his family's regal distillery and bottling company. Earlier in the morning they had brought a dispatch from Prince Quayot's father. The letter informed him that Princess Shayla, this future bride had arrived safely in Renvas. His father, King Helidon had selected the day of the wedding to be the one following the defeat of his uncle's rebel army. All the arrangements for the celebration had been made. Proclamations for the event and gift giving were being distributed throughout the lands.

Their intoxicated merrymaking was interrupted by the sight of an aide who came into the tent and was escorted directly over to the officer of the day, and Grand Marshal Kulfron. The group spoke quietly for a few moments, before the messenger saluted and left the tent to pass the information on to the other senior officers that were not present.

Grand Marshal Kulfron of the Envarian Red Army was Prince Quayot's uncle on his mother side of the family. Quayot and he did not get along with each other, but the old war veteran knew his place. The prince's standing orders were for no less than three tantax commanders to be present in the command tent continually day and night.

Commander Rumgal of the first tantax was always there. His daily duty consisted of planning different campaign scenarios and strategies. Conquering Jeupa was the paramount objective. Immediately following this invasion, the contiguous mountainous territories and fiefdoms would be annexed. Then Worez would declare war on the south western Kingdom of Amrig, and central lands of ancient Zo Tan.

In addition to Commander Rumgal, Commander Arontis of the second tantax squadron was always in attendance. He was tasked to draw and continually re-draw battle maps for the new kingdom as they were conceived and executed under Commander Rumgal's fancifully expanded empire.

Commander Pymondus of the fourth tantax cavalry division was assigned there today as the operations officer. After the aide left the tent the four officers conferred quietly while being watched closely by their suspicious and schizophrenic prince.

Quayot waived Marshal Kulfron over to him after the commanders scattered and went about their business. "What is going on he demanded?" His uncle bent down low and spoke in a soft raspy voice. He did not want the merchants to hear everything that was going on.

Quayot nodded in a drunken stupor and waived him off. "My friends, I have just received some good news, and you will have to excuse me for the rest of the day. Military business you know." The merchants and other guests stood, bowed and were escorted from the command tent. Shortly after being dismissed, most were escorted to their horses, coaches or wagons. Other regal personages were entertained and patronized in the communal mess tent until they could return.

A disheveled looking individual with bludgeoned face was brought into the garrison's command tent by two guards. A frayed, rolled canvas was tucked under the civilian's arm. He was covered in thick road dust and held a bloody rag to his swollen and split nose. While standing with his back against the war table, he and spoke quietly with Grand Marshal Kulfron

The scruffy, vagabond, seaman stood by and waited patiently as the prince finished his wine. Staggering over to the table, the drunkard bumped the side of the war table. The jarring impact knocked over and displaced half of the battlefield pieces. Quayot swayed and gripped the edge of the table for support. Then he grinned contemptibly at the disapproving look on his uncle's face and attempted to stand in proud conceit.

"My lord, this man is Baradic of the Yojan Kingdom. He says that he is an espionage agent in the service of the King Magarus and Worezian's. This spy has brought with him Prince Sesmak's war map along with his plans for the conquest and the retaking of Zarhun City."

Quayot's eyes widened at the news, and his mind seemed to clear from this mornings debaucherous drinking. "When did you get this information," he asked in an anxious, yet slurred voice? Staggering foreword, he took a few steps and tried to compose his thoughts.

Baradic stepped between Marshal Kulfron and the crown prince. Unrolling his cartographer's canvas over the top of the other map on the table, he spoke softly. "Your majesty, I just escaped from Prince Sesmak's encampment late this afternoon. They are breaking camp and packing to move out as we speak. In the confusion of their hasty deployment, they left me near his command tent and I was able to steal this. I know how important it was so I rode right here as fast as I could."

"There will be no way for them to change these plans now; over half of his army was already on the march east." Baradic pointed to the center of the chart he brought. "You can see Sesmak's Army will be entrenched at the outskirts of the southwest ramparts by tomorrow evening. They will be laying siege and attacking the following day at sunrise."

Prince Quayot looked the map over, and then slid it to the side comparing it with the larger geographic chart below. "What do you think Kulfron?" His uncle bent down and looked the diagram over carefully, studying and scrutinizing every aspect of the hastily penned notations for the next ten zestas. The other commanders stood near him watching his hands and fingers moved from one position to the next.

Finally he bent the lower right hand corner over and inspected the back. There were three runic characters in a vertical row. "It is my opinion that it is genuine, sire. This is Commander Ebeston's personalized map showing his proposed deployments and notations for invasion of not only Zarhun City, but the retaking of the central plain."

Prince Quayot's smile widened. "Have the army break camp," he ordered. "We march on Zarhun City!" Marshal Kulfron whispered in the prince's ear. "Sire, your father and King Magarus have ordered us to stay near the Village of Moland on the western side of the plain. We're not to move out until Prince Sesmak has been driven south."

Quayot shoved him roughly aside speaking close to his face with indignation. "What good is for us to wait for him here if he's not coming this way? You heard! He is going to invade from the southwest and retake Zarhun City before the Worezians are ready! Now I ordered you to break camp. We are going to march on my traitorous uncle, and I don't plan on letting him get away again."

The three commanders saluted and left the tent to pass the orders on to the rest of the junior officers. Quayot sat down and quickly wrote a letter to his father; folding it he sealed it in red wax. Handing Baradic a leather purse he said, "Get this to the king as fast as you can. I will see that you are well rewarded for all that you have done." Baradic saluted and walked from the tent. In the sunlight he emptied the draw string bag and counted out twenty large silver coins in his hand. The conniving sailor smiled and waited for the courier escort to bring him a fresh horse.

Three zestars after the order had been given; the Red Army of Envar was ready to move out. All of the military units except for one santax; the two hundred reserves were guarding Prince Quayot. The main body was expected to pull out and march throughout the night.

They would set up a temporary camp twenty thastas southwest of the Village of Rotanis at the "Great Divide." It was the ancient geologic fault line which ran north to south splitting the Zarhun Plain lengthwise. The army would wait for their prince at the gorge, below the base of the twenty foot high escarpment.

The plan was for the troops to eat and rest the following day. Three zestars before the suns set, they would advance over the narrow gorge bridge. The Red Army would march and lead their steeds up the steeply inclined switchback road. Once the warriors reached the eastern side of the plain, they were to regroup into their regimental divisions. Following a short rest, the army would march in the dark until the forward units encountered Sesmak's forces.

The Royal Red Army would attack the forward guard positions using only knives. The main body of the enemy would never know that they were under attack, and would not be called to a battle ready status. It would be a total route and slaughterhouse. Quayot ordered that none of these rebellious prisoners were to be taken alive.

It was the thirteenth zestar when Prince Sesmak called the weary warriors of the southern forces to a halt. The leading edge of his army was getting too far ahead of Marshal Ebestar's and Marshal Traga's forces. Last night he had been informed of their engagement with the enemy in the Splindia Valley. They stopped and rested at one of the few green and sparsely forested areas of this seemingly endless plain. It was a one hundred foot diameter dish shaped geologically depressed area that had once been a shallow lake.

This abandoned farm and cultivated area had twenty to twenty five trees, a deep well, a one room thatched house and a small barn. It was not much of a defensive position but he did not like camping in the openness on this vast savanna. This was a good a place as any they would find. The remainder of his forces would take the rest of the day to catch up. Sesmak sent out cavalry riders and a courier back to inform the rest of his troop their location and intentions.

The main body of the army would be staying here throughout the day and the entire night. Two more days of marching would put his Sesmak's rebel army within twenty thastas of Prince Quayot's Royal Red Army. Sesmak did not like the prospects of engaging the Red Army of his own kingdom. It was not the fact that he was out numbers two to one. It was the realization that he knew most of these warriors and officers personally, and had served with them for many years.

They were the best armed and trained warriors in all of the Envar. It had been a pleasure living with and training these fearless men. It was a sad day for him when the Worezian War broke out. Sesmak was ordered to take command of the Envarian Green Army and not the Red Army.

No camp fires were to be lit at this campsite. It was going to be a cold bivouac. Only jerky, dried fruit, cheese, bread and beer would be served until the army was safely south of the Village of Moland. This is where he expected to be re-provisioned and allowed to rest long enough for his warriors to have one more good hot meal.

Late in the evening riders came into the camp from the south. It was Captain Beligon of the third blue tantax along with a strata of scouts. Prince Sesmak had to be awakened and called to the command tent. The captain stood to attention as Sesmak entered. "Good evening captain, I hear that you have news that could not wait until morning." Sesmak walked over to the wine stand; poured two glasses full to the rim, giving one to Beligon.

"Thank you sir, it has been a long ride." Sesmak indicated the chairs and they sat for a moment while the captain drank. "Sir the Envarian Red Army has moved out and is now in the middle of the plains blocking our way south. They are also running a cold camp, and are preparing for battle."

Prince Sesmak immediately ordered an officers' call, and sent riders to bring the northern marshals and commanders back to his camp. Ebestar, Traga and Kytos arrived three zestars before the sun rose. As soon as Traga was awakened with news of the officers' call, Ciramtis was brought over to him and introduced. He wished that he would have been able to speak to her longer, but he barely had time to read the letter Lord Jedaf had written to him.

She told Marshal Traga that Princess Elona and Diara were safe and currently in camp under Prince Sesmak's protection. He thanked her for all the help and said that at their next meeting he would give her a proper welcome.

This was the first opportunity for Marshal Ebestar and his son to meet. They had not seen each other in four years. Sesmak gave them some time to be alone before everyone sat down in the command tent. In addition to his other instructions, he ordered three stratas of scouts to the west. They needed to find out if they would be able to by-passed the Red Army by going around the main body through the north Moland Forest.

During this lull in activities, Prince Kytos had a chance to find his sister Princess Elona. At first she did not recognize him as he walked over toward her. It was not the darkness; it was the uniform and the way he walked confidently in her direction. She had not been able to sleep, and had been dreaming of Jedaf. All she remembered of the nightmare was that he was hurt and bleeding. She sat at the tailgate of the wagon wiping her eyes and crying softly.

Kytos stepped out from behind Caysa's wagon and said to her, "Every time I see you you're crying." At the sound of his voice, she cried all the louder as she ran over and wrapped her arms about him.

Prince Sesmak, Commander; Quenelyn, Traga, Ebestar, and his son Ebeston sat in the command tent discussing the situation. It would be a senseless waste to attempt a confrontation in the openness of the plain. They agreed that even if escape to the west was not possible, fighting in the woods would offer them some hope. The Moland Forests were large and dense; they could offer sanctuary for many warriors.

Traga and Ebestar sent riders north to have their warriors change directions from a south eastern to a south western line of march. Commander Quenelyn ordered his cavalry and all supply wagons to break camp and immediately ride to the west. Their dust clouds would clear by dawn. The rest of the camp would be marching west as soon as each santax could be formed into squares.

The last of the troops would have less than a zestar to march before the dawn broke. Sesmak wanted to make it perfectly clear, as soon as the suns came up; everyone was to stop where they were and to lie down in the tall grass, until a diversion or an exit strategy could be worked out.

THE ZARHUNIAN CONFLICT

Horastus rose, and to the amazement of Sesmak, his marshals and their scouts, the Red Army had not moved or sent out any scouting parties to the north or west. The rebel leader directed his troops to continue moving west, making as little of a dust cloud as possible. Ebestar's and Traga's forces caught up with the main body and they waited in the forests until the rest of Quenelyn's warriors marched from the plain.

They made camp a half thasta into the woods, and rested. There was no explanation for this mysterious tactic on the part of the enemy troops. Scouting parties were hastily formed and deployed in all directions. There had to be some rationalization for this strange twist of fate, but no one was able to come up with a plausible explanation

After second lunch the morning scouts returned and a second set of scouts were deployed. All the reports that came back were the same. No enemy to the north, no enemy to the east, no enemy to the south. The Red Army of Envar was still camped half way between the western forests and the Village of Rotanis. It had to be some sort of a trap or an ambush was being prepared, but no one could fathom or guess the ramifications.

Quenelyn ordered the cavalry to break camp but to stay in the woods. The horsemen would walk their mounts due south until they reached the end of the Moland Forest. If this was not a trap they would emerge in the grasslands a thasta southwest of the village behind the enemy's army.

Each of the battle formations were given the same instructions and moved out at one zestar intervals. The last to move out would be the supply wagons. They were unloaded and the provisions packed on the backs of the warriors. The wagons were then broken down into shipping parts, and carried through the trees by the draft horses.

Five zestars later Traga's wagon masters walked out of the woods to join the majority of Sesmak's Army. They would have the wagons reassembled and loaded by the time the suns set. The afternoon scouts returned for the shift change. There was still no new information and there were no plausible explanations. What ever the reason was, they could not let an opportunity like this pass them by. Most of the men were well rested, having sat around waiting for Traga's wagons to arrive.

Sesmak ordered his army to re-assemble. They would move back to the flat grasslands and march all night following the western edge of the Zarhun Plain. At day break they would alter direction again and move back into the seclusion of the west woods. They were not as dense as the Moland Forests, and they would end up, being within two thastas of the main road to the capital City of Renvas.

If they were lucky enough to hide in these woods until the next evening they would once again march at night by-passing Envar's Capital and head across the southern plain toward the Zo Tanac Mountains. They would not be driven into the lands of Jeupa; they would end up in the southern Renvary Mountains of their kingdom.

Prince Quayot had been complaining most of the day. No fires had been lit, the food was cold and dry, and the wines were warm from sitting under canvas tarps. His warriors were sleeping and shading themselves beneath their shields or under make-shift blanket lean-to's. Tomorrow he would have another mighty victory. One that would be talked about for generations, and it would be all too his credit and no one else's.

At the appointed zestar King Helidon's son gave the order. The camp was broken and the warriors marched northeast. At dusk they slowly walked up the eastside of the Rotanis ridgeline. This ancient volcanic fault had split the Zarhun Valley almost in half due north-south. The western half of the continental shelf sloping toward Renvas and the sea, the east half remaining almost totally flat until reaching the high mountainous Envarac Forests of the far east.

The armed forces that were camped out on the eastern flat prairie lands had settled in for the evening and everything was quiet. Reports came back to Prince Quayot that the rebel camp was much larger than they had expected. Hundreds of campfires could be seen at the leading edge. Prince Sesmak must have been recruiting in the northern provinces again. Quayot made a mental note; he would have those villages burned to the ground this time. They would never again defy him and support his enemy.

All preparations and plans had been made down to the last minuet detail. Quayot's army was ordered to remove all armor and anything that would rattle or make a noise. They would march slowly and quietly until reaching a distance of two hundred and fifty paces from the enemy lines.

Then they would low-crawl the next two hundred paces and wait for the signal to attack. When the lead tantax reached this location, they would part leaving a twenty pace wide path. The Envarian Red Cavalry was ready to ride into action, with lance, sword and mace.

The zestar had come and Quayot gave the word; hundreds of horsemen thundered past him on their way to the kill. It was a fierce long and bloody battle. Warriors were face to face in the darkness swinging sword and axe in hand to hand combat.

Sketchy reports came back to Quayot that he had lost over half his cavalry during the first two zestars of battle, but the swordsmen had killed more than their share and they were pressing the enemy hard to the east. The renegades had lost many. They had been caught sleeping and were unprepared for his attack.

The first lancemen hit the picket lines about the twenty-fifth zestar creating confusion and havoc. Six zestars of bloody fighting continued while pressing the enemy backwards. Still their opponents had not broken ranks. There were only three zestars left before dawn. Commander Arontis returned to where Prince Quayot had order the command compound tents set up.

While Arontis stood by waiting to make his report, runners came and went quickly. Fighting in total darkness made it imposible for the battlefront officers to report actual loses and determine the locations for the individual regimental units. A dispatch had just been received informing them the enemy was reassembling and attempting to make a counterattack on their north flank.

Grand Marshal Kulfron ordered Commander Rumgal to take command of the tenth tantax auxiliaries and half of the royal body guards to meet this new threat. Arontis stood by watching the activities;

he was weak, having lost blood from two deep chest wounds below his left armpit. Prince Quayot set down his cheese and wine glass and motioned him forward.

Arontis staggered forward holding a bloody compress to his ribs. He could barely speak. "Sire we have lost the second and fifth tantaxes," he said softly. "Another enemy formation has re-grouped and deployed on the battlefield. They have the sixth, seventh, and eight tantaxes boxed in and surrounded on three sides. A large cavalry host has swept threw a gap in the front phalanx of our ranks and has decimated the first tantax, and the last of our ninth tantax cavalry. We are losing this engagement and we should withdraw before we lose this battle."

Quayot went into a flying rage yelling at him and screaming at Grand Marshal Kulfron. "Did you hear what he just said to me Kulfron? We are losing! Eighty thousand warriors against forty thousand and he says we are losing!" Turning his back momentarily on Commander Arontis, Quayot looked at Kulfron drew his dagger and turned back to Arontis.

The prince did not give him a chance to speak further. He drove his sharp blade under Arontis's ribcage, and left it sticking there. Kulfron ran over to his friend, and lowered his limp body carefully to the carpet. The young commander died without another word. "Now you better get those worthless lazy good for nothings back into battle and start fighting like warriors or you will be lying next to him," shouted Quayot!

Grand Marshal Kulfron did not come back until well after sunrise. He was escorted into the command tent by four Worezian junior officers, and the Grand Marshal of the Worezian Blue Army. Quayot walked over toward Kulfron as they entered the tent. The prince was raving mad and still drunk. Eyeing the Worezian officers with contempt he confronted his military's most senior officer and stood arrogantly in front of him while yelling insults.

"It is bad enough that all of your warriors are cowards and don't know how to fight. Now you insult me by going around my back and go slinking over to the Worezians asking for their help!" Prince

Quayot attempted to slap his uncle's face, but his wrist was grabbed in mid air and held forcefully. Prince Quayot glared at the officer that had a grip on his forearm.

"I am Grand Marshal Bythenum of the Worezian Blue Army," the man said as he let go of the Envarian crown prince. The grand marshal nodded to his junior officers. They immediately seized Quayot from behind, twisting both arms behind his back.

"What is the meaning of this," screamed the prince?

"You fool! You stupid, drunken fool! You're so ignorant you still don't know what you have done." Bythenum drew his dagger and sliced Quayot's cheek from hair line to chin. Quayot screamed, and was held tighter as he started to go weak in the knees.

"You have attacked the Worezian Army of the Tan, and killed my best friend, Grand Marshal Malenum. I had to pull half of my army from the eastern plain to support his scattered troops. We have lost over sixty thousand warriors and you have lost seventy thousand!

This has been the most deadly combat engagement in history. Only an imbecile would attack an enemy at night. How were you supposed to know battlefield conditions? The fields are covered with bloody bodies as far as you can see. This is your fault, and even the gods are not going to stop me from killing you!"

He ran the point of his blade down Quayot's face again to the sound of another scream. They were Quayot's last. The two officers holding him let the unconscious prince fall to the carpet unconscious. Marshal Bythenum pulled a chair out from beneath Quayot's war table and sat down heavily. The angry Worezian took two ale mugs and filled them with wine. Marshal Kulfron sat down next to his adversary, and was handed a cup from Bythenum. "Now what are we going to do," he asked?

Looking down at Prince Quayot, Marshal Bythenum spit on him before taking up his mug. Then the Worezian Marshal drained half the wine and slammed his mug down hard. "You know that I am going to have to kill him," he replied. "But my life will still be forfeit. My King, Lord Magarus will be asking me to take my own life for this devastating slaughter. If I do not take the blame for the loss of the Tan Army, he will be taking retribution out on all of my family members."

Marshal Kulfron knew that even though he was a distant uncle and the kings' brother-in-law, his fate would be similar. After the death of his sister Quaya, Magarus had little need for his wife's relatives. The king had received a bridal dowry doubling his wealth, and then managed to acquire the majority of his father-in-laws estates.

There was very little left of the family's fortune, and Kulfron had no children. He sat with his head lowered until a thought, brought a half whimsical smirk to his old weathered face. Looking down at the still form of his nephew Prince Quayot, he said. "I have a way for you to keep your life and your honor if you agree to my terms."

The Worezian Marshal looked at him incredulously. "If I agree to your terms," he asked? "You don't have an army any more."

Kulfron stood and drained his mug. "No, this has nothing to do with this battle. I have hundreds of wounded as do you. We will both be losing our heads for this disaster. What I propose is that you let me kill my nephew Prince Quayot. This way you will not be blamed for breaking any treaty. Your friend Marshal Malenum has already paid the ultimate price and he will be blamed for the loss of his men and your warriors."

Bythenum considered the unusual request. "And what do you get out of this?"

"You let the remainder of my army return home to Renvas with our wounded," said Kulfron. "They are no longer a fighting force, and are no further a threat against you or your kingdom." The old Worezian officer thought a moment, before nodding in agreement. The two of them picked Quayot from the floor and put him in a chair at the head of the war table.

Marshal Kulfron walked to the tent flap and asked the Worezian guard to go to the prisoners and bring Envarian Commander Rumgal back with them to the command tent. The two grand marshals opened another bottle of Quayot's best wine, drank, and waited. Within a half zestar Rumgal walked into the tent. His face was bruised; his left arm had been wounded and was in a sling stained with dried blood.

Kulfron stepped over and stood before his junior officer. "You have no doubt heard what we have done to our allies last night. Marshal Bythenum has agreed to let you take our men home, but first you have to bare witness to what I am about to do. I do this in the knowledge of forfeiting my life." He walked over grabbed Quayot's hair yanking and shaking the prince's head until his glazed eyes opened.

"My lord, I have come to award you another battle ribbon," said Marshal Kulfron. Quayot put his hand to his face and felt the fresh blood running down his cut cheek. He was confused and looked frightened. His lips quivered while tears ran from his eyes. Kulfron drew his dagger and rested the point over Quayot's heart. The prince jerked erect trying to stand and knock the sharp blade away. "Unfortunately my prince you are being awarded the "Star of Rotanis" posthumously."

Kulfron drove the blade to the hilt then quickly pulled it free and sliced Quayot's throat. His nephew sat up straight with an incredulously look on his face, gurgling blood and dying. The old officer handed the bloody dagger to Commander Rumgal, who wiped it clean on Quayot's uniform.

Then saying he was sorry for what he was about to do, the young officer drove the sharpened weapon into Kulfron's heart in a formal execution style manner. His commanding officer and close friend slumped into his arms without another word.

Grand Marshal Bythenum of the Worezian Blue Army gave a wave of his hand and two aides stepped forward. They assisted in lowering Marshal Kulfron's body down to the rug in the receiving area. Then one of the aides pulled the dagger free and handed it back to the Envarian officer. "Escort Commander Rumgal back to the stockade and have the surviving prisoners released."

Rumgal stood to attention and saluted Bythenum. "Sir, I would like to take the bodies of Marshal Kulfron and Prince Quayot home with us, so they can be given a proper burial."

The Worezian officer nodded in agreement. "I will have them wrapped by a priestess of the Order of Divine Justice and the bodies prepared for the journey." Everyone knew members of each royal family belonged to this religious sect and its patron, the Goddess Atrusa.

As soon as Rumgal was escorted from the tent, Marshal Bythenum removed the ceremonial knife of King Sejand from Quayot's scabbard belt and wrapped it in one of the prince's finest silken cloaks. The ancient knife and symbol of Envarian kingship would still be presented to King Magarus as was specified in the treaty agreement between their two kingdoms. It no longer mattered that the marriage treaty had been broken and there would not be an heir to rule over their unified kingdoms and the lands that had been conquered.

Chapter # 28
War Returns to a Devastated Land

Baradic was escorted under guard, to King Helidon's palace in Renvas, Envar. He was surprised that the royal residence was not as elaborate as he had envisioned it would have been. Although far older, the capital of Envar was less impressive than the capital of Worez.

The majority of the buildings were wooden structures needing a coat of paint. Less than half had brick or stucco exteriors. Neither could compare with the city of his birth. The Yojan capital City of Joroca made these two midsized cities look like provincial capitals.

The two ancient metropolises and the cities of the surrounding duchies had not been modernized in more than half a life time. The monarchs and royal families of these hamlets had been squabbling or at war, almost continuously since they broke away from the old Semedian Empire. The newly crowned kings of these divided lands and their relatives had squandered fortunes in silver and gold.

King Helidon's servants had bathed, powdered and clothed Baradic prior to his audience. The soft yellow cotton tunic he wore had long sleeves and white lace ruffled cuffs. His kilt was made of thickly woven brown cotton with a white werna skin hem, waist band and ornamental braided piping. The white stockings and underwear he wore were of fine linen. His low cut boots fit snugly and were made of soft brown leather. Thrown back over his shoulders hung an embroidered green and yellow woolen cloak, with the Envarian crest of a sliver sword beneath a six pointed silver crown.

The chair that he was sitting in had a plush cushioned green satin seat, padded arms and a high back rest. A servant stood by seeing to his every need. While he waited in the royal anti-chamber he drank vintage wines. Baradic's acid etched crystal glass was continually filled from a slender and delicate decanter. It did not matter how long it was going to take for a royal audience to be arranged. He was content nibbling tidbits from the silver hors d'oeuvre tray. The soft cheese cubes, wedges of fresh fruits, and spiced meat strips were the best he had ever eaten.

Baradic was quite pleased and thought that he could easily get used to this kind of a life style. King Helidon was announced, and the spy was escorted into the great hall. Playing the part of the good and loyal servant to the limit, Baradic fell to his knees in front of the throne, prostrating himself. Then he said quietly, "Oh mighty king I bring you news from your great and glorious son, Prince Quayot."

"Since I am his most loyal servant, he entrusted me with the delivery of this auspicious message." Baradic kept his head bowed low and extended his hand with Quayot's green leather correspondence packet. An attendant ran over and fetched it for his sovereign.

Helidon examined the royal seal, broke the red wax and quickly read the letter that was enclosed in the dispatch pouch. He sat for a few quiet moments in contemplation before speaking. "You may go," he said to Baradic folding the note and waving a hand dismissing him.

Two days before Princess Shayla and ten thousand Worezian warriors from their Army of the Tan had entered his city. They had been dressed in full regalia, and following two scores of trumpeters and kettle drum musicians. Wedding plans were being prepared and arrangements for provisioning the Worezian Army regiment were taking place.

Three merchant ships filled with cereal and feed grains had been promised to King Magarus as was specified in their treaty agreement. The merchantmen had just set sail yesterday morning after the princesses' arrival. Now the king read that his son was about to attack

Sesmak's Army of malcontents and vagabonds which were camped outside of Zarhun City.

If Quayot managed to prevent this siege, King Helidon might not have to go through with this marital arrangement. He also would not have to give up half of his kingdom to the Worezian's. Helidon stood to leave the audience chamber and noticed that Baradic was still prostrated at the foot of his dais. "I said, you may leave," he shouted as he waved his arm to the side.

Baradic raised his head slightly. "Sire I have no place to go and no funds to live on while in Renvas. Prince Quayot said you would give me twenty large silvers if I was able to make it through the enemy lines and deliver his letter to you. As you can see, I was thrown to the ground and beaten, but I fought well and did not give up his letter."

Helidon looked at the broken and bloody nose that Captain Odelac had given Baradic. Pausing for a zesta he turned toward his personal male servant. "Get this man his silver, he has done well." Baradic now had more silver coins than he ever imagined. If he were able to find an agent of the Sylakian Kingdom, he knew he could triple his fortune.

The knowledge that King Zaghar's invasion plan for the Histajonies Archipelago were now in the hands of their enemy had to be valuable. He was sure the information was worth at least thirty two rebests, large silvers or the equivalent of two rearus, small golds. He needed to book passage on the first ship leaving Renvas, and he headed for the waterfront.

Argothus and the Worezian first tadleta of the Tan Army was bivouacked a half thasta from the Renvas city gates. Late in the evening, the commander received a rider carrying an urgent dispatch. It was from Marshal Bythenum, his father's oldest friend. The letter notified him that his father Marshal Malenum had been killed in a sneak attack on their armed forces by Prince Quayot and his Royal Red Envarian Army.

It was Bythenum's opinion this stealthy night attack was specifically designed to re-take the regional capital and end the stalemate between their two kingdoms. The Envarian Red Army's surreptitious raid may not have been a mistake by a drunken fool. The dysfunctional and almost totally decimated Tan Army was being re-deployed northeast of Zarhun City. The remnants of his army would be stationed there until relieved by a few tatletas from the Worezian Violet Army.

The letter also notified them of Prince Quayot's death. Due to this covert action all of the Worezian Armies had been placed on high alert. The most likely consequence of this Envarian betrayal would lead to King Magarus once again declaring war. Argothus was ordered to send a detachment into the palace retrieving Princess Shayla and then he was to march back to Zarhun City at all possibly haste.

Commander Argothus was to not engage any of the Envarian military units while the princess was still within the enemy's territory. Three stratas had been sent back into the City of Renvas to protect Princess Shayla and to pack her belongings for the return journey. Princess Shayla had heard the news that the palace spies had been spreading since last evenings' kreb. Her fiancé Prince Quayot had been killed during a battle to retake Zarhun City.

The Kingdoms of Envar and Worez were preparing for hostilities to begin again. She had been fearful that she was going to be held for ransom or sold into slavery. All of her belongings and everything she could steal was hastily packed into trunks and loaded onto wagons as soon as she had heard of his death.

Commander Argothus wasted no time; his tadleta was ready to move out as soon as the princess's coach and her dowry wagons rolled into his camp. She protested about having to continue riding until she was told that preparations had already been made for her capture and sale. The Envarian populace was searching for her and a price of a hundred large silver pieces had been put on her head.

The Worezian Tan Army detachment moved out under the cover of darkness from the suburbs of Renvas. First they retreated due east to the western edge of the Zarhun Plain, then due north toward Zarhun City. They only slowed their military unit's withdrawal just before turning north, on the forced march.

THE ZARHUNIAN CONFLICT

The riders of the Worezian tadleta could see the fires of the advancing Envarian southern Blue Army. They were picketed half a dozen thastas away on the southeast road leading toward Renvas. Commander Argothus was thankful his father's friend had given him advanced warning. His troops would have had forty thousand warriors of Sesmak's rebel army to his north and thirty to thirty-five thousand warriors of Envar's Blue Army to his south and southwest. By tomorrow morning there would have been no escape.

Valadis the spy-merchant and friend of Ciramtis, stood on the southern slopes of the Zo Tanac foot hills. He was looking north through the sparse ponderosa pines down toward the Great Zarhun Plain. He had been commissioned to the rank of captain by the king himself. Following his military induction, Valadis was ordered to reorganize the few troops patrolling the western frontier. The border units were to make preparations, but under no circumstances were they to withdraw. Reinforcements could not be mustered or deployed in less than a half mursa.

It had taken the Jeupan Army of the Blue three days to march from their home base east of the Verengal Mountains, to within a thousand paces of the Noraga Pass. Hopefully King Galthardon of Jeupa would have time to conscript enough easterners to fill the ranks of their Green Army and march it west, before the Worezians invaded their homelands.

Somehow Valadis had doubts this would happen. Four years ago, when the first rumors of war were discussed, the king raised the pay of the warriors in an effort of keeping them in his service. A royal proclamation was sent forth notifying all citizens that a tax increase would be placed on all goods for these additional expenses.

The mercantile and farming guilds protested the royal decree, by blockading the streets and closing the farmers markets. The stevedore guilds refused to load and unload vessels in the harbor. Shopkeepers closed the doors of their retail stores and refused to open them. Taverns and hostels stopped serving hot meals, wines and ales.

These demonstrations and very vocal objections from the gentry lasted until the king agreed to lower the taxes to the old rates, and reduce the amount of the warriors pay increases. If the king wanted the warrior class to be paid more for their loyalty, he would have to pay for them with his own family's funds.

Several hundred warriors from each of the standing armies and a third of the seamen left military service. They offered their loyalties to other kingdoms and some left for the Northern Kelleskarian Wars instead of staying in Jeupa. Mercenaries were being offered twice the rate of pay, plus given land-grant options.

Now the Blue Jeupan Army of the western frontiers had been reduced to fifty thousand and the Royal Red Army which protected the capital City of Hyupeious was down to less than sixty-five thousand. For the most part these disgruntled warriors were older and less likely to fight for the kingdom after the way the mercantile and clothier's guild had treated and regarded them.

The Green Jeupan Army of the eastern boarders was below half strength, and was made up of mostly petty criminals released from debtors' prison. The Blue Army had been given the orders to hold the border at all possible costs, and not to venture out on to the plains. They were not to give the Worezians the excuse they were looking for. They were digging troudeloup pits; sharpening long poles, building stockade fences, rock wall barricades and redoubts for archers.

After escaping from the Worezian Royal Guard, it had taken Valadis six long hard days to drive Lord Jedaf's vegetable cart, the length of the Zarhun Plains. He was glad that Ciramtis made him take the cart instead of a saddle horse. Two times he had been stopped and his cart searched by roving Worezians looking for renegade warriors.

At the southern City of Actiland he traded the cart and stout draft horses for a swift saddle pony and a few silvers coins. Then he rode the remaining five thastas to the frontier, where a small garrison style outpost was located. They sent on Valadis's message alerting their King Galthardon of the Worezian battle plan.

Directly north of his position Val could see two vourtre riders coming in his direction. He knew they were not human because even at this distance they were small in stature. Riding down the hill and out on to the plain, he talked with them at length, and then invited them to come into the camp. The Grand Marshal of the Jeupan Blue Army had been notified of their presence, and was standing outside of the command tent as they rode in.

Walking over to them, he extended his arm to them in formal greeting as they dismounted. He said; "I'm Marshal Stelenus of the Jeupan Blue. I have been told that one of your couriers has already been to my king, and that you have joined us in the war to keep the Worezians from our lands."

The elder of the two took the marshal's wrist in greeting. "They are our lands also," he said. "None are safe as long as Magarus sits on the throne in Worez. Marshal, I am Cul Taric Commander and protector of the vourtre of Amrig and Wurda. This is Ada Hon, Commander and protector of the vourtre of Envar and Jeupa." The other vourtre took the marshals wrist and nodded at the introduction.

Captain Valadis handed over the reins to one of the marshals aides, and led the way to the command center. It was a small, six man canvas shelter usually used along the major roads, at the border crossing outposts. To their left was a canted leanto, the garrison flag and supply tent. Two junior officers were sitting at a table writing out orders. Inside, the main tent there was a rectangular table, six folding chairs, and two small oil lamps.

A serving cart for food and beverages was located in one far corner, and a coat rack for wet cloaks or clothing stood in the other. The marshal's aide poured out four ales and set the pitcher on the stand before leaving the tent.

"I had to ride over to meet you and the rest of the Jeupan's. I needed to inform you that our small forces have reached the Zarhun," said Cul Taric. "There are not as many of us as you humans, but we will do what we can." After taking a sip of ale and clearing the dust from his throat he continued. "We are not fighters of the plains but we can more than hold our own in the woodlands, and foothills."

"Prince Pfitas and King Eneas have five thousand warriors stationed in the Envarac Forests to the north at the Venditch Pass. I have about the same number of warriors camped in the woods, just north of your position at the Zo Tanac Mountain foothills. Commander Ada Hon has three thousand warriors scattered throughout in the woodlands west of here between the Cul Derus and Tollenum Mountains."

Marshal Stelenus wrote notes as the vourtre commander spoke, and marked their locations on his animal skin map with an inked quill. Thirteen thousand warriors were not very many, but it was better than what he had at dawn. "We thank you for any help you can give. We have additional supplies on route, as we speak. If your men need anything, send riders over and we will give you what we can."

The Jeupan marshal poured a refill for Cul Taric, and Ada Hon, as they stretched their legs. Then he thought how ironic it was that they were drinking together, let alone sitting at the same table. Stelenus was old enough to have been in the wars to take the vourtre lands of ancient Semedia. Two of the campaign ribbons on his uniform had not gone unnoticed by his guests. One purple and gold combat ribbon, indicated service during the war and one red and white ribbon denoted more than twenty confirmed kills.

"We will remain in the woodlands and hold both of your flanks for as long as we can," said Ada Hon. "I hope your King Galthardon can convince the kings of the eastern humans to send warriors to support him. If they don't they will be the next ones to face the Worezians. He should also think of sending his Royal Red Army. It will be useless protecting the capital City of Hyupeious if he has no kingdom.

The two vourtre officers exchanged a few words in private before re-mounting. They rode in opposite directions from the Jeupan encampment back to their own units. Having just arrived at the wooded edge of the Plain of Zarhun, there was much to be done. Weapons and supplies were just starting to come into their camps.

There also was hope that the vourtres of Cathon, Tarot, and Rampour would be able to send warriors, and or supplies. Ada Hon had also heard the rumors that King Helidon of Envar ordered his Blue Army to march northwest to protect the coastal Capital of Renvas, while his Red Army pursued Prince Sesmak's rebel army.

THE ZARHUNIAN CONFLICT

The southern Envarian Blue Armies home base was on the northern outskirts of the City of Yoathon. This midsized regional capital was located due north of the Cul Derus Mountain. This was where Ada Hon's warriors were being deployed. The Blue Army had not refused the kings order, but they procrastinated and dragged their feet. The commissary had not started loading any of its perishable supplies and the regimental material goods depot had not made any arrangements for them to march out.

Half of the Envarian Blue Army had previously sworn allegiance to Prince Sesmak. Once they heard of the devastating defeat of their Green Army in the north, they left their post in mass because the king would not order them into battle. The warriors of the southern army, joined up with Prince Sesmak in an effort of keeping the Worezians from seizing their capital without a fight

These deserters were currently with the survivors of the Green Army that had fought their way through to plain after the North Point engagement. The rebel army is still occupying the plain southwest of Zarhun City. For more than two years they have kept the Worezians from invading further south. King Helidon knew if he made an issue of this army's divided loyalties or tried to make any changes in the command structure, he would lose the support of the southern provincial governors, the royal families and their auxiliary fighting units.

Only three zestars had passed since their meeting, when Commander Ada Hon along with four escorts could be seen galloping across the plain back toward the Jeupan command post. The middle aged vourtre officer must have ridden all the way to his armies' base camp between the Cul Derus and Tollenum Mountains, changed horses and ridden right back.

Captain Valadis and Marshal Stelenus of the Jeupan Blue wondered what could have changed so drastically for the vourtre commander to be returning so soon. Ada Hon dismounted and was escorted to a picketed area where the marshal was inspecting some of the recently built berms and fortifications.

"Marshal! The Envarian Blue Army has left Yoathon." Stelenus waived his hand toward the tents and they talked while walking in that direction. News has reached the southern cities of Prince Quayot's death and the night long bloody battle with the Worezian Tan Army. With the City of Renvas now defenseless, Prince Sesmak has ordered the entire Blue Army to make a forced march to the capital.

Sesmak has deployed his few warriors north of Renvas and will attempt to delay the Worezian Army by ambushes and harassment tactics, until the Blue Army reaches the city. Sesmak fears that he will have to evacuate Renvas. He knows that King Magarus will order it burned to the ground. He will also slaughter or enslave all its citizens in retaliation for Quayot's treachery.

They reached the shade of the tent and sat at the map table. Drinks and a hastily put together meal were served as they discussed some new options. The situation for the Jeupans had not changed much. Sesmak had only one option open to him. The prince had to retreat toward the Jeupan Kingdom which is exactly what King Magarus wanted in the first place.

Even though there were less enemy warriors on the battlefield, they would still outnumber the warriors of the southern nations three to one. Dispatches had to be sent to the Capital City of Hyupeious informing King Galthardon and the marshals of the other Jeupan armies.

Ad Hon sent his own riders out notifying the other vourtre commanders. The villages of the eastern Envarac Forests and Venditch Pass Mountains had to be told of Prince Quayot's death. If the scattered vourtre units under the command of Prince Pfitas could be mustered, they might be able to help evacuate the wounded Envarian's warriors and prevent them from being slaughtered on the battlefield.

In the dark, many of the survivors had been separated from their units. They had scattered southeast, seeking refuge in the woods of the Envarac foothills. Envarian warriors of the Red Army were being sought out and put to the sword by the Blue Worezian Army auxiliaries. These men and their woulded comrades needed urgent help. They had to be evacuated further southeast, where the enemy butchers could not find them.

Chapter # 29

Renvas The Capital City of Envar

The eastern scouting strata rode into Prince Sesmak's camp. Most of the wagons and supplies had been loaded, and they were preparing to move out. Dismounting, the first officer waived to the armies point riders for them to halt. "Officers call," said Sesmak. His aides climbed into their saddles and rode off spreading the order. Everyone in the column dismounted while the officers gathered about their commanding oficer.

"First Officer Tharngos has brought us news that Prince Quayot and the Envarian Red Army have attacked our true enemy, the Worezians. We don't have a lot of details, but they have lost the battle and it has cost Prince Quayot, his life." His warrior would have cheered at hearing of Quayot's was death, but for the loss of their many friends and comrades.

"The remainder of our Red Army and most of the walking wounded are retreating back to Renvas. We need to bring the survivors here and tend their wounds. I want the camp set back up, and have the cook fires going. Tharngos send riders to the Villages of Moland, Aruntis, and Blineva requesting help and medical supplies.

Also send me a courier; we need to notify the Blue Army at Yoathon. Our capital of Renvas is now unprotected and the Worezians have ten thousand warriors of the Tan Army camped outside of our cities gates. When they hear the news they may burn Renvas to the ground in retaliation."

Sesmak's Army went into action carrying out the orders. Within no time tents were set back up, kettles were boiling water, and riders were delivering messages throughout the kingdom. Prince Sesmak was worried about the inhabitants of the capital and the exposed flanks of his army. If the Worezian tadleta of the Tan Army that was stationed outside of Renvas remained after burning the capital, they would hold his south western flank.

The rest of the Worezian Tan and Blue Armies would still hold the east flank and the Violet Army would still hold the North Country. It was a worse situation than the one he was in before Quayot's attack. Now their enemy could kill off the rest of the Envarian Army and rule the entire kingdom. The only other escape would have been to sea, but Sesmak knew if the Worezians burned Renvas they would have also burnt or confiscated all the ships in the harbor.

The remnants of the Envarian Red Army had been notified by courier of Prince Sesmak's intensions. Commander Rumgal had ridden to camp swearing his allegiance and that of the remaining junior officers. There were sixteen to eighteen thousand warriors left of the Red Army. Half were too injured to be moved any further.

A quarter of the survivors were walking wounded. Others with leg injuries had been loaded onto carts and wagons. The severely injured, were left on the battlefield to be tended by a few taxt medical units. Less than one tadleta out of eighty thousand warriors remained fit for duty.

It did not sound like a lot but Sesmak's army needed all the help it could get. He now did not have to worry so much about the southern flank. The Worezian tadleta could still burn Renvas but they would not be able to keep him from marching south. During this hectic time, the prince received a courier message from his cousin, the senior officer of the southern Envarian Blue Army. Marshal Fleggian swore allegiance to Sesmak and was following his sovereign's order to march on Renvas.

Fleggian's Blue Army originally consisted of five under-strenght tadletas of less than ten thousand each. Of that eighteen thousand had left their posts to join Prince Sesmak in the northern provinces of Trespaden. His remaining thirty thousand warriors would reach Renvas in four days of forced march.

Prince Sesmak and Marshal Ebestar left Traga's Dragon tadleta to guard and protect the wounded while he and three of his other Envarian tadletas marched on Renvas. He asked Traga, to have Captain Odelac and Ciramtis take charge of all of the tented hospital areas for both of their armies. Prince Kytos and his sister Princess Elona were to take charge of all of the supply wagons and the distribution of all foods.

Odelac tried to protest being put it charge, saying that he was only a ships captain. Traga promoted him to the rank of a commander for the auxiliary supplies unit, so he could no longer refuse; Marshal Traga also promoted Prince Kytos to the rank of first officer. Vadeck, the old marine taskmaster of the Tarpenya was also given a rank as a first officer. He was put in charge of all the camps fires. It was the seaman's task, to see that the wood piles were kept high and dry. Karadis was promoted to the rank of second officer and placed in charge of the medical supply wagons.

It was late in the afternoon when Sesmak sent word back to them. His tadletas and Marshal Fleggian of the southern Envarian Blue Army had met on the outskirts of Renvas. Their combined armed forces were preparing to take the city by force when hundreds of citizens came out waving flags and bringing bread, wine, and cheese to their army.

Sesmak's older brother King Helidon; had been overthrown by the royal centurions and his body was now hanging from one of the balconies near the front entrance to the palace. The rebel prince had been brought the crown and Marshal Ebestar had proclaimed him King Sesmak, Lord of Envar. The tadleta of the Worezian Tan Army and Princess Shayla were nowhere to be found, and no one had died in another useless engagement.

THE ZARHUNIAN CONFLICT

The city should have been in celebration at the news of the coronation, but everyone that lived in Renvas had relatives in the Red Army. Many had several family members in the service. Mourning flags were draped over and hanging from every other household doorway or balcony.

Two generations ago when good King Helagus ruled Envar, he tried to make peace with the neighboring kingdoms. He could not get any of them to sign formal treaties, but as long as his armies were withdrawn from the frontiers there was an uneasy peace.

King Helagus was not a robust warrior like his father or his grandfather. Crowning a sickly thirteen year old was not what the populace wanted and they thought him weak and easily manipulated by his mother.

The teenaged king ordered the four standing Envarian Armies of old, to be reduced to three under-strength battle groups. The border armies of the Blue and Green were assigned the tasks of clearing land, building roads and constructing bridges. Within twenty years the lives of the general populace had improved twofold, and agriculture production had more than tripled.

King Helagus also reduced the acreage of the royal game preserves. He divested his family land holdings by dividing them into small farms for his fathers retiring warriors. Less than a year after his untimely demise, the coronation of his eldest son Helidon took place. Everyone knew this was not an accidental death and everything seemed to revert instantly to the hardships of the past and economic stagnation.

King Helidon swore on his crown that he would bring back the greatness that was Envars after the Eastern Semedian War. He ordered the creation of five standing armies, and sub divided the kingdom into more provinces and duchies. Most of these new territorial regions were to be ruled by rich relatives or merchants who had the money to buy regal status.

The kingdom had been on a war status continuously for the past thirty years. The only peace had occurred during the last two years because the northern war with Worez had ended in stalemate. The

Envarian Army of the Tan had been created for the sole purpose of killing the vourtre and driving them from the eastern foot hills of his grandfather's Envarac Forest and the ancient game preserves of the southern Cul Derus Mountains.

Most of the warriors assigned to this unit had been killed in a twenty year war of attrition. The vourtre burned their own villages and had moved back into the forest like their ancestors. A santax of a couple hundred Envarian cavalrymen would be ordered to ride into the woodlands and forests now and than. They would never be heard from again. The beleaguered Army of the Tan was eventually eliminated and merged with the southern Army of the Blue.

The population of the kingdom was half of what it had been a dozen years earlier. Most of the younger men had been conscripted into the armies or had been taken away from their families and pressed into bondage service for the newly created duchies.

Those that had not been killed in battle had gone to sea seeking a better place to live. The wealthier half of the mercantile guild and their families had relocated to other neighboring kingdoms. The upper middle class divested much of their holdings, reduced the amount of merchandise they carried, closed the majority of their shops, and where known to bury their gold where the tax collectors could not find it.

Renvas itself had a general run down, ramshackle look to it. The buildings that could afford paint and repairs could not find workmen or laborers that were trained or qualified to do the jobs properly. There were a few estates that still had slaves, but most of males were too old or feeble to perform backbreaking field-hand work. The average head of the household barely made a living. Even simple tasks like flower gardening, had been neglected.

Sesmak's first royal proclamation was to pardon all of the warriors of his renegade army. His second decree was to pardon all the villagers that had been fighting at his side or that had been supporting him and his warriors with food and clothing.

The king's next official order was to bring home all the wounded warriors of the Red Army and to declare a week of mourning. During this period of grief and sorrow, Sesmak's senior officers were to review and re-enforce all of Renvas's defenses. They were to scrounge any material that could be used in fortifying the citadel.

The ramparts and buttresses of the outer city walls were still formidable. They had been maintained throughout the war years with Worez, and modifications had continued through this short time of peace. Inside the city itself, the castle and central keep had been stripped. Emergency food supplies, armaments and weaponry had all been sent to the Worezians as part of the dowry arrangements for the new peace treaty.

The earthen dam and ceramic lined aqueducts that King Helagus had constructed over the southern Subarit River were leaking and in poor condition. The floral gardens and park fountains were dry. The flow of the city's drinking water had been reduced as the backwaters were lowered. The port docking facilities, the wharfs, and the piers had warped rotten or missing planking. Most of the pylon supports and balusters were decaying. The wooden floor joists, gussets and x-bracing were filled with sea worm infestations.

The small Envarian Royal Navy based in the north, consisted of four aged galleons, eight frigates, six coastal barks, ten to fifteen flat barges and a dozen coastal freighters. Less then a quarter of those were at anchor in the Bay of Renvas. The few at anchorage, which were stationed protecting the harbor entrance, had not been to open sea in a dozen years or more. Most of the experienced sailors and marines had left the navy to enlist in the service of other kingdoms.

These ships of war were undermanned, undisciplined and in decrepit conditions. Most had barnacle encrusted hulls; their sails and rigging were dry rot from not being unfurled or used in the last three to four years. Very few of them had enough provisions aboard to immediately set sail if ordered to do so.

One competent enemy ship-of-the-line with an experienced crew could defeat the entire Envarian Navy while at anchorage. They could also sink the twenty odd merchant vessels berthed at the piers before they were able to leave their slips. With the defeat of the Royal Red

Army, the kingdom was left with one of the smallest armed forces on the Continent of Zarhun.

The hopelessness of the populous was going to be King Sesmak's biggest problem. The devastated economy and Worezian invasion would be secondary. To make matters worse the weather this year had been unseasonably cold or wet. The spring rains had been heavy at times but they had come late in the planting season.

The harvested grain crops from the first summers planting were yellowed, stunted or withered. A quarter of the sown crops never germinated. A good percentage of the legumes and tubers had been left to rot in muddy fields. Fruits and vegetables had been the mainstay for the population, but now the warehouses were nearly empty.

In the northlands, krastant wheat that should have been waist high, only reach the knees. A lot of the growing seasons first planting had been harvested and confiscated by King Helidon's government officials. The markets had few vegetables and most stands were nearly empty of goods. Over a third of the kingdoms crops had been shipped to the Kingdom of Worez as part of the peace treaty. Soon the month of drought would be upon them and by the end of second summer, starvation would be wide spread.

Now the Worezians occupied the entire north eastern half of the kingdom. Soon they would be taking all of the farmlands south of the City of Zarhun. They had already annexed all of the mountainous forests of the south eastern provinces. By doing this, the enemy prevented the delivery and distribution of heating and cooking charcoal that these communities supplied to the western parts of the country.

In addition to all of the kingdoms other problems, Sesmak had been informed of his enemy's alliance with the evil Sylakian Empire. Some of their battle hardened warriors and foreign mercenaries had already landed on the north coast. These marauding invaders were now pillaging and occupying the north central and north western provinces.

The fertile Valley's of Splindia and Volendale were now occupied and enemy held territory. Dispatch riders also informed him that the villages west of these valleys were being sacked and burned in retaliation and retribution. The new enemy was taking out their vengeance on the citizens of these communities for loss of the Onandonian auxiliary warriors that had been killed by Lord Jedaf's Army during the first battle engagements of this new war.

There was nothing the newly crowned king could do to prevent this ravaging and plundering. Sesmak ordered all of the ships in Renvas's harbor to help evacuate the villagers along the northwest coasts. It was the only thing he could do for these besieged citizens. They would be taken to Palensa or one of the other southern coastal cities of the kingdom.

The Kingdom of Envar no longer had any allies except for the meager forces of the Red Dragon Lord. During his discussions with Marshal Traga and Ebestar he had mentioned his fear that the Worezians would not allow his army to surrender.

A fast schooner was procured and dispatched with orders to seek out the three vessels of the Red Dragon Fleet that were scheduled to rendezvous off the coast of Azzon. This coastal runner was to deliver a message to Captain Cliedeous of the Merimon. Instead of having Jedaf's ships sail all the way back to their home Port of Joroca, the vessels were immediately ordered to alter course and set sail for Renvas, Envar. These large warships would be used to evacuate the capital if it became necessary.

If the Worezian Armies were able to re-group after this battle, they could make an immediate attack on the city. The capital would not be able to withstand the siege. Sesmak would have no choice but to surrender his kingdom to save the people from further death and destruction.

Princess Elona and Diara were hugging each other and crying when Kytos entered the room. "So you told her didn't you," exclaimed First Officer Kytos. Diara tried to hide her reddening face. "Well you should have told her yourself," she said. "I don't think you should go with Commander Odelac and Ciramtis to Jeupa. You should be going with your sister back to Saratam and home to Oppow. That is where you are needed most!"

Kytos diverted his eyes and lowered his chin in deliberation. "You may be right Diara," he said reluctantly. "But I owe Lord Jedaf so much and now that I am an officer in the Dragon Army, it is my duty to stay with the unit. Marshal Traga and all of the Dragon Army will be moving out in two days. It was one of the last orders that Lord Jedaf had written. He directed Marshal Traga to rescue Elona and you, and then to march the army south to Jeupa. They are to help secure the border and build defensive fortifications."

Elona looked at her younger brother in his new uniform. She would never admit it but she was very proud of him. He had seemed to grow up over night, and had lost his boyish face. His arms were showing a lot more muscle, and he stood tall, defiant and confidently before her.

"It's alright Ky," she said. "I was not crying about you leaving me, and I am not worried about sailing to Saratam by myself. King Sesmak has ordered a taxt of warriors to protect and accompany me until I reach home.

I was crying because of our brother Pinthos." She hid her face in a couch cushion for a few zestas blotting the tears, and then she looked back at him. "I don't know how he could sell us to the King Zaghar of Sylak, and have our father and brother Sertron killed?" She choked back another sob and wiped away the last of her tears. "Do you think they could still be alive?"

Kytos sat on the lounge next to her and put his arms around her holding her tightly. She buried her face in his shoulder and started crying again. "I don't know El, Lord Jedaf said that he would try to send word to our father as soon as he could, but Oppow is so far away. It will take months for a letter to reach home. Then there is always the possibility that our father would not believe that Pinthos is after his throne."

"From what Jedaf and Ambassador Ajoris told me, they expected Pinthos to be crowned by the end of this month." Elona cried all the harder. "I am not sure your sailing to Uncle Rastos and Aunt Arna will do any good. I expect that our kingdom will already be at war and under Sylakian control by the time you get to Saratam."

She took her face from his shoulder and wiped her eyes again. "But I have to go Ky, don't you see. I have to try and warn them, and like you said they may not believe the letter you sent to Uncle Rastos, but they will believe me. If father is dead, I can at least warn the peoples of Idecka, Hodek, and Therda that Pinthos plans on invading their kingdoms. Their kings and princes have all had state visits to our home in Jesilla and they know me." She stood, composed herself, straightened her long lacy, rose colored dress and dried her red eyes.

"Now First Officer Kytos, I expect you to escort me and Princess Diara to the dining hall. King Sesmak has put on a feast for the warriors of the Red Dragon's Army and I have been asked to sit at the head table representing Lord Jedaf.

She did not look up at him, but down to the steel dragon headed ring on her finger, which Jedaf had given her aboard the pirate ship Culba. It changed to silver and diamonds for a tenth of a zesta before reverting back to plain steel. She put it to her lips and gave it a quick kiss before taking his arm and leaving for the great hall.

Chapter # 30
Adathe the Capital City of Cathon

Adathe was an old crowded metropolis with extremely narrow cobblestone streets, cramped looking two and three storied brick structures having common walls, and roof top gardens. Most of these building were made of sand colored adobe blocks with dark brown or red mortar joints. Some had been stuccoed but the majority had been painted or glazed in vivid colors.

Goods from all Palestus's continents were piled high on the docks. The markets were full to overflowing with everything imaginable. All the warehouses were packed beyond capacity and storage space was costing a premium price. Business had been the best that it had been in many decades.

If the war between the Kingdoms of Worez and Envar lasted much longer, Cathon would turn out to have the most important and largest seaports on the Continent of Zarhun. As it is now, most nations avoided sailing near the Envarian coast. Although it was once a powerful Kingdom, Worez had very few diplomatic ties, and it was rumored that King Magarius had opened his ports to pirates and renegade shipping merchants from all kingdoms.

Cathon's geological features were different than most of the other kingdoms of Zarhun. It was well protected on three sides by prominent, natural land formations, making any invasion difficult. It was sheltered on the west by the high spires of the Lestran Mountains.

The Kingdom's southern borders were guarded by the cursed hills and valley lands of the ancient City of Tabalis. The east and southeast frontiers were guarded by the lands of Tarot and Rampour. Both of these states owed their allegiance to King Samalis.

Samalis's large navy and marine contingents not only protected the coastal waters of Cathon, they also protected the shipping and coastal villages of the eastern kingdoms. The Archipelago of the Histajonies was only three days sailing north-northeast from Adathe, and Samalis's navy considered the Sea of Askalus their own. Cathon had been a major power in the region for the last ten years, and the king planed on keeping it that way.

In the Histajonies, the island Kingdoms of Jolac and Zurra were sending tribute to him, and King Samalis maintained a separate fleet in the southern Spice Islands. They protected his mercantile shipping and fishing fleets along with making port calls on all the non-aligned nations in the region. This would be the only drawback in telling King Samalis, about Sylak's invasion plan.

The Kingdoms of Bintar and Cathon were trade rivals and not on friendly terms. For the past two years Cathonian cargo vessels had been harassed by the Bintarian fishing flotillas, and by their man-of-wars. Samalis did not feel any sympathy toward them and his kingdoms populous was making a profit selling war supplies to Bintar's neighboring kingdoms.

Moreover King Samalis didn't like the sinister and devious King Zaghar any better. The dark lord and ruler of Sylak had been increasing his influence throughout the archipelago, and he was known to be supplying armaments and military specialists of his own. These advisers have been encouraging the smaller island tribes to unite. The Sylakian diplomat's have also been provoking and inciting the coastal kingdoms into declaring war on Bintar.

Sylakian secret agents and covert sympathizers were interfering with Cathonian trade relations. Some of these kingdoms appeared to be on the verge of signing treaties or making military alliances with

King Zaghar. There were more Sylakian cargo vessels in the harbors of the Gothorian Kingdom than usual, and the Kingdom of Tyjor had recently closed its ports to Cathonian commercial shipping.

The southernmost kingdoms on the continent were known to be enlarging their own naval and mercantile fleets. They were encroaching on century old Cathonian fishing grounds and selling cheaply manufactured trade goods to Samalis's eastern provinces and allied fiefdoms.

Some of Tyjor's mercantile ships were now flying flags of dual allegiance. The tops of their mainmasts were flying their own banner of the black and silver eston whale along side the Sylakian redolga boar's head. The Kingdom of Gothor had decided to do a likewise fashion, except they decided to fly their flag of the banta cave bear in conjunction with the Sylakian commercial flag, of the entire redolga on a blue and white tartan background.

Lord Jedaf and Ambassador Ajoris had been brought to a rather large lounging area in the palace's anteroom. This plush and regal waiting room was adjacent to the main council chamber. The foyer and settee areas were beautifully decorated. Interconnecting paneled doors led from it, to the offices of state, as well as the glazed, French style doors leading to the outside open air terrace and flower garden.

The mosaic flooring was constructed with a combination of varying stones. They were either polished cream colored marble hexagons with brown and orange wavy lines running through them, or a dark chocolate brown with wavy, tan wavy lines.

A thickly woven blue green wool carpet covered a portion of the marble flooring. It had been designed in a pattern resembling the turbulent deep sea. The border depicted shallow rocky shoals with the sea foam and tidewater breaking over them.

Most of the furniture in the waiting area was made of a lightly stained burl hardwood. The individual chair and sofa's had soft, glossy satin overstuffed cushions, portraying sea birds and flowering aquatic plants. The bases of the oil lamp wall sconces were molded in the shape moss covered rocks. They were made of cast copper and had been allowed to green with age.

THE ZARHUNIAN CONFLICT

All the rooms and corridors they had walked through in the palace were similarly decorated in a seafaring motif. The personal assistant and the minister of diplomatic relations had greeted them at the door of the royal residence, and had personally escorted them to the council room. Word had been immediately sent to the king, and his top ministers upon their arrival.

Lord Jedaf was dressed in his formal red and white silks with his finest silver mail, sword and armor. Ambassador Ajoris was dressed in the traditional indigo blue, white silks and satin cloths of the diplomatic guild, and he carried his monogrammed and personalized reddish-brown leather dispatch pouch.

The Lord of the Red Dragon, and the rightful heir to the ancient Kingdom of Semedia, had come on an official state visit. An event like this had not happened in several hundreds of years. The city and palace was alive and buzzing with excited anticipation and rumors. Servants and couriers scurried about like mindless drones. The City of Tabalis and the surrounding cursed mountainous territories were the only remnants of the Semedian Kingdom on this continent.

Over a thousand years ago the wide spread, mighty and decadent empire had been conquered by barbarous hoards that had been supported by minor envious kingdoms of the northern and eastern continents. With ancient Semedia's fall and collapse, civilization on every continent crumbled, reverting to placated stagnation and simple stone aged technologies. Over three hundred palests of brutal uncivilized meager existence followed.

The population on the Planet of Palestus dropped to a quarter of what it had been during the golden years. Starvation, pestilence and the misery created by the greedy local warlords only came to an end through divine intervention. The royal families had been given a stern warning by the merciless and vengeful old gods.

Virros the father of all gods darkened the skies, then rained fire and stones at the planet for six straight days. The vast prairie grasslands and old growth forests were laid waist by gale force winds, and chard black from the firestorms. If it had not been for the individual family vegetable patches and scattered acre sized wheat fields, no one would have survived.

The northern lands of the "Western Empire" had been subdivided and became the Kingdoms of Yoja, Thaygan and Azzon. The western portions of the "Semedian Eastern Empire" had been divided up by the conquering city states of Worez, Envar, Jeupa and Amrig. The foothills and valleys below the mountains had been gobbled up by Samalis's nation of Cathon. All the other bordering fiefdoms and duchies on Zarhun increased their acreage.

If it weren't for the curse on the high mountainous region, the six kingdoms that formed its borders would have annexed these ridges and the central plateau generations ago. Now no humans are known to live south of the foothills, and the Semedian Army of the Red Dragon and its warriors had not been seen in a more than four dozen lifetimes.

A well-groomed dignified gentleman, of medium build and height entered the antechamber. He had long, straight, graying hair and was in his early to mid sixties. Walking into the room, an aura of power and authority showed about him. His pleated white silken tunic along with his dark rich brown kilt and cape were custom made.

The gentleman's weskit was made of the same fine material. The seams were chased in silver thread. On the breast pockets were two individually embroidered coats-of-arms. One of the family insignias was the five pointed silver crown with cerulean tuadur sapphires. It was the crest of the royal Cathonian Family. The other emblem depicted a small burnt orange and dark brown etaoctad fish.

The smaller variety of this gilled sea creature had been adopted by the western Cathonian province and the City of Thaon. The larger brown deep sea grouper like fish was the crests for the Kingdom of Tarot, and the dark green grouper was the crests for the Kingdom of Thour. Both of these kingdoms owed allegiance to King Samalis. His oldest two daughters had married the crown princes and were expected to be crowned queens as soon as their husbands ascended to the thrones.

A thin silver ceremonial sword hung at his side, and a diamond studded knife handle protruded from his finely tooled leather belt.

A well dressed male slave attendant followed closely at his heels. A serving tray in his gloved hands held a crystal wine decanter, along with four matching slender goblets made of acid etched rose glass and trimmed in silver.

"I am Dugartus, the Duke of Thaon, and younger brother of our good King Samalis. Jedaf and Ajoris had risen politely as he approached them. "Please be seated again gentlemen, and have a glass of wine with me, I am sorry for the delay, but on such short notice, it was hard to notify all the ministers. It would not be proper having an audience without all of them being present."

Smiling a little uncomfortably at first, he turned momentarily away from Jedaf and looked at Ajoris. "You know, how complicated some of these diplomatic affairs can be, mister ambassador." The servant set the tray on a low serving table and poured out three glasses of wine, handing one to each of them. They sat down on the lounge taking small sips and smiling back at him politely. It was a crystal clear dry white lusixsa wine, with a slight fruity bouquet, but was one of the best wines that Jedaf had ever tasted.

This had been Ajoris's forth visit to the Kingdom of Cathon, but he had never had a formal meeting with the duke. He had previously addressed the chancellors and economic councilors in the audience chamber, and had met several of the leaders of the guardianship parliament at social functions. The ambassador had also been introduced to King Samalis, and met him once briefly, when he submitted his diplomatic credentials.

Their meeting here was a bit uncomfortable and unorthodox because no previous notification or intensions had been made from the Semedian Empire. King Samalis had sent runners off placing the Royal Red Army on high alert. He and the members of the council were brought together for hastily consultations.

Some were troubled that the ancient empire was here to demand the return of its lands. They were totally confused, worried and frightened. At least ten of the ministers owned large estates in the lower fertile, valleys or mountainous foothills. The only comforting feeling; was they knew the Semedian King would not have come in person if it was to declare war.

Ajoris introduced Lord Jedaf and himself, and after each of them clasped wrists in a warmer and friendlier fashion, the tension in the room seemed to diminish. Dugartus's servant poured another round of wine and left the gentlemen. It was clearly understood that these conversation were confidentially private and they were not to be disturbed.

The ambassador told the duke that King Vestrak of Yoja had given him a letter of personal introduction. Opening his dispatch pouch Ajoris thumbed threw a stack of sealed envelopes. After selecting the right one, he handed it over to the duke.

Breaking the Yojan crested wax seal of the semedian pear blossoms, the duke opened the envelope. The nobleman read the enclosed letter rather quickly. A wide smile appeared on his glowing face. What was written pleased him greatly. He folded it neatly and tucked the parchment back into his purse. "King Vestrak speaks very fondly of you Mister Ambassador, and to come to Adathe escorting such a royal friend, has only added to that esteem. Will Lord Jedaf be attending the wedding ceremonies?"

"I. I," stammered Ajor slightly taken aback, tongue tied and at a total loss for words. "I don't know, sire? It will all depend on the date and a great deal of other factors that I am not at liberty to discuss at this time." Jedaf smiled and was whimsically amused at the older man's embarrassment. On the ride down from the mountains, Ajor had told him of the duke's daughter, and of his friend Kaimmus. It looked like the ambassador had just delivered his own wedding proposal without him knowing about it.

The double stained glass hardwood doors to the council room swung open. Two attendant guards stepped out and stood to attention at the sides. "Ambassador, after the audience, we will go to my family quarters. A date must be set. The day after tomorrow I will introduce you to my daughter Corissa."

The ambassador could not object. After a wedding proposal had been given, the only honorable way out was death. The best he could do was to suggest a delay until after the war. Ajor had every right under the circumstances. In addition he was now in the service of two kings. Not many men had ever been given such responsibility or distinction.

The inner chamber was well lit and as elaborately furnished and decorated as the rest of the palace. Large tapestries covered the two opposite grey stone block walls. Flags of royal families with their coat of arms lined the entrance. The royal dais was located in a large semicircular half domed niche directly opposite the main portal doors to the assemblage hall. The king was seated on a carved hardwood throne that rested on a three step raised adarf, black and red speckled marble platform. Large portrait paintings of his ancestors were on the walls at both of his sides.

King Samalis was a large robust man in his sixties. He had a head full of thick shortly cropped graying curly hair, a small beard and strong looking hands. His deep set eyes, heavy brow ridge and slightly broken and crooked nose gave you the impression he had not come to the throne without having a few confrontations of his own. He was dressed in red and white silk clothing and donning an embroidered cape of purple and gold. There were too many chains of gold about his thick neck, and his broad chest was covered in jeweled brooches.

In the center of the double columned, high cathedral ceiling audience hall was a central hearth. The smoke of the lowly banked blaze of red hot coals rose to vents surrounding ten, three foot diameter skylights. A mosaic tile surrounded the five foot round fireplace making a walkway between the fire and the council members table. They were quietly standing behind their high backed chairs at two semi-circular halves of the table.

The two ring shaped arcs of the table were separated by the wide main aisles. The duke walked over and joined the other members of the council. They nodded a greeting to Dugartus but remained silent. At both halve of the table, eight well dressed dignified gentlemen were standing. Directly opposite their chair a smaller triangular version of the patron's coat of arms hung from the table edge.

The master attendant of the audience chamber took his silver pike and rapped it three times on the marble floor. "Lord Jedaf, King of Semedia and Protector of the Dead," he said. After the echo subsided, Jedaf bowed to the king and then to the Cathonian Councilors. "Ambassador Ajoris of Yoja and Semedia," Ajoris bowed in a likewise fashion as he was introduced. They were escorted to a rectangular table, which stood between the two semicircular table ends. An attendant pulled out their chairs for them and motioned them to the space in front of the table.

Rapping his pike three more times the room quieted. "My Lords, I give you our king, the illustrious Samalis, ruler of Cathon, the eastern Kingdoms of Zarhun, and Lord Protector of the Askalus Sea." Everyone bowed to the king. He waited a few zestas until the noise subsided. Then Samalis bowed his head, first to the council members on his right, then to the members on the left. It was the traditional ceremonial signal for them to be seated.

King Samalis gave a long complimentary speech introducing each member of the council. Then he noted the past deeds of their ancestors and thanked each of them for their invaluable support and community service. They were all inflated with their own importance by the time he was through with their introductions. Each of them wore different family crests. These noblemen were from the richest or the most powerful families in Cathon. A majority of them sported patroon guild emblems on their sleeves.

Jedaf and Ajoris sat and listened patiently, until the king extended his two palms upward toward them. It was the king of ancient Semedia's turn to make a speech, complimenting them for the extreme privilege of this audience and to state his business. Traditionally, an audience was still a privilege, no matter what rank or title a visitor had when visiting another kingdom.

Ambassador Ajoris rose instead of Jedaf. He walked around the low walled central hearth, kneeling before the Cathonian king, and speaking so softly that it prevented the rest of the council members from hearing. It annoyed them, and several were down right insulted. If the king had not been present they would have walked out. King

Samalis stood at last and walked to a private exit at the rear of the chamber. Ajoris rose giving, Jedaf a nod. It was their prearranged way of indicating that a private audience had been granted.

Jedaf stood and followed King Samalis from the great hall. Aioris returned to his table and remained quiet. Servants came in caring trays of spiced tea, hot honey bread, wine, finger bowls and towels. The pastries helped alleviate the anger and kept the noise in the room down to low quiet conversations. Each member of the council talked cordially with the gentlemen seated next to them. No one was happy about the two kings conferring and speaking in private.

One zestar later, King Samalis and Lord Jedaf returned to the chamber. Each took their seats. The room quieted, waiting for the king to speak. "My lords, I know you are all wondering, what we were discussing. I am sorry, but for reasons of state, I can not relay this information to you at this time. Too many ears are about, that I do not wish to hear."

A loud murmur went around and echoed in the chamber. "I know that all of you and the members of your families will be dining with me in a few days. It will be a good time for me to speak to each of you intimately, and inform you of the good news that King Jedaf has given me. Now our guests are tired after their long journey, and they are in need of sustenance and rest. I will see each of you at the feasting tables in five days."

King Samalis rose and the attendant struck his pike on the marble floor. Each of the council members stood and touched his left breast with his right fingertips. Samalis bowed to them and was escorted from the great hall by an entourage of twenty servants and personal attendants. The master chamber attendant that introduced the king escorted Jedaf and Ajoris from the hall. Duke Dugartus followed them closely until they stepped into the anteroom. All the other councilmen left by way of the private side exits.

"Ambassador, will you please follow me?" Ajor looked down at the duke's hand resting on his sleeve, and then back to Jedaf. There was no getting away tonight. He gave Jedaf a knowing glance and followed Dugartus down a side corridor. Jedaf walked in the opposite direction following the attendant. He was led to a large pushily furnished suite of rooms on the third floor of the palace. Inside there were two bed rooms, a bath, a living area, and a dining area. A table was set up in front of a double set of glass doors which led to an open air balcony.

Picking up a wide strip of roasted measan from the table, Jedaf walked over and threw open the glass paneled doors. A good strong, clean smelling breeze came in. There was enough food and wine set out to feed five hungry men. The bath had already been prepared, and the slave women were just adding the scented oils to the heated water. Jedaf insisted on washing himself and he dismissed the three attendants that had been assigned for his and Ajoris's comfort.

It was late in the evening when Ajoris stumbled into the room. He was drunk on his feet and staggering about. Tripping over the carpet edge, he knocked over a stand near the door and broke a hand painted flower vase. Hearing the crash, Jedaf jumped from his bed and ran to the door. Ajoris was laying face down near the entrance. Rolling him over Jedaf could see that he was not hurt, just totally inebriated.

Jedaf carried the older man to the other bedroom; tossed him on the bed, untied his cloak and pulled his boots off. Ajor mumbled waiving his arms and speaking in run on garbled sentences. He was incoherent and not making any sense. After thrashing around in the soft down for a few zestas, he calmed down, closed his eyes and drifted off to sleep. Jedaf threw a light blanket over him, before turning down the lukana oil lamp wick for the night.

Chapter # 31
Worezian Insurrectionists

Ajoris woke with the sunlight hurting his eyes. His temples throbbed, his throat was dried out and still burning from consuming too much strong red wine. He held the top of his head as he walked from his bed chamber. On the table was a teapot with the steam curling upward. He went to it; poured himself a cup, and read the note that Jedaf had I left for him. The young lord was scheduled to have an early morning meeting with the Commander of the Cathonian Red Army and a few junior officers of the royal guard.

Jedaf would be gone all day, but planned on seeing Ajoris around dinner time. The ambassador sat down heavily, tossing the note to the side. He had a hangover and felt miserable. Negotiating all night long for the hand of a woman he didn't want was the hardest job he had ever been given. The duke tried getting him drunk in order for him to make concessions, and it had worked. Ajoris knew better but he finally had resigned himself to the fact that he was about to be married.

Holding his temples, Ajoris sat quietly, trying to think with his eyes closed. He vaguely remembered that the king promised to finalize the contract at the dukes' estate this morning. Tomorrow afternoon he would meet his future bride. Unfortunately it would be the first day of Asursa the same date, as the rite of inheritance ceremony for the daughter of his friend Surmac.

The ambassador thought that he must remember to speak with Jedaf; maybe the young lord would be able to go in Ajoris's place. He sipped the hot tea and ate two honey cakes, before the dukes bodyguards arrived. They would have a suetable change of wardrobe with them. After a long soak in the bathouse, they would escort Ajor to the estate to keep him from from getting lost.

Lord Jedaf met with King Samalis's eldest son Samalic and with Commander Halthus for a breakfast meeting. The king had informed his two sons as to yesterday's private discussions and they had made all the preparatory arrangements for today's mission. Crown Prince Samalic was the Marshal of the Cathonian Red Army and Halthus's commanding officer. After a brief chat, he introduced Commander Halthus and left the dining room to see to some other unfinished details.

The commander was a muscular man in his early forties and standing about five foot eight. He had dark eyes and the hard emotionless face of a gambler. There was a sparse dark brown scraggly beard about his chin, and he had a gravely and raspy voice which sounded like he had been used to drinking strong liquors. Jedaf and Halthus finished eating a plate of fruit topped hotcakes and downed their tea. They wanted to be in the mercantile district before the crowds arrived.

Commander Halthus and his three taxt of royal guards located the Worezian merchant carts after searching the inner commercial district for the first three zestars of the morning. The enemy warriors had set up their sales stand in a street at the edge of the mercantile area near a crossroad leading to the shops of the tanneries.

Jedaf had to move up wind to keep from gagging. The strong smell of the tannic acid fumes, the rancid dye pits, and the piles of fly covered bloody animal skins and hides were making him nauseous. The Commander and Jedaf stood outside at a street corner linen shop. From this vantage point they could look in each direction and keep an eye on the Worezians.

The merchants placed one of their carts perpendicular to the lane so that their guild emblem of the loom, faced both directions of the widened bazaar area. Jedaf pointed out Ukam and Dorat standing in front of their merchandise wagons. They were folding carpets and stacking them on a sales display table.

The rest of the disguised Worezian warriors had scattered throughout the city. The only thing for Jedaf and the Cathonian guards to do was to wait. Commander Halthus and his band of men had removed their uniforms and donned their street clothing before leaving the barracks this morning.

The Cathonian's were stationed in different locations throughout the shopping district. Standing outside or in the doorways of the retailers, they could see in both directions. Two men stood loitering across the street from Jedaf and another four warriors were stationed down the same street, outside of a small inn.

The first men to show up in the marketplace were Renya and Bothar. They were dressed in Cathonian military uniforms of the Blue Army. They stopped at the vendor's wagons and spoke with their friends while casually looking around. Ukam handed each of them two large katmet crocks of purified and thinned lamp oil, along with a small throw rug that was to be cut up and used in making torches.

The Worezian handed Ukam a few coins, and headed through the crowd toward the cities southern gate. Halthus leaned against the building and folded his arms, giving the signal. Renya and Bothar were less than fifty feet from the stand, before two warriors in the packed street, stepped up on them from behind.

The two spies set the oil crocks down carefully, after they were poked in the back with the sharp point of a broadsword. The Cathonian guardsmen led them away without any noticeable change in the atmosphere on the "Street of the Weavers."

Lord Tavay showed up a half zestar later, along with Gentuc. They stopped at the stand briefly asking a few non specific questions, before continuing their walk toward the "Street of Tanners." The two men located on the opposite side of the street followed them slowly until the Worezians reached the corner at the next intersection. Two other guardsmen stepped out of the recessed front doorway of a yarn shop. Having already drawn and leaved their swords, they blocked the tradesmen's way. Lord Tavay instantly panicked and turned about to run.

The other Cathonian guards had also drawn their blades. There was nowhere for the Worezian's to escape. Gentuc dropped his sword and knife. Tavay decided that he was not going to be taken alive; he turned the point of his knife at his chest, trusting hard. He slumped to his knees, and then fell to his side. It was a quicker and less painful death than the others would receive.

Hasto and Learic never made it to their companion's sales stand. Jedaf identified the two warriors from quite a distance away. The two of them had created a seen in front of a bedding shop that was having a clearance sale. The young lord saw the two men shoving a woman to the paving stones. He also saw them knocking her two children out of their way as they made an opening in a tightly packed throng of shoppers. The two roughnecks made the kind of commotion that Lord Tavay would have punished them for, had he lived.

Other women standing nearby tried to muscle their way into the vacant space created by the warriors. The irate bargain shoppers started screaming and hitting the men until they stepped from the four inch high raised sidewalk planking, and onto the cobblestone street. Jedaf crossed the narrow thoroughfare and walked over to the inn where Halthus's men stood by outside sipping ale. Pointing out the Worezians, he returned to the lookout position that he had taken up with the commander.

The guardsmen walked down the street until they came face to face with the enemy agents. The Cathonian guards never slowed their pace. The pseudo merchants didn't suspect anything, until it was too late. They were jumped on and pulled into the alley where they were beaten, gagged and bound. The last insurgents to show up were the darker skinned Omaleian musclemen that looked more like stonecutters or farriers.

Jedaf knew that they were no fools and would not come willingly. He was thankful that they were the last of Lord Tavay's warriors to show up. If a large ruckus had broken out earlier, word would have spread and they might not have been able to round everyone up. Sindo and Oryel walked over to the sales stand. They appeared to be interested in purchasing one of the larger carpets. Finally after being reassured that everything was alright, they made their selection.

Sindo tossed four coins on the counter, and lifted his end of the carpet to his shoulder. Oryel picked up the other end, leading the way through the crowd. Suddenly something caught their eye, and they became suspicious. Both of them noticed Cathonian guardsmen closing in on them. Throwing the rolled carpet at the first two guards, they drew their swords and stood in a back to back defense. They were seasoned veterans and knew what they were doing. Their friend's merchant cart was less then fifty paces from where they decided to defend themselves.

At the first sounds of clanking steel; men, women and children started running. Ukam and Dorat, seeing and hearing the attack dropped what they were doing. If they were to slip away, it had to be now during the altercation. The two salesmen ducked down crawling under the carts furthest away from the skirmish. The commander's men saw them, as they converged on the whole area closing off the escape exits. The carpet retailers were not armed, and were taken into custody without a fight.

It was not so with the other two strongmen. Oryel killed three guards and wounded a bystander that got in his way, before he took a deep sword thrust in his side. Sindo killed two guardsmen and grabbed a hold of a woman using her as a shield. She was the wife of the shopkeeper, whose stand they had wrecked during the fight.

Backing his way through the crowd he saw his opportunity to make his getaway. He pushed the woman into the enemy soldier's arms and jumped onto some crates that had been stacked against a six-foot high stone wall. He jumped belly up on it and started to swing his leg over. Another zesta and he would have been over the wall, escaping and running away down the back alley. A sharp pain in his back ended his hopes.

Halthus had thrown his bone handled dagger. Sindo teetered on the top of the wall. The blade was deeply imbedded, between the ribs of his lower back. He coughed up blood and died before hitting the ground. The bodies were immediately covered and hauled away. In less than twenty zestas, the street had returned to its normal hustle and bustle.

The commander and Jedaf took over the mercantile stand, and carried on business as usual. None of the owners of the other booths or stands seemed to note any difference and wouldn't have cared one way or the other if they had. It was turning out to be a big sales day for the retailers, and the two new comers learned to have three eyes like all the other shopkeepers.

There were an awful lot of pickpockets and thieves out there, and Jedaf was beginning to think they all came over to practice at his carts. His biggest fear was that word had gotten back to First Officer Futhey. If that were the case, the Cathonians would be having an even longer couple of days trying to locate this faceless officer and the other nine covert warriors he had brought with him.

About the ninetieth zestar; two time periods after second lunch, the Worezian gentleman showed up. He and his strata of men walked down the street, five to a side. Some had bags or parcels under their arms. Some had an arm full of clothing, and some had bushel baskets of vegetables, or fresh fruit. Looking at them; they didn't appear to be different from any of the other shoppers. Futhey left the four men that he had been walking with, at the inn down the street and came on ahead alone.

Jedaf instinctively knew this individual was the man that they had been expecting. Futhey stopped in mid stride for a moment and then re-crossed the street. Something had alerted him or he had changed his mind and decided to make contact at another time. He sorted threw the stack of capes and cloaks at the clothing stand directly across the street from where Jedaf stood.

The anxious teenager cautiously looked around. An off duty warrior from the royal household, walked up to the carpet stand. He idly pawed through the throw rugs and carpet runners. Turning his back quickly the commander of the royal guard let the boy wait on this customer. Halthus did not want to be recognized, and knew this guardsman, to be a loud-mouthed braggart.

Luckily he didn't stay very long and he moved off down the street. First Officer Futhey followed two women over to Jedaf's stand. He walked so close behind them, that one might have thought they were together.

Jedaf could see that he was not one of the average border guards. He was well groomed, clean shaven without sideburns and handsome despite the tattered and frayed clothing he wore. His apparel could not hide the fact that he was not a peasant. His stance and mannerisms reflected wealth and status. He sneered occasionally and showed little regard for people of the lower classes as he stood among them.

One of the customers bumped into him as she rummaged through a stack of door mats. He glared at her and bushed his elbow as if to remove dirt or lice. He examined blankets in one cart, speaking casually, asking the prices and where the goods were manufactured, before moving on to the next. He was a careful intelligent officer. Two words from Jedaf's experiences denoted an oxymoron and never seemed to fit well together, intelligence and officers.

Finally Futhey appeared to feel it was safe enough for him to make contact. Making up his mind he picked up a small floral throw rug, made in the region of Lestra, and carried it over to the sales stand. Before he had a chance to speak, an elderly balding man stepped between him and Jedaf. The old man set his carpet down. Then he started to argue and negotiate price, as was traditional.

Futhey stood behind fidgeting and waiting impatiently for about three zestas. Finally he had enough. He pushed the old man to the side and tossed Jedaf a small silver coin. "I want to buy this rug." He looked sternly at the old man; "If you're not going to buy that carpet go to another stand," he said forcefully making a mean grimacing face.

The wrinkles on the old man's cheeks smoothed, as his face tightened. His eyes betrayed him and he appeared about to do something stupid. His hand moved warily into the folds of his cloak.

Futhey was faster. He had drawn his dirk, pressing the sharp double edged short blade against the old mans neck, in the blink of an eye.

The man's wrinkled; weathered hand came slowly out from below his cloak. It did not have a weapon in it. It had three bronze coins. He leaned warily forward a little with the knife still pressed at his throat and dropped them in Jedaf's palm. Then backing away, he lifted the carpet to his shoulder and disappeared into the crowd.

"My father should hire you as a salesman," said Jedaf with a whimsical smile on his face. The officer glared back at teenager. He did not appear to be amused. "I'm interested in this rug. It's marked three bronzes two coppers. I will take it." The small rug was over priced. It had been marked that way for the sales argument.

Jedaf opened his purse and dropped in the small silver that Futhey had tossed him. Taking out one bronze, eight coppers he handed over the change. First Officer Futhey tucked the rug under his arm, and then dropped the coins in his purse.

"I have got a long ride out of the city and then I have to return later this month," he said. "I hope that I will be back by the fifth. It is the fifth day of Asursa that the celebration is to begin," he asked questioningly? Jedaf looked from side to side. The two women that Futhey had crossed the street with stood nearby sorting blankets. "That's not very good timing sir," replied Jedaf. "If you come back on the fifth, the fires will all be out by then."

The woman finished unfolding every blanket on the stand, shook their heads and moved off to disassemble some other shopkeeper's wares. Futhey stepped closer, bending low, placing his elbow on the counter. "Has Lord Tavay set up lodging for us," he whispered?

Jedaf took a hand towel and casually cleaned the road dust from the counter. "Yes. Follow my friend Dorat here." He will take you to a boarding house that has been rented.

Commander Halthus finished refolding and stacking the blankets at the other cart, and then stepped over to the sales counter. "Take First Officer Futhey and his men to see Lord Tavay," said Jedaf. "See to it they are fully briefed on our plans." Halthus did not say anything in response; he just nodded and pointed his index finger down the street. It was the same direction that the Worezian officer and his men had come from. As they walked off Futhey's men fell in behind following them. Jedaf remained at the carpet carts until they were out of his sight.

In the other direction he could see some dirty children which were dressed in tattered clothing. They were gathering together a pile of their parents' tunics and stockings that had been scattered about in the middle of the street. Walking over to the stand and clothing racks that had been knocked over and ruined in the brawl earlier, Jedaf could see the amount of lost goods would cost them dearly.

The woman was still shaken and crying while her father or a much older husband attempted to nail the legs back on their display table. The merchant were of the weaver's guild and too poor to have much of a selection.

The cotton tunic tops that they had come to sell were now soiled and dirty. They had been stepped on and kicked about in the gutter during the scuffle with the Worezian warriors. Some of the merchandise was blood splattered and the children were sorting the ones they thought could be washed out and still be sold. Jedaf taped the owner of the stand on the shoulder and waited for him to stand up before speaking.

"Good sir. This is indeed your lucky day!" The owner let go of the wobbly table he was attempting to fix, and it collapsed again. He stood up, brushed the dirt from his hands and looked at the customer as if he were crazy. Jedaf didn't give him a chance to speak, he just kept rambling on. "You see the men that wrecked your stand were wanted outlaws with a price on their heads. For your help in their capture, the commander of the guards has decided that you be allowed to take the carts and all of their wears as a reward."

Jedaf escorted him by the arm, leading the shopkeeper over to Lord Tavay's mercantile carts. "These are now all yours. Take them and move them over in front of the alley with your other goods." Jedaf gave him a hearty congratulating pat on the back. Picking up the purse with the days sales he walked off down the street. The shopkeeper was left standing in front of the stacks of carpets at the display table. His mouth was open and a he had a dumbfounded look on his face.

First Officer Futhey and his men followed Commander Halthus for about a quarter of a thasta beyond the market district. The further they walked the less suspicious they became. Halthus led them up an alley between the avenues of the travelers. Cathonian warriors were waiting in all the building's recesses. They struck when Futhey's party was half way up the street, closing off both exits.

Commander Halthus threw the officer roughly to the ground and stood on his sword arm. He along with three others of his taxt of nine warriors was captured during the engagement. All the others left the alley belly down stacked in carts. The bound prisoners were all assembled in one group and marched to the palace dungeons for interrogation. The ones that were willing to talk were to have their lives spared. They would be sent to the tin mines north of Lake Vella.

All the Worezian's decided that the mines were better than death. The exception was that of, First Officer Futhey. King Samalis questioned him personally. After trying to persuade this pompous officer to talk for over a zestar, the king lost his patience and finally gave up. He used his whip to nearly strangle the Worezian officer before tossing his limp body down into the dark recesses of the oubliette.

The king was quite pleased at the way everything had worked out, and he pledged his sword to Lord Jedaf for having saved his kingdom. Permission to hire two ships and three hundred and fifty men was given and paid for by Samalis. The king also ordered the Cathonian Second Army of the Blue to break camp on the southern woodland border. They were to march to the foothills of the western Lestran Mountains.

The Cathonian First Army of the Red, camped outside of the Adathe city gates would meet them there. The navy was also alerted by small pilot boats with dispatches to all ships in the fleet. They would stand at the ready to sail for the northwest coast. King Samalis had given his word, that on the day of his celebration he would declare war on the Kingdom of Worez and march his armies west.

His troops would be laying siege to Woreza, the enemy's capital city. While the main body of Worezian troops were away fighting on the central Zarhun plain, the Cathonian Navy would blockade the entire north coast, seizing any ship not willing to turn about, or head for other ports. Jedaf knew what King Samalis meant by other ports; they were to either to sail to Adathe or one of his kingdoms other seaports or they would be sunk.

    The king did not do all of this solely out of gratitude. In their private conversation and negotiations, Jedaf had promised King Samalis that at the end of the campaign, he would see to it all the land east of Port Giehan would be given to Samalis. This stretch of coastal land and its villages amounted to one forth of the present Worezian Kingdom's north coast.

Chapter # 32

The Eye of the Storm

Lord Jedaf awoke early. On the railing of his open air balcony, birds were perched and chirping. Their song brought a long absent natural smile to his face. He reached his arms as far apart as possible stretching once before rolling out of bed. It was one of the largest that he had ever seen or slept in. It was overstuffed with down, covered with silken sheets and tightly woven woolen blankets. At least four different kinds of scented animal furs were at the foot rail for colder nights, or if cuddling up in ermines were to your liking.

Jedaf had not slept this well this since leaving Traga's home in the City of Joroca. Washing and dressing at a leisurely pace, he watched the sky out of his window. The teen thought that this could easily become habit forming. It was a clear blue bright morning without a cloud in the sky. He also noticed that it must be very early. There were not even the beginning wisps of smoke from the ies cook fires. It was going to be a beautiful day; he could feel it in his bones.

Outside of his bedroom door he could hear the stamping around of clumsy feet. The sounds had to be coming from Ambassador Ajoris. From the looks of his physical condition and the way he came stumbling into their chamber suite the night before, it was a wonder he had woken this early. Jedaf opened his bedroom door quietly and stepped out into the adjoining combination dining-parlor room.

The teenaged lord was right. It was the ambassador, and the middle aged man looked like hell. Ajoris had large dark circles and bags under his blood shot eyes. Both of his hands were trembling as he tried to drink down a cup of hot tea, and look up at Jedaf at the same time. He still had the wrinkled lines of worry on his brow, and had slept in his clothing.

Later this morning Ajoris was scheduled to meet his future bride, Corissa for the first time. All he could think about was what his friend in the embassy had said to him when describing her. "She has a charm about her that makes it hard for any man to keep from starring at her."

Ajoris kept picturing a short, plump, ogre of a woman about four foot nine, dark brown knotted hair, large moles and blemishes on her face, and a two-ton granite ringed trinket chained about her neck. He closed his eyes tightly and shuttered trying to drive the images from his mind. He took a deep sip of his tea burning his tongue and the roof of his mouth. Coughing and chocking he held his throat and swallowed hard before speaking.

"Duke Dugartus's escort will be here soon Jedaf," he said in a raspy anxious voice. "What am I supposed to do?"

Jedaf laughed, and than thought better of it. "I am sorry Ajor. I really haven't got any suggestions."

The elder man began to pace about frantically while waiving his arms about as if he were clearing the air. He had made up his mind at that moment; he would get even with Vestrak despite the fact that he was his uncle and the King of Yoja. This royal plot and intrigue was all his doing, and the ambassador wanted no part of it.

Ajoris was interested in the daughter of one of his father's old friends that he had met at several social functions, but had not made his intentions formally known. The thought of her was one of the few things that had kept the diplomat going while he was a captive aboard the pirate ship Culba. Her name was aptly chosen by the gods. Aranan, meant beautiful daughter, and she certainly had the eyes and face of an angle. Ajor had vowed that he would speak with her father on the return trip. Now all his future hopes had been crushed.

King Vestrak had crushed his dreams and made it impossible for him to make this commitment. A formal proposal of marriage had been offered to the daughter of a stranger, and he knew the wedding contract would shortly be accepted. All Ajoris was supposed to do on this diplomatic mission was to carry dispatches to King Samalis, and a simple letter offering friendship to Duke Dugartus for his hospitality and assistance during the negotiations.

Ajoris was led to believe; his assignment was to seek permission for remodeling the Yojan embassy and gardens. The estate was currently unlivable and had been abandoned since his predecessor had died over five years ago. The other task that he was given was to look into the possibilities of enlarging the property and grounds by purchasing the adjacent property that was owned by the Dugartus family. That was all he was told, and he expected to be home by the end of Asursa.

It looked like Captain Sedran's pirate ship and King Vestrak's wedding proposal had changed his future overnight and Ajoris did not like the prospects. "If you can think of any way for me to get out of this fiasco, I would appreciate it. In the mean time, I guess I will wash and get dressed. I'm supposed to have ies with the duke and king."

Jedaf didn't know what else to say, and he did not want to make the older man feel more miserable than he was already. Giving advice to a man almost thrice his age made him feel uncomfortable. He just gave the diplomat a sympathetic look and shrugged his shoulders.

They had spoken briefly before last evening's kreb, and Ajoris knew that yesterday Jedaf had a long hard day rounding up and interrogating the Worezian spies. Today the young lord talked about doing very little and had said he needed the rest. Ajoris did not want to burden him further with his own dilemma. The ambassador seemed to read the young lord's mind and walked quietly back to his own bedroom.

Jedaf had planned to spend a quiet day just walking the cobblestone streets of Adathe. He thought of buying a few new set of clothes, or maybe he would just relax and do some window shopping. The Cathonian people normally wore a kilt that was two inch longer at the lower hem. Their stocking were a softer weave and above knee length. The leathers of their boots were higher, and the soles and heals were thicker than the other peoples of the Zarhun Continent.

Their tunic's woolen fabrics were of a heavier cloth, and some had thin leather strips woven into the fabric. Generally speaking the Cathonian's wardrobe consisted of more intricate checkered patterns and a majority of their clothing had a cabled look to them. All the materials seemed to have brighter and more vivid colors, than the dull oranges and brown earth tones of the Dolfinian Continent.

The other most notable change in apparel was the fact that a lot of the men and women wore hats. Most were pull-over caps made of cloth fabrics, but there were a few made of leather or sported an animal hide or fur trim. Most head covering looked like skull caps with a double or triple banding at the hair line. None of the hats had brims, ear protection or chin ties. He thought the change in style was probably due to the colder and crisper air that dropped from the shear spires of the southern Tabalis Mountains.

There were still quite a bit of cultural differences between each of the continents. What better way to learn them, than to just stroll the streets and listen to its inhabitants. He had already made arrangements to purchased two ships, and had hired crews to man them for the voyage to the Histajonies Continent. King Samalis said he would supply the warriors that would protect Lord Jedaf until he reached the Kingdom of Bintar.

The Cathonian king also provided a contingent of royal ships marines to fight any sea engagements. The vessels would not be ready until the end of the week at the earliest, and possibly another week for outfitting the men with gear and provisions for the voyage and expected overland trek.

A zestar after eating breakfast Jedaf was leisurely strolling about the boardwalks and through the avenues, streets and lanes when he heard the shouts and yells from an angry mob of shoppers. An unruly and noisy crowd was gathering at one of the street corners ahead of him.

Commander Halthus of the Cathonian Red Army Guard was standing on the steps of a haberdashery arguing with a group of pushing buyers and ordering them to disperse. At his side were three vourtre warriors dressed in battlefield attire and having their long knives drawn.

The olive green skinned humanoid warriors appeared to be from two different military contingents. The leader wore a dark green leather tunic with copper chain mail rings on his chest and sleeves, and a kilt of the same dyed green leathers.

Malleable iron banding strips had been sown into the pleats and folds of the leather. The other two warriors were dressed in similar fashion but their leathers were dyed a pale orange with alternating light brown colors. Neither of the vourtre warriors had chain mail or any visible iron protection. From what little Jedaf knew of the military dress codes, rough iron applets signified the status of a junior ranking officer, but he was not sure if vourtre warriors followed these human traditions.

One obnoxious loud mouthed rabblerousing bystander was kneeling on the steps and binding up a slashed and bleeding forearm wound. Another was backed up against the support post to the porch roof. He had dropped all his resent purchases. The packages had been scattered about and stepped on during the scuffle. A sharp edged curved knife blade was pressed to his jugular and he was pleading for his life in a whining high pitched voice.

The battle hardened vourtre warriors had enough of the shoving and racial insults. They had chosen the leaders of the trouble makers to demonstrate how quickly these flabby human villagers could be killed if they did not keep their comments to themselves and mind their own business. Jedaf elbowed his way through the tightly packed crowd to the forefront and stepped up onto the porch next to Halthus. Facing the mob he asked the royal guard commander, "Need any help?"

The Cathonian commander pushed a man backward that tried to follow after Jedaf, and kicked a second in the ribs that had the same thought. "Lord, you couldn't have come at a more opportune time. We have been searching for you since early this morning. Ambassador

Ajoris told us you were out shopping but he did not know which of the guild markets you were going."

Jedaf pulled his sword from his scabbard and leveled it at the group of angry faces. "Which one do you want me to cut in half first," he asked loudly? The men standing at the front of the throng thought he meant every word and decided to back up. Halthus yelled at them again. "The next one that is dumb enough to set foot on the steps, you can cut in half!" The threat worked; the mob started to thin and scatter.

The vourtre officer released the man that he held at knife point and threw him roughly to the ground. The townsman scrabbled to his feet and gathered his packages. He ran off and did not slow down until reaching the corner of the nearest alley. The wounded man on the steps looked around and saw there was no one left to back him up. Using his teeth, he hurriedly pulled the end of his bandage tight, grabbed the two cloaks he had purchased and ran off trying to catch up with his friend.

"Captain Ra Zonis of Am Hass, this is Lord Jedaf of Dolfi." The hardened middle aged surly vourtre officer looked skeptically at the thin, but muscular young human. He had expected to meet a much older man. This six foot tall, bare faced boy with jovial smile did not even look like a warrior.

If it had not been for the sword, the captain would have taken him for the son of a farmer. Jedaf sheathed his blade and extended his arm. The captain grasped the teen's wrist briefly, and bowed his head deftly. "This is Su Chadis the elder and At Wegus," Haltus said with a wave of his hand. "They're from the north-western Jeupan Mountains." The warriors nodded at the introductions, but still faced away protecting their backs, with their knives still drawn.

Captain Ra Zonis reached into his travel bag and pulled out a finely tooled leather dispatch pouch. Opening it he handed three letters to Jedaf. Each parchment was thrice folded, and one was sealed in red wax and having the impression of his dragon crest on it.

Jedaf knew he had given one of his pinkie rings to Princess Elona and had given the other one to her brother Prince Kytos. The large signet ring that had made these impressions did not come from either of them. The only normal sized ring he had given away was to Commander Traga of his Red Army.

Across the street, and down two shops from where they stood, was a small two story rooming house with a café storefront. The stucco was painted a bright canary yellow and having forest green trim, shutters, balcony balusters and roofing tiles. Jedaf pointed at the octenoma with the painted teacup marquee. "Let's get a cup of hot herbal tea; it is a bit early for ale."

They walked over to the tradesman's hostel and lingered for a moment in the entry hall as they chatted and looked about. The rooming house clerk looked up at them from behind the reception counter when they came through the front door. He was a brash muscular twenty year old that acted as a greeter most of the day and a bouncer if one was needed later in the evening. In a fit of anger he tossed his dust rag to the side of the counter in a disgusted manor and stepped out from behind it, yelling at them. "You can't bring those dirty animals in here!"

The vourtre warrior's did not have time to react to the insult. Commander Halthus did not hesitate, he immediately grabbed the man by the full of his face with one of his beefy hands, and the clerks waist belt with the other. Lifting the maitre d' easily overhead he tossed the receptionist over the counter against the rear wall, breaking two shelves of stemmed glassware. "Thanks we'll seat ourselves," said Halthus in a deep raspy tone.

It was still a little early for hora, the Palestusian first lunch period and only one other table was occupied. A middle-aged couple was seated infront of the bay window. Hearing the crash and seeing the vourtre, they decided not to stay. The gentleman tossed a few steel coins on the table before leaving the room. An older woman dressed in a single piece blue dress and tied back graying hair, ran out of the kitchen. She heard the glassware breaking, and stood nervously near the doorway with her mouth open. "We will have a large crock of tea and a platter of honeyed raisin cakes," the commander said to her as they walked by.

Entering the dining area the five men took one of the round tables for six, that was located off to the side of the louvered swinging doors to the kitchen. It had a cream and light brown checkered tablecloth with ocher colored linen napkins and flatware laid out. The owner did not reply to them, but ran immediately back into the food preparation area yelling for the waitress.

A young, brunette with braided hair and intertwined pink ribbons came out of the kitchen. The frazzled bond servant was wearing a bright yellow apron over her full length pink dress. She was carrying a heavy tray of dishes. One side of the tray held a wide double stacked cobalt blue katmet teapot with oil lamp warming base. Stacked in the center were six tea cups, saucers, and plates having a light blue and lavender flower patterns on the rim. On the opposite side of the tray was a matching patterned charger with ten to twelve steaming hot buns covered in honey, brown crusted sugar, and toped with crumbled adotaks, a sweet almond shaped nut.

Setting the tray on the table near them she timidly poured out a cup of tea and placed a honey bun on a small plate for each of them. She kept her lips pursed tightly and did not say a word to anyone while serving. Then she nervously hurried back to the safety of the kitchen. It was obvious the matron or owner had warned her not to make any snide comments or remarks. The captain and the three vourtre warriors ate and drank quietly while cordially speaking to each other. Lord Jedaf broke the seal on the one letter and began to read the correspondence.

The sealed letter was not from Commander Traga as expected. It was from Eneas, the newly crowned king of the Zarhun vourtres. Where he received a dragon headed signet ring, Jedaf could only guess. It had to have been a gift from one of his predecessors. The letter briefly described what was happening in eastern and southern Kingdom of Envar and why the vourtre had historically been allied with the Lords of the Red Dragon. In the letter the king pledged his and his people unending loyalty and support.

The message went on relating King Eneas's intension of declaring war on King Magarus. The vourtre warriors would not be fighting on the battlefield, but would remain at the edge of the eastern mountains, southern woodlands and forests along the Zarhun Plain. This is where his people could be the most effective. The vourtre would prevent Worezian Army units from encircling the Envarian refugee's or making any flanking attacks against the Jeupan Kingdom's defenses.

The king of the vourtre had received dispatches informing him, that the Worezian Army of Violet had recently crossed the northern border of Envar. They were making revetments and a fortified encampment before merging with the Sylakian invasion force that had just landed at the City of Trespaden. It was the king's opinion that because of the resent engagements the Worezians had with the Royal Red Army of Envar and the battle the Red Dragon Army had with the Onandonians, the Violet Army was planning on staying at this location for an extended period of time.

The months of first summer were coming to an end and Vergus; the month of drought would soon be upon them. Invading the great grassland Zarhun Plain at that time of year would be foolhardy and difficult. High winds and dust storms were frequent. Most if not all of the smaller wadies and rivulets would be bone dry. King Eneas expected the enemy armies to act prudently and would not advance until the first week of second summer.

The second and third unsealed letters had been forwarded from Marshal Traga and Princess Elona. Traga's letter described the engagements in the north against the Onandonian and Otaskan warriors. It noted and informed him that Princess Elona and Diara had been rescued by Captain Odelac and Ciramtis, the sorceress of Iblac.

At this time, Jedaf's small Red Army of the Dragon was on the march south pursuant to his orders. They would meet with the Jeupan border guards to formulate plans for both strategic defenses as well as any offensive tactics. It was unlikely that they would march out onto the Zarhun plains; because their combined meager forces were still out numbered three to one.

The letter further related what Traga had learned about the Envarian Red Army's incursion and defeat against the Worezian Tan Army. King Helidon and his son had been killed and Prince Sesmak had been crowned the new King of Envar. The capital City of Renvas was being fortified but would not be able to withstand a long siege.

King Sesmak with the remnants of his army, planned on making a stand east of the city. They would fight a holding action until all the citizens that wanted to leave could do so. After the evacuation the rear guard units of the Envarian Army would retreat to the southeast toward Jeupa unless honorable surrender terms could be negotiated.

The last letter was from Princess Elona. It was brief and written with a delicate hand in a flowery style script, but in a formal almost impersonal manner. She thanked him for saving her brother Kytos, and for sending his friends to rescue her and Princess Diara. Then she chastised him for not informing her that he was not a servant or bond slave as she had been led to believe during their entire voyage to the City of Woreza.

The Oppowian princess informed Jedaf that she would not be traveling south with Captain Odelac's crew and the Dragon Army. Princess Diara was too afraid to board another ship, and would remain with them and assist Prince Kytos. Instead of going along with them, Elona planned on immediately sailing for the Kingdom of Saratam.

It was her intension to personally inform them of her brother Pinthos and the Sylakian's plan to pillage their homelands. She would warn the kingdoms of the southern Kelleskarian Continent that they should prepare for an invasion

The way she signed her letter did not fail to bring a joyful smile to his face. At the bottom was written, "Caskan Cokul Ire, Elona," except it had a line through it, crossing it out. It was the same way he had ended the letter he had written to her when she was a captive in the palace of King Magarus in the City of Woreza.

At the time he had thought, "Your eternal slave," was a more appropriate ending than "Ibun Jedaf." The word love was only used between spouses, their children or other close immediate relatives. Her letter was signed; "Ibun Elona, Jedaf ja velgor iejras arast," Love Elona, wife of Jedaf the Lord of the Red Dragon.

Jedaf refolded the letters and tucked them into his tunic. It seemed Ambassador Ajoris was not the only one that was engaged to be married. Unfortunately his first duty was to make the pilgrimage to the City of Tabalis as the Council of Elders had directed. He was sure that his teachers had not anticipated the quandaries and difficulties the gods were going to put him through. Six other Lords of the Dragon had made this religious sojourn and had lived long productive lives serving the peoples of Palestus.

After the audience with Cathonian King Samalis, Ambassador Ajoris was supposed to buy provisions and make arrangements for them to journey to "The City of the Dead." If the Dragon Lord was able to survive the ordeal and tests of the gods, Jedaf planned on sailing within the next two weeks to the Archipelago Continent of the Histajonies and would be disembarking in Port Multarus, the Bintarian Kingdom's capital city.

Jedaf thanked Captain Ra Zonis and asked him and his warriors to stay and have lunch with him before returning to the vourtre City of Am Hass with a reply. Jedaf needed some time to think. He yelled out for the waitress, stood up and moved over to the empty table next to the warriors. The young woman returned from the kitchen, but stayed by the doorway and away from their tables. "We will be staying for lunch," said Jedaf. "Clear the table and get these men anything that they want to eat or drink."

The waitress did not move right away and had a worried look about her. "Is there a problem," he asked? The brunette timidly walked over to the young lord and whispered quietly in his ear. "My mistress has told me to get rid of these creatures before they stink up the place." He reached into his travel pack and took out a folded stack of parchment, an ink bottle and an eco quill pen. Then Jedaf handed her his empty tea cup and whispered back to her, "Go tell your mistress that if we are not served quickly, I plan on burning this building to the ground with her in it."

The bond servant ran back to the kitchen as fast as she could and returned with two trays of freshly baked bread loaves, crocks of soft yellow sharp skukat cheese, and an assortment of sliced fruit. A male waiter came out of the kitchen a zesta later, carrying a tray of bowls with hot celba and white rena soup, along with a mug of ale for everyone.

Jedaf knew it was to their liking; most of the vourtre were vegetarians. They ate the bread and thick white pea-bean and green tomato soup quicker than he was able to finish writing his letter. The waiter came back to their table and dropped off another tray of krastan bread loaves and another round of ale, while the young lord re-read what he had written.

In his correspondence he thanked King Eneas for delivering Traga's and Elona's letters. He also thanked Eneas for his kingdom's support in this war. Jedaf noted that he was going to be leaving for the City of Tabalis in two to three days, and if his expectations were met, he would be back to the City of Adathe in eight to ten days.

The young lord told Eneas that King Samalis and the Cathonian people were now their allies. They would also be declaring war on the Kingdom of Worez and blockading the ports of all of their cities. If he was not able to return from Tabalis, he asked Eneas to continue supporting the Jeupans and the Envarians in their battle to regain their freedom.

Then he wrote, making a final and solemn request of the king. Jedaf wanted Eneas to send a messenger to Marshal Traga of the Red Dragon Army at the Jeupan frontier passes informing him that Jedaf had received the letters from his friend and that he sends his prayers. If no further contact could be made before the war began, Traga was to use his discretion whether or not to endanger the lives of his men, and continue fighting on the side of the Envarians.

Folding up the parchment he thought of Elona and wished there was some way to communicate with her. If she were not so far away, he could have sent her an enchanted paper airplane letter like he had done once before. At least she was safe, and that made him feel better than he had in a long time. He sealed the letter in red wax and pressed his ring into it. "Captain, when you are finished eating, you can deliver this back to your king." Jedaf handed the letter to Ra Zonis who slipped it into his dispatch pouch.

"Commander Halthus, after escorting our friends and allies to the city gates, I would appreciate your help in buying some supplies. The Ambassador and I will be leaving the city, the day after tomorrow and I don't think Ambassador Ajoris has had time to make any of the purchases necessary for our trip."

Halthus gave him a quick salute. "It will be a pleasure lord. I will be glad to help anyway that I can. Do you need a contingent of men to escort you south?" Jedaf had thought about this possibility when he and Ajor had discussed their travel plans, but he did not want to put anyone else's life in jeopardy. He felt bad enough just taking the ambassador along, but he knew it was going to be next to impossible to be able to talk the older man out of it.

Not coming along, would have prevented the diplomat from having an excuse not to get married. "No Commander, that will not be necessary, I am sure we will be able to find our way. I'm going to sit here for awhile and then pick up a few items that I know we will need. I will meet you after mya in the street of shops at the farmers produce market." The three vourtre warriors gave the young lord a salute. Commander Halthus stood with the others finishing their ales and leaving the dining area.

Lord Jedaf finished his soup that was now pasty and almost cold. He sipped remorsefully at his ale while gazing out the front window in an absentminded fashion. Devastation was coming to this land and there was nothing he could do to prevent it. Two armies had already clashed in a minor skirmish and a prelude to this conflict. A thousand men had died already.

How many more would have to die to satisfy the gods in their warped quest for converts and devotees. He was beginning to think, these meaningless deaths might not be his fault after all. Then again he pondered his reasoning. Maybe the Council of Elders was right after all and he had been the catalos that had caused these events.

It seemed that it was just as easy for him to use this as an excuse and blame all the ills of this world on them as it would have been be to honor or pray to them. There had been too many unnatural and unexplained events since he had been brought through the void to this world.

These global conflicts seemed to be part of a preordained fate of the Palestusians. This war was not about human glory or the conquests of new lands. It was about good verses evil and the continued existence of the old gods. If they could not be placated and revered, they would not be remembered and would perish to the oblivion of time.

The Zarhunian Conflict
Glossary

Word: Definition
- Acotaxarus: An award given to warriors for courage and valor. Made of a five pointed gold star and trimmed with orange ribbons.
- Actiland: A small city of the Kingdom of Envar. It is located of the Continent of Zarhun at the far southern end of the "Great Zarhun Plain."
- Adarf: A hard granite like stone; black with red speckles. It is a very expensive building material.
- Adathe: The capital city of the Kingdom of Cathon, located on the Continent of Zarhun.
- Adotak: A sweet almond shaped nut.
- Adufa Tar: A weight scale.
- Agortha: A kingdom on the Continent of Agortha.
- Alia Stambur: The cloth used to wrap bodies for burial.
- Am Haas: The capital city of the vourtres of Zarhun. It is located near the east-central border area of the Kingdom of Envar, west of the eastern Semedian capital City of Tabalis.
- Amrig: A kingdom on the southern Continent of Zarhun. The capital City is Amaric.

- Arisdi: A thin wild vine with small bright yellow buttercup like flowers.
- Aruntis: A small farming village of the Kingdom of Envar. It is located on the northwest Zarhun Plain.
- Askalus, the Sea: The sea north of the Continent of Zarhun, between the Continents of Kelleskar and the Histajonies Archipelago. It was named after Askalus a flag ship commander of the ancient Kingdom of Cathon in 0295 KC.
- Asursa: The fifth month of the Palestus Calendar. The 2nd month of 1st Summer. It was named after Asursa the Goddess of Flowers.
- Athamus: The God of Water. One of the eight Major Gods.
- Athca: A large brown and black vulture like carrion bird with curved bill and sharp talons. An egg tooth.
- Atrusa: The Goddess of the Wind. One of the eight Major Gods.
- Ayesa: A kingdom on the Continent of Kelleskar.
- Azzon: An east-central kingdom on the Continent of Dolfinia. The capital City is Tansac.

- Banta: A very large, short faced, carnivorous cave bear. They are dark brown or black in color; having tough skin and thick fur.
- Bintar: A kingdom on the west-central Continent of the Histajonies Archipelago.
- Blineva: A village of the Kingdom of Envar known for their saw mills and Uberan hardwoods of the woodlands of Gothom.
- Blyga: A vegetable pepper that is shaped long and thin like that of a feather. They are green, yellow, red, or purple in color.
- Bolusa: The soul or the liver.
- Burkat: A hardwood tree with smooth thin bark growing to a height of approximately thirty feet, and having a girth of about thirty inches. Its branches are in the upper most part of the tree leaving its base bare. The limbs extend outward, shading an area of about forty feet in diameter. The leaves are soft, light green color in the shape of a webbed hand twelve inches

across. Its bark sheds annually and is used for weaving baskets, and mats.

- Cama: An offering.
- Caskan Cokul Ire, Elona: Your eternal slave, Elona.
- Caspasi: A major city of the ancient Semedian Empire. It is located on the Continent of Dolfinia, east of the Great Desert.
- Cathon: A kingdom on the north central Continent of Zarhun. The capital City is Adathe.
- Celba: A green smooth skinned tomato like fruit, which has a round shape. It has many small seeds that run down your face when you bit into it.
- Celban: The plant of the celba fruit. They have dark green stems and light green leaves. The plant grows to a height of two feet. These fields are where Ceratus are known to hide.
- Ceratus: A large greenish brown puma like cat of the forested areas. They are found all over the Planet of Palestus.
- Chavna: A leathery pancake with chopped dried fruit inside (usually avna apricots). The food is used mainly by merchants and travelers.
- Claura: A priest or religious cleric.
- Clotis: A very tall straight hardwood tree growing to forty feet and having a girth of two feet. Used mainly in the timber and shipping industry. It is also used for firewood.
- Culba: A forth class merchantman and passenger ship with two masts, 80 ft long and having a 30 foot beam. It is currently sailing under the Onandonian flag. This is Captain Sedran's privateer. The name means - Fast sailing.
- Cul Derus Mountains: A mountain range (It means an alter cloth covering a mountain. They are sacred vourtre lands). They are located on the south western Continent of Zarhun in the Kingdom of Envar.

- Dakalug: A six segmented loaf of round bread.
- Darius: The God of the Trees. One of the sixteen Lesser Gods. Pertaining to the seven first trees of Palestus.
- Dastus: The God of Fate. One of the eight Major Gods. To be fair or impartial.
- Dedeok: A kingdom on the Continent of Kelleskar. One of the entrances to hell is thought to be located here. This is where many demons, creatures of the night, and spirits congregate.
- Delclot: A wooden platform.
- Delmet: A dais or stone platform (Stand-Stone)
- Diezra: The Goddess of Water Plants. One of the sixteen Lesser Gods.
- Diezra: The third month of the Palestus Calendar. The 3rd month of Spring. It is named after Diezra the Goddess of Water Plants.
- Dolfi: The capital city of the ancient Kingdom of Dolfius on the Continent of Semedia.
- Dolfinia: The third largest continent of the Planet of Palestus. The continent was renamed from Semedia in the year 0170 K.C.
- Dorretta: A small city on the southern border of the Yojan Kingdom.
- Dujiak: A small, short legged, scavenger pack dog, having razor sharp teeth, and a curly tail. The animal is dull yellow in color and is similar to that of a hyena.
- Duera: A small southern village of the Kingdom of Yoja, on the Continent of Dolfinia.

- Eco: A pen. A quill pen made from a picrican feather.
- Emen: Cooking salt.
- Envar: A kingdom on the western most Continent of Zarhun. The capital City is Renvas.
- Envarac Forests: A dense forest and game preserve located in north-east Kingdom of Envar on the Continent of Zarhun.
- Esella: The Goddess of Plants. One of the fourteen Minor Gods.

- Eston: A large black whale like fish with silver underside, inhabiting all of the seas of the Planet Palestus.
- Eurkus: A kingdom in the east central Continent of Kelleskar. The capital City is Lysesam.
- Everro: The Goddess of Rain. One of the fourteen Minor Gods.
- Everro: The second month of the Palestus Calendar. The 2nd month of Spring. It was named after Everro the Goddess of the Rain.

- Featga: A large wolf of the woodlands.
- Femelis: A three inch diameter onion like vegetable plant. They are red or white in color.

- Gass: A rodent. This animal is a river rat.
- Giehan: A small fishing village of the Kingdom of Envar located on the north coast of Zarhun between the capital City of Woreza and the Lestran Mountains.
- Gleggas: A forth class merchantman having two masts, 80 feet long and a 25 foot wide beam.
- Gothor: A kingdom on the southwest central Continent of the Histajonies.
- Gothom: A village and uberan woodland hills of northwest Kingdom of Envar.

- Hampt: A kingdom on the southern Continent of the Histajonies.
- Hesboth: A second class man-of-war, 200 feet long and having a 50 foot wide beam. This vessel has three masts, and is sailing under the Yojan flag.
- Hespa: A fresh water spring with healing waters located in the Kingdom of Bintar on the Continent of the Histajonies. To be made welcome.
- Histajonies: The sixth largest continent on the Planet of Palestus. A large archipelago shaped continent that was re-named in the year 0275 K.C. It was originally named after Gorthorius, the God of Animals.

- Hodek:A kingdom on the Continent of Kelleskar.
- Hora:First lunch period of the Palestus workday. It is usually served at the 12th zestar. It is named after horastus the larger of the two suns. It is more than a lunch but less than a full course meal.
- Horamya:The Palestus day, is made up of 28 zestars. 16 horomya make up a palestus month or Mursas. 240 horamya make up the Palestus year or palests.
- Horastus:The larger of the two suns in the Odea Solar System. Created by Virros the God of Fire.\
- Hydos rayos exparos eastra:A spell which controls a persons mind. Do not touch! Take your hand away!
- Hyleren:A pigeon like meadow bird, dark brown body and head, white breast with brown speckles, yellow and white wing and tail feathers. The bird is an insect eater.
- Hyupeious:The capital City of Jeupa on the Continent of Zarhun.

- Iblac:A kingdom on the west-central Continent of Kelleskar. The capital City is Arunca.
- Ibun Elona, Jedaf ja velgor iejras arast: Love Elona, wife of Jedaf the Lord of the Red Dragon.
- Idecka:A kingdom on the south-central Continent of Kelleskar. (Looks like the shape of an-ink bottle) The capital City is Antika.
- Iles:The first meal of the day usually served from about the 6th, to 7th zestar. It is named after lesta Goddess of life.
- Iesta:The Goddess of life. One of the eight Major Gods.

- Jakib caska fa ata eiantan mu azzatus xin caskan gos: Thank you for picking out the best horses and keep the wind in your face.
- Jes:Rice.
- Jesilla:The capital city of the Kingdom of Oppow, on the Continent of Kelleskar.

- Jeupa: A kingdom on the southeast coast of the Continent Zarhun. The capital City is Hyupeious.
- Jolac: A kingdom on the Continent of the Histajonies.
- Joroca: The capital city of the Kingdom of Yoja, on the Continent of Dolfinia.

- Kartbaco: A ship's log book.
- Katmet: Ceramic.
- Kaybeck: The written language of Palestus, having three rows of ten pictogram character runes, or 30 letters.
- K.C. The time after "Kaybeck's Arival." The Year Zero.
- Kebran: The God of War. One of the fourteen Minor Gods.
- Kelleskar: The largest continent on the Planet of Palestus. It was re-named in the year 0310 K.C. It was originally named Iesta.
- Krasta en: A strong whiskey made from white krastant wheat grain.
- Krastan: A coarse, yellow bread made from krastant wheat.
- Kreb: The evening meal of the Palestus day. It is named after Krebolus, the God of Death and Darkness.
- Krebolus: The God of Death and Darkness. One of the eight Major Gods.
- Krebolus: The fifteenth month of the Palestus Calendar. The 4th and last Month of Winter, It is named after Krebolus the God of Death and Darkness.
- Krem Rocala: A funeral pyre.

- Lestran Mountains: The north central mountain range on the Continent of Zarhun.
- Locern Plain: A large plain of the east central Kingdom of Worez. It is located on the Continent of Zarhun.
- Locises: The Goddess of Peace. One of the eight Major Gods.
- Locisies: The eleventh month of the Palestus Calendar. The 3rd month of Fall. It is named after Locisis the Goddess of Peace.
- Lukana: An oil lamp.

- Lusarus:A bright, yellow, sweet grape, which makes a golden, colored light wine.
- Lusemtus:A blue-green grape of western Kelleskar and Agortha.
- Lusumak:A deep purple grape of Zarhun and Zureathon, which makes a strong, dark purple wine.
- Lusverus:A blood red grape of the Continent of Agotha and the Histajonies.
- Ly:A cooked fruit that is spread on breads, hardtack and preserved meats.

- Measa:A cow or the meat of a cow.
- Measan:A bull or a steer. The meat of a bull or steer.
- Medorus:An island off the southeast coast of the Continent of Kelleskar. Part of the Kingdom of Saratam. The island is located at the southern part of the Straits of Aturius.
- Megath:The fourth largest continent on the Planet of Palestus, it was re-named Zarhun in the year 0301 K.C.
- Merimec:An amulet or blessed medallion.
- Merimon:A forth class merchantman and passenger ship with two masts, 80 ft long and having a 20 foot wide beam.
- Mokan:A kingdom on the Continent of Zureathion. The people practice ritual sacrifice and are rumored cannibals.
- Moland:A village of the north central Envarian Kingdom. It is located south of the Moland Forests along the north western Zarhun Plain.
- Multarus:The capital city of Bintar on the Continent of the Histajonies Archipelago. The name means, the odor of a heavy perfume.
- Mursa:The Palestus month, made up of sixteen horamya. 15 mursas make up one Palestus year, or a "palest".
- Mursas:The largest moon of the Planet of Palestus. The fourth planet in the solar system of Odea.

- Mya: The second lunch period of the Palestus day. It is usually served at the 16th zestar. Named after Myastus the smaller sun. Mya is a very light snack opposed to a meal.
- Myastus: The smaller of the two suns in the Odea Solar System. It was created by the Virros the God of Fire.

- Naros: A kingdom on the west-central coast of the Continent of Kelleskar. The capital City is Jakibeg.
- Nedaka: A blue, leather medical bag of the healing guild.
- Nefren: A waist high bush with yellow variegated green leaves. Used medicinally as a sleeping potion.
- Nestagin: A brown, long furred, and eared kangaroo like rabbit.
- Norga Pass: A pass between the southern Zotanic Mountain foothills and the northern Verengal Mountains. The pass is the major route from the southern Zarhun Plain of the Kingdom of Envar and the eastern lowlands of the Kingdom of Jeupa. The pass is located on the western Continent of Zarhun.

- Ocrotiej: A prayer
- Octenoma: A café (Eating-House-Small).
- Odea: The solar system and galaxy in which the Planet of Palestus is located. The Home of the Gods. Odea, the Book: The "Holy Book" of the Gods, relating the creation.
- Onando: A kingdom on the Continent of Kelleskar. The capital City is Adros.
- Oolet: A fat tuberous white potato like vegetable with reddish skin. They can grow as large as a grapefruit.
- Oppow: A kingdom on the central Continent of Kelleskar. It is located on Lake Iesta. The capital City is Jesilla.
- Otaska: A kingdom on the Continent of Kelleskar.
- Oyaltan: One of the nine races on the Planet of Palestus. They only inhabit the south-eastern and central plains of Iesta, now the Continent of "Kelleskar." A yellowish brown skinned people, with wide strong backs. They grow to a height of 5'-0" to 5'-6." Their straight dark brown hair and sparse beards

hide the weathered faces of these nomadic people. They have wide faces and wide spread apart dark brown eyes. Their facial features are gentile and they speak with softness in their voice. They are known for their animal breading and herding abilities. These people are the greatest horsemen of Palestus.

- Palea:The smallest moon of the Planet Palestus, the fourth planet in the solar system of Odea.
- Palensa:A southern Envarian coastal city on the Continent of Zarhun.
- Palestus:The fourth planet in the solar system of Odea. It has two moons, Mursa the larger and Palea the smaller. The yearly rotation is 240 days.
- Pharlon Isles:A group of six islands off of the coast of the Continent of the Histajonies Archipelago. These islands are part of the Kingdom of Bintar.
- Picrican:A small pheasant like game bird with brown, green, and yellow feathers.
- Pligma:A stone high in lye content. Used for making concrete and soap.
- Pligolg:Lye soap.

- Quayga ja:A large red hawk.

- Rampour:A kingdom on the Continent of Zarhun. The capital city is Ramusa.
- Rearus:A small (arus) gold coin shaped like a diamond, ½" wide and 1" long. Its value is equivalent to sixteen rebest (large silvers). Sixty four (64) reest (small silvers). Two hundred fifty six (256) splig (bronzes) and five hundred twelve (512) garja (coppers). Two thousand and forty eight (2048) garja (coppers), or eight thousand one hundred and ninety two (8192) galt (steels).
- Rebarus:A large (Reb) gold coin shaped like a diamond, ½" wide and 2" long. Its value is equivalent to four (4) rearuses

(small golds). Sixty four (64) rebest (large silvers). Two hundred fifty six (256) reest (small silvers). One thousand twenty four (1024) splig (bronzes) and two thousand forty eight (2048) garja (coppers). Eighty one thousand and ninety two (8092) garja (coppers), or thirty two thousand seven hundred and sixty eight (32,768) galt (steels).

- Rebest: A large (est) silver coin shaped like a diamond, ½" wide and 2" long. Its value is equivalent to four (4) reest (small silvers). Sixteen (16) splig (bronzes) and thirty-two (32) garja (coppers). One hundred and twenty eight (32) garja (coppers), or five hundred and twelve (512) galt (steels).
- Redolga: A thin-legged wild pig like animal with four front tusks weighing as much as 100 pounds. Its meat is sweet and lean, not fatty. The animal has coarse bumps on its back. Its dull yellow skin has brown spots on the sides. There are three varieties.
- Rena: A vegetable bean that is round on the top, like a half pea, and flat on the bottom. The bean is brown, red, or white in color.
- Renvas: The capital city of the Kingdom of Envar on the Continent of Zarhun.
- Roomaris: A village of the Kingdom of Envar on the Continent of Zarhun. It is located on the north western coast of the Sea of Tenolfo, west of the Roomaris Hills.
- Rotanis: A village of the Kingdom of Envar on the Continent of Zarhun. It is located southeast of Zarhun City on the northern Great Zarhunian Plain.
- Rut Ana: Incense oil.

- Santax: An army group of approximately 175 warriors.
- Saratam: A kingdom at the southeast most end of the Continent of Kelleskar. (A study-Industry). A college. The capital City is Kartaras.

- Sebus: A light green leafy cabbage like vegetable with reddish highlights. It's used mostly for stews or soups and sometimes is chopped into salads.
- Semedia: The ancient name for the Continent of Dolfinia. It was re-named from Semedia in the Year 0170 K.C.
- Semedia: The light green pear like fruit with large yellow pomegranate seeds and a thick scale like skin from the Semedian tree.
- Sestra: The Goddess of the Sky and Heavens. (Sky-The space between the planets).
- Sku: Cheese.
- Spli: The color brown. Tree brown.
- Splindia Valley: An east-west valley of the north central Worezian Kingdom on the Continent of Zarhun. It was named after the many varieties of splindia flowers. The valley is known for its pligma mining.
- Strata: A group of approximately 35 warriors.
- Stramus: A venomous snake similar to a horned viper.
- Subarit River: A small river south of the capital City of Renvas in the Kingdom of Envar on the Continent of Zarhun.
- Sulaga: A fifth class merchant ship.
- Sydolla: A small passenger ship. Owned by Captain Zabus Tay of Worez.
- Sylak: A kingdom on the northwest coast of the Continent of Kelleskar.

- Tabalis: The capital city of ancient eastern Semedia on the Continent of Zarhun. Abandoned for thousands of years, it is now known as the "City of the Dead."
- Tadleta: An army unit of approximately 910 heavy infantry warriors.
- Tansac: The capital city of the Kingdom of Azzon on the Continent of Dolfinia.
- Tantax: An army group of approximately 10,100 warriors.

- Tark: A kingdom island off of the north-central Continent of Zureathion.
- The capital City is Yalmoth.
- Tarmeg: A measure of weight equal to 100 tarmets or approximately 600 pounds.
- Tarmet: A counter balance stone weighing approximately six pounds.
- Tarot: A kingdom on the Continent of Zarhun. The capital City is Zharot.
- Tarpenya: A fourth class merchant ship. Captain Odelac's vessel.
- Tatla: A shrub with bright red bitter berries. Growing to a height of six feet, it is the common home of many small birds. The roots can be used for a hallucinating drug that is addicting and eventually causes madness.
- Taxt: A group of approximately 10 warriors, and a leader.
- Taxzy: A sailor.
- Tenolfo, the Sea: The sea between the Continents of Dolfinia and Zarhun. It is named after Tenolfo, an ancient King of Yoja.
- Tenolfis: A small fishing village on the north point of the Kingdom of Envar, on the Continent of Zarhun. It is named after the Yoyan King Tenolfo.
- Tessa: A large, fat, slow, brown and yellow honey bee.
- Thaon: A coastal city of the Kingdom of Cathon. The home of Duke Dugartus.
- Thasta: A land measurement equal to 2500 paces. It is approximately one mile or 5,208 feet.
- Theodian Steel: Hardest a best steel with the most tensile strength. Made in the forges of the island Continent of Theod.
- Therda: A kingdom on the western shores of the Bay of Jo Horac, on the Continent of Kelleskar. The capital city is Metatga.
- Tia: Berries.
- Tollenum Mountains: Mountains of the south western Continent of Zarhun. They are located on the western side of the "Great Divide" in the Kingdom of Envar.

- Treskul: The five evil creatures created by the God Kebran to teach man the need to honor and praise the gods.
    - 1st — Thagmar Demon of Death.
    - 2nd — Indwok Demon of War.
    - 3rd — Motaluk Demon of Pestilence and Disease.
    - 4th — Raslikon Demon of Famine and Starvation.
    - 5th — Lufarus Demon of Hate and Envy.
- Treskuls curti yie enom fasic: Dry up and go to live in the deep recesses of the treskul's home.
- Trespaden: A small city on the north coast of the Envarian Kingdom. It is located on the Continent of Zarhun.
- Tyjor: A kingdom on the Continent of the Histajonies Archipelago.

- Uberan: The most common tree on the Planet of Palestus. It is a hard wood tree that grows to a height of about twenty feet. It appears to be almost flat on top with wide thick limbs that are widely spaced. Its leaves are large spade shaped, providing a lot of shade. The wood is used for almost everything. It is strong, light colored and easily workable.
- Umsath Ra: Ancient kingdom of the vourtre on the continent of Zarhun. King Dracar.
- Uthamus: The God of Sea Serpents. One of the sixteen Lesser Gods.

- Veajak, nosta ieja Esella: The Goddess Esella's blessings and serenity.
- Vellastran Mountains: The mountain range separating the Kingdoms Worez and Cathon on the Continent of Zarhun.
- Vellastran Passes: The large passes separating the mountain chain at two locations. The northern most pass leads from the Great Zarhunian Plain to the Vellastran Plain of Cathon. The southern pass leads to the ancient City of Tabalis before heading north to the Kingdom of Cathon.

- Vellestran Plain: The large fertile delta plains of the Cathonian Kingdom on the north coast of the Zarhunian Continent.
- Venditch Pass: The mountainous pass leading east from the central Zarhun Plains of Envar through the northern Zotac Mountains to the ancient Kingdom of Zo Tan.
- Verengal Mountains: The Mountain of the south western Zarhun Continent separating the Kingdoms of Envar and Jeupa.
- Vergus: The sixth month of the Palestus Calendar. The month of drought. It is named after Vergus the God of Reptiles.
- Vlatok Mountain: A small mountain of the north central Kingdom of Envar or the Continent of Zarhun.
- Volendale: A valley and a village in the northwest kingdom of Envar, between the Gothom and Roomaris woodland hills on the Continent of Zarhun.
- Vourtre: An emerald green bird of central Continent of Zarhun. It has long, wings and tail feathers of red and yellow. The vourtre race was named after these birds, because of the color of their green eyes.
- Vourtre: One of the nine races on the Planet of Palestus, mostly inhabiting the south-eastern and central Continent of Megath, now the Continent of Zarhun & the eastern and central Continent of Arvaya, now the Continent of Agortha. A light brown skinned people with straight black shinny hair, growing to a height of about 5'-0." Their eyes are a sharp piercing emerald green and there is a distinctively pointed-ness to their ears. Their physical frames are slight but they are stronger then most of the other Palestus races. Their faces are generally thin with high cheekbones, and thin eyebrows. Vourtres live longer than all the other races except for the elgos. Some live as long as 160 years. They are known for their agricultural and forest management abilities. (They are named after the forest green vourtre birds).

- Warkmeg: An iron cleat or fastener.
- Watull: Cornmeal.

- Werna: A stocky reddish or brown antelope with straight horns.
- Worez: A kingdom on the north central coast of the Continent of Zarhun. The capital City is Woreza.
- Woreza: The capital city of the kingdom of Worez on the Continent of Zarhun.
- Wurda: A kingdom on the southern Continent of Zarhun. The capital City is Enembus.

- Xinu Stramus: The intestines.

- Yara Zo: A ritual death.
- Yoathon: Southern regional capital of the Envarian Kingdom on the Continent of Zarhun.
- Yoja: A kingdom of the north-eastern Continent of Dolfinia. The capital City is Joroca.

- Zarhun: The fourth largest continent on the Planet of Palestus. It was re-named Megath in the year 0301 K.C.
- Zarhun City: A city state on the northeast Zarhun Plain in the Kingdom of Envar, on the Continent of Zarhun.
- Zarhunian Plain: The largest plain on the Zarhun Continent. Located in the central and western Kingdom of Envar. It was named after King Zarhun in the year 0300 K.C. by his son.
- Zesta: 1/28 of a zestar. It takes 28 zestas to make a zestar; this is the Palestus equivalent to a minute. They are approximately equal to two earth minutes.
- Zestar: 1/28 of a Palestus day. It takes 28 zestars to make a day or horamya, this is the Palestus equivalent to an hour, and they are approximately equal to 56 earth minutes.
- Zongra: An abandoned pligma (Lye) mining town of the kingdom of north Envar. The town is located at the western end of the Splindia Valley, on the Continent of Zarhun.
- Zo Tanac Mountains: Mountains of the western Continent of Zarhun separating the Kingdoms of Envar and the ancient Kingdom of Zo Tan.

- Zurra: An island kingdom off the coast of the Continent of the Histajonies.
- Zureathion: The fifth largest continent on the Planet of Palestus. It was re-named from Thama in the year 0450 K.C.

Would you like to see your manuscript become a book?

If you are interested in becoming a PublishAmerica author, please submit your manuscript for possible publication to us at:

acquisitions@publishamerica.com

You may also mail in your manuscript to:

**PublishAmerica
PO Box 151
Frederick, MD 21705**

www.publishamerica.com